THEIR FINAL ACT

Alex Walters

D1448619

Also By Alex Walters

DI McKay Series

Candle & Roses (Book 1)

Death Parts Us (Book 2)

Praise For Alex Walters

"I really enjoyed this new crime series and will definitely be looking to read the next book when it comes along." **Joanne Robertson – My Chestnut Reading Tree**

"Alex Walters' crime debut is a great read, it is exciting and intriguing and I simply loved this detective novel." **Caroline Vincent – Bits About Books**

"Superb!" **Chris Nolan – Goodreads Reviewer**

"This is the first book in a new series for Alex Walters which I am positive will gather quite a following very quickly, myself being one of them." **Susan Hampson – Books From Dusk Till Dawn**

"Dark, powerful and utterly absorbing with a satisfying ending I didn't see coming. Loved it." **Deborah – Goodreads Reviewer**

"A book of many threads that are skillfully drawn out and all solved by the novels end - a definite, must read." **Sue Gale – Goodreads Reviewer**

"The pacing & smooth prose makes for effortless reading, one of those books where you're surprised to see how far you've gone when you finally look up." **Sandy – Goodreads Reviewer**

"A fantastic thriller that I would have no hesitation to recommend and will be keenly keepin g an eye out for more books featuring Alec McKay!" **Kate Noble – The Quiet Knitter**

"This is a fast paced easy read full of twists and turns that I didn't see coming not to mention the OMG moments." **Shell Baker – Chelle's Book Reviews**

"I thought that this was a brilliant book and as soon as I finished I knew it was going to have to be a 5 stars read and up there with my top crime reads of the year!" **Donna Maguire – Donnas Book Blog**

"A great detective thriller and I look forward to McKay's next investigation!" **Clair Boor – Have Books Will Read**

"This book was a nail biting ,crisp dark read...that keeps you guessing all the way through...." **Livia Sbarbaro – Goodreads Reviewer**

CHAPTER 1

'That you, Jimmy?'

Jimmy McGuire winced, hearing yet again the beginning of the accidental catchphrase from the days when he'd been half a double act. As always, it was called out in a parodic version of the already exaggerated Glasgow accent he'd used on stage in those days.

Christ, couldn't the buggers even let him have a piss in peace?

'Aye,' he responded wearily. 'It's me. Here to serve.' It had never been funny, or even intended to be. It was just the throwaway opening of some routine, which for some reason had got a laugh. They'd used it again, more incongruously, in some other piece and the laugh had been bigger. So it popped up more frequently, initially as an in-joke between the two of them. But somehow it had gained a life of its own, ensuring a round of applause at the start of every show. In the brief golden period when they'd attracted the interest of television commissioners, the producers had been obsessed with concepts based on 'here to serve'. Unsurprisingly, none of the programmes had ever been made.

The phrase had become a bloody weight on his shoulders, reminding him of where he was and how far he'd come. Here to bloody serve.

'Great show, pal,' the voice said from somewhere off to his left. 'You still got it.'

'Aye, well, thanks,' he muttered. Rule one, he thought. Never engage in conversation in a public toilet. Rule two: never look anywhere but down into your own urinal. There were more rules they'd once developed a routine around, but he couldn't immediately remember what they were. That one hadn't been particularly funny either.

He finished off and zipped up his fly, turning to survey the small room. His unwelcome admirer had already left, though Jimmy hadn't heard the door open. That was something. At least he wouldn't have to wash his hands while making awkward small talk about how brilliant his set had supposedly been.

His set had been okay. He'd enough experience to wring the laughs out of the pissheads who frequented this kind of comedy club. He could deal with the hecklers and get the audience on his side. He gave them a good time. As far as he could tell, the only person not enjoying it was him.

He didn't even know why he'd come back up here. Because he'd been invited, he supposed. That and curiosity. See how much the place had changed. Spoiler alert: it hadn't, or at least not in any ways that really mattered. He'd thought he might look up a few of the old crowd, but in the end he didn't have the energy. All he wanted was a quick bite to eat if he could find somewhere still open, a walk along the river for old time's sake, and then bed. In the morning, he'd get an early train south.

He stepped back out in the bar. The show was still going on – he hadn't even been top of the bill – so most of the punters were in the main room. A few of the more hardened drinkers were scattered along the bar, most apparently drinking alone. One of them turned and scrutinised him as he passed. 'You're him, aren't you?' the man said, his voice slightly slurred.

Always be polite to the paying customers, Jimmy told himself. Even if they were probably paying to see someone else. At least this one hadn't come out with the bloody catchphrase. 'Probably, pal.'

The man squinted at him through bloodshot eyes. 'Saw you were on tonight. What you doing playing a shithouse like this?'

McGuire forced himself to laugh. 'It's a living. And it's not so bad. These clubs are the future of comedy now.' That was the line his bloody manager had fed him, anyway, when Jimmy had started playing this circuit.

'You used to be big time though,' the man said. 'Well, bigger than this.'

'Long time ago, eh?' McGuire made to move past him.

'You were good though,' the man persisted. 'Back in the day. Better than a lot of the shite around. Better than this place.'

'Thanks, pal. Appreciated.' McGuire finally managed to make his escape. Truth was, he didn't want to spend another minute in that place. The noise. The smell of sweat and booze. The raucous laugher that would grow increasingly uncontrolled and humourless as the night went on.

He pushed his way out into the street and stood for a moment drinking in the chill night air. It was only just after nine, but, apart from one or two smokers outside the bars, Church Street was deserted. Most people didn't come out on a school night.

His intention had been to find somewhere to eat. It had always been a challenge, at least outside the biggest cities, to find anywhere still serving after a gig – even more so in the days when they'd been last on the bill. Indian or Chinese restaurants were usually the best bet, if you didn't mind sharing the place with groups of pissed-up youngsters.

Now, though, his appetite had deserted him. The thought of scouting round for somewhere still open, having to go through the rigmarole of choosing and ordering – all that left him feeling exhausted. He'd managed to grab a sandwich at the start of the evening, so he'd survive till morning. All he wanted was a bit of peace and an early night.

He turned off the main street into one of the narrower roads leading down to the river. He'd loop round that way, enjoy the night air and the views over the waterfront, and then head back to the charms of his budget hotel.

Off the main street, the night felt eerily quiet. He glanced at the shadowy doorways, wondering if this was a wise move. But it was still relatively early. The only danger here would be from some wee ned looking for a fight after a few too many pints, and none of that would kick off till later.

He could see the river glimmering with reflected light. Down there, there'd be other pedestrians. Dog walkers, people coming out of the restaurants. The usual passers-by.

It had been warm when he'd left the hotel earlier, and he hadn't bothered with a coat, just the trademark jacket he wore on stage. It had turned colder, a stiff breeze blowing up from the river. He found himself increasing his pace to keep warm.

Halfway down, he thought he heard footsteps. He stopped and looked back, but the street was deserted. Just a scrap of paper fluttering in the wind.

As he turned back to continue, he heard the words hissed from the shadows beside him. 'That you, Jimmy?'

McGuire was a big man. A little overweight, but more than capable of looking after himself. There wasn't much scared him. 'When you've died on stage in front of a crowd of hen parties, there is no other death,' he used to say.

He turned to respond and, if necessary, defend himself. But he never had the chance. Before he could move, something whipped around his head.

He stumbled backwards, fumbling at his collar, trying in vain to loosen the cord tightening around his throat.

It took him only seconds to lose consciousness.

CHAPTER 2

They'd had the conversation a couple of months before in DCI Helena Grant's office. 'You're joking.'

'Do you see me laughing, Alec?' she'd responded.

DI Alec McKay had leaned forward and peered at her face, as if taking the question seriously. 'Not now you mention it. But you've one of those poker faces. I'd never want to call your bluff.'

'You call my bluff all the bloody time, Alec. Mostly you get away with it.'

'But not guilty. How's she expect to get away with that?'

'By playing the victim card for all it's worth, according to the Procurator.'

McKay had been sitting in front of Grant's desk. Now, he rose and wandered about the office, occasionally stopping to gaze at her bookshelf or pick up some paper she'd left on the table. This, Grant knew, was a sign that McKay was feeling agitated. She'd once found the habit irritating. Now, she'd mostly learned to ignore it.

'She can't play it very far though,' McKay pointed out. 'She killed two people.'

'One of whom, according to her, had abused her physically and sexually since her childhood. And she's saying the other was a serial rapist who'd abused her repeatedly and similarly in adulthood.'

McKay was silent for a moment, clearly trying to make sense of this. 'Denny Gorman, a serial rapist?' he said, finally. 'Even if the inclination was there, the capability wouldn't be.'

'You know as well as I do, Alec, that rape's not about sex. It's about the abuse of power.'

'That's my point. Gorman didn't have any power. Ach, no one had a lower opinion of Denny Gorman than I did. He was a slimeball of the first order. But he was an utterly ineffectual one.'

'Most rapists are ineffectual slimeballs,' Grant said.

'Elizabeth Hamilton's original claim was that Gorman raped her when she'd had too much to drink. There was nothing in her statement about repeated abuse.'

'Apparently she wants to make a new statement. She claims that when she made her original one she was still too traumatised by what had happened and wasn't in a fit state to give an accurate account.' Grant paused. 'Not helped by the fact that the police officer leading the interview was…' She paused again and looked down at the notes she'd scribbled when talking to the Depute Procurator earlier. 'The phrase was "acerbic and unsympathetic". Does that sound like anyone we know?'

McKay dumped himself back down on the chair by Grant's desk and snatched up her stapler. For a moment, Grant thought he might throw it through the window behind her, but instead he just tossed it from hand to hand. 'For fuck's sake, Helena. This is utter shite. Grade A bollocks from start to finish. They must see that.'

'Not up to them, is it? If this is the line she takes, it'll be up to the jury.'

'Aye, but the Procurator will tear it to shreds, surely?'

'He'll do his best. But he's clearly rattled.'

'Jesus Christ, I thought this one was cut and dried.' McKay was still gently tossing the stapler as if about to use it as an offensive weapon. 'We caught her red-handed with the two fucking bodies, for Christ's sake. Even the bloody Procurator ought to be capable of making that stand up.'

The case went back to the previous summer, the climax of an extraordinary series of multiple killings over on the Black Isle. Elizabeth Hamilton had been the daughter of John Robbins, who was now assumed to have committed the original murders. Hamilton herself had been a victim of Robbins' abuse and had had suspicions about his behaviour. The exact sequence of events had always been unclear, but it had appeared that, with the balance of her mind disturbed, Hamilton had sought revenge on both her abusive father and on Denny Gorman, a local publican, who she said had raped her at the end of a drunken evening. The story was messy and far from clear, but Hamilton had apparently drugged the two men and somehow pulled their bound bodies into the sea off Rosemarkie Beach with the intention of drowning them. Hamilton had been intercepted by DS Ginny Horton, a member of Grant's team, but by then Robbins and Gorman had already been dead.

There had seemed little doubt that Hamilton would be convicted of murder, albeit with considerable extenuating circumstances. The assumption had been that she would plead guilty with the aim of seeking the shortest possible sentence. Now it seemed as if Hamilton, or her lawyers, had chosen a bolder route.

McKay finally grew bored with the stapler and dropped it back on to Grant's desk with a clatter. 'So how's she trying to justify this shite?'

'It goes back to how she ended up at Robbins' house that last time. She was vague about that when we interviewed her. Our assumption was that she'd finally lost it and gone back there to take her revenge on Robbins.'

'Or that she'd gone back there to try to screw some more money out of him. Maybe she lost it when he said no.'

Grant nodded. 'We never quite got to the bottom of it though, did we?'

'She reckoned she couldn't remember how she'd ended up there. All just a blank. Doc told me that was not uncommon. Dissociative amnesia.' As always, McKay spoke the polysyllabic words as if chewing a mouthful of nuts. 'The mind makes you forget traumatic events. Never works for me.'

'She could have been telling the truth,' Grant said. 'But she's claiming to remember more now.'

'Like what?'

'Like the fact that she didn't go to Robbins' house voluntarily.'

McKay sat up straight in his seat. 'What?'

'That's what she's saying. Reckons she was just walking in the centre of Inverness when Robbins drew up beside her in that van–'

McKay had picked up the stapler again. 'Van?'

'The van he used for the killings.'

McKay nodded. 'Aye, I know. The one we found at the rear of the house.'

'As far as Robbins knew, he'd bunged Hamilton a few quid and shipped her off to Aberdeen after she threatened to blackmail him. So when he saw her back in Inverness he wasn't best pleased.'

'This is what she's saying?'

'This is what she's saying. He told her to get into the van then drove her back to his house. When they got there, he grabbed her then tried to use the chloroform on her, the way he had with the other victims. She fought back, somehow managed to turn the tables and forced the chloroform soaked cloth across his mouth.'

'And this is what she's saying?' The note of scepticism in McKay's tone was growing with each repetition of the question.

'Aye, Alec. This is what she's saying. This is what she'll apparently be saying in court under oath.'

'So why did she get into the van with this man who she reckoned had already threatened her if she returned?'

'Maybe she was scared. Maybe he made nice and said he'd changed his ways. I don't know. I assume the Procurator will challenge her on that.'

'Let's hope so. So she says Robbins attacked her. She fought back, managed to give Robbins a taste of his own medicine. Then what?'

'She says that that was when she really lost it. The trauma of being attacked again. The knowledge of what Robbins had done and the realisation that she'd almost just become another of his victims. The memories of the abuse she'd suffered.'

'Blah, blah, blah.'

'So she wanted to get her own back on him. She tied him up, dragged him into the back of his car, and then headed off to Rosemarkie Beach.'

'Stopping to pick up Denny Gorman on the way. Also drugged and tied up.'

'We're getting back into the territory she claims not to be able to remember. All she can say is that the balance of her mind was disturbed and she didn't know what she was doing.'

'Conveniently enough.'

'There's more.'

'Spare me.' McKay had put down the stapler again but was back to wandering around the room. 'No, tell me the rest. I need a laugh.'

'She reckons she never intended to kill either of them. Just wanted to give them a scare. Robbins used to dump her in the sea at Rosemarkie when she was a child. Knew she was scared witless even in shallow water because she couldn't swim. Her plan was to drag them into the rising tide, with the bodies weighted down. She'd assumed the cold water would wake them, and either they'd be able to drag themselves clear in time.'

'Despite being tied up?'

'It's possible. But she also says she'd intended to drag them clear if they didn't respond.'

'So why didn't she?'

Grant was silent for a moment. 'She's claiming that was partly our fault.'

McKay had been staring intently at Grant's poster of the Cairngorms as if it might provide some unexpected insights. Now he turned. 'Our fault?'

'Ginny's, to be precise.'

'So it's my fault she didn't tell her story accurately. And it's Ginny's that she killed Robbins and Gorman.'

'You're getting the hang of this, Alec.'

'Oh, for fuck's sake.'

'She reckons she'd been on the point of pulling Robbins and Gorman clear when Ginny turned up and dragged her away. She says Ginny had got the wrong end of the stick and thought Hamilton was trying to kill them.'

'I wonder what might have given Ginny that idea. For fuck's sake, is Hamilton actually going to say this shite in court?' McKay said. 'You've read Ginny's statement. When she got there, Hamilton was sitting staring into space. Ginny didn't even realise what she'd done at first. Then when she discovered the bodies, Ginny was the one who tried to drag them out of the water. Until Hamilton hit her over the bloody head.'

'That's apparently not how Hamilton remembers it.'

'Then Hamilton really is bloody doolally–' McKay stopped. 'Ach, but that's the point, isn't it? She wins every which way. Just sows confusion and if others challenge her it only confirms she was off her head.'

'The balance of her mind was disturbed, it says here. But, aye, that's about the size of it.'

'You think she'll get away with this?'

'Who knows? Like I say, it's got the Procurator rattled. He doesn't like to be wrong-footed by smartarse lawyers. They were already gearing themselves up for some negative press when Hamilton was convicted and sentenced. You know, the abuse victim who's punished by the state. Her lawyers have been winding up the media to influence the tone of the trial coverage.' Grant paused. 'I'd never say it outside these four walls, but there's a part of me thinking good luck to her. I mean, murder's murder, but Robbins and Gorman won't be missed by anyone, and Hamilton had suffered a hell of a lot. We had no option but to charge her and I want to see justice done, but if she avoids a long sentence, however she does it, I won't be entirely sorry. The one who deserved to rot in prison was Robbins, and he never will.'

McKay was uncharacteristically silent for a few moments. 'Aye, I take your point. But there is one other thing.'

There was something in McKay's voice that sounded an early warning to Grant. She'd heard that tone before, usually when McKay was about to confess to some particularly egregious flouting of procedure. 'Go on.'

'Something I haven't told you.'

CHAPTER 3

'God, you scare me, Alec,' Helena Grant said. 'What is it this time?'

'Probably something and nothing. But I've always had a niggling doubt about that case.' McKay was standing in front of Grant's desk, with the air of a defiant schoolboy who'd been summoned to the headmistress's office. He was a short wiry man, with slicked back greying hair and a faintly intimidating presence. 'It was those last interviews we did with Hamilton–'

'The ones where you were,' Grant looked back down at her notes, '"acerbic and unsympathetic"?'

'I was sweetness and light,' McKay said. 'Actually, I really was. You ask Ginny. Anyway, it's true that Hamilton seemed away with the fairies half the time. It was difficult to get her to focus or to tell her tale coherently. But halfway through she mentioned the candles and roses.'

Robbins' victims had been found, sometimes buried, sometimes not, always accompanied by an apparent tribute of candles and roses. 'So what?'

'You remember,' McKay said. 'That was a detail we haven't released to the general public. It was only afterwards that it occurred to me to wonder how she knew about it.'

Grant rubbed her temples as if to ward off an incipient headache. 'You're not suggesting that Hamilton was involved in the killings?'

'I'm not suggesting anything. I'm just telling you about a question that's been troubling me. And which set off a whole chain of other questions in my mind.'

'Such as?'

'Such as whether Robbins had really put her on a train to Aberdeen in the way she told us. Maybe he gave her that clapped out old van to get rid of her, or maybe she just took it. He wouldn't have wanted to run the risk of reporting her, given she'd been threatening to blackmail him.'

Grant was looking back at her notes. 'Did you check on any of this at the time?'

'A little, but I didn't think anyone would thank me for rocking the boat.'

'That's untypically considerate of you, Alec. You're normally only too happy to rock the boat just for the sheer hell of it.'

'Aye, well. There's fun and there's fun. Robbins was dead. Hamilton was likely heading for prison in any case. There didn't seem much point in opening up another can of worms. Don't tell me you'd have been happy.'

'I'd have given you the bollocking of all bollockings. But you should have said something, Alec. If you had any doubt.'

'Maybe. But where would it have got us?'

'Nowhere probably,' she conceded. 'Did we find any trace of Hamilton's DNA in the van?'

'I did check that. There was nothing mentioned in the report, but that wasn't what they were looking for. At the time, I decided not to pursue it. In any case…'

'In any case, she's now saying she was in the van anyway, when Robbins picked her up in Inverness.'

'Exactly. So it would prove nothing.'

'I'm struggling to get my head round this, though. Why would she have killed those women?'

McKay nodded. 'That's the question. But another, related, question is why would Robbins have killed them.'

'Because he was a violent, sadistic, controlling bastard?'

'Aye, he spoke highly of you too. You're right, obviously. He was all that. But he was also smart. He manipulated these women to get what he wanted, then when he was bored he "disposed" of them, to use Hamilton's elegant phrase. But previously, as far as we know, he'd disposed of them by paying them to bugger off out of his life. We've no evidence he killed anyone before this, although Hamilton was happy to let us think he might have done.'

'So why would he start? Is that what you're asking?'

'He was a successful man. If he had been responsible for previous killings, he must have carried them out very discreetly. So why kill three women he'd not seen for years? And why leave their bodies displayed so ostentatiously?'

Grant was feeling as if she really was developing a headache. 'Maybe they were trying to blackmail him, like Hamilton wanted to.'

'It's possible. But we've found no evidence of that. We've found nothing to suggest Robbins had had any contact with those women in recent years.'

'Okay,' Grant said. 'But I come back to my first question. Why would Hamilton have wanted to kill those women? They were fellow victims of her father's.'

'I'm not a psychologist,' McKay said. 'Thank Christ. But they were all brought back to places where they'd been happy in their childhood. They were all commemorated with the display of candles and roses. We know Hamilton herself had been living a miserable solitary life. We know that the victims were all living alone with no obvious friends. Maybe Hamilton thought she was saving them from a life like her own.'

'For someone who isn't a psychologist, you're more than capable of talking your own brand of fluent bollocks, Alec.'

'Aye, well, I've had plenty of chance to listen to it over the last few weeks.'

'How's that all going?'

At the insistence of his estranged wife Chrissie, she and McKay were having another shot at couples counselling. McKay had been resistant, given their previous negative experience, but had finally recognised that Chrissie would never agree to a reconciliation otherwise. 'It's going,' he said bluntly. 'Not much sign of Chrissie flinging open the door to invite me back into the marital home though.'

'Give it time, Alec. Give her time.'

'Not like I've much choice, is it? Anyway, I'm happy enough in my little Black Isle bachelor pad.'

Grant knew better than to challenge that, and decided it was probably safer to move the conversation back to their original topic. 'Do you seriously think that Hamilton might have been the killer?'

He was silent again, as if giving her question serious consideration. 'Everything pointed to Robbins. The van, his business life and his trips down to Manchester. And everything we knew about his history. With Robbins dead, we were all more than happy to put a lid on it. Case closed.'

'But?'

'But a lot of what we've got on Robbins came from Hamilton. She was the one who painted the picture of him as the serial abuser, the one who picked up young women and discarded them.'

'We found some corroboration of that from other witnesses,' Grant pointed out.

'We did. I'm not for a minute suggesting that it's not an accurate portrait of Robbins. He was a nasty manipulative bastard. Christ, I experienced that for myself. But it's a big step from that to saying he was a multiple killer. We didn't find much evidence in his house.'

'We found stuff in his van. The chloroform. Ties, plastic sheeting. Stuff that matched what was used with the victims.' Grant stopped. 'But you're saying that it might have been Hamilton using the van all along.'

'I'm saying it's a possibility.' He'd risen to his feet again and was pacing up and down the narrow office. 'It's been keeping me awake. Well, not exactly. It's other stuff keeps me awake, but this is one of the things that troubles me in the wee small hours.' He'd stopped behind her desk and was staring out of the window. Outside, it was a glorious spring day, one of the best they'd had so far, although at this level the view largely comprised a string of unprepossessing retail and business parks.

'You think we should reopen the enquiry?'

'Ach, I don't know. I'd persuaded myself it didn't matter. Hamilton was likely to be sent down for a fair few years in any case. Like you say, she was probably doing a public service by ridding the world of Robbins and Gorman. But if there's a chance she might walk away scot-free…' He turned and gazed back morosely into the room. 'On the other hand, all my original reservations still hold true. No bugger would thank us for reopening this can of worms. Even if we could persuade the Procurator we've reason to.'

'Aye, and good luck with that one,' Grant agreed. 'Given the sensitivity of this, they're not going to be rushing to stick their necks on the block. Imagine the media reaction if she manages to walk away from the original charges, only for us to open a new enquiry implying she was actually the original killer all along.'

McKay nodded. 'And even if we could persuade our Procurator buddies that it was the right decision, how likely are we to make any progress? We've got nothing substantive on Hamilton other than one passing comment in the interview. And, aye, there are countless ways she could have found out about the candles and roses. This place leaks like a fucking sieve, and she could just have heard some officer or staff member mention it while she was in here. That's what she'll claim anyway if we challenge her. We could try to prove she'd driven the van, but even that wouldn't be anything more than circumstantial. Her partial amnesia is extremely convenient because, unless we find some hard evidence, she can just be vague about anything that might incriminate her. What else can we do? Disinter the bodies, assuming any of them haven't been cremated? Hope to find some DNA evidence linking the murders to Hamilton? It's a massive long shot.'

'There may have been more victims,' Grant said. 'We're not exactly short of missing persons over the years.'

'Maybe. But nothing's emerged since the original story broke. We'd just be chasing shadows.'

'All of which suggests there's really bugger all we can do. Except wait to see how this pans out.'

'Looks like it, doesn't it?'

'Most likely she'll go down anyway, at least for a while. The Procurator might be getting a touch of the jitters, but he still thinks this strategy of theirs is a hell of a gamble that'll probably backfire on them. He reckons she'd have been better just pleading guilty, setting out all the mitigating factors and throwing herself on the mercy of the court. That way, she'd probably have walked away with a relatively short sentence. This way – well, it's all or nothing.'

'Aye, but the Procurator's the sort who only ever bets on the favourite. Hamilton strikes me as one who likes playing for the higher odds.' McKay was still staring blankly into the room, his expression suggesting he was thinking back to those last interviews with Elizabeth Hamilton. 'And,' he added finally, 'she also strikes me as someone who likes to win.'

That had been two months before. Now, with the trial completed and the verdict delivered, it looked as if, as so often, McKay had been right. Hamilton had played against the odds, and had somehow managed to come out on top.

CHAPTER 4

J ane had never been up here before as far as she could remember. Or maybe that wasn't true. Perhaps she had, years before, as a child. She had no memory of that, nothing really before the age of ten or eleven. It was quite likely, she thought, that there had been a time when she'd been happy, when her only cares had been childish ones. She had no reason to think that wasn't true. It was just that she could recall none of it.

Occasionally, in her dreams at night, she'd felt a trace of it. She could remember nothing of the dream later, only the aftertaste of an emotion. A sense of freedom. An absence of anxiety. The opposite of anything she felt in her daily life.

They were only a little way north of the city, and had been driving for no more than twenty minutes but it already felt as if they'd entered a different world. She was beginning to realise how constrained her life had been, how little freedom she'd really had. She'd been aware of the mountains in the far distance, but they'd always seemed little more than a backdrop, a stage setting, something unreal and unreachable that had nothing to do with her life. Now they were close enough that she felt she could reach out and touch them. Yet they'd travelled such a short distance.

Jane glanced back at the young woman sitting in the rear seat of the taxi. When they'd left the centre, Jane had climbed into the front without really thinking, and the other woman had sat in the rear. They ought to have tried to make conversation, given they'd presumably be living together for some time to come. But they hardly knew each other, except to nod a greeting as they passed in the corridor. Jane had not known how to initiate a conversation, and the other woman had shown no inclination to try. The taxi driver had made a half-hearted attempt to engage them both in some diatribe about local politics, but had quickly realised he was talking to himself. The rest of the journey had passed in silence, the two women staring out of the window at the passing landscape.

Jane wondered whether the other woman had ever been this way before. She looked more confident, more knowing. It probably wasn't the first time she'd travelled over the Kessock Bridge, seen the Beauly and Moray Firths stretching away on the two sides, the green hills and afternoon sunshine reflected in the strangely still waters. All this was a wonder to Jane, but she guessed that, for the other woman, this was just another taxi ride.

Jane wondered what her story might be. Jane had been in the centre for long enough to know that every story was different, even if, in the end, they all amounted to the same thing. They'd all come there by a different route, sometimes short, sometimes long, always painful. Most looked worn down and diminished by what they'd been through. Sometimes you could almost see them come back to life as the days went by.

This woman, though, had a different look to her. Yes, she looked as if she might have been through a lot, as if she might have even more of a story to tell than most of them. But she also looked confident, assured, as if she was now the one in control. There was nothing browbeaten in her demeanour or behaviour. Jane had noticed her from the day she had walked into the centre. Most of the women looked as if they were trying to hide themselves, disappear into the background, avoid being noticed. That was how they'd survived before. Jane had been the same. It was only now that she was beginning to regain some confidence. In herself. In her right even to exist.

The woman also looked familiar. Jane was sure she'd met her somewhere before, though she'd not been able to pinpoint where. Maybe just around the city, although Jane had spent little enough time out and about. That had been one of the rules in the old days. Then, after she'd left, she hadn't been able to go out for fear of running into him and being dragged back into that hell.

Even so, she'd come across this woman somewhere. Jane had the sense of having seen her close up, having heard her talk, but hadn't been able to work out where or how that might have happened. Perhaps, if they had the opportunity to talk more in their new home, she'd get to find out.

Jane was still staring out of the window, trying to make sense of their journey. After another mile or so, they came to a roundabout, with the driver continuing on the A9 north, the road reducing to a single carriageway. There was woodland on both sides of the road, and no clue as to their destination.

A farm, Jane had been told. A working farm, though she hadn't had much of an idea what that might mean. She had a vague idea that farms involved animals – sheep, cows, chickens, maybe. Then there were farms growing crops – corn, maize, barley, that sort of thing. But that was the limit of her knowledge. She couldn't imagine what it might be like actually to live on a farm.

She knew also that they would be expected to help out. Nothing arduous, she'd been told, but the owner was looking for some assistance with daily tasks. That was how she was able to offer accommodation rent-free to those who needed it. Jane had worried about this at first, concerned it might just be another way of exploiting her. She'd had more than enough experience of that.

But, no, they'd reassured her. This wasn't like that. The owner of the farm was a decent woman, they'd said. A bit of a character, with a history she'll be keen to tell you about. But all she wants is a bit of practical help, some company, and in return she'll take care of you till you're ready and able to take care of yourself.

It had sounded too good to be true, and maybe that would turn out to be the case. But Jane hadn't had much to lose, and little real option other than to rely on the kindness of strangers. And, if the offer really were genuine, she'd do her best to reciprocate.

'This is the one,' the taxi driver said, breaking the silence for the first time since his initial attempts at conversation. 'Not far now.' He signalled right, and took the next turning off the main road. Ahead of them, Jane could see another stretch of water, with a line of hills and mountains beyond.

They passed what was clearly a farm, with a couple of trailers and other farm machinery cluttering a yard beside the road. Jane wondered if that might be the one, but they continued past. The water was on their left, just visible beyond a stretch of fields and woodland. The whole place looked glorious in the spring sunshine.

After another half mile, they entered a more populated area, with the occasional house or bungalow visible on both sides of the road, and signs warning of an impending thirty mph speed limit. There was a sign indicating the name of the village, though it had passed before Jane had a chance to read it. She'd been told the name previously, when they'd first been talking about her coming here, but it had meant nothing to her.

The village itself seemed to comprise very little. They passed a couple of small new-looking housing estates, some larger houses with views out over the firth, and a small village general store and post office, with a pub opposite. That seemed to constitute the heart of the village.

A few moments later, the driver turned left into a single-track road leading down in the direction of the water. 'Have to be careful down here. You get a few speed demons who don't realise there's no way to pass.'

A few hundred yards further on, he turned right into a gateway. There was a sign to the left of the gate, but again Jane was too slow to catch the name, though she recognised the word "farm". This was presumably their destination.

A rough track, laid only with roadstone, led them across an open field towards a cluster of buildings ahead. 'Does nothing for my bloody suspension, this,' the driver said, clearly talking mainly to himself. As they reached the first building, the track widening to form a turning space, he pulled to the right and then looped round until he was parked in front of what appeared to be the front door. 'Here we are.'

Jane glanced back at the other woman, who was already climbing out of the taxi. It was impossible to read her expression. Jane nodded to the driver. 'Thanks. Do we owe you anything?'

'All taken care of, hen.' He was an elderly man, slightly overweight, with a kindly expression. He was probably a good granddad to someone, she thought. 'Don't worry,' he said. 'Netty'll take good care of you.'

Jane nodded, unable to think of anything else to say, and then pushed open the passenger door. 'Thanks,' she said again.

Outside, she stood blinking in the sunshine, while the driver retrieved their luggage from the boot, just a couple of small bags between them.

Jane looked around, wondering what would happen next. There didn't seem to be anyone to greet them. The building in front of them was clearly the farmhouse, an old brick-built edifice that looked as if it had seen better days. The front door was closed.

'Good morning! Welcome!' The voice came from around the side of the house, unexpectedly loud.

A moment later, its owner emerged into the sunshine. 'I'm so sorry,' she said. 'I meant to be here to greet you, but I lost track of the time.'

The woman speaking was a short slightly squat figure dressed in a shapeless grey cardigan and tweed skirt. Her unkempt hair was a matching shade of grey. But she had an oddly ageless air, as if she might always have looked that way. Her accent was English, though with a burr that suggested she'd lived in the Highlands for many years. She fumbled in her pocket and then thrust a hand out towards the taxi driver. 'Thanks as always, Archie. Something for your trouble.'

He smiled and took the crumpled note. 'You don't need to, Netty. All paid for by the centre. But I know there's no point in arguing with you.'

'Glad you've finally learned that lesson, Archie. Buy yourself a pint.'

'Aye, and I'll be drinking to your health.' He turned to the two younger women, as he climbed back into the car. 'Best of luck, ladies. You're in safe hands.'

'Welcome to you both. In case you hadn't guessed, I'm Netty Munro.' She waved a hand around her to indicate the buildings and land around them. 'This is Muir Farm in all its spring glory.'

Jane felt overwhelmed by Munro's ostentatious manner, welcoming as it was. For a moment, Jane wished she could climb back into the taxi that was already disappearing across the field. But Munro was already grasping her by the hand, as if about to drag her physically into the house behind them. 'You must be Jane and Elizabeth. Right, let's get you both inside. You're probably both gasping for a cup of tea. I know I am.'

Without waiting for a response, she picked up both of the women's bags and strode towards the front door of the house. The two younger women glanced at each other, Elizabeth giving a barely discernible shrug, and then followed in her wake.

Inside, the house was gloomy and cool, but with a welcoming air. The hallway was shabby, dominated by a heavy oak dresser which had clearly seen better days. But there was a lingering scent of freshly baked bread, and another faintly perfumed smell which Jane couldn't place but which immediately made her feel at home.

Munro dropped the two bags in the hall and proceeded through a door at the far end, beckoning the other two women to follow. They found themselves in a large farmhouse kitchen, with a pine dining table, an imposing-looking Aga, and a mismatched array of cupboards and work surfaces. It looked like a practical workspace rather than any kind of show kitchen, and Munro seemed more than at home here. She filled an old-fashioned kettle and placed it on one of the rings of the Aga, waving for Elizabeth and Jane to seat themselves at the table. 'Tea? Coffee?'

'Tea, please,' Jane said timorously.

'Coffee,' Elizabeth said, adding 'Please' as an apparent afterthought. She had already sat down, and was watching Munro with a glint of amusement in her eye. Like someone watching an eccentric animal in a zoo, Jane thought.

Munro talked as she busied herself preparing the drinks. 'So, welcome to you both. You're no doubt wondering quite what you've let yourself in for coming here. I hope more than anything you've let yourself in for a good time. I'll need you to do some work, of course, but nothing unreasonable, and you'll have plenty of time to relax. Enjoy the fresh air, enjoy the scenery. Enjoy the food, I hope. Speaking of which...' She crossed the room to what looked to be a pantry, leading off the main kitchen, and returned a moment later, bearing a plate holding a large sponge cake. 'I baked this to celebrate your arrival. So I insist you both have a piece.'

Jane was still looking around her, amazed that she should even be here in this extraordinary kitchen, listening to this equally extraordinary woman. Elizabeth might be unimpressed, or at least pretending to be, but Jane could hardly believe her own eyes or ears. It was as if she'd entered a world she barely knew existed.

'So,' Munro went on, once they were all seated with their drinks and slices of cake, 'I've had a few dozen young women up here over the years. All recommended to me by the centre, like yourselves. Some stayed just a week or two, others for the whole summer or longer.' She held out her hands expansively. 'You're both welcome to stay as long as you wish. But when you choose to leave, that's entirely your business.'

'But why do you *do* this?' Elizabeth said. To Jane's ears, the question sounded abrupt, discourteous. But Munro appeared not to notice.

'Why do I *do* it?' she said. 'That's a good question. I suppose partly just because I can. I have the space and facilities to accommodate people without it being intrusive. I suppose partly because I do need some help with the farm as I get older. I have some paid support for the heavier tasks, but an extra pair of hands or two is always useful.' She paused. 'And because I do have at least an inkling of what the two of you might have been through. I can tell you about that sometime when we've got to know each other better. And you can tell me your stories, if you wish. But there's no obligation.'

'We're very grateful to you anyway, Mrs Munro,' Jane said, ignoring the look that Elizabeth was giving her. 'It's very kind.'

'It's Netty,' Munro said. 'The last part of it is that I do enjoy the company. It's good to have some younger blood around the place. Keeps me young as well.'

'So what is it we have to do while we're here?' Elizabeth said. 'I mean, what's the deal?'

Munro gazed at her for a moment, and then smiled. She'd clearly encountered Elizabeth's type before, Jane thought, and wasn't going to be fazed. 'You don't need to worry, my dear. I'm not going to take advantage of you. The deal is simply this. You're welcome to stay as long as you like and to leave whenever you wish. While you're here, I'll provide you with a comfortable bedroom each – I'll take you up and show you those in a minute – and more food than you'll be able to eat. You can also be assured that you'll be safe and secure here. In return, all I ask is that you do a little work for me – mainly just cleaning, some light gardening, and other similar jobs. Just what I need to keep the place in order, really. I have very few rules, the main one simply being that you treat me and the farm with respect.' There had been no change in Munro's tone as she spoke the last sentence, but Jane was left in little doubt that this was not a woman who would brook any nonsense. Elizabeth looked as if she'd also taken on board the message. 'But mostly,' Munro went on, 'while you're here I just want you to relax, leave your worries behind and enjoy yourselves.'

To Jane, all this sounded far too good to be true. Her life didn't deal these kinds of cards. She just lurched from one crisis to the next, escaping one disaster only to find herself stepping into something worse. When she'd met Iain, she'd thought everything was finally going to be all right. But it had all turned out worse than ever. And so here she was.

She fully expected that this would turn out the same way. Something would go wrong. Netty Munro would be just the next in line to take advantage of her. Jane had little doubt about that, and she could see from Elizabeth's expression that she thought the same. But it wasn't as if there were other options, other than staying in the centre, and that wasn't feasible in the longer term. All Jane could do was go with the flow, and hope that finally her luck had changed.

Munro took a last mouthful of tea and pushed away her mug. 'Okay. Assuming you're both happy to stay, let me show you your bedrooms. You can get settled in, freshen up if you want to, and then I'll give you the grand tour of the estate.'

CHAPTER 5

'Garrotted?' DS Ginny Horton looked up at Alec McKay who was looming over her desk. 'Did you say garrotted?'

'Aye. You know, like strangled. With a thin cord.'

'I know what garrotting is, Alec. I just didn't know it was much practised in the Scottish Highlands these days.'

'They're all a bunch of *teuchter* heathens. You never know what to expect of them.'

'Everyone up there sings your praises too, Alec. But you're serious about this?'

'Deadly. Body found this morning. Just off Bank Street, by the river. Tucked away in a doorway. Suspect a few people had already walked past it, assuming it was some homeless guy or drunk asleep there.'

'So who found the body?'

'Couple of restaurant workers from the one of the places by the river apparently. Stopped for a smoke before heading in to work.'

'But – garrotted?' Horton had a fresh-faced appearance that suggested she might be disturbed by the prospect of a gruesome murder. McKay knew that this was far from the case. He'd even discovered, disconcertingly, that she was much less English and more Scottish than she appeared to be. That, he'd decided, would explain a lot.

'The examiners haven't arrived yet, so it's not confirmed. But there doesn't seem to be much doubt.'

'Not just an ordinary strangling?'

McKay laughed. 'The common or garden fucking stranglings we get so many of in the streets of Inverness. No, I spoke to one of the uniforms I know. Looks like very thin cord or even wire. Cut right into the neck. Genuinely nasty piece of work.'

'So we picking this up?'

'Helena's tossed it in my direction. Keep us busy while we've still got some resources here. At least till she gets overridden and they send some wet-behind-the-ears kid up from Edinburgh.'

'Is that on the cards?'

'Increasingly. Fucking centralisation. Only reason we're getting away with it at the moment is because they don't believe there's life after Perth.'

'Or death. In this case.'

'Exactly. So, you just going to sit there shuffling computer files, or do we get down there to find out what's what?'

'I take it I'll be driving?'

'Do I look like fucking Parker, your Ladyship?' He was already out of the room, leaving her with no option but to grab her coat and follow.

At the end of the corridor, he stopped and looked back, waiting for her to catch up. He sometimes had the sense that this was the only time he felt alive. Those rare times when he had a proper new case on the horizon, something he could get his teeth into. He had a growing paranoia that all the really serious stuff would soon be syphoned off down south.

Aye, well, he thought as he led Horton down the stairs, just let them fucking try.

***

'You've done a decent job,' McKay said. 'Considering.' He turned and peered along the riverside. The uniforms had cordoned off a lengthy stretch of Bank Street, as well as the streets leading down to the river. There'd be some grumbling at the restaurants, given that the area was unlikely to be reopened for the lunchtime service.

'We did our best,' the uniform said. He was a relative youngster, but everyone looked young to McKay. 'Bit short of bodies–' He stopped and glanced involuntarily over his shoulder to where the forensic tent had been erected. 'If you'll pardon the expression.'

'Where's the two who found the body?' McKay asked.

'Two gents over there.' The uniform gestured to the men standing by the river looking as if they were itching to be somewhere else. 'On their way into work.'

They almost certainly wouldn't be able to tell him anything useful, beyond what time they'd found the body. He might as well go and put them out of their misery. He turned back to the uniform. 'See our examiner friends are here. Who's drawn the short straw this time?'

'The old guy,' the uniform said, then, clearly noting McKay's raised eyebrow, he added, 'The tall one, I mean.'

McKay glanced over at Ginny Horton, who had been watching the exchange with her usual amusement. 'Jock Henderson, presumably. He only stays in the job to keep running into me.'

'That'll be it,' Horton said. 'Want me to talk to our two witnesses over there, while you exchange pleasantries with Mr Henderson?'

'Pleasantries? That would be a first. No, Jock won't thank me for interrupting him till he's finished. Let's have a chat with yon two first. See if there's anything useful they can tell us.'

McKay imagined that, in normal circumstances, the men would be cocky wee buggers. They had that air to them. It was clear though, that much of that bravado had been knocked out of them first by the experience of finding the body and second by being left to cool their heels for the last half hour.

The taller of the two looked up as McKay approached. He was dark-haired, skinny, with a complexion that had suffered from the ravages of acne. The other man looked barely out of his teens with a pale complexion and a mass of ginger hair already showing signs of thinning.

'You the police?' the first man said.

'Aye, I'm the police,' McKay said. 'As is my colleague here. DI McKay and DS Horton. You two were the lucky winners of our daily "find a body" competition, I understand?'

The first man nodded. 'Over there.'

'That must be why they've stuck a bloody great tent over the top,' McKay observed. 'What's your name, son?' McKay's manner tended to disconcert witnesses, but it was far from accidental.

'Gavin Murdoch,' the young man said. 'This is Billy. Billy Farrell.'

'Well, Gavin Murdoch,' McKay said, 'what brought you and Billy here down to these parts so early in the morning?'

'We both work at the restaurant on the corner there,' Murdoch said. 'In the kitchens. We start at seven thirty so we can do the prepping for the lunch service.'

'So what time did you stumble across the body?'

Murdoch looked at Farrell. 'Must have been about quarter past, twenty past, something like that. We both get the bus in. That's supposed to get to the station at ten past. Then maybe five minutes to walk over here.'

'You walked down from Church Street?' McKay pointed to the street where the body had been found.

'We usually walk down that way. If we've time, we stop for a quick ciggie on the corner. We're not allowed to smoke outside the kitchen, so it's last chance we have before break time.'

'Near where you found the body? That where you usually stop?'

'More or less. Depends a bit on the weather. If we're pushed, we'll just grab a smoke as we're walking over. If we've got a few minutes to spare. It's nice to stop and get a break before we get sucked into the madness, you know?'

'Aye,' McKay said. 'Busy life in the kitchen, I imagine.'

'Never stops,' Murdoch agreed. 'Not till after lunch anyway. Then we get a bit of a break before we start prepping for dinner. It's a long day.'

'I don't envy you, son. Okay, so tell me exactly what happened this morning. Sounds like the bus got in on time?'

'More or less. So we weren't in a hurry. It was shaping up to be a decent day, so we thought we'd stop and have a smoke looking out over the river.'

'Always good to appreciate the joys of nature,' McKay said.

Murdoch blinked. 'We'd just got to the bottom of the street, when it caught our eye. Billy spotted it.'

Farrell looked disconcerted at having the narrative tossed in his direction. 'I guess I saw it first,' he said. 'Just out of the corner of my eye. Thought it was just someone dossing in the doorway, you know?'

'I know, son,' McKay said. 'Too many in that position around this city. So what made you realise it wasn't just that?'

'I don't know, exactly. Something about it didn't look right. There was an old coat thrown across it as if it might have been someone asleep. But somehow it didn't look like that…' He stopped, as if overcome by the memory.

'I understand,' McKay said gently. He'd already changed his tone, recognising that Farrell would need a different kind of prompting. 'So what did you do?'

Farrell looked awkward. 'At first we just kind of laughed about it. Gavin thought I was making a fuss about nothing. But the more we looked, the more we thought there was something funny about it.'

'Funny in what way?'

'I don't know exactly. The way he was lying. It didn't look natural somehow. Not the way you'd lie if you were just asleep or even out of it on drugs or booze.' He stopped and it was clear he was reluctant to continue.

'So you went to look?' McKay prompted.

'Aye. I mean, I just twitched back the coat thing that was lying on him. Then I saw his face…'

'Go on,' McKay said.

'It was dead white. Almost blue. And there was blood around his neck and collar…' Farrell trailed off. 'Didn't have much doubt he was dead.'

'Did you touch anything else?'

Farrell shook his head, his expression suggesting he might not want to touch anything else ever again. 'No. Just dropped the coat back over him. Then went to call 999.'

'Good lad. Anything else you can tell us?' The question was directed at both young men.

'I don't think so,' Murdoch said. 'Like Billy says, we just left it after that.'

'Did you see anyone else around?' McKay's assumption was that death had probably occurred some time before the two men found the body. But it was always worth asking the question.

'Not really,' Murdoch said. 'It was early. There were a few people on the main roads, but not much down there. Reckon some people might already have just walked past without spotting it. It was only because we stopped for a smoke.'

'You're no doubt right, son. Okay, we'll need to get a formal statement from you both for the record. And we'll need to take your fingerprints and a DNA sample, just so we can distinguish yours from anything else that might be on the body. Are you planning to head into work?'

'I've already phoned in so we didn't get a bollocking,' Murdoch said.

'We won't get this lot clear in time for your lunchtime service anyway,' McKay said. 'So we might as well get the formalities sorted, and then we can let you on your way.'

Taking her cue, Horton took a step forward. 'You come with me. We can sort out the statements and other stuff in the car.'

McKay knew that if there was any other information to be gleaned from these two, especially from Farrell, Horton's gentle persuasion was more likely to tease it out of them than his own brand of blunt interrogation. 'I'll leave you to it, Ginny. I'll go and see whether I can drag Jock Henderson away from his new best friend.'

CHAPTER 6

Jock Henderson, true to form, was propped against the corner of the building, pulling on what was no doubt only the latest in a long line of cigarettes he'd already smoked that morning. He was a tall ungainly figure with a shock of greying hair that gave him the air of an off-kilter academic.

'Morning, Jock. Practising the fine art of delegation, I see?'

'Aye, Alec. At least some of us know how to delegate. The kids have to learn.'

'And safer if you're not in there trying to teach them? I can see that.'

This type of exchange was standard between the two men – ostensibly humorous but with an edge that neither could entirely explain. McKay had sometimes wondered whether one of them had inadvertently caused the other some deep offence in the far past, but he had no recollection of anything that satisfactorily explained their relationship.

'Always a joy to see your smiling face, Alec. Makes a change from looking at corpses. Though not much.'

'What's the story then, Jock?' McKay gestured towards the tent.

'Male. Fifties, I'd guess. Reasonably smartly dressed. Dark suit, white shirt. Well, white blood-stained shirt. Tallish. Five eleven or six foot. Clean shaven.'

'And I heard garrotted? Or was that little detail not worth highlighting?'

'That what you call it then? Is that the technical term for having a piece of piano wire or cheese wire or whatever the hell it was pulled tight around your fucking neck? Aye, I was coming to that.'

'It's true then? Jesus.'

'Aye, it's true, right enough. Nasty old way to die.'

'What do you reckon happened?'

Henderson looked up and down the street, as if envisaging the scene. 'From the position of the body, my guess would be that our friend was walking down from Church Street. He must have stopped for some reason as he reached the corner. Then some bastard threw a piece of wire round his neck and pulled tight. He'd almost certainly have died from asphyxiation first, which is some blessing, but the fucking wire almost decapitated him.'

'Not an accident then.'

'I think we can fairly safely say, Alec, that this wasn't an accident.'

'Any sign of the murder weapon?'

'Nothing. It was removed from the body, which must have been a task in itself, given how deeply it was embedded.'

McKay frowned and looked around. It was still relatively early but there were already plenty of passers-by on Church Street above them, some of them pausing to peer curiously down the alley at the cordoned area. 'Any thoughts on time of death?'

'Nothing precise. That's for the doc. But not that recent, I'd say. Last night, rather than this morning.'

'Any idea who the poor bugger is yet?'

Henderson's smug expression suggested he'd been waiting to be asked. 'Aye, well, that's quite interesting. We've got ID right enough. There's a wallet with all the usual stuff – credit cards, driving licence, a few quid in cash. Even his passport, just to make our life easier.'

'Go on, Jock. You're dying to tell me. Is it maybe the Chief Constable? Or the Secretary of State for Scotland? Or is it somebody who might conceivably be missed?'

'Does the name Jimmy McGuire mean anything to you?'

'McGuire?' There was a vague bell ringing somewhere in the back of McKay's head, but he couldn't immediately place the name. 'Should it?'

'Dingwall and McGuire?'

'Jesus, really?'

'It's him sure enough. Being garrotted's not done a lot for his complexion, but he's recognisable.' Henderson stubbed out his cigarette under his shoe, immediately lighting up another. 'I've just been looking him up on my phone. He was playing that new comedy club on Church Street. Not even top of the bill, would you believe.'

'Sounds like the mighty have fallen quite a long way,' McKay observed. 'Never liked him though. Arrogant wee prick, I always thought.'

'Takes one to know one, Alec.'

McKay ignored him. 'As for the other one. Jack fucking Dingwall, for Christ's sake. What sort of name's that?'

'A stage one, if I recall correctly,' Henderson said. 'One of those Equity things, because there was some other bugger already using his real name. McGuire was real enough though. Or at least his name was.'

'You're obviously an expert, Jock.' Every now and then, McKay found a reason to reappraise Henderson's character. Not for the better, usually, but at least in a different light. 'It was Dingwall who got sent down, wasn't it?'

'Aye. Five years, for rape.'

'Unpleasant bloody story.' It was gradually coming back to McKay. 'When are we talking? Early nineties?'

'Something like that. Don't get me wrong,' Henderson added, as if suddenly realising that he was giving McKay material for future satire. 'I wasn't a huge fan. But I saw them live a couple of times.'

'Scotland's answer to Hale and Pace,' McKay mused. 'As if that was ever a question that needed a fucking answer.'

'They came up through the alternative comedy circuit. Reckon it was mainly just because the telly up here was looking for some home-grown talent. They fitted the bill at the time. Never really took off though.'

'Would that have been because they were crap?' McKay offered.

'Let's say they weren't all that original. They were okay live, if you'd had a few bevvies. But they never broke into TV properly. They got overtaken by all that *Absolutely* and *Chewin' the Fat* stuff.'

'I'll take your word for it, Jock. I remember the bloody rape story though. Some wee groupie, wasn't it?'

'Not sure groupie's quite the right word. But, aye, a young fan. Went with Dingwall back to his hotel room in Glasgow, she'd had a few drinks. He reckoned it was consensual. She didn't. Jury believed her.'

'Praise the Lord,' McKay said. 'Evidence must have been strong, given how successful we generally are at convicting in rape cases.'

'Don't recall the details,' Henderson said. 'But there were a couple of witnesses who said he'd been trying to coerce her earlier on, and there was bruising and suchlike which indicated it hadn't been consensual. On top of that, there were suggestions he'd tried to drug her, but she'd been smart enough not to take it.'

From someone who didn't recall the details, McKay thought, that seemed a fairly thorough account. 'Even so, professional performer like Dingwall might have pulled the wool over their eyes.' He'd seen it too often in his career. The defendant who turns up in the smart suit, looking eminently respectable, and claims he can't for the life of him understand why this unscrupulous young woman should be victimising him.

'Judge was pretty scathing about Dingwall's evidence,' Henderson went on. 'He went to pieces in court. Inconsistent, rambling, didn't match up with the other evidence presented. The victim was straightforward, clear and stuck to her story. He was lucky to get five years, if you want my opinion. I'd have strung him up.'

It was unusual for Henderson to express such a strong view, particularly about an issue like this. He had a couple of daughters of his own, McKay recalled. Maybe that was the reason. Henderson wasn't a man with a strong imagination – which, in fairness, was one of the qualities that made him an effective examiner. He wasn't fazed by even the most gruesome of crime or accident scenes, and didn't generally speculate beyond the available evidence. For the same reason, he could come across as insensitive to the sufferings of others. He wouldn't care much about an issue unless it was really brought home to him.

'Must have put a dampener on their comedy partnership though?'

'It was the end of all that. I suppose you have to feel sorry for McGuire, though they were already past their peak by then. There'd been talk of a TV series. But it never happened. They were still doing okay live, but my guess is it was dwindling by then. Then McGuire was left on his own, with no prospect they'd be able to resume when Dingwall came out. Hard to get laughs if you're a convicted rapist.'

'So what happened to McGuire?'

'Far as I remember, he went to ground for a while. Bobbed up in a few straight roles in Scottish TV dramas and the like. Hadn't realised he'd gone back to comedy, but it looks like he was performing solo now. Would have been interesting to see.' Henderson sounded genuinely regretful.

'What about Dingwall? He must be out by now.'

'Oh, aye. We're talking twenty or more years ago.'

'Any idea where he is?'

'Not a scoobie. I have a feeling he came back up north somewhere. Kept his head down, which I suppose is all he could have done.'

'We'll have to track him down,' McKay said.

Henderson raised a bushy eyebrow. 'You reckon he might be involved in this?'

McKay shrugged. 'Who knows? But can't really see it, can you? If anyone had reason to bear a grudge, it was McGuire. And why wait so long and then do something like this?'

'Unless there was more to the original story than met the eye.' Henderson was already moving on to his third cigarette since

McKay's arrival. McKay ostentatiously pulled out a packet of gum, unwrapped a strip, and popped it in his mouth. He proffered the pack to Henderson, who had already lit up. 'Never grows old, does it, Alec?'

'You reckon there might have been more to the story? You seem to know the ins and outs.'

'Just a casual observer. No, not really. At the time, it was a surprise, I remember. It all seemed out of character for Dingwall. More the kind of thing you'd expect from McGuire, to be honest. But then that was just based on the way they came across on stage. Probably quite different in private.'

'I remember Dingwall's trial was a pretty big deal, even though they were Z-list celebs by then.'

'Someone off the telly gets sent down's always news,' Henderson agreed. 'Even if it's someone you've never heard of. They made a lot of the double act. I can't imagine that some of the tabloids didn't try to get McGuire to tell his side of the story, but I don't think he ever did.'

'So no motive there then. Still, we'll need to track down Dingwall for a chat anyway. You know if McGuire was married?'

'No idea.' Henderson was clearly beginning to resent being treated as the fount of all knowledge relating to Dingwall and McGuire. Quite possibly, McKay thought, because he'd realised by now that McKay was only extending the conversation to take the proverbial. 'They were single at the time of the trial, because the defence made a play of that, as if their lifestyle might somehow provide a justification for raping a young woman.'

'Aye, and no doubt *her* single lifestyle was used to try to justify her being raped,' McKay said. 'How it always fucking works.'

'I've no idea if McGuire might have got married since, though. Don't imagine it would exactly have made the front page of *The Scotsman*.'

'Another avenue for us to pursue anyway.'

'You reckon this was targeted then? Not just some mad bastard picking on someone at random.'

'Christ knows,' McKay said. 'It's a fucking weird one, isn't it? Most likely some lone lunatic, and McGuire was the unlucky bugger who was walking by.'

'It'll be a big story, either way,' Henderson observed, with a note of glee in his voice. 'McGuire's not exactly a household name any more. But someone off the telly gets garrotted is an even bigger story than someone off the telly gets sent down.'

'Aye, Jock. You always know how to cheer me up, don't you?'

'My role in life.'

'At least it's a role you carry out, unlike your bloody examining,' McKay said. 'Go and chivvy up your lads. Some of us have got real work to do.'

CHAPTER 7

'The two rooms are pretty similar,' Netty Munro said. 'I don't know if either of you has a preference?'

Jane tried to catch Elizabeth's eye, but she was staring through the open doorway with a bored expression, showing no interest in any of the accommodation being offered.

To Jane's eyes, both rooms looked lovely. They were small farmhouse bedrooms, with varnished wooden floors scattered with rugs. Three of the walls were plastered. The fourth, with its window looking out over the firth, was bare stone. Both rooms were simply furnished, each with an old oak wardrobe and dressing table and a large brass double bed. 'I don't mind. They're both beautiful.'

'I'll take this one then,' Elizabeth said, apparently at random. She picked up her bag and strode into the room, as if about to undertake some purposeful activity.

'You're happy with that?' Munro said to Jane. 'There's not much to choose between them.' She gestured to the vacant room. 'This one might be slightly larger.'

Jane guessed this was meant to make her feel better about Elizabeth's peremptory choice. In truth she hardly cared. Both rooms were infinitely better than anywhere she'd slept before. 'I'll be very happy in here.' For the first time since her arrival, she'd begun to think that this might actually be true.

'Excellent.' Munro was speaking loudly so both women could hear her. 'There are towels in your wardrobes. If you need more, there's a pile in the cupboard at the end of the landing. When they're dirty, drop them into the laundry basket in the bathroom.' She pointed to a closed door on the opposite side of the landing.

'The bathroom's there, with the loo next door. Oh, and this is Alicia's room.' Munro gestured towards another door.

'Alicia?' This was from Elizabeth who was gazing out of the bedroom window at the view beyond.

'Our third guest. She's been here a few weeks.'

'Is she–?' Jane stopped, unsure how to frame the question.

'She's from the centre, like yourselves. It's up to her whether she wants to tell you her story. Just as it's up to you whether you want to share yours. It's your business. Some guests find it helpful to talk about their backgrounds. Others don't.'

Jane didn't know whether this was intended as an invitation or a warning. 'It'll be nice to meet her,' she said.

'She's just gone for a walk,' Munro said. 'I think she was a little nervous at meeting you. But I'm sure you'll get on with her.' The last sentence appeared to be directed at Elizabeth, who was still staring out of the window. 'Right, I'll leave you to it for a short while. If you'd like a shower, feel free. Otherwise, just have a bit of a rest and freshen up, and then pop back downstairs when you're ready. Then I can give you the tour of the rest of the farm.' She turned back to Jane. 'You should have a look at the view. You're really seeing it at its best today.' She ushered Jane into the bedroom, and then disappeared back down the stairs, humming a tune that Jane recognised but couldn't place.

Jane's first thought was to try to talk to Elizabeth. The other woman seemed a little older and, Jane thought, much more streetwise. Jane was keen to know what Elizabeth was thinking about this set-up. Was it really everything it seemed, or was it too good to be true? But when she emerged from her room she saw that the other bedroom door was already closed. It seemed as if, for the present at least, Elizabeth had no desire to talk.

Jane returned to her own room and walked over to the window. A green meadow ran down to a hedge, with a newly sown barley field beyond. From there, the land dropped away towards the waters of the Cromarty Firth. The firth itself was extraordinarily still, a large mirror reflecting the surrounding hills and the clear blue of the sky.

To someone who had rarely ventured out of the city, the scene was breathtaking. Jane felt as if she could stare at it all day, slowly drinking in the details. The clusters of woodland, the scattered houses and bungalows that gave a human dimension to the landscape, the pylons, polytunnels and wind turbines dotting the countryside. The mountains in the distance, the summits still patched by the last lingering winter snow.

She turned back to survey the room. Here too there were details she hadn't initially noticed. A vase of daffodils on the dressing table. Paintings on the wall which she guessed depicted local scenes – a woodland landscape and a harbour with fishing boats. Above the bed, there was an ornate crucifix and a large framed photograph which appeared to show an aerial view of the farm. On the adjoining wall was another, more intriguing, photograph. It depicted a young woman holding an acoustic guitar, standing in what looked to be a desert landscape, two men of a similar age standing close behind her.

Jane crossed the room and peered more closely. The woman was clearly Netty Munro, perhaps twenty or so years before. Her eyes were hidden behind sunglasses and her long hair was black rather than grey. But the figure was the same, if slightly slimmer, and there was no doubting her expression.

Jane walked back across the room and opened the wardrobe to unpack her small collection of clothes. Apart from the stack of towels on the top shelf, the wardrobe was empty and still seemed so when she'd finished hanging up her few items. It felt wrong, she thought. A wardrobe like this was designed to be full of clothes – thick jumpers and skirts for the winter, shorts and T-shirts for the summer, rows of shoes and accessories. She had barely anything, and the handful of clothes she possessed felt inappropriate whatever the time of year. Once again, she was feeling as if she'd arrived here only through some administrative error. Tomorrow, or probably even later today, someone would inform her there'd been a terrible mistake, and that she had no option but to return to the life she'd lived before.

She shook her head, trying to drive away the fear. Time to go down, she thought, and find out what this place really held in store for her. She wondered about trying to have a quick shower – the showers in the centre had been too busy that morning for her to shower before she'd left – but decided she could wait till the evening. Perhaps use up one of her few changes of clothes before they had supper or tea or dinner or whatever they were likely to call it in a place like this.

As she closed her bedroom door behind her, she saw that Elizabeth's was still closed. Jane already had the impression that Elizabeth was someone who did things in her own time and her own way. How well that would go down with Munro remained an open question.

Jane made her way down the stairs, feeling awkward and ungainly. There was something about the stillness and calm of the house that made her feel, inexplicably, both welcome and out of place. The hallway was eerily quiet, the only movement the drifting of dust motes in the shafts of sunlight through the windows.

All the doors off the main hallway were closed and, with no real idea of where to go, Jane made her way through to the kitchen. Munro was standing at the Aga, stirring a large cast iron pot with a wooden spoon.

'Hello, dear,' she said, not glancing up from her task. 'I didn't expect you quite so soon.'

'I'm sorry…' Jane began, taking the words as a criticism.

Munro looked up and smiled. 'Don't worry. You're free to come and go as you please here. I just thought you might want more of a rest before coming down. I think our friend Elizabeth might be having a nap. She seemed a little tired.' She left the last word hanging, as if freighted with greater meaning.

'She hasn't been down?'

'Not yet. We don't need to disturb her. Would you like some more tea?'

'Shall I make it?' Jane said, keen to be of some use.

'That's very kind of you.' Netty gestured at the pot with her wooden spoon. 'I'm making some venison stew for this evening.'

'Venison?' Jane had taken the kettle from the top of the Aga and was filling it at the sink. The sink was like everything else in the house. Old-fashioned, a little worn, functional. 'I don't think I've ever had venison. That's deer, isn't it?'

Munro nodded. 'The centre told me that both you and Elizabeth were meat eaters. Not vegetarian, I mean. That's right, is it?'

'Oh, yes. I eat meat.' *When we were able to afford it*, she added to herself. 'I don't know about Elizabeth though. I hardly know her.'

'We can check when she comes down. I can rustle something up if she can't eat this. I hope you're not squeamish about the idea of eating deer.'

'No, not at all.' Jane held out the kettle. 'Where do I put this?'

Munro lifted the lid on one of the other rings on the Aga. 'There's fine.'

Jane did as she was told, and went to fetch the teapot from the kitchen table. She was already feeling slightly intimidated even by this simple task. She'd forgotten till now that when Munro had made the tea earlier she'd used proper tea leaves, rather than the bags Jane was accustomed to.

Munro had obviously registered her discomfort. 'Just tip the old leaves into that green compost bin by the sink. Then rinse the pot. When the kettle's boiled, pour a little hot water into the pot to warm it up. Then throw that out and spoon in the new leaves.' She pointed to the shelves to the right of the sink. 'They're in that blue container. Three teaspoons should be enough, if you then just fill the pot halfway with boiling water.'

All this was more complicated that Jane's previous experience of making tea, which had essentially involved dropping a teabag into a mug. It sounded straightforward enough though. She busied herself following the instructions, hoping she was doing everything right.

'That's perfect, dear,' Munro said when Jane had finally placed the teapot on the mat in the centre of the table. 'There are mugs in that cupboard and milk in the fridge. Let it brew for a few minutes and then I'll come and join you.'

Jane sat herself at the table and watched as Munro finished preparing the stew. It was like no cooking she'd ever witnessed, let alone carried out herself, concluding with the addition of half a bottle of red wine, various herbs and other ingredients that Jane couldn't even recognise. 'Dried juniper berries,' she had explained, in response to Jane's question. 'They add a scent and a kind of bitterness, I suppose.' Jane had nodded, accepting that, if Netty Munro said so, this must be a desirable quality in a venison stew.

Finally, Munro slid the pot into one of the Aga's ovens. 'There. That can just cook away for a couple of hours, and we'll be ready for supper.' She sat herself down beside Jane and poured the tea, adding little more than a teaspoon or so of milk. 'You're feeling a little uncomfortable here, aren't you, Jane?'

Jane hadn't been expecting such a blunt question. For a second she had no idea how to respond. 'A bit,' she said finally, her voice little more than a whisper. 'It's all very new.'

'You're not the first, you know, Jane. A lot of our visitors feel like that at first. But you'll settle in. Everything I said was true. I want you to feel at home while you're here. And you're welcome to stay here as long as you wish.'

Jane was silent for a further moment. 'I still don't quite understand why you do this.' she said. 'Letting strangers into your home, I mean.'

'People are only strangers until you get to know them,' Munro said. She laughed. 'God, that's not the sort of stuff I normally come out with. But it's still true. As I said, Jane, I like to have a bit of life around the place. A few young people to liven the place up. It's generally worked out very well.' She paused. 'Once or twice, people have tried to take advantage. But I can handle that.' She took a sip of her tea and then continued, as if changing the subject. 'I'm not sure about Elizabeth though. I don't know whether she'll settle in. She strikes me as the independent type.'

Jane nodded, wondering how to respond. 'She seems quite… confident, I suppose. Sure of herself.'

'She certainly seems that,' Munro agreed. 'And that's excellent. As long as she's not *too* sure of herself.' She gazed down into her mug, as if thinking. 'So, Jane, shall I tell you about the farm?'

'Please,' Jane said, doing her best to sound interested.

'It's a working farm. A fairly large one. When I first bought it, I used to run it myself, but I'm getting a little old for that. I rent out most of it to one of my neighbours. He grows barley and wheat, and we've got some livestock on the lower fields.' She rose and walked to the kitchen window, beckoning for Jane to follow her. 'You see that line of trees. That marks the far boundary of my land. Then it runs round to those hedges over there.'

'That's huge,' Jane said, thinking of the postage stamp gardens she had once envied.

'Not compared with some of the places round here,' Munro said. 'But it's more than enough for me. I don't make a lot of money from it, but enough to keep ticking over, with the other stuff.'

Jane didn't feel able to ask what the other stuff might be. She had already been wondering how someone like Netty Munro had been able to afford a place like this. Perhaps she'd find out eventually, if Netty chose to tell them. For the moment, Jane was happy just to accept everything as it came along.

'I'll take you for a walk around the place in a minute,' Munro said. 'We should take advantage of this glorious weather while we can—' She broke off as the kitchen door opened.

Jane turned to see Elizabeth standing in the doorway. She had clearly showered, her hair still damp and uncombed, and she was wearing a fresh T-shirt, emblazoned with a face that Jane didn't recognise. Elizabeth's expression seemed to be a mix of awe and accusation.

'I've only just realised,' she said. 'It's been troubling me since we got here. Then I saw the picture upstairs. You are, aren't you?'

Munro looked back at her, a faint smile playing on her face, as if she were amused at some game that Elizabeth was playing. 'I...'

'But you are, aren't you? You're not Netty Munro. You're Natasha Munro.'

CHAPTER 8

Slightly to McKay's surprise, the front doors were unlocked, though it was clearly some hours before the place would be open for business. He pushed his way inside and stood in the gloom, looking around. The place had once been a cinema, he assumed, though that had been before his time in Inverness. He remembered it going through various incarnations as a bingo hall and then as a succession of nightclubs that had seemed to generate more trouble than business. It had stood empty for lengthy periods, including for most of the previous couple of years. A few months earlier, after some delays on the licensing front, it had finally reopened, this time as a stand-up comedy club.

McKay supposed there might be a market for that, though it wasn't his kind of scene. A couple of the local bars had run comedy nights, attracting decent crowds. The new owners, two brothers called Baillie, had a successful track record, already operating two other hostelries in the city, so McKay guessed they knew what they were doing. Even more remarkably, as far as McKay was aware, the Baillie brothers seemed to have no reputation for criminality. Maybe they were clean, or maybe they just hadn't been found out yet. As a cynical copper, McKay's inclination was to think the latter.

'Can I help you?' a voice said from somewhere in the gloom.

'I hope so, son. Though only time will tell.' McKay walked forward and saw a youngish man standing just inside the open inner doors. 'DI Alec McKay.' He waved his warrant card, knowing full well that the man was too far away to read it.

'Police?' the man said suspiciously. 'What can I do for you?'

'You are?'

'Drew Douglas. I'm the manager.'

'Good to meet you, Drew.' McKay walked past him into what was clearly the main performance area. There was a low stage running from the far wall into the centre of the room, surrounded by tables set out cabaret style. There was a bar stretching the length of the left-hand wall. McKay imagined the place might look quite glamorous when properly set up and lit. At the moment, it looked gloomy and slightly shabby, reeking faintly of beer.

'Is there something you're after?' Douglas prompted from behind him.

McKay turned, smiling. 'How's business? Not been open long, have you?'

'Just a few months, yes. We're doing all right. Bit of a slow start, but now people are beginning to find out about it. Look–'

'Nice to see something a bit different in the city,' McKay said. 'I'll have to give it a try some night. I like a laugh.'

'You'd be very welcome. Look–'

McKay could see that Douglas was growing nervous, afraid he might be about to be raided or have his books turned over. He wondered whether the club might have something to hide, but dismissed the thought, at least for the moment. Even if there was something dodgy going on, it was difficult to see how that might result in the death of one of its performers, here on a one-night stand. But, as with everything he came across in the course of an enquiry, McKay mentally stowed the thought away for later consideration. 'You seem to be getting some decent names performing here.'

Douglas had clearly accepted that, whatever McKay's reasons for being here, he wasn't going to explain his presence until he was ready. 'Aye, not bad. It's a bit of a challenge when you're this far north. The acts don't realise they can fly up here more quickly and cheaply than they can get to a lot of places in the north of England. But we're gradually educating them. We've persuaded a few to make the trek up here after Edinburgh this year so we're trying to set up a bit of an event around that.'

'Good stuff,' McKay agreed. 'See you had Jimmy McGuire on the bill last night. Not bad.'

Douglas frowned, still clearly wondering where this was heading. 'Not sure Jimmy really counts as a big name these days. We didn't even have the confidence to stick him on top of the bill. That didn't go down well, as you can imagine. In fairness, though, he did a decent set and we reckon he brought in a few extra older punters. Those who remembered him in his prime.'

'Dingwall and McGuire?'

'Aye, Crap name, wasn't it? Different times, I suppose.'

'So who was top of the bill last night?'

'Maggie Laing. Up-and-coming. Done a few of those panel shows on TV. Bit challenging, bit near the knuckle. Gets the men feeling uncomfortable sometimes. She went down a storm.'

'Glad to hear it,' McKay said, without any obvious sincerity. 'Did McGuire enjoy her set?'

'McGuire? Shit, is that what this is about? Don't tell me he's been causing some trouble. I was told he'd put those days behind him.'

'Those days?'

'The drink. He had a reputation for it at one stage. Not a good reputation.'

'That right?' This was something that seemed to have escaped Jock Henderson's all-seeing eye.

'Aye. A couple of years after the other guy – Dingwall, or whatever he was really called – got sent down, McGuire tried to make a comeback. He managed to get himself a few parts in daytime soaps and that sort of stuff, and then decided to make a solo comeback on the circuit. Just low key at first, till he found his feet. Dingwall and McGuire didn't really have a straight man as such, but if you've been part of a double act it's not easy to find your solo voice.'

'I'll take your word for that. I've always had a solo voice.'

'He went down pretty well at first,' Douglas went on. 'I mean, he's a funny guy. Good sense of timing. But he started to get a reputation for being unreliable. Used to knock back one too many before the show sometimes. It's not that uncommon. Helps overcome the nerves. Loosens the inhibitions. But the best ones either don't do it – at least not till afterwards – or know how to control it. Maybe McGuire needed a prop to replace his old partner, I don't know. But it affected him on stage. He began not turning up for gigs, or turning up late and, well, not in a condition to go on stage.'

'But you booked him anyway?'

Douglas shook his head. 'This was a while ago. He disappeared off the scene again for a good few years. Then, a couple of years ago, he began to make another comeback. Mainly just unpaid open mic slots at first, apparently. Just to get back into the swing of it, and get himself noticed, I suppose. The word was he'd kicked the booze and was fully sober, and that seemed to be evident in his performances. Like I say, he's a genuinely funny guy. Knows how to work an audience – nice balance between getting them behind him but gently goading them. Never too cosy. Can handle the hecklers. So he gradually worked his way back. I was more than happy to give him a go. Not that much of a risk, to be honest, because even if it had been a car crash, the punters would have enjoyed seeing him die–' Douglas stopped, reading McKay's expression. 'What is it?'

'I'm sorry, Mr Douglas. I should have made it clear before now. Mr McGuire's body was found early this morning. Just round the corner from here, down on Bank Street.'

Douglas was silent for a moment. 'Shit. I mean, I heard the sirens. What happened to him? Some sort of accident?'

'That's what we're trying to ascertain. But, no, at present, we don't think that it was an accident. We believe he was unlawfully killed.'

'Christ. You're kidding.' For a moment, Douglas looked genuinely shaken.

'I think even Mr McGuire might struggle to make a joke out of this,' McKay observed solemnly. 'Was there anything notable about Mr McGuire's behaviour in here last night? You mentioned he didn't respond well to not being top of the bill.'

'Yes, but that was just a few acerbic comments when he first arrived. To let me know he wasn't happy. After that, he was professional enough. Did his set. Went down well, as I said. Not sure after that. I saw him in the bar briefly afterwards, but he was only drinking fizzy water. You get thirsty up there on stage. I didn't see him later, so assumed he'd pushed off to his hotel.'

'Do you know if he had any contact with your top of the bill?'

'Maggie? Not particularly, as far as I know. I mean, they might have rubbed up against each other backstage, as it were. There's not a lot of space back there. But I didn't see them talking or anything. She was with me after the gig. We had a bit of a chat over a few drinks in the bar. I was trying to persuade her to take part in our post-Edinburgh shindig.'

'Do you know what time she left?'

'It was after midnight. I offered to walk her back to her hotel but she was insistent I shouldn't.'

'Where's she staying?'

'Place just along the river. We have a deal with them. Here...' Douglas ducked into the box office and returned holding a business card. 'This is the place. She and McGuire were both staying there.' He glanced at his watch. 'Don't know if she'll be up yet. She was planning to have a wander round the city today and then fly back this evening.'

'London?'

'Aye. She's from Glasgow originally, I think, but lives down there now. It's where the work is.'

'You've presumably got contact details in case we can't catch her at the hotel?'

'I've got a mobile. Otherwise, it's through her agent. Do you really need to speak to her?'

'We'll probably need to talk to anyone who might have had contact with McGuire last night. Including your staff here and any other acts.'

'There were just the two of them last night. Thought that would be enough to attract an audience. I can give you a list of the staff who were on duty.'

'I'll get someone to pop in and pick that up later. Any punters we should be talking to? Regulars, or anyone you saw talking to McGuire?'

Douglas hesitated for a moment. 'Not really. When I saw McGuire in the bar, he was very much on his own. He didn't come across as someone who liked to shoot the breeze, if you get my drift. We have a few people we see in here regularly, but I couldn't tell you their names, let alone give you any contact details. It's a varied crowd. Students, stag and hen parties, office get-togethers or just couples or groups looking for a different night out. And people who are just fans of a particular comic. Maggie's got some dedicated followers, and I dare say a few people came to see McGuire out of curiosity.' Douglas paused. 'Well, it'll be a small claim to fame, I suppose. Being present at his last gig. Poor bugger. Unlawfully killed, you said? You mean murder?'

'Too soon to say that.'

'I mean, he's had his issues over the years, but I can't imagine why anyone would want to kill him.'

'We don't know that anyone did. We don't know if he was targeted deliberately. Or if he was just in the wrong place at the wrong time.'

'Was it a mugging?'

McKay held up his hands. 'Best if I don't say any more for the moment, Mr Douglas. We'll no doubt be issuing a statement in due course. It's still early days. I'm just following up the most immediate leads for the moment.' He turned towards the door, indicating that the conversation was over. 'Many thanks for your time. We may well need to speak to you again. I take it we can find you here?'

Douglas nodded. 'Aye, I don't get much time away from this place.'

'Ach, well. At least you get a few laughs.'

***

McKay stepped back out into the street, blinking at the bright sunlight. Church Street was already looking busier, a mix of late commuters heading into work and early shoppers stealing a march on the day. He hadn't really been expecting to learn much new at the club, but he was still kicking his heels waiting for Henderson and his team to finish their work and it had seemed the obvious place to start.

The one new thing he'd learned was that McGuire had had a drink problem. Even if he'd put it behind him, it might be a line worth pursuing. In McKay's experience, drunks were often prone to making enemies or storing up trouble, especially if they ran up debts chasing their habit. The next question was whether McGuire had any family – a wife or partner who might, eagerly or otherwise, be awaiting his return home. McKay had already set someone checking that out back at the office. Apart from anything else, they'd need to get a formal identification as soon as they could.

He walked slowly down towards the river, enjoying the feel of the unaccustomed sun on his face. Like most Scots, McKay was instinctively mistrustful of warm weather, always assuming that the dreich days would follow. If the fine weather went on for too long, he felt uneasy, as if it was a breach in the natural order of things. For the moment, though, he was content, energised as he always was by the prospect of a major enquiry. He could see Ginny Horton waiting for him at the end of the street.

'Assume Henderson and his gang haven't finished yet?' McKay said as he reached her.

'Reckoned they weren't far off.'

'Probably dragging his heels deliberately just to annoy me.'

'I imagine so. Anything new from your visit to the club?' McKay had briefly interrupted Horton taking the young men's statements to update her on McGuire's identity.

'Not really. Other than that McGuire had had a drink problem, though was supposedly back on the wagon now. And that he was second on the bill last night. Or, given there were only two acts, bottom of the bill. Top was someone called Maggie Laing.'

'I've seen her on TV. On one of those panel shows. She was pretty good. Made the male comics squirm, which is always good to see.'

'I'll take your word for it. Different generation from McGuire, presumably.'

'Very. How'd McGuire go down last night?'

'Not bad apparently. Guy up there reckons he was a decent comedian, even if past his best. But wasn't entirely happy at not being top of the bill.'

'You think that might be relevant?'

McKay shrugged. 'Who knows? He wasn't the easiest of characters, by all accounts, so I suppose he could have had a run in with someone. Take a lot for that to escalate to this level though. The guy up there hadn't noticed him talking to anyone in particular.'

'So what next?'

'I need to update Helena, especially as it looks as if this might be of some interest to the media. And we need to set up the enquiry properly, now we know what we're dealing with.'

'Do we know what we're dealing with?'

McKay grinned. 'Nothing straightforward anyway.'

'Which is just how you like it. Want me to have a chat with Maggie Laing while you're briefing Helena?'

'Aye, that would make sense. Be good to catch her while she's still at the hotel. I don't imagine she'll have much to tell us, but don't want to be chasing across the country trying to get a statement from her.' He handed over the business card that Drew Douglas had given him. 'This is the place.'

'Okay. Let me know if you decide to head back before I'm done. If you take the car, I can always get a lift from one of the lads here.'

'Don't get a lift with Henderson. You never know where he's been. Well, you do. That's the trouble.'

She shook her head indulgently. 'Have fun, Alec.'

'Oh, I will. I promise you that.'

CHAPTER 9

There was a long silence before Netty Munro responded. 'I've always been Netty,' she said. 'To my family and friends. Natasha was just for the public.'

Elizabeth came further into the room. 'Yes, but Natasha Munro. That's awesome.'

'I'm delighted you think so, dear. It never really felt that way to me, though it had its compensations.' She was gazing at Elizabeth with an odd expression, as if they were engaged in some contest that Jane couldn't appreciate. She had the sense that there was some game being played, but she couldn't imagine what it might be.

'I can see now how you can afford a place like this. How you can afford to do what you do.'

'Perhaps,' Munro said. 'Though this place was an inheritance originally. An uncle of mine who died childless. I thought at first I'd use it as a holiday home. Maybe even turn it into apartments and let it out. But I came here and fell in love with it.'

Jane, sitting beside her, was looking baffled, as if the other two were speaking a language she didn't understand. 'Who's Natasha Munro?'

'I am, dear. Or at least I was.'

'She was famous,' Elizabeth said. 'One of the first big female country rock stars. And an actress. I don't know why I didn't recognise her straightaway.'

'Probably because I'm much older than I was then. And all of that is something of an exaggeration. I was hardly a star. Just a Christian singer-songwriter who got lucky and had a few hits. And then got asked to appear in some largely mediocre films. To be honest, I'm surprised that someone as young as you even recognises my name.'

'My father was a huge fan.'

'Ah, well, that makes more sense. He'd have been the right generation. It's nice to be remembered.'

Jane was gazing at her, her expression even more awestruck than Elizabeth's. 'You were a singer?'

'I still am, from time to time. I might even inflict it on you, if you're not well-behaved.' She laughed. 'I just don't do it in public for money any more. Which is a great relief.'

'But it must have been amazing.' Elizabeth pulled out a chair and sat down at the table next to them. 'Travelling the world. Meeting all those other stars. You must have millions of stories.'

'A few,' Munro said. 'A few of them even repeatable in polite company. And I might inflict some on you too if you're not careful. You're right though. It was exciting at first. When you're young and you get the chance to go places you've never dreamed of. But after a few years it gets wearisome – just an endless trail of tour buses and planes and airports and identical theatres. I was big in the US Bible Belt, and frankly it doesn't get more tiresome.'

'Is that why you stopped?' Jane asked.

'Partly, and partly because people weren't listening anyway. I had some hits on the US country charts. A couple of them crossed over and I sold a lot of records on the back of them. But then the hits dried up and I wasn't selling as many records any more. Fashions had moved on, and people were listening to other things. And my Christian stuff was perhaps just a bit too wholesome.'

'But your stuff was timeless,' Elizabeth said. 'I used to love it as a teenager.'

'That must have been a good few years after my heyday. You're right, in that it wasn't really just chart material. The hits were flukes initially. The first one was almost a novelty record. But they sold my albums. I imagine I could have continued a career if I'd wanted to. Focused on the songwriting and selling smaller venues on the basis of people vaguely remembering my name. But I'd really had enough by then. Wanted to jump off and do something different.'

'Farming?' Elizabeth said.

'As I said, that was mainly an accident. Most of my life has been really. One chance encounter or event that's led me from one thing to the next. I've tended to go with the flow. While this place fell into my lap, I decided to try to make a go of it. I had a fair bit of money stashed away, so I was able to invest in new machinery and carry out some repairs that were needed to the building. I knew nothing about farming, but I found a man who did, so I paid him to run the place and, in the process, teach me what he knew. Or at least the most important bits of what he knew. And that's how it happened.'

'You don't regret giving it all up?' Jane asked.

'Not in the slightest. It's not as if I was ever going to be a megastar. I'd had my moment in the sun, and it was time to move on. It was hard work, getting the farm back up to speed. But it was so different from what I'd been doing that it hardly felt like work at all. I wish that were still true, but I think now I'm beginning to be really past it.'

'Do people recognise you in the street?' Elizabeth asked.

Munro laughed. 'Not often these days, I'm relieved to say. Once upon a time they did, when I was appearing on *Top of the Pops*. I occasionally see people do a double take, as if they know they've seen me from somewhere but can't think where.'

'That was how I was,' Elizabeth said. 'When I first saw you outside. I thought you must be someone I'd met somewhere.'

'Is that right?' Munro said. There was an edge to her voice, Jane thought, though she had no idea of its significance. 'I've had people engage me in conversation about their family or their pets or what they did on their holidays, because they think they already know me but can't work out how. But I can bore you with my wealth of fascinating stories some other time. Shall we take a walk outside so I can show you what we have?' Without waiting for any response, she rose and picked up a pair of walking boots she'd left in the kitchen doorway. 'What kinds of shoes do you have?'

'I've just got a pair of trainers,' Elizabeth said.

Jane nodded. 'Me too.'

'That should be okay for the moment.' Munro stooped to pull on her own boots. 'The ground will be dry, given the weather we've been having, so if you avoid the very muddy patches you should be fine. Go and get them on and we'll go outside.'

A few minutes later, they were standing outside the back door of the farmhouse. There was a large open storage barn on their right, containing various farm machinery. To their left, a newly seeded barley field stretched away, slowly descending in the direction of the firth. 'So,' Munro explained, 'the fields over here are given over to barley and some wheat. The barley is used in the whisky industry, so it goes to a good home. Some of it eventually makes its way back here in liquid form. We've just planted this year's crop. That faint sheen of green across the surface is the first shoots beginning to appear.'

'It's huge,' Jane said, staring out in the direction of the water.

'We have a fair few acres.' Munro led them further down the farm track, past the barn. Behind the barn, Jane could see a small shanty town of other wooden buildings, presumably more storage. There was another large barn across the field. Munro gestured to their right, where grassland stretched up towards the elevated horizon. 'We have sheep grazing up there normally. They've been taken inside in preparation for lambing.'

'You have lambs?' Jane said. 'Will we be able to see them?'

'Of course. You can even have a go at feeding some of the smaller ones, if you like.'

To Jane, this just seemed like further proof that she'd stepped into a different world. Up to now, farming had meant little to her. A word used on supermarket packaging. Something she'd seen on TV in a documentary or a soap. She was standing in the middle of one, gazing in mild wonder at the tractor in the barn, the array of imposing but unidentifiable machinery beside it. It looked as if there would be livestock for her to gaze at and even to touch.

'It's not a large farm by local standards,' Munro said. 'But it's enough to eke out a living, especially after I invested to bring it up to modern standards. So that, combined with my royalties from songs and recordings, keeps me comfortable enough.'

'She must be loaded,' Elizabeth whispered to Jane. 'Place like this.'

'I–'

Munro clearly had sharper ears than the two girls realised. She turned to gaze at Elizabeth 'I wish I were,' she said. 'But you don't make big money in farms. Not up here. I've a little stashed away from my previous life. But mostly in investments and probably nothing like as much as you'd think.' Her eyes were fixed on Elizabeth, as if she were issuing a warning.

'I'm sorry, I didn't mean–'

'No, dear. I know you didn't mean anything. I just like to make things clear.' She had already turned and was heading back towards the farmhouse. Elizabeth tried to catch Jane's eye, but Jane had decided that she didn't want to appear complicit with Elizabeth. She had no idea what Elizabeth's game might be, but it seemed unlikely that she would remain as a long-term guest. Jane wanted to do nothing that might place her own position at risk.

As they reached the corner of the farmhouse. Munro paused and waved her arm airily in the direction of the firth below them. 'That pastureland down there belongs to the farm too. Now, let's go inside, and I'll get us a cold drink. We can take advantage of the fine weather and sit out on the decking for a while.'

She led them back into the cool of the kitchen, and busied herself getting items out of the fridge. 'We can have something stronger later, but maybe just some home-made lemonade for now? I made this earlier.' She placed an earthenware jug on the kitchen table and fetched some tumblers from one of the cupboards. She poured lemonade into each of the tumblers and pushed them towards the two young women. 'Let's go outside. I'll open the patio doors in the living room.'

They followed her back into the sitting room. The sun was streaming in through the large windows, and for a moment, after the relative gloom of the kitchen and hall, Jane was dazzled. As she blinked, she heard Munro saying: 'Ah, there you are. There's some lemonade out in the kitchen.'

As Jane's sight cleared, she saw that a woman, perhaps even younger than herself or Elizabeth, was sitting on the sofa. Her body was curled around itself, as if preparing to ward off an attack, and she looked terrified at their presence. She was staring down at the floor, her mousy blonde hair concealing her face.

'Is everything all right?' Munro was suddenly looking concerned.

The woman mumbled something inaudible. There was a book butterflied face down on the sofa beside her. Some kind of romantic novel, Jane thought looking at the pastel cover, though she couldn't make out the title.

Munro was moving to sit beside the woman, but she paused. 'Perhaps the two of you had better go out and sit on the decking. I'll come and join you in a moment. This is our third guest—'

'Aye, I know her,' Elizabeth said. 'Alicia Swinton. How you doing, Alicia?'

There was a moment's silence as the two women stared at each other. Then, suddenly and unexpectedly, Alicia Swinton burst into tears.

CHAPTER 10

'She's finishing breakfast,' the receptionist said, only the merest hint of disapproval in her voice. 'We don't normally serve it at this time, but she was working late last night apparently.'

Ginny Horton nodded. She imagined this place wouldn't bend the rules for anyone who wasn't, at the very least, a minor television celebrity. 'Would you see if I can have a word with her?' For the moment, she thought it better to keep matters as discreet as possible.

'You're the police, you say?'

Horton hadn't just said. She'd actually shown the woman her warrant card. 'Yes. I'd like a word.'

'No trouble is there?'

'No trouble. I just need a word.'

The receptionist stared at her for a moment, as if trying to contrive other reasons to prevent Horton entering the hotel. 'Can I tell her what it's about?'

'It's a private matter. It shouldn't take very long.'

'Okay.' The tone implied the request was anything but okay but the receptionist turned and disappeared into the restaurant, returning a moment later. 'She's sitting by the window.'

As it turned out, not only was Maggie Laing sitting by the window, she was also the only person in the room. She looked up as Horton approached.

'Good morning,' Horton said. 'Ms Laing?'

'That's me. Maggie, though.'

'DS Horton. Ginny,' she added.

'Well, Ginny,' Laing said, 'it's quite exciting to be interrogated by a police officer over breakfast. Did I finally manage to offend the wrong person?'

'If you did, that's not why I'm here. I'm afraid I've some bad news.'

'You'd better sit down then. Would you like some coffee?'

'I'm fine, thanks. But don't let me stop you drinking yours.' There was a cup of coffee and a half-eaten slice of toast in front of Laing.

'It'd take more than you to stop me, this time of the morning. Okay, fire away. I'm intrigued by what sort of bad news would have led you to track me down at my hotel breakfast. Not just last night's reviews, presumably?'

'How well did you know Jimmy McGuire?'

Laing raised an eyebrow. 'Jimmy McGuire? I didn't really. Met him for the first time last night. Though he seemed to think differently. Don't tell me he's got himself into some sort of trouble.'

'In a manner of speaking,' Horton said, feeling able to talk more freely with the knowledge that Laing and McGuire hadn't been friends. 'He was found dead this morning.'

'Dead? Bloody hell.' Laing took a sip of her coffee. 'Not in the hotel, I'm assuming. If it had, Sybil Fawlty out there wouldn't have been able to resist bursting in with the news.'

'No, not in the hotel. Look, Ms Laing, I'd prefer if you kept this confidential until we've formally confirmed the identity and made a public statement. He was found just along the road here. At the bottom of the alleyway leading down from Church Street to Bank Street.'

'Poor bugger. Great Hibernian heart attack, was it? He looked the type.'

'We don't think so, no. We think he was killed.'

'Killed? Fuck me. I've died a few times, but not like that. Who'd want to kill a comedian? Apart from other comedians, obviously.' She stopped, realising what she'd said. 'That was a joke. I'm sorry, It's what we do.'

'You implied McGuire thought he'd met you before.'

'Yeah, he reckoned he was sure of it. At least once, he said. Some comedy awards do a few years back. I mean, it's possible. Everyone always gets well pissed at those things, so I couldn't swear we hadn't come across one another. But I'd no recollection of it. I took it as a half-hearted chat up line. I'd been told McGuire apparently had a bit of a reputation in that department, especially with younger women. He was wasting his time in my case, for a number of reasons.'

'Can I ask who told you about this supposed reputation of McGuire's?'

'It was just the word on the street, you know. There's quite a grapevine in the business. If you're performing with someone, you ask around a bit in case there's anything you ought to know.'

'What sort of thing?'

Laing shrugged. 'It can be anything. The ones who are unreliable so you end up having to cover for them. The ones who try to sabotage the other acts. And the ones who are not safe in taxis, to use that quaint old phrase. With the emphasis on quaint, if you get my drift.'

'Which category did McGuire fall into?'

'Are you trying to get me to confess to his murder? I bet you're like Columbo. Just one more thing, Ms Laing…' She laughed. 'I felt for the poor bastard. He'd been a name once. Not a huge star, but a big fish up here. To be honest, Dingwall and McGuire were one of the reasons I got into comedy in the first place. I taped one of their TV appearances, and I used to watch it all the time as a kid. That was their skill. A bit edgy – well, for the time anyway – but mainly just silly. Went down well with kids. It was humour we could get, but something we knew our parents wouldn't entirely approve of.'

Horton had no recollection of the double act and could only nod. 'And McGuire?'

'Like I said, he'd apparently always had a bit of a reputation as what some might call a ladies' man. And I might call a creep. That went back to the Dingwall and McGuire days. From what I've heard, some people were surprised it was his partner who ended up inside. Maybe McGuire was more careful.' She stopped. 'I'm sorry. This isn't much more than gossip.'

'That's fine. 'I'm just trying to get an impression of what sort of a man McGuire was.'

'I'm not really the one to tell you. This is all rumour. I was told he'd had a bit of a drink problem when he first tried to make a comeback. Unreliable. But everyone reckoned he'd put that behind him. Recent word was pretty positive. Desperate to make a proper comeback, wasn't going to let anyone down. Didn't mind not headlining. Just as well as he probably didn't have any choice on that front.'

'How did you find him last night?'

'I didn't speak to him for long. We had a bit of a chat before the show. He was fine. A bit gushing, if anything, and prone to invading your personal space. Like I say, I thought he was trying to chat me up and I wondered if he'd try to make a move after the show. I've had that a few times. Though most men are able to take a knee in the balls for an answer. But he was maybe just trying a bit too hard because he saw me as the new kid on the block, you know? The up and coming talent who was bound to see him as a has-been.'

'Did you? See him as a has-been, I mean?'

Laing shook her head. 'He's obviously seen better days and some of his stuff was a bit dated, but he was an influence on me. Not in my act – we're chalk and cheese – but in making me want to do this. He's still a good comic.' She blinked. 'Sorry – was a good comic. Christ. No, he was good last night. Went down well.'

'Did he resent you being the headline?'

'If so, he hid it well. There were a couple of little jibes, joking but not entirely joking. Enough to remind me who he was. But all good-natured, to be honest. He said a couple of generous things about me in his set. Probably partly to get my fans on his side, but that's how it works. We all do that stuff.'

'Did you see him talking to anyone else? Anyone it might be worth our talking to, I mean.'

Laing thought for a moment. 'He didn't strike me as the gregarious type. But most of us tend not to be before we go on.

Too busy getting into the zone and running through various bits of routines.'

'It's not all improvised then?'

'Christ, no. Not even by those who pretend it is, with a few honourable exceptions. It's smoke and mirrors. Everyone's different. Some learn it line by line. I'm not in that camp. I have routines I expect to use during the set, then I improvise around them to some extent. I might drop some or expand them, depending on how it's going, and there's a bit of reacting to what the audience throw at you. The set evolves every time you do it. You find a funnier way of saying something or a better line, or some smart thought pops into your head unexpectedly.'

'Is that how McGuire seemed last night? Wrapped up in himself before going on?'

'I'd have said so. He wasn't unfriendly.' She hesitated. 'There was one of the club staff he was talking to at some length. Early in the evening, just after they'd opened the doors. Quite a lengthy conversation, at least by comparison with anyone else I saw him talking to.'

'I don't suppose you caught her name?'

'She was introduced to me as Morag. I didn't get her surname. Short blonde hair. She was working behind the bar later, but seemed to have some sort of admin role as well. She was the one who'd organised the hotel here. That might have been why McGuire was talking to her, if he had some query about the arrangements.'

'That's very helpful,' Horton said. 'I'll leave you to your breakfast. We probably won't need to bother you again, but do you have a contact number just in case?'

'Sure.' Laing fumbled in her pocket and produced a glossy business card. 'It's all corporate these days. Even us more radical types. Especially us more radical types, probably.'

'It's the same everywhere,' Horton said, handing over her own business card in return. 'Even in the police. If there's anything else you think might be of use to us, just give me a call. Thanks for your time.'

'No problem. It's a bit of a shock though. I hardly knew him, but he was part of the reason I'm doing this. Poor bugger. Good luck with finding who did it.'

'We'll do our best.'

Laing took another sip of her coffee, then grimaced. 'Ach, cold.' She looked back up at Horton. 'He had his problems, Jimmy McGuire. Everybody knew that. But he was a decent comic and he deserved better. This business can eat away at your soul if you let it.'

Horton nodded, unsure how to respond. 'Thanks again,' she said, then turned and made her way out into the hotel foyer, suddenly feeling overwhelmed by a sense of claustrophobia.

CHAPTER 11

Horton arrived back at the crime scene to find McKay still waiting. 'Wee Jock's only just finished his good works,' he said, 'so I thought I might as well hang around for you. I've got the uniforms carrying out a search of the immediate area to see if there's any sign of the weapon, though my guess is it's probably at the bottom of the Ness. Whether it's worth getting the divers out is another question.'

'Presumably we're talking about something not much more than a piece of wire?'

'Would need some means of gripping it but, essentially, yes.'

'Won't be easy to find.'

'No, even assuming it was thrown in around here. The killer could have hung on to it and disposed of it further downstream.'

'Or somewhere else entirely. Or not at all.'

'I always knew I could depend on you to lead us rigorously through all the fucking options, Ginny.'

'Here to help.'

'In that case make yourself useful and drive us back to the office. Three-line whip from Helena.'

'About this?'

'Partly. I filled her in on what we had so far. Especially about McGuire's identity. Can't say it exactly made her morning in the present circumstances.'

'Elizabeth Hamilton, you mean?'

'Aye. The last thing Helena needs is another enquiry that's going to get us plastered all over the media.'

'We don't have a lot of choice. McGuire's not exactly a household name these days, but he's still familiar enough to sell a few papers.'

They made their way back to the car. McKay waited till they were out onto the main road before continuing. 'Means there's going to be even more pressure than usual to get it right. And even more vultures circling if we fuck it up.'

'So what about Elizabeth Hamilton? We're both potentially in the frame there. That bastard in court threw as much mud as he could in our direction.'

McKay shrugged. 'That's his job. None of it will stick.'

'You're sure of that, are you?'

McKay was silent for a moment, which was answer enough. 'You can never be entirely sure, can you? In the end, the chiefs'll want to cover their own backsides. If that means throwing a few minions to the wolves…'

'You always know how to reassure me, Alec.'

'But Hamilton's story made no sense. By the time you got there, Robbins and Gorman were most likely already dead. Hamilton was just sitting there. She wasn't trying to rescue them. You didn't stop her doing anything. You didn't even know the bodies were there until it was too late.'

Horton shivered, thinking back to the windswept night on Rosemarkie Beach when she'd encountered Elizabeth Hamilton sitting soaked to the skin at the sea's edge, apparently oblivious to the world around her. Oblivious too to the two bodies she'd tied up and dumped in the rising tide only metres away. 'That's what happened. But there are no other witnesses. It's my word against Hamilton's. There was no one to corroborate my account.'

'You're a serving police officer who wrote up a dispassionate account of the event, whereas Hamilton's the fruitloop's fruitloop.'

'Remind me not to let you represent me if this becomes a disciplinary matter, Alec.'

'It won't,' McKay said confidently. 'Like I say, her story makes no sense. Why would she tie them up just to release them? And if she had been trying to release them, why would you have wanted to stop her?'

They'd rehearsed these arguments endlessly since the trial. Even knowing the line the defence had been planning to take, they'd both found the cross-examination challenging. Not because they had any doubt about the veracity or accuracy of their own accounts, but because the defence counsel had been so adept at twisting their words and adding a spin they'd never intended. Too often, they'd found themselves on the back foot, trying to explain what ought to have been self-evident. Horton had felt afterwards that they should have prepared better, but McKay just saw it as part of the game. 'They're smart smooth-talking bastards. What can you do?'

'Whether it makes sense or not isn't the point though, is it? The point is they managed to sow enough doubt in the jury's mind that she wasn't convicted.'

'Not fucking proven. Not fucking proven. This fucking country.'

'Whatever. The fact is she got away with it, and showered us in ordure in the process. And that bloody press campaign…'

In parallel with the trial, though with care to stay within the confines of the law, one of the national papers had initiated a campaign about the horrors of sexual abuse in the family and employment. As far as Horton had been able to ascertain, the campaign had been the joint work of a well-intentioned MSP who'd long campaigned on the issue and Hamilton's legal team, who'd seen an opportunity to highlight some of the issues that lay behind her trial. During the trial itself, the paper had been careful to keep its focus very general, drawing on a range of historical cases. After the verdict, though, they'd interviewed Hamilton to discuss the impact on her as a survivor of abuse. The implication had been that the Procurator Fiscal had been wrong even to bring the case to trial in the first place. The headline had been: Blaming the victim.

At the time, McKay's response had been succinct. 'Fuck me, so it's politically incorrect to prosecute fucking murderers now, is it?'

Horton's own feelings had been more nuanced. She appreciated everything that Hamilton had been through – some of which resonated with her own childhood experiences. But ultimately Hamilton had been directly responsible for the deaths of the two men she alleged to have been her abusers. It was right and necessary to take the background into account as mitigation, but it was equally right and necessary for Hamilton to be tried for the offences she'd committed. Horton had no problems with the outcome of the trial – she'd always hoped Hamilton's sentence would be as lenient as possible – but she was unhappy that the truth and her own reputation had been trashed on the way to that outcome. 'Has Helena said anything about what's going to happen with the Hamilton case?' she asked.

McKay shook his head. 'There's been no formal complaint from Hamilton or her representatives about our handling of the case. I suspect they'll just keep their heads down now they've got the verdict they wanted. If they open it all up again, we might uncover something that's not in their interests. Procurator grumbled a bit and wanted to have a further look at the case notes, but they accept our version is right, whatever smokescreens might have been thrown up in court. And it's not as if they did a brilliant job on the day, so they probably don't want to open it up again either.' He paused. 'Some of the higher ups were talking about referring it to complaints as a sop to the media. Show we're doing something. But Helena managed to talk them out of that, on the basis that it would give credibility to something that's basically bollocks. Other than that, we've just played a straight bat with the media.'

'It's still a blot on the copybook though, isn't it? Even if it goes nowhere,' Horton said gloomily.

'When you get to my age, the copybook's so blotted no one can read the bloody story.'

In McKay's case, that might well be true, Horton reflected. But it wasn't how she'd seen her own career going. 'Hamilton's handled it smartly though, hasn't she? The not proven verdict indicates that there were doubts about her innocence, but that'll all be forgotten in the wake of the newspaper campaign. And the media are always looking for sticks to beat Police Scotland.'

'We usually manage to provide them with plenty of ammunition without the need to make stuff up,' McKay said. 'Forget it, Gin.

This stuff will blow over and the wolves will move on to tear apart some other poor bastard. It's how it goes.'

'Except the McGuire killing's going to keep the spotlight on us that bit longer.'

'Aye, there is that. We need a result quickly. So let's hope there's something personal behind this we can pin down, rather than just some lunatic picking off random passing stand-up comics.'

Horton nodded as she pulled into the car park behind the office. 'Amen to that.'

CHAPTER 12

'You're already acquainted then?' Netty Munro said. Her voice was toneless, revealing nothing.

Elizabeth nodded. 'Aye, We go way back, me and Alicia. Don't we, Alicia?'

Alicia was wiping her reddened eyes, staring up at Elizabeth. 'Aye. Way back.'

Munro sat herself on the sofa next to Alicia. 'I think it's best if Elizabeth and Jane go and sit out on the decking, while I speak to Alicia.' She looked up at Elizabeth, as if daring her to disagree.

After a moment, Elizabeth nodded and pulled open the patio doors to step outside. Jane followed, with a brief glance behind her.

Munro waited until the two women were seated, then pulled the window shut before turning back to Alicia. 'It's not my business to pry into any of your backgrounds but is there some problem with Elizabeth being here?'

Alicia shook her head. 'It's not Elizabeth's fault. I knew her at school. We were friends as teenagers. I mean, not best friends, but we hung around in the same groups and knew each other pretty well. She was – okay, I suppose. It was her dad–'

'Ah.' Munro sat up straighter on the sofa. 'You don't need to tell me if you don't want to.'

'I used to go round to her house sometimes. Her dad was pretty well off, and they had some biggish place. Nice bit of Inverness near the river. Plenty of room so we tended to congregate there a bit. He never seemed to mind. Seemed to welcome us being there. But… then he caught me on my own, in the kitchen. And he tried to touch me. You know?'

'I know. Did this happen more than once?'

'I was stupid, looking back. But I was very young…'

'How old were you?'

'Only fourteen.'

Munro nodded, her face expressionless. 'I see.'

'He… he chatted me up, I suppose. I was flattered that he was even interested in a wee girl like me. He was decent looking for his age, and quite sophisticated, I suppose. So I let him do things–'

'I'm sorry, Alicia.'

Alicia shrugged. 'I think Lizzie – Elizabeth – knew what was going on. She warned me off. At the time, I was angry about it. Thought she was interfering. I thought it was her dad's business what he did.' She laughed. 'I didn't realise she was trying to protect me. We had a blazing row and didn't speak after that. I haven't seen her since I left school. Until now. Brought the whole thing back.'

'I'm sorry,' Munro said again. 'If you think it's better that Elizabeth doesn't stay here–'

'It's not her fault. It would be good for us to get to know each other again. Put that behind us.'

'I think Elizabeth's got as much to put behind her as you have. I know that your experience with her father wasn't the only instance of that behaviour.'

'Do you mean–?'

Munro held up her hand. 'I don't mean anything, except what I said. But you're both survivors, in your different ways. I imagine you'll be able to help each other, if you allow yourselves the time and the space. Jane too. But Elizabeth may not be the easiest person to deal with.'

Alicia nodded. 'She was always a bit like that. Strong-willed. Took the lead, and knew what she wanted. It's difficult to think of her as – well, as a victim.'

'Sometimes it's people like that who suffer most of all. Because they don't want to admit they're not in control. Are you ready for us to go out and join them?'

'I think so.'

'You've every right to your privacy. I've told you all that you don't need to share anything about your background if you don't want to. I have very few rules here, but that's one of them. Don't let Elizabeth badger you into sharing things that you don't want to. If you feel pressurised, tell me straightaway.'

Munro pushed herself to her feet and led Alicia out on to the decking. Elizabeth and Jane were sitting at the large table, sipping their lemonades in silence, gazing out at the vista of the firth and the mountains beyond. 'Alicia tells me you were at school together,' Munro said to Elizabeth.

'Yeah. We were good friends then, weren't we, Alicia?'

Alicia sat herself down beside the other two young women. 'Aye, pretty good. It's been a long time.'

'It has that,' Elizabeth agreed. 'How've you been keeping?'

'You know. Not so bad.'

'That's the story of all of us, isn't it?' Elizabeth said, glancing over at Munro, who was watching them both, her face revealing nothing. 'Not so bad. Considering.'

CHAPTER 13

'Jimmy McGuire?' Helena Grant said. 'Is that supposed to mean something to me?' They had already been through a variant of this conversation over the phone, but Grant never believed in making life easy for McKay.

'Dingwall and McGuire?' McKay offered.

'Firm of solicitors? I think I used them to buy my house.'

'Comedy double act from the nineties. I believe they were fucking hilarious.'

Grant frowned. 'Now you mention it, they do ring a vague bell. On telly a bit, weren't they?'

'Aye, so I believe. To be honest, I don't remember them either. But I'm told they had their moment in the sun.'

'It's all we need, isn't it? McGuire may be a long-forgotten no-mark, but I can see the headline: TV celebrity murdered.'

'You always know it's a long-forgotten no-mark when they don't put the name in the headline,' McKay agreed. 'But still everyone buys the paper to find out which particular long-forgotten no-mark it is.'

'And in the current climate the media will act as if he was the new Billy Connolly, just so they can use it as a stick to beat us.'

'You don't think you're getting a mite paranoid, boss?' McKay enquired innocently.

She gazed at him for a moment, as if considering a more forthright response. 'No, Alec, I really don't. Not considering that we're still dealing with the flak from the Elizabeth Hamilton case. They've still got that bloody media campaign going. Linking it to all the "Me Too" stuff in the US now.'

McKay shrugged. 'It's not unreasonable. Robbins and Gorman were precisely that kind of sleazebag. I'm sure there are plenty more of those bastards out there.'

'I'm not denying it. But there's also a political agenda here. In particular, an anti-Police Scotland agenda. They're just using it opportunistically. In part anyway,' she added as an afterthought. 'Jesus, if I'm not careful I'll find myself defending the likes of Denny Gorman.' She gave a mock shudder.

'Ach, it's always the way with those bastards. Even when they do the right thing, they do it for the wrong reasons. All we can do is keep buggering on.'

'And hope we don't bugger up. Aye, I know.'

'Any more word on the Hamilton case?' McKay enquired.

'Nothing. I'm hoping we've headed the Chief off at the pass with regard to getting complaints involved. Trouble is, they're always keen to get their arse covering in first just in case. But he recognises the Not Proven verdict implies that our testimony was accepted as credible. It was mainly just that there was no one to corroborate Ginny's version of events. And enough sympathy for Hamilton to swing the verdict.'

'Meanwhile, we're the bad guys because we dragged her into court.'

'Not our decision. All we do is present the evidence. Which is why I don't think the Procurator will be wanting to open this up again, either.'

'The danger is we all play the blame game. It's always a risk when you've got fuckwits in charge.'

'Expressed with typical diplomacy, Alec. Okay, so what about McGuire?'

'The key question is whether McGuire was targeted for some reason, or whether this was just some crazy picking a victim at random.'

'I don't think that's the politically correct term, Alec.'

'Aye, I'll let you know when I start worrying about the sensitivities of someone who garrottes random passers-by.'

'Pretty bizarre way to kill, whatever the motive.'

'Which is why my initial inclination is to think it's some nutter. Sorry, differently sane individual. I guess it's possible they didn't even realise what the consequences would be, though that's hard to believe. But it's also an efficient way to top someone in a relatively public area. Silent. Easy to target. Gives the victim no opportunity to respond or probably even make much of a sound. Simple to dispose of. If you wanted something quick and quiet, it might be what you'd choose.'

Grant thought for a moment. 'Could it be a pro job?'

'No idea. I mean, I suppose it's possible, for all the reasons I've just said. I've never heard of a pro using this method, but maybe this one's just pushing the envelope. Your more innovative hitman. But why would anyone take out a contract on Jimmy McGuire? He can't have been that unfunny.'

'Maybe he owed money. Maybe this was a warning *pour encourager les autres*.'

'Seems an extreme way of doing it. A good kicking would have sufficed. But we can look into that possibility.'

'Current wife? Ex-wife? Spurned girlfriend? Someone else with a grudge?'

'Anything's possible. It sounds as if he wasn't the easiest person to deal with, so he might have made a few enemies. I've got someone looking into his family circumstances. We don't even know yet if he was married. There doesn't seem to be any reference to a wife in any of the online stuff about him, but then there isn't all that much about him, full stop. He might have had his moment in the sun once, but the clouds have closed on him pretty thoroughly over the last decade or so.'

'What else?'

'We're talking to people at the club, though I don't know how much we'll get from that. We're doing some door to doors in the area where he was found, but most of the property round there is retail or commercial, so there's not much chance of finding anyone who saw anything. Beyond that, our best bet is to follow up any personal or domestic connections.'

Grant nodded. 'We can't keep this one under wraps. If this was a random killing, we potentially have a threat to public safety. We'll have to issue a warning.'

'We can keep McGuire's name out of it for the moment. The body's not been formally identified. That at least buys us a little breathing space.'

'Maybe. I'm willing to bet this has already been leaked. Some bugger here will have accepted a quiet backhander for revealing the identity. I'll talk to comms. I'd aim for a low-key warning – there's no point in stirring up too much panic – but it's their call.'

'I'll leave you to deal with those smooth-talking buggers. Not really part of my skill set.'

'You do surprise me, Alec. How are things on the home front just now?'

'Ach, you know, pretty much the same. Still enjoying the bachelor lifestyle, if that's what you want to know. Young, free and single. Well, single anyway.'

'Tell me about it.' Grant had been widowed at a relatively early age and lived by herself in North Kessock. 'How's Chrissie seem?'

'She's thawing a bit. Though still not giving any strong signs of encouraging me back. But we're both getting better at talking about things.'

The way McKay was shifting in his seat suggested to Grant that this improvement didn't extend to discussing personal matters with her. She felt the same discomfort when anyone tried to talk to her about her late husband. 'It'll work out in the end.'

'Aye, one way or another,' McKay agreed fatalistically. He pushed himself to his feet. 'I'd better see how Ginny's getting on. I've left her drumming up resources for us.'

'Let me know if anyone won't play ball, and I'll crack the whip.'

'Ginny's very persuasive.'

'It's going to be a big one, this. We need to make sure we don't screw up.'

McKay nodded. 'I'm thinking of having those very words emblazoned on a motivational poster above my desk.'

CHAPTER 14

'Right, we've got everything pretty much in place,' McKay said. 'We've a team doing door to doors round the area where the body was found. There are a few private flats and stuff tucked in among all the shops and offices, so someone might have seen something.'

'I'm not holding my breath. What about the club?'

'I've sent Josh Carlisle. If there's anything useful, he'll get it out of them.'

'Aye, I can see those wee lasses fawning over young Josh,' McKay said. Carlisle was a relatively inexperienced DC who had gradually been earning McKay's grudging respect. Not least because he'd emerged largely unscathed from the fiery baptism to which McKay subjected young officers.

'I was thinking more of his interviewing skills,' Horton said.

'Aye, those too.'

'I sent someone to check out McGuire's hotel room. I wondered about doing it while I was there, but thought it best to get it done properly so I just told them to make sure it wasn't touched till we got back.'

'Anything?'

'Not really. It looked as if he'd hardly been in there. The receptionist reckoned he checked in, dropped his bag, and pretty much went straight back out again. Which ties in with the time he arrived at the club. They brought his bag over and I've had someone go through it, but it's just a change of clothes really. No documents to add to what was in his pockets.'

'Which was?'

'Usual stuff. Wallet with a driving licence, a few bank cards, fifty quid in Scottish notes, and a few receipts and stuff. Driving licence gave us an address at least. Outskirts of Edinburgh.'

'How did he get up here?'

'Looks like the train. There's a return ticket in the wallet.'

'Anything else?'

'I've been doing a bit of digging into his personal circumstances. He was divorced. Not long after it all went pear-shaped following Dingwall's conviction. But there's also apparently a current partner. I found some story about McGuire online. A new future for funny-man Jimmy. You can imagine.'

'I can imagine right enough. Okay, we'd better get someone to go and break the news to his new partner. Then see if we can get her up here to do the formal identification.' McKay shook his head. 'That bit's always a bastard.'

Horton nodded. 'There was a card in his wallet for what I assume is his agent. Also Edinburgh based. Thought we shouldn't set any hares running till we'd spoken to the partner. Don't want this leaking out inappropriately.'

'Quite right.' McKay paused, thinking. 'If there's two of them down there worth talking to, maybe we should have a trip ourselves, rather than delegating it to the local plods. If I can get Helena to clear the lines.'

'You think it's a good use of our time?'

'Who knows? If anyone can tell us anything useful about McGuire, personal or business, it ought to be those two. And never does any harm to see the whites of their eyes when you break the news. Just in case they've got anything to hide.'

'You think they might have?'

'I don't think anything. But I don't discount anything either. Always keep an open mind.'

'That's you all over.'

'Anyway,' McKay went on, ignoring her, 'we've got the routine stuff underway here. If I get Helena to make the necessary calls today, we could have a drive down first thing. Always good to do a bit of missionary work among the lowland heathens.'

'You're not even a highlander, Alec. You're from Dundee.'

'Aye, but they don't know that, do they?'

'Okay, Alec. I'm game. As long as you don't get us into any trouble.'

McKay threw open his hands in mock outrage. 'When have I ever got us into trouble?'

'If that's a serious question,' she said, 'then let me count the ways.'

***

The woman sitting before him was tall, slim and attractive enough to make DC Josh Carlisle feel seriously out of his depth. She obviously recognised the effect she was having on him and wasn't going out of her way to minimise it. He could already feel a blush rising to his sensitive cheeks.

'Morag Bruce?' he said finally. His voice felt croaky and he had to clear his throat.

She smiled. 'That's me. And you're…?'

'Sorry.' He cleared his throat a second time. 'DS Carlisle. Josh,' he added, immediately realising that he'd sounded pompous.

'Good morning, Josh.'

'You've presumably been told why I'm here?' None of this was going quite the way he'd intended. He was wishing he could start the conversation again, like rebooting a computer.

'Drew just told us that – well, something had happened to Jimmy McGuire.'

Carlisle guessed that Drew Douglas had probably told the staff more than that. He couldn't imagine that the word about McGuire's fate hadn't spread rapidly through the grapevine. 'That's right. We just want to talk to anyone who might have spoken to Mr McGuire last night.'

'I spoke to him. I imagine a number of us did.' There was something in her tone that Carlisle couldn't immediately interpret.

'That's fine. We just want to build up as full a picture as possible of his movements. So anything you can tell us will be useful, no matter how trivial it might seem.'

She nodded slowly, as if considering the significance of his words. 'So what do you need to know?'

Carlisle was trying to avoid staring too obviously at her. She really was rather good-looking, he thought, with her short blonde hair and slightly mischievous smile. He had the sense that she was teasing him in some barely perceptible way, but decided he didn't care too much. 'We understand he arrived at the club around six. It would be useful to know who he spoke to. What sort of things he talked about. Anything he said that might be pertinent to our enquiries.'

'How will I know what's pertinent to your enquiries?'

Morag was definitely making fun of him, he thought. 'You won't, necessarily. And we might not, at this stage. Sometimes things that seem trivial at the time turn out to be significant later. If you see what I mean.' He knew he was on the point on descending into gibberish. 'So, really, anything you can remember.'

She nodded solemnly. 'That makes sense. He arrived here around six like you say. I didn't register the time particularly, but it was early in the evening. We open the doors at seven, so people can have a drink or two. Then the acts normally go on around eight or eight thirty, depending on how many people we've got on the bill. We normally have more than two, but McGuire and Maggie Laing were both biggish names in their different ways, so we didn't want to dilute the bill too much. Drew comperes and usually kicks off with an introductory set to warm the audience up. McGuire went on about eight thirty and did an hour. We had a break and then Maggie took us through till just before eleven.'

Carlisle had already noted she called McGuire by his surname and Laing by her forename, and wondered whether that was significant. 'What did McGuire do between getting here and going on stage?'

'To be honest, he arrived a bit earlier than we'd expected. We encourage acts to get here in plenty of time so we're not fretting about whether they're going to turn up or not. We've had one or two who've cut it fine or even been late, which doesn't do a lot for our blood pressure. At one point, McGuire had got himself a reputation for unreliability so I think he's keen to prove a point these days.' She stopped. 'Sorry. Was keen, I suppose.'

Carlisle was momentarily tempted to make a joke about the late Jimmy McGuire, but recognised this wasn't the moment. 'So what did he do between his arrival and going on stage?'

'Not a lot. The other worry we have when acts arrive early is that they might hit the bar. You'd be surprised by how many acts like a drink or two before they go on. Mostly, it's okay. Loosens them up a bit. But we've had the odd one who's had a dram or two too many, and believe me it showed. We were worried about McGuire, given his previous reputation, but he stuck to fizzy water all evening as far as I could see. When he first got here, he was asking if there was anywhere he could get a snack. Reckoned he didn't like to eat too much before going on so just wanted a sandwich. The local cafés were mostly shut by that time, so I sent someone to get whatever they had left at the Co-op.'

'And after that?'

'Jimmy sat around in the bar for a while. As far as I could see, he didn't say much to anyone, apart from, you know, exchanging pleasantries.'

'Anything else?'

There was a noticeable hesitation this time. 'Not really.'

Carlisle had been briefed in advance by Ginny Horton. 'Maggie Laing said he spent a bit of time talking to you.'

'Me?'

'That's what she said. Do you remember what he talked to you about?'

'I…' She looked less confident than at the start of the conversation, Carlisle thought. 'Yes, you're right. He did. I look after the admin here. I help Drew with the bookings, and do stuff like organising hotels if the acts need them, arranging taxis. That kind of thing. McGuire came up to me and complimented me on the choice of hotel. They pay their own costs, but we try to find them inexpensive places that are a bit friendlier than the chain hotels. We've got an arrangement now with the one where McGuire and Maggie Laing stayed. It's a comfortable place and they do a decent breakfast.'

'You said he began by complimenting you about the hotel. Anything else?' Carlisle was beginning to sense that her blether was keeping something back.

She was silent for a moment. 'Aye, there was, if I'm honest. It started with him getting a bit too close, if you get my drift. Then it felt as if what he was really trying to do was chat me up. It wasn't what he said to start with, it was just the tone.'

'Maggie Laing said something similar apparently.' Carlisle wasn't sure whether he should say that, but he had the sense Bruce might need a little encouragement.

'That right? Doesn't surprise me. But I bet Maggie had the sense to tell him to bugger off. I'm my own worst enemy. I went along with it for a bit. You know, flirting. It's just what I tend to do with the male punters. Flatters them a bit, and makes them feel good about the place. But they mostly realise I'm not serious.'

'And McGuire didn't?'

'No. Or at least he pretended not to. To give himself an excuse to push it a bit further, you know? Pestered me about what I was doing later in the evening. If I fancied going for a bite to eat with him. I said I couldn't, that I had to stay here clearing up afterwards. Which is true. He got a bit more pushy. Said he'd clear it with Drew. I said that wasn't the point, that it was my job.' She hesitated, and Carlisle realised that she had something more to tell him.

'Go on.'

'He got even pushier then, and it felt a bit nasty. He didn't quite say it in so many words, but he hinted that, if I didn't say yes, he'd tell Drew it was me who'd come on to him – to McGuire,

I mean.' She took a breath. 'That I'd offered my services to him, if you like, for a fee.'

Carlisle could feel himself blushing again. 'You're kidding.'

'No. I mean, like I say, it wasn't as explicit as that. He knew if I tried to make a scene about it he could claim he'd been misunderstood. But that's what he was suggesting.'

'What did you do?'

'Just very quietly told him to fuck off. Then I told him, if he tried anything more, I'd tell Drew exactly what he'd said, word for word, and Drew could judge for himself. And that if I knew Drew, he'd make sure everyone on the Scottish circuit knew exactly what McGuire was like.'

'Good for you. What was McGuire's reaction?'

'He looked baffled. Said he didn't know what the hell I was talking about. Then he turned and went off to his dressing room and I didn't see him again after that. Thank Christ.'

'Did you say anything to Drew – Mr Douglas, I mean?'

'I did afterwards. In case McGuire tried anything. But Drew and I go back a way. We trust each other. I just wanted to make sure it was all out in the open.'

Carlisle nodded. 'Mr Douglas didn't mention this when we spoke to him this morning.'

'It was all something and nothing, really. McGuire had always had a bit of a reputation as a womaniser.'

'This is a bit more than a chat up though, isn't it?' Carlisle said. 'This was harassment.'

She smiled. 'Most of us women are more than accustomed to that. Especially in an environment like this. We know how to deal with it.'

'You shouldn't have to,' Carlisle pointed out.

'Has anyone ever told you how sweet you are? I wish I was a few years younger.'

'I–' Carlisle had opened his mouth but couldn't think how to finish the sentence.

'The other reason Drew didn't say anything,' she went on, ignoring Carlisle's increasingly reddening face, 'is that he was a bit afraid it might make us look like suspects.'

'Suspects?' Carlisle said, relieved to be scrambling back onto safer conversational ground.

She shrugged. 'I know. It's daft, isn't it? But Drew's a bit paranoid. He thought this gave us a possible motive for wanting to harm McGuire. I said to him you don't kill someone just because they've tried it on.'

Carlisle could think of murders committed for more trivial motives, but nodded. 'Even so, I suppose I should ask you and Mr Douglas if you can account for your movements after the end of Mr McGuire's set last night.'

Her eyes opened wide. 'You don't seriously think–'

'Just for elimination purposes. We'll be asking everyone here the same.'

'I was behind the bar all evening. Drew was coming and going like he does, making sure everything's running smoothly. Then, like I say, we make sure we've cleared up at the end of the evening. We close the bar at eleven, so it's usually after midnight before we've got everything sorted. Think last night it was about twelve thirty before we got finished.'

'Who was here then?'

'Drew and me, along with a couple of the bar staff.'

Carlisle nodded. They didn't yet have a confirmed time of death for McGuire, so this didn't entirely let Morag Bruce or Drew Douglas off the hook, but he accepted Bruce's view that McGuire's behaviour at the club was hardly the motive for a garrotting. Both Douglas and Bruce had said they hadn't seen McGuire after his set, but no one else had so far been able to confirm his departure time. 'Anything else you can tell me? Did you see McGuire talking to any of the customers?'

Morag shook her head. 'Not really. He was still in the bar when we opened up, but it was pretty quiet at first. I didn't really see him after that, except on stage.'

'Thanks for your time, Ms Bruce. We may want to talk to you again as the enquiry progresses, but that's fine for the moment.'

'I hope you don't really think that me and Drew might have—'

He held up his hand in the way he used to when controlling traffic. 'We don't think anything yet. It's very early days in the investigation and we're just gathering as much information as we can. The most important thing is that people are open with us.'

'Okay,' she said. 'We'll do whatever we can to help. Apart from anything else, it doesn't do the club's reputation much good if an act literally dies on us.'

'They reckon any publicity's good publicity.'

'Let's hope so,' Morag Bruce said. 'Because I've got a feeling that there's going to be plenty coming our way.'

CHAPTER 15

Jane wasn't sure what to call the meal. Netty Munro called it dinner, because she was English and, truth be told, just a bit posh. Jane would normally have called it tea or supper, but then she wouldn't normally have been part of a group that ate as late as this. And she wouldn't normally have been eating this kind of food.

Munro had insisted that it was just a simple dinner, but it wasn't like anything that Jane was accustomed to. She'd had stews before, of course. She remembered her mother cooking stews sometimes using the cheapest cuts of meat, which they could still afford only occasionally. They'd been a treat then, and she'd enjoyed them. But they'd been thin and watery and flavourless compared with what she was eating now, bulked out with potatoes and whatever other cheap veg they could get their hands on.

This food was nothing like that. This was a rich casserole, heavy with red wine and aromatic with herbs and other flavourings she'd never tasted before. There was an edge there that she assumed was from the juniper berries that Munro had mentioned. And on top of it was a light but flavoursome crust, which Munro had said was a cobbler made from some local smoked cheese. There were boiled new potatoes and a selection of vegetables, only some of which were recognisable to Jane. Most unexpectedly of all, there was wine served with the meal.

This was something else that Jane had never really encountered, though she knew it was normal enough. Her dad and Iain had both been beer drinkers, but that had just been something they knocked back as much as they could, whether or not there was food involved. Quantity, not quality. And any other booze they could get their hands on. It had killed her father, and it would kill Iain, not that she cared about that.

Wine in a nice-looking glass over dinner was something else again. Something she'd never expected would be part of her life. But there she was, sitting out on the decking, working her way through a rich venison casserole with a glass of rosé sitting, beaded with condensation, beside it.

When Munro had offered her a choice of wines, Jane hadn't known what to say. She'd assumed she wouldn't like wine anyway – she'd never cared for beer – so she thought it probably wouldn't matter. She picked the rosé mainly because it looked the prettiest, and Munro had nodded as if in approval at her choice, although Jane noted that she'd subsequently been drinking red wine.

But Jane was happy with her choice. With the first sip, she'd been unsure, finding the wine sharper and less sweet than she'd expected. But then she detected the flavours and aromas that people always talked about – something floral, something more fruity like strawberries, she thought. By her third or fourth sip, she'd decided that she really did like this drink after all.

She was still feeling uncomfortable here, though her discomfort was lessening with every mouthful of wine. She, Elizabeth and Alicia had been joined by another guest for the meal, a middle-aged woman called, rather unexpectedly to Jane, Henry Dowling. Munro had explained that Henry was really short for Henrietta, but Jane still couldn't understand why someone would choose to saddle themselves with a man's name. Like Netty Munro, Dowling was English and posh, so Jane had decided it was just one of those eccentricities that the posh English are prone to, like shooting grouse and choosing to holiday in Scotland when they could clearly afford to go anywhere.

'Henry and I go back years,' Munro had explained. 'We used to perform together in the early days. Henry was much more talented than I was.'

Dowling had raised an eyebrow. 'But Netty was much more successful,' she said. 'So go figure.' She was a tall slender woman, with long black hair and pale skin. She might have been a hippy in her day, Jane thought. Certainly that was still how she was dressed tonight, in a long brightly coloured dress that reminded Jane of clips she'd seen on TV of 1960s fashions.

'You just never sold out the way I did,' Munro countered. 'I chased the dollar, not even particularly successfully, while you held on to your integrity.'

'If you say so, dear,' Dowling laughed. It was clear to Jane that the two women were fond of one another, for all their jibes. She wondered where Dowling lived. She'd arrived on foot, so presumably somewhere nearby. It seemed odd that she and Munro had ended up living in the same small Highland village.

The weather had remained fine, and Munro had arranged for them to eat out on the decking at the rear of the house. As they'd sat down to eat, the sun had been low over Ben Wyvis, the Cromarty Firth dazzling gold in the low sunlight. The landscape over the firth was hazy, the patchwork of fields and trees pale in the early evening. As they sat eating, the sun's last crimson gradually disappeared behind the mountain, leaving the sky translucent in the gloaming. The whole scene was more beautiful than anything Jane had seen before.

As the evening drew on, it remained warm enough to sit outside. They finished the meal with a rhubarb crumble made with fruit grown on the farm. This was food that Jane at least loosely understood, but there were still flavours she didn't recognise. Fresh ginger, Munro had suggested, and some other spices. After the dessert, she had produced a cheeseboard laden with what she said were all local cheeses. Some of the others sampled them, but Jane found the array intimidating and, already full, she was content simply to sip a cup of coffee. Even that, she realised, wasn't the instant stuff she'd drunk all her adult life, but something different – richer, sharper, leaving small granules in her mouth. She'd had enough of the wine not to worry too much and simply accepted the experiences that life was, for the moment at least, throwing in her direction.

Elizabeth and Alicia had been unexpectedly quiet all evening. Jane had assumed that Elizabeth would use an occasion like this to demonstrate her superior understanding of this type of lifestyle, but she'd largely sat in silence, other than to respond to direct questions. Munro had clearly been doing her best to engage Alicia in conversation, but for the most part Alicia too had seemed content merely to participate passively in the exchanges between Munro and Dowling. She'd looked relaxed enough, Jane had thought. Unlike Elizabeth who, even in her silence, had managed to convey an air of resentment at having to be part of the dinner.

As the sky slowly grew dark, Munro had risen and disappeared into the house, returning a few moments later carrying two guitar cases. Dowling shook her head. 'Oh, Christ, darling, you're not going to inflict that on your poor guests?'

'They've got to earn their supper somehow,' Munro said. 'Anyway, I need the practice. You and I haven't played together for too long.'

Dowling gave a mock sigh and then took one of the guitar cases. The two women moved their chairs back from the table, and removed the guitars from their cases. After a few moments spent tuning the instruments, Munro began to play.

For Jane, the effect was magical, a culmination of everything she'd enjoyed during the evening. She didn't recognise the tune and had no idea whether or not Munro was a skilled player. The music began with a repetitive finger-picked figure but then Jane could feel the melody growing more complex, Munro's fingers moving with increasing rapidity across the fretboard.

After a few moments, Dowling nodded, recognising the tune, and played, adding a further level of complexity. 'I'll do this in Henry's honour,' Munro said. 'One of her favourites.'

Munro explained to Jane afterwards that the song was a traditional Scottish ballad which she sang as "Auchanachie Gordon and Lord Saltoun" though it was better known to contemporary folksingers as "Annachie Gordon" from a version recorded by an English singer called Nic Jones. Dowling had loved that version and always included it in her acoustic sets but had gradually reverted to the Scottish title and words. Jane hadn't really understood that, given that both Munro and Dowling were themselves English, but Jane decided it was just another of those eccentricities.

The song itself she found utterly entrancing. She wasn't entirely able to follow it on that first hearing, but it was a sad tale about a young woman forced by her father to marry some nobleman rather than her true love. The story had ended badly, with the true love returning from a voyage to find the woman had died on the day of her marriage. Jane hadn't been sure whether that was really better or worse than if he'd arrived home to find her alive but married to someone rich and powerful. It sounded like a tragedy either way. There was something about the story that, oddly, resonated with Jane. Not that she'd ever been forced to marry a nobleman or was ever likely to be. But she knew about being forced into marriage with someone she hadn't even liked. She wondered if things might have been easier if she'd simply dropped dead on her wedding day. Mind you, she thought, the registrar would have been pretty pissed off.

Jane suspected that Munro's voice might have seen better days – she'd have to try to hear some of her recordings – but she was still a remarkable singer. It was as if she somehow managed to get inside the song, as if she were singing words she'd written. As if she were singing about herself and her own experiences, rather than something that had happened hundreds of years before. Yet there was a strangeness to it, especially on an evening like this when everything felt so unworldly, as if Netty Munro was calling to them from another place or time.

After the first couple of verses, Dowling joined in on the harmonies, her voice unexpectedly higher than Munro's. The effect was even eerier, the two voices much more than the sum of their individual parts, the notes intermingling with the guitar accompaniment to create an oddly choral sound.

When the song ended, there was silence for a moment, disturbed only by the faint chirrups of the night's last birdsong.

It was as if no one knew how to react. Applause seemed almost inappropriate, too trivial. But finally Alicia clapped and Jane felt able to join in. Munro smiled and gave a mock bow, holding out her arm to acknowledge Dowling's contribution.

Then the smile faded from Munro's face. 'Are you all right, Elizabeth?'

Jane turned to see that tears were streaming down Elizabeth's cheeks. The expression on her face, though, was very different from that of the sobbing Alicia earlier. Alicia had looked distressed, anxious, perhaps even afraid. There was no sign of distress in Elizabeth's eyes. Instead, she looked furious with the world around her.

Munro had placed her guitar against the railing around the veranda and was rising to her feet, but Elizabeth had already left the table and was heading back into the house.

At the last moment, she stopped and turned back to face the group still gathered round the table. 'That bastard,' she said. 'That bastard father. He killed her.' She took a breath, as if struggling to hold back more tears. 'She should have killed the bastard. She should have killed *him*.'

CHAPTER 16

'So what's this, Alec? Date night?'

McKay was studying the whitebait on the end of his fork as if it might be a clue in some ongoing enquiry. 'Just thought it would be good for us to get together on neutral ground.'

'I can't remember the last time you took me out to dinner.' Chrissie looked around her at the small bistro. 'Decent place too. You come into some money?'

'Hardly. What with paying rent on top of a mortgage.' He regretted the words even before he'd finished speaking. Smart move, Alec, he thought. Give Chrissie some ammunition right from the start. He could feel this was already beginning to drift the same way as every other time they'd been together over the last couple of years.

'That what this is all about then,' she said. 'You trying to get back into the marital home to save a few quid on rent.'

He was tempted to say it was more than a few quid. But he bit back the words. Otherwise, they really would get locked back in the same old tit for tat. 'Don't be daft. I'm not trying to do anything. I just thought it was time we had an ordinary conversation.'

'There's the couples counselling,' she pointed out. 'We're making some progress there.'

'I'm not disagreeing,' he said, though his view of the counselling was still more negative than hers. He'd learnt not to say that too often though. 'But that's – well, it's an artificial set-up, isn't it? It has to be. The whole point of it is to talk about things we wouldn't talk about day to day. I don't want to talk about any of that stuff tonight.'

'You don't want to discuss Lizzie?'

He felt as if he were being led gently into a trap. In the counselling sessions, they tended to focus on little other than Lizzie. The truth was that tonight he wanted to talk about almost anything else. But he could hardly say he didn't want to discuss the daughter who'd died, alone in London, in what might have been an accident or might have been suicide. 'That's not the issue,' he said finally. 'But we're adults. Middle-aged. We have our own lives and futures.'

'Unlike Lizzie.'

He took a breath. 'Chrissie, don't. I'm not trying to downplay what happened to Lizzie or deny we need to deal with it. But we're better talking about that when we've got a professional there to help us through it. Tonight, I just wanted us to get back to the small talk we used to have.'

'Did we used to have small talk?'

'You know fine well we did. We used to make each other laugh.'

For the first time that evening, she allowed him a faint smile. 'Aye, I suppose we did, once upon a time.'

'We could do that again, you know, Chrissie. We could get back there.'

'You reckon?'

'I reckon it's worth a shot.'

'I'm not sure this is neutral territory anyway,' she said. 'This is more your stamping ground than mine these days.' Since he'd moved out of the house he'd shared with Chrissie, McKay had been renting a small bungalow in Rosemarkie on the Black Isle, just a few hundred metres from where they were sitting. 'You in here often then?'

'Chance would be a fine thing,' he said. 'Last time I was in here, I was offering a consoling coffee to Jackie Galloway's grieving widow.' Galloway had been one of the victims in a major murder enquiry a few months earlier.

'You always went for the older woman, Alec. Present company excepted.'

For the first time, McKay felt able to smile back. 'She's still living there up on the High Street. By all accounts having the time of her life now she's got rid of that bastard Galloway.'

'There's a lot to be said for dumping your bastard husband, I hear.' Her face was deadpan, but, perhaps for the first time in recent years, McKay felt comfortable that she really was just joking.

'So I've heard.' McKay gestured towards his starter with his fork. 'This whitebait's excellent. How's your soup?' Chrissie had ordered the Cullen Skink, the smoked haddock soup ubiquitous in these parts.

'Really good,' she said. 'One of the best I've had. Not bad having a place like this on your doorstep. Impressive location too.' Crofters Bistro was set on the seafront overlooking Rosemarkie Beach, with a fine view of the Moray Firth. The sun was low in the sky behind the building, casting long shadows across the water, the Eastern sky already turning a deeper blue.

'Aye, not bad. Romantic,' he added, chancing his arm.

'I suppose it might be in the right company.' She gave him another smile. 'We'll have to see.'

'Do you want another glass of wine?'

'Why not?' Chrissie had been dropped off here by her sister, and had already planned to get a taxi back into town. 'If you want some more we could get a bottle.'

'Let's go mad.' He lifted his head to catch the eye of the waiter.

'As long as you're not trying to get me drunk, Alec McKay.' She was already looking happier and more relaxed than he could remember seeing her.

'Like I say, I'm living in reduced circumstances. I can't afford what it would cost to get you drunk.'

She laughed, and he wondered how long it had been since he'd heard that sound. They'd always got on well together, he thought. Best friends as well as lovers. She hadn't even worried too much about the amount of time he devoted to the job, which was what destroyed many police marriages. She'd known what she was marrying, and although she'd occasionally grumbled at the long hours and late nights, she'd never really resented it. It had only been after Lizzie's death that things had changed. That had brought them up short, made them reflect on what parental failings might have led their daughter to leave home and to die alone in a far-off city. They'd both felt guilty, and they'd each sought to offload their guilt onto the other. And neither of them had been able to talk about it.

The waiter came and brought them the requested bottle of red wine, and then their main courses. Outside, the twilight was thickening, and they could see the lights of Fort George and Ardersier on the other side of the firth. Chrissie was right, McKay thought. In the appropriate company, this place was romantic, true enough.

'Long while since I've had chips as good as these,' Chrissie said. It wasn't exactly the romantic utterance that McKay might have hoped for, but at least it showed she was enjoying herself. 'How's yours?'

'Terrific.' They still weren't really into the season and it was midweek, but the restaurant was almost full. This was something else he'd missed, he realised. The company. Not just Chrissie – though mainly Chrissie – but the whole experience of being out in a crowd of people. He'd been to the pub a few times since he'd been staying there. They were welcoming, but the locals knew who he was after the Galloway enquiry, so he was always treated with a degree of wariness. They weren't exactly unfriendly but they tended not to be very forthcoming either, so too often he'd found himself sitting alone in a corner nursing a pint. Though maybe, he reflected, that was just because he'd always been an inhospitable bastard.

Tonight, though, was going well. Better so far than he'd hoped.

They finished the meal, declined desserts but ordered coffee with a single malt for each of them. McKay sipped gently at the whisky and said, 'Sorry you came?'

She was still smiling, which he took as a good sign. 'I nearly didn't, you know. I'd told myself I wouldn't meet you outside the counselling sessions until I was sure I was ready. And I wasn't at all sure yet. Then, when you phoned and left that message – my first instinct was still to say no. Then I had a chat about it with Ellie.' This was Chrissie's younger sister. 'She said we needed our heads banging together. She said it was clear as day to her that we were desperate to get back together, but were too proud to admit it.'

'And was that true? In your case, I mean.' McKay wasn't at all sure this was the right question, but it was too late to withdraw it.

She was silent for a moment. 'Was it true in yours?'

'Aye. And I'm a stubborn old bastard. Took me a lot to pick up that phone, you know.'

She nodded. 'Aye, I know. And, yes, it was the same with me. I mean, desperate might be overstating it. I don't want you getting ideas above your station. But Ellie was right.'

'You reckon this might be the start of something then?'

'I think it just might if you play your cards right, Alec McKay.'

'I won't be taking anything for granted.' He held up his empty glass. 'One more for the road.'

'Better not. I don't want you to have to carry me. You're too old for that.'

'Thanks for that.' He paused. 'You could come and have a drink back at the bungalow, you know. I've a decent bottle in the cupboard.'

She was silent for a moment, watching him, and he half expected she was going to say no. But finally she said, 'Go on then. I haven't seen this palatial residence of yours.'

'I'll have to give you the grand tour. If you've thirty seconds to spare.' He hadn't really expected that Chrissie would be prepared to visit the place, but he'd given it a rare tidy-up just in case.

He paid the bill and they stepped out into the night. It was still unexpectedly warm for so early in the year, and the light lingered even though the sun had long set behind the Black Isle. They walked along the seafront then paused to gaze across the firth at the line of lights on the far shore. The tide was low, and the beach stretched out below them.

'I see that Hamilton woman was acquitted,' Chrissie said. 'That was along here, wasn't it?'

'At the far end. Where the café is.'

'That going cause any trouble for you? Her getting off and all.'

'I hope not. It was Not Proven. Everybody knows she did it. It was clever lawyers got her off. But fair play, maybe she'd suffered enough.'

'Aye. There is that.'

'Anyway, I didn't invite you out to talk shop.'

'Maybe you should do it more often, Alec. You bottle that stuff up too much.'

They were leaning on the railing overlooking the beach. McKay turned to her. 'You reckon I'll get the chance then? To talk about it more often, I mean. With you.'

She was silent for a moment, then laughed. 'I reckon that's where we're heading, you numpty. Don't you?'

It was McKay's turn to be silent. Then he leaned forward and, somehow, the next moment they were kissing. Like teenagers, McKay thought. Like fucking teenagers.

CHAPTER 17

Ginny Horton finally felt she was getting back into some sort of a rhythm. The dark mornings were long past so she found it much easier to drag herself out of bed for a decent run before getting ready for work. Her partner Isla was planning to work from home today, so Horton had left her sleeping peacefully in their bed. She'd felt a brief pang of regret as she'd stepped out into the chill air, but her mood had brightened immediately at the sight of the low morning sun glittering on the dewdrops.

She'd always found it difficult to keep up her running through the winter, though she tried to maintain the discipline. It was just that much harder to force yourself out of the house into a chill black morning or a wet dark evening. This winter had been much worse though. She'd spent those dark months fearful of leaving the house, worried about the presence of her stepfather in the area. Thankfully, all that was behind her, though the experience had been traumatic.

Isla had persuaded her she needed to get back into the routine. 'You know it makes you feel better,' she'd said. 'If you sit in here scared of every shadow you'll never get back into it. Just get up, get out and start running again.'

The days rapidly lengthened up here, and as soon as the mornings were sufficiently light she followed Isla's advice. At first, she'd wondered how she'd ever managed to do it at all, let alone achieved the speeds and distances she'd been accustomed to. She started with short runs, just heading down to the army camp at Fort George, enjoying the mirror-like sheen of the Moray Firth in the early morning light and the taste of the cold air in her lungs.

Within a few days, she could feel herself slipping back into her old routines, slowly building up her pace and stamina. The initial aches were receding, and she found she could do it after all. Soon she was planning longer and longer circuits.

Her mind entered a different space when she ran. There was something about the rhythm, the sense of isolation, that allowed her thoughts to move into new channels. It was almost as if she wasn't thinking, as if she were surrendering herself to the unconscious. But she also knew it was often where her brain worked most effectively. Sometimes, if she was facing a particularly intractable issue at work, this would be where the solution would jump, unbidden, into her brain.

She could feel herself entering that zone. The sky was cloudless and there was almost no wind, and she could see the landscape of the Black Isle opposite mirrored in the firth. She gradually picked up speed, heading past the fortifications of Fort George and then out along the coast towards Whiteness Point in what had become her usual circuit. She could complete it in the time needed to allow her to shower, dress, and grab a bite of breakfast before she headed into the office.

This morning, she was feeling mildly guilty. They had a major enquiry kicking off and part of her wanted to be in the office early, getting things moving. Alec would almost certainly be there first thing – although that tended to be the case most mornings now he was living by himself – and would express mock-disapproval at her arrival.

But she also knew she worked much more effectively if she'd been for a run. Her head felt clearer, her brain sharper. She knew too that it was important to maintain her routine. If she allowed it to slip, she'd struggle to get back on track again.

As a compromise, she'd pulled herself out of bed even earlier than usual, giving herself an extra half hour. It had been the right decision, she concluded. She needed this. It was becoming a form of addiction, but at least it was healthier than the temptations coppers usually succumbed to.

Her circuit took her along the edge of McDermott's Yard. It was a former fabrication yard, responsible for building and maintaining oil platforms during the boom. McDermott's had closed years earlier as demand had declined, and the site had been empty ever since. It had been sold a couple of years earlier, with plans for its redevelopment, but nothing had so far materialised.

Even on a bright spring morning, there was something eerie about the place. Some of the buildings were still standing, and in some cases had not been fully cleared out. Old-fashioned computer monitors and office equipment were visible through the broken windows – as if the employees had simply risen from the desks and benches and simply walked away. She had no idea what ghosts might haunt the place, but it always felt to her as if something must be lurking in there.

She was approaching along the edge of the yard when she saw the figure standing ahead of her. At first, her mind still reflecting on McDermott's ghosts, the sight unnerved her. A lone figure, motionless, slightly unreal in the early morning haze.

As she drew closer, she saw the figure wasn't alone, but was accompanied by an equally motionless dog. Just an early morning dog walker. She didn't often encounter them on this stretch because she was generally out too early, but she sometimes saw them as she was returning back into the village.

The man was elderly, dressed in a flat cap and a raincoat that looked too heavy for the weather. He raised his hand as if to command her to stop. In his other hand was a mobile phone.

Her first thought was to ignore him. She didn't have the time to stop blethering with some old bloke about what a nice day it was or how lovely his dog might be. But something in the man's expression caught her attention. She slowed, allowing herself a moment to recover her breath. 'Are you okay?'

The man held out the phone. 'I was trying to use this,' he said. 'My son bought it for me. Reckoned it was very straightforward. But I've not managed to get it working yet.'

She took the phone from his hand. 'You'll need to turn it on first.'

'Oh,' he said. 'What do you do?'

She examined the phone and found the off/on switch. 'You press this.' She waited a moment while the screen came to life. 'Then you need a password.'

'That'll be Scott,' the man said. 'That's my dog.' He gestured to the animal sitting beside him. 'Named after Sir Walter.'

She keyed in the password and handed the phone back. 'There you go.'

The man looked back at her, his expression still baffled. 'So do I just dial 999 now like I would on a real phone?'

Horton frowned. 'Why do you want to phone 999?'

'Because of what Scott found.'

Horton looked around them at the bleak deserted yard, the clusters of decaying buildings, the sparking waters beyond. 'What did Scott find?'

'The body.'

Horton blinked. 'I'm sorry. What body?'

'The one that Scott found.'

Horton took a breath. 'Yes, of course. What I mean is, where is this body?'

The man gestured into the heart of the yard. 'Over there.'

'Right. Perhaps you'd better show me first.' Whatever this man had found, it most likely wasn't a body. Maybe something that had been washed up. Someone sleeping rough.

'I don't think that would be right. A young girl like you. You shouldn't have to see that sort of thing.'

Horton reached into the pocket of her track suit for the warrant card she made a point of always carrying, mainly on the off-chance of an incident like this. 'I'm a police officer, Mr...?'

'Stewart. Gordon Stewart. You're a police officer?' There was a note of amazement in his voice, as if the concept of a young female officer was beyond his comprehension.

'I am, Mr Stewart. A Detective Sergeant. If you could show me what you've found, I can decide what's best to do.'

'Aye, of course. It was Scott who found it.' The man led the way back into the yard. 'I don't really like him coming in here because there's a lot of glass and rusty metal around. I always worry he might hurt himself. He was off his lead but he's normally quite obedient.'

Horton was happy to let Stewart talk. Whatever it was he'd found, he sounded shaken and she sensed he wanted to keep talking until they'd reached their goal.

'Anyway, this morning,' he went on, 'he suddenly went tearing off. It wasn't like him at all. I wondered what had attracted him. He's not normally like that even with rabbits or rats.' They had reached the first of the buildings. Stewart led them around the corner and then, clearly reluctant to proceed any further, he gestured ahead. 'There. That's where I found Scott.'

Horton didn't need to go any closer to see that, despite her previous scepticism, Stewart's judgement had been correct. The haze of flies around the body suggested it had been lying for some time there in the spring sunshine. 'You stay here, Mr Stewart. I need to take a closer look but if it is what you think, we'll need to ensure that the site isn't disturbed.'

'You think...'

'I don't think anything, Mr Stewart. But if there's an unexplained death we have to treat it as suspicious until we can ascertain otherwise.' The usual police jargon, she thought. The reassuring code you used with the public. 'Do you live nearby, Mr Stewart?'

'Ardersier,' he said. He gave her an address which she recognised – a new-build estate mainly comprising small bungalows. 'I'm parked just up there. I usually drive over here with Scott for his walk in the morning. I used to work here, you know? In the yard. Long time ago.'

'A different place now,' she said.

Stewart wanted to talk, understandably enough given what he'd just stumbled upon but she needed to be calling this in, getting things moving. 'There's no point in keeping you here. We'll need a statement from you in due course...'

'A statement?'

'Just routine. For the record. All you need to do is tell us what happened, anything you might have seen or noticed. If you leave me your address and telephone number, we'll send an officer round to talk to you later today. Is there anyone else at home?'

'My wife.' Stewart glanced at his watch. 'She'll be getting concerned. I'm normally back by now.'

Horton nodded, relieved. She'd been afraid that Stewart might live alone. 'Leave me your details and you can get straight back. You'll be okay to drive?'

He looked puzzled at the question. 'Aye, of course. It's not far.'

'No, of course.' She didn't have her notebook with her, so she keyed his details into the note facility in her phone as he painstakingly spelled out his address and, inevitably, a landline phone number.

She waited till he'd disappeared back up the path towards his car, then dialled the number of the control room. This, she thought with a sigh, would be the first of several phone calls and the start of another very long day.

CHAPTER 18

'That's your phone,' Chrissie said, her voice muffled by the duvet.

McKay said something incomprehensible from under the covers. He rolled over, fumbling for his phone on the bedside table, succeeding only in knocking over a glass of water. He sat up. 'Fuck.'

'Just like old times,' Chrissie said. 'I'd forgotten how much fun it was.'

The phone was buzzing away beside the bed. McKay snatched it up.

'It's work, isn't it?'

'It's Ginny.' Finally waking up sufficiently to work out what he ought to be doing, McKay took the call. 'Ginny?'

'You okay, Alec? You sound a bit hassled.'

'You woke me up.' His tone was intended to sound accusatory, but he knew it simply came across as petulant.

'I thought you'd have been up hours ago.'

McKay looked at his watch sitting in a pool of spilled water. *Not hours ago*, he thought defensively, *but she's right. I should have been up*. 'You in the office?'

'No, I'm still out in Ardersier.'

'Glad to hear it. Thought you might be getting too keen.'

'I went for a run this morning, out by McDermott's Yard.'

'You don't need to give me a status update, you know, Ginny. I'm not fucking social media.'

'This is serious, Alec. I was out by McDermott's Yard and I found a body–'

'This some sort of elaborate practical joke?' He glanced over at Chrissie, who was listening to his side of the conversation with obvious curiosity. He wondered momentarily whether to mention what exactly Horton had interrupted, but decided neither woman would forgive him if he did.

'No, Alec,' Horton said patiently. 'There's a body. It wasn't me who found him, to be accurate. It was some old guy walking his dog.'

'It's always the fucking dog walkers,' McKay said. 'Do you realise how much quieter our lives would be if people weren't allowed to walk their fucking dogs?'

'That would really make you happier, wouldn't it? Anyway, there's a body. It's been there a day or two, given the state of it, but I can't tell you much else.'

'You've called it in?'

'No, I thought I'd wait a few more days so it could get really decomposed. Yes, of course I've bloody called it in. Got some uniforms coming over to protect the site, examiners supposedly on their way.'

'You think it's suspicious?'

'No real way of knowing at the moment. I've not approached any closer than I needed to confirm it was really what it appeared to me. I'd say male, but that's about all I can tell you and I'm not even certain of that. But it's an odd place to find a body.'

'It is that,' McKay agreed. 'But people, especially kids, do go exploring that place. Somebody might have had an accident. Or some jogger or fucking dog walker having a coronary. Or some junkie sleeping rough…'

'I know. It's all possible. No point in speculating till we know the circumstances. But given we've one unexplained killing on our hands.'

'You thought you might as well add to the list. Fair play, I suppose. But, you're right, might not be a bad idea to be on the scene just in case there is a link. We've got everything in place on the McGuire enquiry now, so that'll trundle on for an hour or two.' McKay and Horton had initiated a variety of activities the previous afternoon, ranging from door to doors in the vicinity of the crime scene through to collecting CCTV footage and ANPR data from cameras around the city. They were still waiting on sign-off of their proposed trip to talk to McGuire's partner and agent in Edinburgh, and hadn't yet managed to track down the elusive Jack Dingwall. 'You spoken to Helena yet?'

'Yes, I thought I'd better brief her before I called you.'

'Smart move. Always keep your arse covered when you're working with me.'

'We've been together a few years now, Alec. That's one lesson I learnt a long time ago. Anyway, Helena thought the same. Apart from anything else, if it turns out this is connected, it shows we're on the ball.'

'Aye, I imagine the shite will be hitting the proverbial this morning with the McGuire killing.' They'd made that public the previous evening in time for the later TV and radio news bulletins, but the real coverage would come this morning. The full details hadn't been revealed, but there'd be enough for the media to get their teeth into. 'I'll be over as quick as I can.'

'Can't be soon enough,' Horton said. 'Apart from anything else, I wouldn't mind someone relieving me a bit so I can get some clothes on. I'm still in my running gear.'

'Always told you no good would come of all that fitness bollocks. I'm on my way.' He ended the call and looked down at Chrissie, who was lying next to him with a faint smile.

'It brings it all back.'

'Murder investigation,' he said. 'And now we've another body, which may or may not be connected.'

'All go, isn't it?'

'Look, Chrissie, I'm really sorry. Especially after... you know.'

She laughed. 'I've never minded this, Alec. I know it goes with the job. It's what I married. It's one reason I love you.'

He noted the present tense. He couldn't remember the last time she'd said that, even in the counselling sessions. 'But still.'

'That's never been the problem. The problem's been what's been going on between us.'

'I quite enjoyed what was going on between us last night.'

'Only quite? Alec, this is the best it's been between us since… since as long as I can remember.'

'You think we're on our way back then?'

She hesitated so long he thought she was going to say no. 'On our way, yes. But we're not there yet. I don't want to rush it.'

'But…'

'I'm serious about this, Alec. Last night was terrific. All of it. It feels like we've turned over a new leaf. But let's have a day or two to reflect before we take the next step, eh?'

'This your way of letting me down gently?'

'You know me better than that. If I were going to let you down, there'd be nothing gentle about it. Look, give it a day or so. Just so we're both certain where we want to go next. Then you come round to supper at home.'

'Home?'

'Aye, home. Our home. Not this dump.'

McKay looked around the tiny bedroom. 'You know how much time I've spent on this place?'

'Aye, bugger all. Come round tomorrow night. Have supper with me. We'll take it from there.'

He nodded, knowing this was the best offer he was going to get. 'It's a deal. I'd better get up, get showered and go and relieve Ginny. And see whether we've got another killing on our hands. You want me to give you a lift in?'

'If you've got time,' she said. 'I could get a cab.'

'I'll drop you off. It's not really out of the way.' He paused. 'In any case, it'll be good to get a glimpse of home.'

CHAPTER 19

J ane had no idea what had happened the previous evening after Elizabeth's outburst. After a few moments, Netty Munro had followed Elizabeth into the house. It had been a long time, perhaps half an hour or so, before she'd rejoined them. In the meantime, Henry Dowling had continued to strum away at her guitar, singing them what Jane assumed were folk songs. Dowling's voice was lovely, smoother and more resonant than Munro's but without the same ability to bring the songs to life. Or perhaps, Jane thought, it was just that the moment had passed, the intensity dispelled by Elizabeth's unexpected reaction.

The night had grown dark around them, the decking lit only by the second-hand glow from the living room. Below them, Jane could make out the lights on the far side of the firth, the dense cluster of houses in Dingwall, the line of the A9, the occasional passing of a car across the Cromarty Bridge. The sky had remained clear and the first stars were visible. Between Dowling's songs, the night felt eerily quiet, with no birdsong or breath of wind. To Jane it felt as magical as ever, but there was something else. A sense of threat. A sense of unease. Something not quite right. She didn't know whether it was what Elizabeth had said, her oddly disproportionate response to that first song. Or whether it was the songs themselves. The sound of something old and primitive, the stories whose full meaning remained tantalisingly out of reach.

When Munro finally returned, she told them Elizabeth had retired to her room. 'She was exhausted, poor thing. Today must have taken more out of her than she'd realised.'

Jane wasn't sure she really believed this. Elizabeth hadn't struck her as the type who would be affected by the experience of moving there. Her behaviour had reminded Jane of something different. It was like the outbursts of anger she had encountered sometimes from her dad or with Iain, a response triggered by almost anything. In their cases, the anger was often fuelled by drink, but it was always an undirected fury at a world they felt had never treated them fairly. Elizabeth's sudden emotion had felt similar – an explosion of something that had been building for a long time.

Munro had emerged from the house clutching a bottle of single malt, and was now pouring a glass for everyone. Jane wanted to refuse – she was already feeling light-headed from the wine – but felt it would be impolite. She hesitated then copied Munro in adding a splash of water from the jug on the table.

She'd had whisky before, of course. Iain would sometimes come back with a bottle he'd acquired from some dubious source. But he rarely got his hands on anything but cheap blended stuff and, on the few occasions he'd managed to obtain something better, he wasn't inclined to share it with Jane. This was a local whisky, Munro had proclaimed. That, as with the food, seemed important to her for reasons Jane didn't entirely understand. She took a nervous sip, expecting the spirit to burn the back of her throat.

It did, but there was a flavour and warmth there she realised she liked. It felt right for that time on a warm spring evening, a soothing and comforting end to an unexpected day. Munro had picked up her guitar again, and she and Dowling were playing together, a tapestry of sound that somehow matched the complexity of the whisky.

For a few minutes, Jane allowed herself to be lost in the experience. She was no longer thinking, no longer worrying about what tomorrow might bring. About whether this would really last. She couldn't recall when she'd felt more content than this, and she decided she might as well just go with it.

It was another half hour or so before the party finally began to break up. Munro and Dowling both seemed still full of energy, but Jane could see that Alicia was beginning to wilt. Munro had clearly spotted it too, and, putting aside her guitar, said, 'You're looking tired, dear. Do you want to be getting off to bed?'

Alicia blinked as if the question had been unexpected. 'I think I'd better. Can hardly keep my eyes open.'

Jane decided to take the opportunity to say her own goodnights, not wanting to find herself alone with the two older women. 'I think I'd better call it a night too, if that's okay.'

'Of course,' Munro said. 'You can leave us two oldsters to put the world to rights.'

'Do you need any help with the washing-up?'

Munro shook her head. 'Not tonight, dear. That's another one of my rules. The first night is always down to me. In the future, you can give me more of a hand, but we'll take that gradually.'

'Are you sure?'

'It's one of my rules. And my rules are rock solid.' It wasn't entirely clear whether she was joking.

'Okay. I won't argue. What time do you want us up in the morning?'

'Sleep as long as you need to tomorrow. Again, we'll get into a routine before too long, but you need time to rest first. Come down when you're ready. I'll be around somewhere.'

Jane nodded, feeling slightly uneasy with this response. She wasn't used to it. She was used to people telling her what to do. Sometimes pointlessly, sometimes arbitrarily. Sometimes backed by the threat of violence. But never leaving space for her to argue or express her own views. 'Thank you. Goodnight then.'

She made her way back into the house, Alicia following silently behind her. They climbed the stairs to the first floor without speaking, but as they reached the landing Alicia said, 'I'm glad you're here, Jane. You seem nice.'

The words were unexpected, not least because Alicia had said almost nothing to her all evening. 'I try to be,' Jane said awkwardly, unsure how else to respond. 'What do you make of this place, Alicia?'

Alicia always seemed nonplussed by a direct question. 'I don't know. Netty's lovely. I've only been here a few weeks, but she's been very kind. I'm not really used to that.'

'Me neither. I just wonder what it is she wants. Why she's doing this, I mean.'

'I don't know if she wants anything. I think she's just doing it because she thinks it's the right thing to do.'

Jane wanted to believe it. She still had an awful fear that she might wake up and find herself back in the centre, that she'd somehow dreamed or imagined it all. 'What about the work? What is it she gets you to do?'

'Not much so far. I mean just helping round the house and doing a bit of stuff in the kitchen. I've helped her peel potatoes and that sort of thing, and done a bit of cleaning. But nothing very difficult so far.'

'Doesn't sound bad. Let's see what tomorrow brings.'

Alicia nodded. 'Goodnight. I hope we can be friends.' She sounded like a character in a children's book, Jane thought. She'd borrowed some of those books from the library as a child – the kind of books where posh girls went to boarding schools and lived a perfect life. Her mam had always encouraged her to read, but she'd had to hide the books from her dad.

'Sure we will be, Alicia,' Jane said.

She entered her bedroom, feeling more relaxed once she'd closed the door behind her. She had no nightwear, so she'd have to sleep in her T-shirt. The room was warm and she pushed open the window to breathe in the night air, fresh with some floral scent that Jane didn't recognise. Her room was above the decking area, with the same view of the firth they'd enjoyed over dinner.

As she leaned over, she realised that Munro and Dowling were still sitting out there, the bottle of single malt between them. Their voices carried upwards with unexpected clarity. Jane's first instinct was to withdraw her head, feeling guilty at the prospect of eavesdropping on her host.

She hesitated a moment too long, and heard part of the exchange from below.

'What do you think of them?' Munro was asking.

'Jane and Alicia seem okay. Good material.'

Jane didn't want to hear any more. She pulled her head back into the room and firmly drew the curtains, leaving the window open for air. She could still hear the two women's voices, but could no longer work out what they were saying.

She finished undressing and climbed into bed, astonished again by how comfortable it was. As she turned off the light, she could still hear the murmur of the two voices outside.

She wondered what they were saying. Good material. That was what Dowling had said. Good material for what?

She'd expected to fall asleep quickly after the drink and the stresses of the day. But instead she found she was tossing and turning, kicking off the covers because she felt too hot, her mind working over everything she'd seen and heard since arriving here. Her conversations with Munro. Her interactions with Elizabeth and Alicia. The dinner and the music. Most of all those last words she'd heard.

Good material.

When she finally managed to sleep, her dreams were disturbed, incoherent narratives of imprisonment and slavery which felt real and vivid, but which by morning had fled her mind, as insubstantial as the early mist on the firth. It was only then that it occurred to her to wonder why, in that late-night exchange, Munro and Dowling had not mentioned Elizabeth.

CHAPTER 20

McKay pulled into the entrance to the Yard and stopped before the line of police tape. One of the uniforms was already striding towards him. McKay wound down his window and waited.

'I'm sorry, sir, but this area's–'

'You do this on purpose, Benny? Pretend not to recognise me just to wind me up?'

'Oh, aye, sorry, sir. It's just we've already had a couple of people here rubbernecking. Think the guy who found the body hasn't been exactly discreet. Probably blabbed to one of his neighbours.'

'Great. No doubt someone's been on the phone to the *Press and Journal* just to spread the word further.' That would mean another call back to Helena, and another conversation for her to have with comms. 'You going to let me past then, or do I have to join the rubberneckers?'

'Aye, come through. Your wee lass is over there.' The uniform gestured towards the corner of the nearest building.

'My wee lass? Oh, DS Horton, you mean.'

The uniform seemed impervious to McKay's irony. 'That's the one.'

McKay sighed theatrically then, hardly giving the uniform time to pull back the tape, drove into the yard and parked up close to where Horton was standing. He climbed out and walked over to join her, nodding to the uniforms, who clearly recognised when they weren't wanted and moved to rejoin their colleagues taping off the remaining area.

'Cavalry's arrived,' McKay said. 'Save you being bored to death by the boys in blue. What's the story?'

'Examiners arrived a couple of minutes ago. They're setting up.' Horton gestured towards where two figures in white suits were constructing the protective tent. 'Rather them than me in this case. Body's been there a day or two. And it's been a warm couple of days.'

Though he'd never admit as much to Jock Henderson, McKay had nothing but admiration for the examiners' resilience in the face of a scene like this. He supposed eventually you just became inured to it, but he couldn't imagine how you managed to get to that stage. Police officers had to deal with a fair amount of unpleasantness, and often they were the first on the scene, but they rarely had to work in such demanding conditions. 'There are times when even Jock Henderson earns his pay. Speaking of whom…'

'You're spared the pleasure of his company today. Pete Carrick's on the job.'

'That's something.' McKay could see now that Carrick was one of the two figures in white. He was a heavily built, slightly lumbering man, with a shock of red hair and an expression that seemed permanently surprised. Given some of the situations he had to deal with, McKay supposed the surprise might be genuine. 'You want to get off for a bit?' he said to Horton.

'I wouldn't mind grabbing a shower. I was only supposed to be going out for a run.'

'You'd come some distance. You getting back into it now?' McKay made constant fun of Horton's running, but he knew how important it was to her and how difficult she'd found the events of the previous winter.

'Pretty much. It's easier now the days are getting so much longer.' She paused. 'And when my abusive stepdad isn't banging on the window.'

'I can see that. Look, you take the car. I'm going to be here for a while, I imagine. So take your time.' On his way, McKay had dropped Chrissie back at what he still, perhaps now with a little more hope, thought of as home. Then he'd called in at the office to swap his own vehicle for one of the pool cars.

'I just need a shower and a quick change of clothes and I'll be back.' She regarded McKay with curiosity. 'Incidentally, none of my business but not like you to be late out of bed on the first morning of a major enquiry. Don't tell me you got lucky last night?'

McKay laughed. 'Bugger off, Horton. You're absolutely right. It's none of your fucking business. But, for what it's worth, I actually got lucky twenty-odd years ago. I'd just forgotten.'

She nodded. 'I'm hoping that's good news.'

'We'll see.'

'Good luck with that, Alec. You've both been through a hell of a lot.'

He nodded, vaguely, his expression indicating that he'd already said more than enough. 'You go and get yourself cleaned up. I'm told you scrub up okay.'

'Fuck off, Alec,' she said amiably. She turned to go then paused. 'You want to speak to the guy who found the body while I'm gone? I can give you his details.'

'Is he likely to tell me anything useful?'

'I doubt it. It was the dog found the body. He only stayed around long enough to see what it was and call the dog off. He brings it down here most mornings though, so I suppose it's possible he might have seen something over the last few days.' She was silent for a moment. 'We've had a couple of visitors here already, so it looks like he must have blabbed when he got back home. I did have a word with him about being discreet, but maybe I should have kept him here. I just thought he was likely to be more trouble than he was worth.'

McKay shrugged. 'He'd have blabbed as soon as we let him go anyway. So it would only have bought us a bit of time. And the longer we'd kept him here the more he'd have to blab about. As it is, all he knows is we've found a body. If it gets to the media, we can just play a straight bat till we know what we're dealing with. Which may well be not much if chummy over there died from natural causes.'

'Yeah, you're probably right. Okay, shower, clothes and then I'll be back. Don't have too much fun in my absence.'

'If you say so,' McKay said. 'Though having a chat with the examiners should remove any risk of that.'

CHAPTER 21

'Is this what they call glamping?' McKay called. He'd stopped sufficiently far from where the examiners were working to ensure he didn't risk contaminating the scene.

'It's supposed to erect itself instantly,' Pete Carrick said, gesturing to the tent beside him. 'But it never bloody does.'

'We've all been there. How's it looking?'

'Not good.' Whereas Jock Henderson seemed to be perpetually gloomy, Carrick was normally a bundle of cheery enthusiasm. Even faced with the prospect of an already decomposing corpse inside an overheated tent, his good nature seemed undented. 'Body's in a bad way. I'd say it's been here at least a couple of days. Decomposition fairly well advanced, and it's been attacked by one or more predators.'

'Lovely. Any clues as to identity yet?'

'Not really. White. Male. Probably middle-aged, though I wouldn't swear to that till we've had a closer look. And–' He stopped as if waiting for a cue from McKay.

'And?'

'I heard from Jock about the Jimmy McGuire case. The cause of death. It looks as if this might be the same.'

'That right?'

'Again, I don't want to speculate before I've looked properly.'

'You buggers never do.'

'But it looks like there's a narrow lesion around the neck. That could well be the cause of death.'

'Another garrotting?'

'Another garrotting.'

118

'Jesus,' McKay said. 'So when did that become the dispatch method of choice? Still, it might help us reduce the knife crime figures. You sure about this?'

Carrick hesitated. 'Pretty, to be honest. Like I say, I need to have a closer look once we get started. But that's what it looks like.'

'Which means that, unless garrotting really has become unexpectedly fashionable, there's a connection between this and yesterday's killing.' McKay intended his tone to be suitably serious, but it was difficult to disguise the excitement in his voice. 'You think he was killed here?'

'It's too early to say. The body might have just been dumped here. But it should be possible to tell once we've examined the scene properly.'

McKay knew when he was being warned off. Carrick was easier to deal with than Jock Henderson, but none of the examiners liked being rushed or to speculate ahead of the evidence. 'Aye, son, fair enough. Not asking for guesswork. Just want to know as much as I can before I brief the powers that be. If we do have two related deaths, this'll need some managing.' *There's my shot across your bows, son*, he added to himself. *Don't rush, but don't be sitting around on your arse either.*

'You'd best let me get on then,' Carrick said with a grin. 'I'll tell you as soon as we've got something solid to report.'

'You do that, son.'

McKay walked slowly back to where the uniforms were clustered. They seemed to have the site effectively cordoned off, and most were just standing chatting. McKay stopped and looked about him. The yard was an extensive area, comprising little more than an empty concrete expanse with a few abandoned and derelict buildings. Assuming that Carrick was right – and for all Carrick's reticence, McKay had little doubt that he was –they'd have to institute a thorough search of the place, a major task in itself. Quite probably fruitless, McKay thought. If the murder weapon wasn't in the vicinity of the body, it could easily have been tossed into the sea in the natural harbour within Whiteness Point. The divers were likely to have even less luck down there than in the Ness.

McKay wasn't prone to be over-imaginative but this struck him as a strange place. It was partly just the sense of lost industry – a site that had once been so central to the local economy, now given over to grass, weeds and wild flowers. He thought of the people who must have passed through here, the business that had been conducted, the sheer hard work of those who'd kept the place going. Then its moment had passed, and the place had vanished into history. *It's what awaits us all*, McKay thought.

He walked over to the cluster of uniforms.

'What's the story, sir?' one of them said.

Sir. You didn't get that too much these days, though McKay tended to get it more than many of his colleagues. He was always happy to let his reputation go before him, for good or ill. 'Too early to say, son. But we'll be treating it as suspicious until Pistol Pete over there tells us otherwise. Some of you lot keen to get off?'

'Not if we're needed here. But you know what it's like these days, sir.'

'Aye, only too well, son.' He raised his voice to speak to the rest of the group. 'I'll need to keep a couple of you here to protect the site. Especially if we're getting rubberneckers. Rest of you can bugger off back to proper work until we know what we're dealing with.'

While he was speaking he noticed that, as if summoned by his reference to rubberneckers, a car had drawn up just off the road at the site entrance. 'Okay, people, you sort out among yourselves who's staying and who's going. I'll go and have a little chat with our friend over there.'

He walked slowly over to the car, watching as an elderly man climbed out of the driver's seat. 'Can I help you, sir?' McKay asked, in a tone that suggested the answer was unlikely to be in the affirmative.

The man was looking slightly bewildered. 'I'm sorry. I was talking to one of your colleagues earlier.'

'Is that right, sir?'

'A young lady. She was very helpful. I was trying to phone–' The man stopped, as if conscious he was rambling. 'Stewart. Gordon Stewart.'

It took McKay a moment to work out that this must be the man's name. 'You were talking to DS Horton?'

'That's right. After Scott found–'

'Scott?'

'My dog. He was the one who found it.'

'You found the body?'

'As I say, Scott–'

'Yes, of course. How can we help you now, sir?'

Stewart hesitated, as if not sure why he was there. 'Your young lady…'

'DS Horton.'

'Yes, she said someone would be coming round to take a statement from me.'

'We'll need to do that, sir, yes. Just routine.'

'That was what she said. She said I should include anything I can remember that might be relevant.'

McKay nodded, wondering whether there was a point to any of this. 'That's right, sir,' he said, patiently. 'Sometimes things that seem trivial can turn out to be useful to our enquiries. So anything you remember–'

'That's the point. I hadn't remembered but my wife did.'

'Go on.'

'She thought it might be important. That I should come and tell you straightaway.'

'Tell us what?' McKay was beginning to pray that Horton would reappear to relieve him of having to deal with this apparent dotard.

'It was a couple of days ago. Not yesterday, the day before. I normally walk Scott twice a day. I bring him here in the morning, and then just walk him near the house in the evening.'

McKay nodded wearily, having finally accepted there was little point in trying to hurry Stewart. Whatever he might have to say, he'd say it only in his own good time.

'But that day I needed to pop into the shop for a couple of things so I thought I might as well take the car out. So I brought Scott up here for his walk in the evening as well.' He stopped, as if his story was now complete. It took him a moment to realise he hadn't yet mentioned the salient point. 'There was a car here. Parked where I am now. There sometimes are. Other people come up here to walk their dogs.'

Or just dogging, McKay thought, *though probably not at the times when Stewart was here.*

'I remember thinking it was a bit odd,' Stewart went on. 'It was an estate. One of those big Volvo things. The boot had been left up. There was a plastic sheet spread out inside.'

'In the boot?'

'Yes, spread across the bottom of the boot. Thick plastic. Industrial stuff.'

This was beginning to sound more interesting, McKay thought. 'Did you see anything else?'

'Not really. There seemed to be something spilled on the plastic. Some sort of staining. At the time I thought it might be someone fly-tipping. We get a bit of that down here.'

'You didn't see anyone with the car?'

Stewart shook his head. 'To be honest, I decided to make myself scarce. I've had one or two run-ins with fly-tippers before. Some of them are nasty pieces of work. So I just drove on and parked further along.'

'I don't suppose you noted the car registration?'

'No. I should have done, shouldn't I?' Stewart looked genuinely distraught at his own failing. 'I realised afterwards I should have taken the number and reported it, if they really were fly-tipping. But I was keen to get out of there and I didn't really think about it till too late. By the time I got back, the car had gone.'

'You said the car was an estate?'

'Yes, one of those big ones. Not new, I'd have said. A good few years old. It was a dark colour, blue or black.'

If you were looking to dump a body, McKay thought, you'd probably wait till dark. On the other hand, the nights were already growing short up here, and it wouldn't be fully dark until ten or even later. Maybe there was more risk of running into doggers than dog walkers round here. They couldn't afford to discount the sighting anyway. Although Stewart hadn't given them much, it might be enough to pick out the car on any CCTV on the surrounding roads. 'What time of day would this have been, Mr Stewart?'

'About five, I think. I usually take Scott out before we have tea. I left the house a bit earlier than usual so we could call in at the shop. So probably just after five when we got here.'

'Thank you, Mr Stewart. That's very useful.'

'You think they might have brought the body here then? Whoever was in the car, I mean.'

'We don't even know the cause of death yet, Mr Stewart. So it's too early to say. But your sighting may be useful, especially if the death does seem suspicious.'

Stewart nodded. 'I should have mentioned it to your colleague earlier. But it had slipped my mind. It was only because I'd mentioned it to my wife after I got back – you know how it is.'

'Aye, I do,' McKay said sincerely. 'We're none of us getting any younger.' In his own case, he felt he'd aged several years in the last few minutes. 'But I'm very grateful that you reported this. As I say, we'll be sending someone round to take a formal statement, so if there's anything else you remember in the meantime...'

McKay gently ushered Stewart back to his car, certain that if left to his own devices the elderly man would stay there blethering all day. It was only after Stewart had finally driven away that McKay turned to see a couple of the uniforms standing grinning at him.

'We've had a few of those this morning,' one of the uniforms said. 'Bloody time-wasters. We just told them to bugger off.'

McKay walked over until he was standing only a metre or so away from the uniform. McKay was a short, slight man but the uniform took a half step back as if expecting a physical blow. 'That right, son?'

'I–'

'Thing is, son, that fine upstanding pillar of the community has just given me what might turn out to be a useful lead. I wonder if any of those worthy citizens you told to bugger off might have had any useful intelligence to share with us?'

'I don't think–'

'Aye, well, try not to. It doesn't seem to be your strong point. Now, if anyone else turns up here, I want you to be polite, listen to anything useful they might have to tell you. And then, and only then…' He paused theatrically, before treating the uniforms to one of his rare smiles. 'Then you can tell them to bugger off.'

CHAPTER 22

J ane had no watch, so at first she had no idea what time it was
when she awoke. It had taken her a while to get to sleep, and
she'd felt restless for most of the night, waking occasionally
to see the light brightening in the gaps around the curtains. She'd
fallen into a deeper, more relaxed slumber after that, and now felt
as if she'd overslept. Munro had said she should rise whenever she
was ready, but Jane thought that really she should have been up
early to do something useful.

She dragged herself out of bed and fumbled for her mobile
in her bag, which she'd left by the bed. To her surprise, it was
only just past eight, earlier than she'd expected. Tomorrow, she'd
remember to set an alarm before she slept.

She walked over to the window and pulled back the curtains. It
looked as if it was set to be another fine day. The sun was behind
the house, casting long shadows down towards the firth. A faint
mist lay on the water, but the surface was extraordinarily still,
reflecting the hills and trees on the far shore.

There was a towelling dressing gown hanging on the bedroom
door, presumably intended for her use. She pulled it on and
stepped out onto the landing, standing still for a moment to listen
for any sound.

She could hear nothing. Elizabeth's and Alicia's bedroom doors
were closed, and there was no movement from below. It occurred
to Jane that she didn't know where Munro slept. There didn't seem
to be another bedroom up there, but there were presumably rooms
downstairs she hadn't been shown.

The bathroom door was ajar. Jane hadn't had an opportunity
to shower the previous day either before leaving the centre or since

her arrival, and she'd felt bad about that the previous evening, wishing she'd spruced herself up more for the dinner. That had been one of the problems at the centre. There were too few showers for the number of women staying there, and often none available in the mornings. Too often, she'd taken the path of least resistance and simply not bothered. But she knew from experience where that could lead. You stopped caring about yourself, and then you stopped caring about much else. If you didn't care about yourself, no one else was likely to.

There was a walk-in shower as well as a bath. Maybe she'd brave the bath when she felt a little more at home. It took her a few moments to work out how the electric shower was operated, and then a little longer to adjust the water temperature to her liking. Finally, she undressed and surrendered herself to the streams of hot water, feeling, for the first time since she'd climbed out of bed, as if she was waking up. She was tempted to turn the water to cold just to feel the shock through her body, to remind her that she had begun a new life, that everything from here on would be different. In the end, she did the opposite, turning the water as hot as she could bear, enjoying the sting of the near-scalding liquid on her skin.

She finished washing her hair and body, and then, turning off the water, stepped out of the shower, reaching for the towel. As she did so, there was a banging at the door. She stopped, feeling as if she'd been caught out in some inappropriate act.

'You going to be long?' It was Elizabeth's voice from the far side of the door.

Jane could feel her initial guilt curdling into a mild resentment. It wasn't as if she'd been in the bathroom for long. And it wasn't as if Elizabeth had any more right to be in there than Jane had. She called back, 'Won't be a minute.'

'Hope not. I'm dying for a wee.'

Jane wondered whether to point out that there was a separate toilet next door, as well as the one in here, but decided it wasn't worth the effort. Maybe the other toilet was already occupied. Still damp, she pulled on the dressing gown and drew back the bolt on the door.

Elizabeth was standing directly outside, her expression suggesting she'd been considering forcible entry.

'Sorry about that,' Jane said, unsure why she was apologising. The door of the adjacent toilet was standing open.

'No worries. You sleep well?' Elizabeth's apparently urgent need to use the bathroom seemed to have vanished.

'A bit restless. New bed and all that. Are you all right?' Jane thought back to Elizabeth's odd behaviour of the previous night, and wondered what sort of state she might be in.

'Ach, I slept fine. Out like a light. I always do.'

'That's good. I thought you might be a bit under the weather…' She trailed off.

'Last night, you mean? That was just me being a wee bit daft. Probably a glass of wine too many.' As far as Jane could recall, Elizabeth had drunk very little. Jane had watched the other diners carefully because she hadn't wanted to do anything inappropriate herself. 'Just get a bit sentimental with those old songs.'

Elizabeth's response had sounded anything but sentimental, Jane thought. 'We were all a bit more tired than we realised too. Long day.'

Elizabeth gazed at Jane as if about to challenge this assessment. 'Aye. I'll let you go and get dressed. If you're down there first, tell Netty I'll be down shortly.' She gestured towards Alicia's door. 'No sign of Princess Alicia, I'm assuming?'

'I've not seen her,' Jane said, wondering whether the nickname dated back to Elizabeth's previous acquaintance with Alicia, or was a comment on Alicia's status there. Either way, Jane had no intention of being complicit in whatever joke Elizabeth might be making.

'See you downstairs.' Elizabeth disappeared into the bathroom, and Jane returned to her own bedroom. Elizabeth's presence was one of the factors that left Jane still feeling uneasy. She had the sense that Elizabeth wasn't playing by the rules, even though Jane had no idea what those rules really were.

Then there was the previous night's conversation between Munro and Dowling. Good material. What had that meant? Good material for what?

CHAPTER 23

Jane dressed quickly, increasingly conscious how few clothes she had. She'd have to find out from Netty Munro what the arrangements here were for washing. Jane also wondered about the possibility of getting into Dingwall or Inverness to buy something. She still had a little stashed away from the money she'd managed to take with her when she'd finally left Iain. The money he'd never known about that had enabled her to make the break. She assumed she wouldn't be able to claim any benefits while staying there, and at some stage that could become a problem, especially when she wanted to move on. But that was a problem for the future, and she couldn't bring herself to worry too much about it for the moment.

Closing the bedroom door behind her, Jane stood on the landing, listening. The bathroom door was still closed and she could hear the sound of running water from inside. She suspected that Elizabeth had already been in the bathroom as long as she had been.

Apart from the hiss of water, the house was silent. She made her way downstairs and stood in the hall, wondering where to go. The door to the living room was open and the patio windows pulled back, but there was no sign of life. Feeling slightly nervous, she continued through to the kitchen.

Henry Dowling was sitting at the table, a copy of *The Guardian* spread out before her. She looked up as Jane entered. 'Morning. I'm still here, I'm afraid.' She gestured towards a mug sitting on the table beside her. 'Netty said to help yourself to anything you want for breakfast. Coffee's in that cupboard, real and instant, I think. Milk's in the fridge. Sugar's… actually, I've no idea where sugar is.'

Jane stood in silence for a moment, nonplussed by Dowling's manner. 'Can I get you another drink?'

'I'm good for the moment. If you're hungry, there's bread over there for toast. Cereals in the cupboard. Other stuff in the fridge, I think – bacon and suchlike…' She stopped as if she'd exhausted her knowledge or inspiration.

'I'll be happy with a slice of toast,' Jane said, as she filled the kettle. She certainly had no intention of trying to prepare anything more complicated. 'Is Netty not around?'

'She's out in the wide acres of the estate somewhere. She's had some workmen here doing stuff on the fencing, so she's gone to check what they've done. Reckoned she wouldn't be long.'

'Looks like another lovely day.'

'It does. Though I hadn't intended to be up this early to enjoy it.'

'Do you live in the village?' Jane wasn't sure whether she was being overly inquisitive, but it seemed a harmless enough question.

'Yes. It's not far. But I didn't trust myself to walk back in the dark after Netty and I had finished punishing the Scotch. So she found a bed for me.'

Jane nodded, unsure how else to respond. 'I feel slightly hungover,' she offered. She wasn't really sure this was true. Her mouth felt a little dry and she was still a little woozy, but otherwise she was fine. It was just what people said. Grown-ups, she thought. People who understood how life ought to be lived.

'You're not used to it, darling. I never seem to get hangovers these days, though I'm not sure that's anything to be proud of.' She yawned and took another mouthful of coffee. 'Didn't expect to wake up so early. I can normally sleep through anything. Even Netty bustling about.'

Jane had found the bread and was trying to work out how to operate the toaster, which seemed more sophisticated than any she'd come across before. 'Netty said that you help out on the farm?'

'I do a few bits and pieces where I can. I'm good with my hands so I've done a few carpentry jobs and the like for her.'

'Carpentry?' Jane didn't quite manage to conceal her surprise.

'The day job's building guitars, these days. I have my own workshop, making high-end acoustics. So hammering in a few nails is child's play by comparison.'

'I suppose so.' Jane had finally persuaded the toaster to work, and was waiting for her slice to pop up. 'Was the guitar you were playing last night one of your own? One you made, I mean.'

'Certainly was. And Netty's too. I gave her that one for her birthday a few years back. She reckons it's the best guitar she's ever played. But then she has to say that, doesn't she?'

'I'm no judge but they sounded lovely to me. Netty doesn't make guitars as well then?'

Dowling laughed. 'No, there are only a few of us about. But Netty makes songs, which is just as important. If not more so.'

Jane didn't know quite what to make of that, and was almost relieved when they were interrupted by the kitchen door opening. She expected Elizabeth to join them, but it was Alicia, blinking and looking half awake, still in her dressing gown. 'I'm sorry. Am I very late coming down?'

'Christ, no,' Dowling said. 'What's wrong with you people? This is not a civilised time to be awake.'

'Would you like some coffee?' Jane asked. 'I'm just making some.'

'Please,' Alicia said.

Dowling turned and held out her mug. 'Actually, I've nearly finished this. If the kettle's boiled...'

'That's fine.' Jane could feel she'd already slipped back into her familiar domestic role. Provider for others. She immediately felt a little more comfortable, as if she'd found a niche to slip into. It was what she was accustomed to. Providing for her dad and her younger siblings when her mother hadn't been able to. Providing to Iain. Even in the centre, she'd often been the domestic one – the one who'd bring cups of tea and coffee to others, the one who'd clean up when no one else could be arsed, the one everyone turned to if they needed something. At times she'd been taken advantage of, but she hadn't minded too much. She'd felt she had a legitimate place, that she could justify her presence. She needed that and she thought she'd still need it there, however kind and generous Netty Munro might be.

She finished making the coffees and brought them over to the table. Alicia had sat down and was staring blankly at the tabletop. Dowling had returned to her newspaper and was chuckling gently at whatever she was reading. Jane found a plate and a knife for her toast, and carried them over to join the other women. There was butter in a dish on the table and a jar of marmalade. 'Sleep well?' she asked Alicia.

'Pretty well,' Alicia said. 'Took me a while to get off, but then I don't remember anything till I woke up just now. I thought it must be later than it is.'

They lapsed back into silence while Jane spread butter on her toast. She hesitated, then added marmalade.

'That's Netty's,' Alicia said.

For a moment, Jane thought she was being accused of stealing their host's marmalade but Alicia added, 'She makes it, I mean. It's really nice.'

Jane nodded, still chewing. She'd never been sure whether she liked marmalade, but like everything else in this house, this was better than any she'd had before. It tasted of fruit rather than just bitterness. 'It's very good.'

'Netty's a dab hand at pretty much anything in the culinary department,' Dowling said. 'Sweet, savoury. Bread, cakes. Jams. You name it.' She paused, glancing between the two younger women. 'Did you both come here from the centre?' She held up her hand, as if to prevent them replying. 'Sorry. Tactless. Netty's rules apply, as always. You don't need to tell me anything unless you want to.'

Alicia shrugged. 'I came from the centre. It's nothing to be ashamed of.'

Jane nodded in agreement. 'Me too. They were pretty good to me, as good as they could be.'

'I'm sure they were,' Dowling said. 'Most of Netty's visitors tend to come from there. And that's pretty much what they all say. That they felt safe. And well looked after.'

Alicia laughed, though it wasn't clear how much humour was in the sound. 'I spent my first week or so there certain my ex was going to track me down. They were very cautious though. I don't suppose they could keep away someone who was determined enough, but they do pretty well.'

'And they're smart enough to know that most violent types are just feckless no-marks when it comes to it,' Dowling said. 'They wouldn't have the gumption to track anyone down.'

That had been true enough of Iain, Jane thought. After she'd walked out, he'd gone round to her sister's – the only one of her relatives he'd actually met – and started causing trouble. But Mo's hubbie had shown him the door, and Jane hadn't heard a word from or about him since then. Even so, she'd been relieved to see the quality of security at the centre. On the rare occasions some bastard did manage to track his ex down, they hadn't been able to access the interior of the building and the police had been called before they could proceed any further.

'They do good work there,' Dowling said. 'What was it in your two cases? Boyfriends? Husbands? If you want to tell me.'

'Boyfriend,' Alicia said. 'Nasty piece of work. I can always pick 'em.'

'Husband in mine,' Jane said. Was Iain a nasty piece of work, too? She'd never thought of him in those terms. Theirs had never been what you might call a great romance, but they'd initially liked one another well enough. Then, just like her dad, he'd started drinking and getting violent. There'd been enough times when he'd scared her. But she still couldn't bring herself to think of him as a bad man. A stupid man, definitely. A weak man, almost certainly. An overgrown child – well, she thought so. But under all that he was maybe okay, she thought. Or at least he could be. She'd hoped she could help him make that change, but by the time she'd left she knew it wasn't going to happen. There was too much booze, not enough work. Too many pressures he thought it was okay to take out on her.

One day he might change, but someone else would have to help him through it. She had no intention of being there. She'd already spent too long making excuses for him. Whatever the future might hold, she was moving on.

'We've all been there,' Dowling said. 'Me and Netty too.'

Jane looked up in surprise. She'd never envisaged that that kind of thing happened to the likes of Netty or Henry. Apart from anything else, they weren't shackled to a relationship by lack of money or other opportunities. If there were problems, they could just walk.

But even from her own experience, Jane knew it was rarely that simple. She'd stuck around with Iain partly because the alternatives were always going to be challenging. But something else had kept her there. She hadn't wanted to give up on what she and Iain had once had. She hadn't wanted to admit she'd got it wrong, that he wasn't the man she'd thought. So she'd hung on, hoping to rekindle a magic that had never existed in the first place. It was a kind of madness, she could see that. But, talking to others in the centre, she'd discovered her feelings were far from unique.

'Is that why Netty does this?' Alicia asked. 'I mean, takes in people like us.'

'I suppose that must be part of it,' Dowling said. 'But Netty's a complex woman. And a generous one. She does things because she wants to. She genuinely likes the company. She likes having young people here. It helps her to stay young.' She stopped suddenly and looked towards the back door. 'Talk of the devil.'

Jane had heard nothing, but Dowling had been right.

A moment later, the back door rattled open and Netty Munro stepped inside. She was wearing jeans and a faded T-shirt with the logo of a band that Jane vaguely recognised. 'Buggers!' she exclaimed to no one in particular.

'Problems, dear?'

Munro looked around the room, as though surprised to see the other women there. 'Oh, not really. Just that they haven't done everything they were supposed to on the fencing. I'm going to have to get them back again.'

'Anything we can do?' Dowling asked.

'They were supposed to do it and I'll make bloody sure they do.' This sounded to Jane like a different woman from the Netty Munro she'd met the previous day – much more focused and businesslike. 'Is there a cup of tea going?'

'I'll make it.' Jane jumped up. 'How do you take it?'

'Strong. Splash of milk. That's all.'

Jane crossed to the sink to fill the kettle, hearing Munro saying behind her: 'I'm glad to see you all in such fine fettle this morning. Henry and I certainly don't deserve to be, given the whisky we knocked back.'

'We pickled our constitutions long ago,' Dowling said.

'True enough. We must be careful not to corrupt these innocent young things. Speaking of which, where was Elizabeth off to in such a hurry this morning?'

'I haven't seen her,' Dowling said.

'I saw her upstairs,' Jane added, as she placed the kettle nervously on one of the Aga's rings. 'She was just heading into the shower. She didn't say anything about going anywhere.'

'Plays her cards close to her chest, young Elizabeth,' Dowling commented.

'Which she has every right to,' Munro said. 'I'm assuming she wasn't walking out on us for good, as she wasn't carrying any luggage. Her business. For the moment at least.' The last words were added apparently as an afterthought, but they sounded meaningful to Jane. Not exactly threatening, but serious.

Jane waited for the kettle to boil, and then prepared Munro's tea. She wondered if she ought to be doing something more complicated with leaves and a teapot, but Munro declared herself content with a teabag stewed in a mug.

'So what do we do if she doesn't come back?' Jane asked.

'Don't you worry yourself about that,' Munro said. 'That's my problem.' This time, Jane thought, the undertone of threat was more obvious. Munro might well be as kind and generous as Dowling had indicated. But it struck Jane that she wasn't someone you'd want to get on the wrong side of.

Good material, she thought again. Whatever that might mean, she imagined that Munro would have the strength to shape that material in whatever way she wanted.

CHAPTER 24

'Just had a friend of yours here,' McKay said.

'I saw him,' Horton said. 'We passed on the road. I had to pull in to let him past on the single-track bit. I was keeping my head low, but he made a point of stopping to wind the passenger window down and call across to me that he'd been talking to "my boss". I think he imagined I was the secretary or something.'

'I *am* your boss,' McKay pointed out.

'You keep telling yourself that, Alec. What did chummy want anyway? Had he just come back for another gawp?'

'He actually came back with some additional information.'

'Wonders will never cease. Anything useful?'

McKay recounted what Stewart had told him. 'So, maybe useful,' he concluded. 'Or maybe three-fifths of fuck all. Who knows?'

'Worth following up,' Horton conceded. 'Any other news while I've been gone?'

'Not really,' McKay said. 'I was planning to have another chat with young Pete Carrick in a second. He must have made some progress by now. After all, he's not Jock Henderson.'

'What is it with you and Jock anyway?' Horton said as they walked across the site towards the crime scene.

'Ach, it's just friendly banter.'

Horton looked sceptical. 'It doesn't always sound like it. You sure there's nothing more behind it?'

'If there was, it's so long ago that Jock and I have both forgotten what it was. I just like to keep him on his toes.'

'If you say so, Alec.'

Carrick and his fellow examiner – whom McKay vaguely recognised but didn't know – were standing by the tent as McKay and Horton approached.

'Shirking on the job again, Pete? Don't let Jock catch you.'

'Aye, funny how when it's a job like this it's always me pulls the short straw. Jock seems very adept at avoiding them.' Carrick's tone was light-hearted. No one, not even McKay, seriously believed that Henderson hadn't tackled more than his fair share of unpleasant jobs.

'Must be pretty grim in there,' Horton commented.

'Aye, I'd say so. Two-day-old corpse. Plenty of flies. The odd maggot or fifty. Over temperature, in case the body wasn't decomposing fast enough. Oh, and the smell. Did I mention the smell?'

McKay had never quite worked out how people like Carrick stayed so cheerful in the face of a task like this. 'You didn't really need to. I can get a nice whiff of it from here.'

'To experience the full delights, you need to stick your head in the tent. But I wouldn't recommend it.'

'I'll just wait for your TripAdvisor review,' McKay said. 'How's it going anyway?'

'Reckon we're not far off done.'

'Headlines so far?'

'I was right about the garrotting, you'll be delighted to hear. Same MO as yesterday's – I gave Jock a quick call to compare notes. Thin wire. Maybe piano wire or something like that.'

'Any sign of the murder weapon?'

'Nothing with the body.' Carrick looked around them. 'Might have been dumped anywhere round here. But if you were going to dispose of it, you'd head over to the firth, wouldn't you?'

'I'd have thought so,' McKay agreed.

'In any case,' Carrick went on, 'I don't think it was done here. Think the killing occurred somewhere else and the body was transported here after death. There's not a lot of blood around.'

McKay exchanged a glance with Horton. 'So maybe chummy's Volvo's relevant after all?' He explained to Carrick what Gordon Stewart had told them.

'That would fit with the likely timing,' Carrick said. 'Though I can't be very precise on that, given how the temperatures have been over the last couple of days. Doc'll probably give you a better idea.'

'You always were the optimist, son,' McKay said. 'If the body had been transported here, would you expect a lot of blood in the vehicle?'

'Again, you'd have to ask the doc. But maybe not too much. The actual incision is pretty fine. Death would probably have resulted from asphyxiation.'

McKay nodded, absorbing this. 'Any ID?'

'Aye, well, that's interesting, given yesterday's victim.'

'Is it, son? Okay, keep me interested.'

'Your man yesterday was that comic guy, wasn't he?'

'Jimmy McGuire,' Horton confirmed.

'This one looks like he's a musician.'

'Christ,' McKay said. 'Any more and we'll be able to put on a show at the fucking Glasgow Empire.'

'Do we have a name?' Horton asked.

'Ronnie Young.'

'Ronnie Young?' McKay said. 'That rings a bell.'

'Aye, it did with me too. Bit before my time though, so I asked Jock.'

'If Jock remembers him, he must have done a turn in the music halls.'

'Not exactly. He was big in the eighties. Biggish. At least by Scottish standards. Part of the post-postcard scene, if you get my drift.'

'Not really, son. Never really been my thing.'

'He was lead singer and guitarist with a band called The Money Pit.'

'I've heard of them,' Horton said. 'They had a couple of hits, didn't they?'

'Jesus, Ginny. Are you older than you look?' McKay said.

'I've heard of Shakespeare,' she explained patiently, 'and he was even before your time. You're just ignorant, Alec.'

'Happy to stay that way if the alternative is knowing about bands called The Money Pit. What a fucking name.'

'From what I remember, it was all too accurate.' This was from the other examiner who'd been standing silently listening to the conversation. He was older than Carrick, probably nearer McKay's age. 'Like you say, they had a couple of minor hits with an indie label up here, signed with one of the majors who thought they had star potential. Label poured a fortune into their debut album which the band largely pissed up the wall, and the whole thing disappeared without a trace. Got lousy reviews everywhere and sold about five copies. I've got one of the five, and it's still worth bugger all,' he concluded, proudly.

'What's Young being doing since?'

'The band went on for a bit. There was a second album, I think. Much lower budget. Still went nowhere. They split up. After that, from what I remember, Young did various things – bit of record producing, bit of management, bit of a solo career.' He paused, thinking. 'There was some scandal with the band, if I remember.'

'Scandal?' McKay glanced at Horton, who was clearly following the same train of thought.

'Aye, something about underage groupies. The band weren't much more than teenagers themselves, but even so… I remember that one of the Sunday papers made a bit of a splash of it at the time, but nothing much came of it. But I've a recollection that one of the other band members – not Young – got sent down for some kind of sexual assaults a few years later.' He paused, shaking his head. 'Can't remember the details. But it was something along those lines.'

'Thanks for that, son,' McKay said. 'Sounds like we might have some sort of pattern emerging. Showbiz types. Has-beens. Hint of sex-related scandal in their past. Oh, and garrotting. I nearly forgot the garrotting.' He paused, then added, as if to himself, 'I wonder why garrotting.'

'Don't envy you lot this one,' Carrick said. 'Media are going to have a field day, aren't they? Not one, but two minor celebrities they can stick on the front page.'

'You're not wrong,' McKay agreed. 'So you'd better get your arse in gear and get the job finished, hadn't you?'

***

'You okay?' McKay asked.

'I'm fine, Why?'

'Only that it must have been a bit of a shock stumbling across a corpse like that.'

Horton shrugged. 'It's not exactly what I go looking for on a run. But it's not like it's the first dead body I've seen.'

'Aye, I suppose.'

They were heading back into the city, and for once McKay was driving. Another concession to her welfare, Horton thought. 'I get what you're saying though. It's taken me a while to get back into the routine after what happened with my stepdad and everything.' She still tended to use that shorthand, even though technically he never had been her stepfather. It was easier than having to explain the whole sordid story. 'But today wasn't like that. I didn't feel threatened. Except that I might die of boredom listening to Gordon Stewart.'

'Must have been a shock for him too. I'll remind whoever interviews him to go gently.'

'What did Helena have to say?'

'Mainly a few choice expletives. I said we'd debrief her properly when we got back. She's not best pleased at having another dead Z-list celebrity to deal with though. Apart from anything else, if we don't make progress quickly, chances are it'll be taken out of our hands.'

Horton suspected that this possibility might be more of a concern for McKay than it was for Helena Grant. McKay lived for cases like this, something he could get his teeth into. Grant probably had more than enough on her plate anyway. 'Any more on the fallout from the Elizabeth Hamilton trial?'

'Not that I've heard. Hamilton seems to have gone to ground somewhere. Maybe working on her autobiography with some tabloid hack.' McKay paused. 'Makes me nervous that we don't know what she's up to. I wish we'd kept her under surveillance.'

Horton glanced across at him, but his eyes were fixed on the road. 'On what grounds? Even if we think the verdict was wrong, it's not as if she's likely to be a danger to the public, is it?'

'She killed two people.'

'She was responsible for two people's deaths. In very specific circumstances. There's no reason to suppose she's a danger to anyone else.'

McKay made no response as they turned off the Raigmore roundabout, and then made their way around to police HQ. There was something on his mind, Horton thought, but he clearly wasn't ready to share it yet, if at all.

Grant was standing in the corridor waiting for them. 'I've just been talking to comms,' she said, as she led them back into her office. 'We've not said much about the McGuire case so far, except that a body's been found and that we're treating the death as suspicious. We've still not formally ID'd him, so we're not revealing the name just yet. We've arranged for someone in Edinburgh to visit his partner so we can get her up here as soon as possible–' McKay had opened his mouth to protest, but Grant didn't allow herself to be interrupted. 'Aye, I know you were planning to go down there, Alec, but this morning's finding changes our priorities a bit, don't you think?'

'I suppose,' McKay conceded. 'But there's his agent to talk to, as well.'

Horton had sat herself in one of the seats before Grant's desk but McKay continued to roam around the room in his usual way.

'We can speak to him on the phone in the first instance,' Grant said, 'once we've confirmed the identity. If he has anything useful to say, we can arrange for someone to go down.'

'What about Ronnie Young?'

'We need to get him ID'd too. I'm told he was living up in this neck of the woods with his wife. Out near Beauly somewhere. That's probably your next task. We're not going to suggest there's any link between the two bodies at this stage, at least not till we've got a clearer idea from the doc.'

'Aye, they could be just two random garrottings,' McKay said 'Like buses. Always come along together.'

'It's a fine balance. If there is some multiple killer out there, the public need to know. But there's no point in raising unnecessary concerns.'

'But we're going to treat them as one enquiry?'

'You know better than that, Alec. We can't jump to any conclusions. But, aye, we'll have the same team working on both, unless it becomes evident that they're not linked. I've been drumming up some resources. We've got a uniformed team going out there this afternoon to do a search of the area. We'll do some door to doors in the vicinity to see if anyone else spotted anything suspicious. Another sighting of this Volvo might be useful. I've set someone on to checking all the CCTV and APNR footage for the relevant period.'

'Sounds like you've been busy.'

'Like you said, Alec, we need to make fast progress on these. We'll be under a microscope already, and there are parts of the press that would love another stick to beat us with.'

'Don't I know it.'

'So don't you go blabbing to any of your mates on the locals.'

McKay held up his hands in mock offence. 'Moi?'

'Aye, toi. I know you, Alec McKay. If you think there's a chance of getting a useful lead from it, you'll do it. Just make sure you clear anything with me first, eh? I don't want any surprises.'

'Message received. You want us to go and talk to Ronnie Young's wife next then?'

Horton could see that he was itching to get out of the office and back to what he thought of as real work.

'Widow, I suppose I mean,' he added as an afterthought.

'That would be good. At least it'll keep you out of my hair for a couple of hours.'

'You'll miss me when I'm gone.'

She shook her head. 'Alec, when I was thirteen, I had my appendix removed. I miss that more than I'm likely to miss you.'

He grinned and turned to Horton. 'Okay, Ginny, it's clear we're not wanted. Let's hit the road. Your turn to drive, if I'm not mistaken.'

CHAPTER 25

McKay was fiddling with the satnav, occasionally swearing under his breath.

'You not got that thing working yet?' Horton asked. 'Do you want us to stop so I can do it?'

McKay looked up and gave her a look that told her the answer was definitely no. 'Bloody technology. What we need is a teenager. Someone who understands this kind of thing.'

'Look, all you do, Alec, is tap in the postcode–'

'What do you think I've been bloody trying to do? But this bloody touchpad keyboard…' He uttered a couple more profanities for good measure, then finally sat back. 'There,' he said. 'Simple when you know what you're doing.'

'I imagine it would be,' Horton said. She glanced over at the screen. 'Shouldn't be all that much further then.' The address they had for Ronnie Young and his wife had turned out to be between Muir of Ord and Beauly, just within the western boundary of the Black Isle. They'd taken the A662 along the south side of the Beauly Firth, intending to head north through Beauly itself with the satnav guiding them for the last few miles. It wasn't an area Horton knew well, though she'd been to Beauly with Isla once or twice. There were a couple of decent cafés to grab a bite to eat and the ruins of Beauly Priory to wander through.

'Must be somewhere around here,' she said, after they'd passed through Beauly and were heading out towards Muir of Ord. The satnav had just informed them, in its mellifluous tones, that in two hundred yards they would have reached their destination. The only problem was that they were in a stretch of open country with no obvious houses around them.

'It's always the bloody problem up here,' McKay said. 'Postcode covers half of each fucking village.' He peered out of the passenger window. 'Not that there's any sign of a village.'

'What about that?' Horton pointed to a narrow metalled track running off to their left between two fields. 'Reckon there might be something down there?'

'Worth a look,' McKay said doubtfully. 'But there's no sign.'

'I can't see anywhere else that looks possible,' Horton said, as she turned off onto the track. 'And if it's not the right place we might at least find someone who can give us directions.'

McKay nodded, still looking doubtful at the wisdom of this decision. They bounced down the track for a half mile or so, still with no obvious sign of life. Then there was a sharp right turn as the road dipped further downwards. Horton was hoping there wasn't a tractor waiting to meet them round the bend.

As they turned the corner, the road opened up into what had presumably once been a farmyard with a squat old house positioned at the far end. Its farming life looked to be well behind it. The yard had been turned into an impressive-looking garden, dotted with tubs full of daffodils and other spring blooms, a large central lawn, and, to their left, a patch of woodland with a decking area standing beside what Horton took to be a substantial brick barbecue. The place was clearly lovingly, and probably expensively, maintained.

The farmhouse had been upgraded in similar style. The building looked to be nineteenth century or older, but it had been recently renovated and redecorated. There was a Land Rover Discovery standing in the driveway ahead of them.

'Nice place,' Horton said. 'You reckon this is it?'

McKay gestured to a sign beside the front door. 'The name matches. It looks as if Young wasn't doing too badly, if he could afford a place like this.'

Horton pulled up behind the Land Rover and they climbed out into the afternoon sunlight. Somewhere behind the house they could hear a dog barking.

McKay pressed the doorbell and they heard the ringing from distantly inside. There was no other sound. He waited a moment and pressed it again, holding it for longer this time.

'Can I help you?' The voice came from somewhere to their left, the tone suggesting that the answer to the question must almost certainly be no.

'Mrs Young?' McKay asked, squinting to make out the figure walking towards them.

'Who's asking?'

'Police,' McKay said, holding out his warrant card. 'DI McKay and DS Horton.'

The woman walking towards them was tall, with long blonde hair. She walked with the catwalk stride of someone who'd once been a model. She looked as if she was used to being in the public eye, though her face was unfamiliar to Horton. 'I'm Bridget Young,' she said. 'How can I help you?'

'Could we perhaps go inside, Mrs Young? I'm afraid we may have some bad news for you.'

Bridget Young looked them both up and down, as if considering whether she really did want them in her house. 'You'd better come round. I was just doing some tidying up out the back.'

They followed her round the side of the house into the smaller rear garden. It had been cultivated to create the air of an outdoor living space, with an artfully arranged gap in the trees to allow a view of the mountains beyond. McKay assumed that adjoining fields had once belonged to the farmhouse but had been sold or let for agricultural purposes. Whatever its origins, the building did not have the air of a working farm.

'Would you like some tea or coffee?' Bridget Young said over her shoulder. McKay was intrigued that, despite being told they were bearing bad news, she seemed so far unperturbed. People responded very differently to that kind of announcement, but they were usually keen to hear what you had to say.

'I think that had better wait till you've heard what we have to tell you, Mrs Young,' he said. She had led them through a set of patio doors into a stylish kitchen. Substantial money had been spent there, McKay thought, and relatively recently. She gestured for them to take a seat at a large oak table.

'I'm going to put the kettle on anyway,' she said. 'I'm parched. Been in the garden all morning.'

McKay looked across at Horton, who shrugged. McKay waited till Young had filled the kettle and set it to boil, then tried again. 'Can I ask whether you know your husband's current whereabouts, Mrs Young?'

She turned back to them. 'Is this something about Ronnie then? He's in Edinburgh as far as I know. Why?'

'When was the last time you spoke to him?'

'Couple of days ago, I suppose.'

McKay took a breath. 'As I said, I'm afraid we may have some bad news, Mrs Young. About your husband. This morning my colleague here, DS Horton, responded to a report of a body being discovered.'

'A body? You mean Ronnie?'

'It looks as if that may well be the case, Mrs Young. I'm sorry.'

The kettle had boiled and for a moment, Bridget Young continued to prepare the tea, pouring boiling water in a pot, as if she hadn't heard McKay's words. 'I can't exactly pretend I'm surprised,' she said finally. 'The bugger could certainly pick his moment though.' She looked up at McKay. 'Was he found in the hotel?'

McKay frowned, then shook his head. 'I'm sorry, Mrs Young. I think you may have misunderstood the circumstances. The body was found locally. Near Ardersier. In McDermott's Yard, if you know that.'

Bridget Young stared at him, clearly baffled. 'McDermott's Yard? I don't understand. What the hell would he be doing in McDermott's Yard?'

'We were hoping that you might be able to shed some light on that.'

'You've got the wrong man. You must have. Ronnie's in Edinburgh.'

'If you feel able to, we'd like to ask you to confirm the identity. It's possible there's been a mistake, but we found ID that indicated it was your husband.' McKay had hesitated before acknowledging the possibility of a mistake, knowing the tendency of grieving relatives to cling to any remnant of hope. But so far Bridget Young did not seem the typical grieving relative.

'Of course.'

'What was your husband doing in Edinburgh?' Horton asked.

'Producing a record. New young band from that neck of the woods somewhere. Not really my sort of thing, but Ronnie reckoned they had a lot of potential.'

'You say you spoke to him a couple of days ago?' McKay said.

'He called me just to say he was fine and that everything was going well. He was expecting to get back here around the end of the week.' She shrugged. 'I can see you're wondering why we wouldn't have spoken since then. But that's how he is when he's working on a recording. He's a hard taskmaster with the artists. He reckons that's how he gets results. So they work long days and he sticks with them in the evenings. So they keep the vibe going, as he puts it.' There was an edge of irony in her tone. 'If you want my opinion, a lot of it's about trying to claw back his lost youth. Partying down with the kids. But then he comes back up here and loses himself in bucolic tranquillity with me, so it seems to work okay.'

McKay noticed they were all still speaking in the present tense. 'Does he spend a lot of time away?'

'It varies. Producing's his main line of work these days. He's not exactly A-list, but he's in demand. Enough to be able to pick and choose the work anyway. He tends to avoid stuff that's likely to require him being away for weeks on end, unless it's someone he particularly wants to work with or in some location he's keen to visit. Mostly, it's the up and coming bands, and it's a week or two in London or Edinburgh.'

'Does he still play himself?' Horton asked.

'A little. He did a solo album a couple of years back, and did a low-key tour to promote that. He's been talking about doing another – has the songs all ready – but hasn't managed to find the time. He does the occasional one-off gig if he's asked.'

McKay felt as if he'd allowed the conversation to drift away from their purpose, Young's likely death barely acknowledged. 'When I told you we'd found a body, you implied you weren't surprised, Mrs Young. Why did you say that?'

She blinked, as if she'd forgotten why the two police officers were in her house in the first place. 'Ronnie's – well, he's prone to burn the candle at both ends. He's not as young as he'd like to think he is. It wouldn't surprise me if he'd had a heart attack or a stroke.'

McKay wondered whether Young's methods of maintaining the vibe might have included the use of Class A drugs. His own knowledge of the music scene was as sketchy as Bridget Young's appeared to be, but he assumed such practices were still not uncommon. Something for the post-mortem, maybe, assuming that the body really was Young's. 'Can you think of any reason why he might have returned up here without letting you know?'

'Anything's possible with Ronnie. His head's sometimes in a different place. If he'd finished earlier than expected, he'd often just turn up back here without warning. So that wouldn't be surprising in itself.'

'How would he normally travel?' Horton asked.

'To Edinburgh he'd get the train. London, he'd fly down.'

'Can you think of any reason he might have been in the vicinity of McDermott's Yard?'

'You're really serious about this being him?'

'As I say, Mrs Young, we found items with the body that indicated it was your husband, so we have to start by checking that out. Have you tried to contact him since you last spoke?'

'I called his mobile this morning to see if he had any idea when he might be back, but it went straight to voicemail. But again that's what I'd have expected. He never has it turned on in the studio and mostly forgets to switch it on when he gets outside. I just left him a message on the basis that he'd eventually pick it up and get back to me. But that will be in his own good time.'

'And McDermott's Yard?' McKay prompted. He was struck by Bridget Young's ability to deflect the direct questions they were asking. He couldn't decide whether this was a deliberate tactic or just her usual way of interacting with others.

'I don't think Ronnie's been back there for the best part of twenty years.'

'Back there?'

'Aye, it's where he worked when he first left school apparently. Did an apprenticeship there. He was still working there during the early days of the band. Only gave it up when it looked like they might make the big time. Which they never did, of course, but I don't think Ronnie ever regretted leaving that job.'

'When did you meet your husband, Mrs Young?'

'About ten years ago. From what he's told me, he went through some lean times after the band folded. Scraped a living performing solo but it wasn't easy. He got into the producing side pretty much by accident – some mate asked him to produce a few demos and he got the bug. He was always a bit of a techie – that was his background and he was into the electrical and IT stuff – so he just got his head down and learned how to do it. It took off from there. Began to work with some relatively big names and make some decent money from it.' She made it sound as if that was the main basis of her interest in Ronnie Young. 'Funnily enough, I'd travelled a similar route. I started out as a model. We're supposed to be airheads, but a lot of us aren't. I was getting a bit long in the tooth to be in front of the camera, so I decided to get behind it. It had always been a bit of a hobby, and I'd worked with some of the best so I'd learnt a lot. I ended up doing some publicity shots for a band Ronnie was producing, and there you are.'

McKay nodded. This seemed to be another of those unfathomable marriages. But most seemed to be that way, and he was in no position to cast the first stone. He was growing increasingly conscious that, during the whole of their discussion, Bridget Young had still failed to acknowledge the possibility, let alone the likelihood, that her husband might actually be dead.

'Are you able to come with us to confirm whether the body we've found is that of your husband, Mrs Young?' Fairly brutal, he thought, avoiding Horton's eye, but he sensed Bridget Young needed dragging back to reality.

'Now, you mean?'

'If you're able. I think the sooner we confirm this one way or the other the better.' McKay had checked before he and Horton had left the office that the body was in a state to be seen. Despite the problems of decomposition, he'd been told the face was presentable. He really hoped that the bastards in the mortuary weren't going to let him down on this one. There were other routes to confirming the identity but this was likely to be the quickest.

'Yes, of course,' she said. 'Look, let me try to phone Ronnie first. I'm sure you've got this wrong.'

'By all means.' McKay was coming to the conclusion that Bridget Young's apparent calm was nothing more than a remarkable ability to deny reality. Maybe it went with the territory, he thought. If you spent your working time constructing fantasies, perhaps that's where you ended up living.

She pulled out her mobile phone and dialled the number. Then she shook her head. 'Just gone to voicemail. Still switched off.'

That was another question, McKay thought. No mobile had been found on or near the body. So what had happened to it? Would they find it elsewhere in the yard or had it been lost or taken wherever the killing had occurred? Either way, they'd need to get access to the account and call log.

'Okay,' she went on. 'I still think you must be wrong, but as you say the sooner we sort this out the better. Do you want me to follow you?'

'We'll drive you down and bring you back. It's just to Raigmore.'

She had risen to her feet, but suddenly she sat down again, as if she'd only now been struck by the reality of the situation. 'I'm not sure I can do this. If this really is Ronnie.'

'You don't have to, Mrs Young. We can use dental records or DNA to check the identity. It's your choice.'

She looked up at him, her face blank, as if she was unable to understand what he was saying. 'I should though, shouldn't I? Otherwise, I'll just be sitting here, waiting for him to call but not knowing.'

McKay nodded, not wanting to steer her one way or the other. His instinct was that, if the body really was that of Ronnie Young, it would ultimately be easier for his wife if she were to see the body. Otherwise, McKay had a sense that, whatever method they used to confirm the identity, she would remain in denial. But it had to be her decision.

After a long silence, she stood up again. 'Okay. Let's do it.'

CHAPTER 26

'Is there something I can do?' Jane asked. 'To make myself useful, I mean.'

She had already collected all the breakfast crockery and, under Netty Munro's instructions, had helped stack the dishwasher. That was another new experience for Jane. She'd ever actually used a dishwasher before, and found it hard to believe that the appliance could be as effective as washing by hand.

Alicia had been trying to help too, following a step or two behind Jane, picking up the odd item that Jane had been unable to carry. Jane had the sense that Alicia was well intentioned but, so far, not particularly effectual. That was perhaps unfair. Alicia had a cowed air, as if life had beaten any spirit or energy out of her. Jane had no idea what Alicia might have experienced. And not everyone was as resilient as Jane herself.

At first, Munro had seemed surprised at Jane's question, as if she hadn't seriously expected the younger women to provide any assistance. She'd been sitting at the table, idly scanning through Dowling's copy of *The Guardian*. She looked up. 'Okay. If you're really keen, we'll start with the garden, shall we? I was planning to work out there this morning. Any help always welcome.'

Jane nodded her nervous assent. This was further unknown territory for her. She'd never worked in a garden before. She'd grown up in flats, and her only experience of horticulture had been the plastic packages of petrol station flowers that Iain had occasionally bought when he'd been trying to make up for whatever mental or physical harm he'd done her. 'Happy to try. But you'll have to tell me what to do.'

'Oh, I'll do that,' Munro said. 'I don't want you tearing up my prize blooms.' The tone was light-hearted but as so often there seemed to be a serious undertone.

Jane and Alicia followed Munro out of the back door into the bright morning sunshine, leaving Dowling still perusing the newspaper over another cup of coffee. It was already turning into another fine day, with just a few white clouds scudding briskly across an otherwise blue sky. The firth looked different this morning, Jane thought. The previous afternoon, the waters had filled the broad stretch between here and Dingwall on the far side. Now they had receded, leaving wide stretches of uncovered earth along each shore.

Munro followed Jane's gaze. 'It's surprisingly tidal,' she said. 'The waters are shallow there, so when the tide goes out it drains rapidly. It's one of the things I love about it. It changes so much, not just at different times of the year but even across the day.'

The area to the side of the house below the decking had been turned into a proper domestic style garden, a contrast with much of the rest of the land which remained a working farm. There was a neatly trimmed lawn, and flowerbeds laid with spring flowers that, with the exception of some scatterings of daffodils, Jane couldn't recognise. Munro gestured towards the beds. 'I could do with some help weeding those, if that's okay.'

'As long as you show us which are weeds and which aren't,' Jane said.

'They say a weed is just a flower in the wrong place. But, yes, I'll show you what's in the wrong place.'

In the event, it all seemed fairly straightforward. Munro explained carefully which plants should be removed and which left, and Jane found it easier to distinguish between the two than she'd feared. Alicia looked more nervous but, as in the kitchen, seemed comfortable to follow Jane's lead. Jane sat down on the lawn beside the bed and systematically worked through the plants, indicating to Alicia that she should do the same a little further along.

It was the kind of work Jane enjoyed. Not exactly mindless because she had to concentrate on which plants she was removing, but sufficiently repetitive that she could lose herself in the process. It wasn't physically taxing, but she knew it would be more tiring than it seemed. Again, she wanted that. Something that would distract her from her own thoughts and anxieties. Her own memories.

'Am I doing it right?' Alicia said, keeping her voice low. Netty Munro was kneeling by one of the beds at the far side of the garden, carrying out the same task.

Jane peered over, checking the plants that Alicia had tossed into the bucket they were both using. 'That looks right to me.'

'I've not done this before,' Alicia said.

'No, me neither. But we'll be okay.' It was odd, Jane thought. She had found herself taking on a maternal role with Alicia, even though she suspected that the other woman might be older. But that was the kind of person she was. That had been part of the difficulty with Iain. He'd wanted to treat her as a substitute mother rather than a girlfriend or wife, and initially she'd allowed that to happen because she felt comfortable with the role. But then he'd grown angry with her supposedly because he thought she wanted to replace his mother. Go figure, she thought.

'Still no sign of Elizabeth,' Alicia said.

That was true, but hardly surprising. It was less than a couple of hours since Munro had apparently seen Elizabeth striding down to the gates. It was possible she'd just decided to go for a short walk before rejoining them, but Munro's description had made her departure sound more purposeful than that. There was something about Elizabeth that Jane had been unable to fathom. 'I suppose it's her business,' she said.

'We used to be friends,' Alicia said. 'Same crowd and all that, you know.'

Jane thought back to the friends she'd had in school. They were all still living locally, she assumed, but she'd lost touch with all of that. That had been Iain's doing too. His petty jealousies. It wasn't even that he was concerned about her and other men. He just resented her enjoying herself with anyone other than him. And it had been a long time since she'd enjoyed herself with him. 'Did you fall out?'

Alicia hesitated, as if unsure what to say. 'No, not really. Not with Elizabeth.' Alicia was silent for a long time, still carefully tugging away at the weeds, and Jane thought she wasn't going to say any more. 'It was her dad. He… did things. I let him do things.'

'Jesus, that's awful. Did you tell anyone?'

'No, that's the thing. At first, I didn't really realise it was wrong. Or maybe I did but I didn't want to think it was. Then I felt bad about it. I thought it was my fault that it had happened. Elizabeth tried to warn me off. I thought she was pissed off with me, and we had a row. I mean, a real big row. We stopped being friends and so I stopped going to her house. I tried to contact her dad a couple of times but he never responded.'

'Probably lucky for you he didn't.'

'Aye, I know that now. Elizabeth was just trying to protect me. But I didn't realise it.'

'So you think she's okay then? I mean, you like her?' Jane realised that these were the questions she'd been unconsciously asking herself since she'd first encountered Elizabeth. There'd been moments when she'd thought Elizabeth must be decent, well-intentioned. Others, often almost at the same time, when she'd decided Elizabeth was an utterly ruthless bastard. Jane had no real evidence to support either judgement, and with most people the question wouldn't even have occurred to her on such a short acquaintance. There was something about Elizabeth that generated a more extreme response.

Alicia hesitated again. 'I don't know, to be honest. She makes me feel… I don't know… uncomfortable. I don't trust her. That's awful, isn't it?'

'I don't know,' Jane said. 'I've felt the same about her. There's just something–'

'How's it going?' Munro said, from behind them.

She'd approached without either of the two younger women noticing, and Jane wondered how much she might have heard of their conversation. 'You'd better check we're picking out the right plants,' she said.

Munro peered into the bucket, and then sifted through it with her hand. 'That looks fine, dear. And the bed's beginning to look good. Getting rid of all the ones we don't want.' As so often with Munro, there was an edge to her words that Jane couldn't interpret.

She was about to offer some response when there was a shout from across the lawn. She turned and saw Henry Dowling waving to Munro. Munro waved back and then strode across the lawn to meet her.

'Thought I should let you know,' Dowling called, her voice carrying clearly across to Jane and Alicia. 'I was just heading home when I saw Elizabeth.'

'Elizabeth? Where was she?'

'Waiting at the bus stop in the village, would you believe? I asked where she wanted to go. She was being a bit optimistic. She'd just missed a bus and the next one isn't for ages. She didn't seem particularly worried. Said she needed to get into Inverness to do a bit of business. I didn't really know what to do. Hadn't time to drive her in myself. In the end I took her back home to pick up the car, then drove her down to near the Tore roundabout. There are more buses go past that way so I thought she'd got more chance of getting one without having to wait forever.'

'That's good of you, dear,' Munro said. Her voice was noticeably quieter than Dowling's had been, but Jane could still just about make out the words. 'Did she say what sort of business?'

'No. Not a word. I didn't press her.'

'I don't suppose it matters. I just hope she's not left waiting too long.' Munro paused. 'Since you've come back, do you want to have a look at those fences with me? Give me your expert view?'

Dowling nodded. 'If you like. Nothing spoiling.'

Munro smiled and turned back to the two other women. 'You two carry on up here. If you need a break, there are cold drinks in the fridge.'

Jane watched as the two women disappeared off into the farmyard, then she turned back to Alicia, who was still busily tugging away at the weeds, concentrating as if conducting some highly complex task. 'I wonder where Elizabeth's gone.'

Alicia frowned. 'She's always seemed to me like someone who has secrets. Even when she was at school.'

'Maybe one of them was her father. From what you told me.'

'I thought that. Not at the time. At the time I just thought he was interested in me. God, I was stupid. But then, later, I wondered whether that was one of the secrets that Elizabeth was keeping. She always seemed like someone who was – I don't know – juggling different lives. As if there was more than one Elizabeth.'

'Maybe that was how she coped with her dad,' Jane said, thinking how often she'd lied to neighbours and family about what Iain was really like. How her mam had told the same lies about her own father.

'Maybe,' Alicia said doubtfully. 'But it felt the same yesterday. As if she was holding things back. As if she wanted us to talk about ourselves, but wasn't prepared to do it herself.'

That didn't sound particularly surprising to Jane. Elizabeth had struck her as someone who was very self-protective, who'd been damaged before and didn't want to be damaged again. She could sympathise with that, even though she knew she'd never be able to achieve the same detachment.

Oddly enough, she'd had the same feeling about Netty Munro. That she wanted her guests to talk about themselves and their experiences – even though she'd insisted that it was their own choice whether to do so – but she'd been reluctant to discuss her own past. She'd revealed a little when Elizabeth had identified her, but Jane guessed she'd said nothing that wasn't already in the public domain.

Jane wondered also about Elizabeth's motives in revealing Munro's identity. Her father had been a fan, she'd said. The same father who'd abused Alicia and probably Elizabeth herself.

Alicia was right, Jane thought. It felt as if there was an undertone to whatever Elizabeth said, as if there was some meaning she wasn't articulating. Some secret never quite revealed.

Jane turned back to the weeding, recommencing the mindless task of clearing the soil. Her brain was already elsewhere, struggling to find answers to questions she barely understood.

CHAPTER 27

'She was certain?'

'Afraid so. From the way she'd been behaving, I thought she might say no. That she might not even believe her own eyes. But it only took her a second. Now you're telling me I needn't have bothered putting her through all that.'

Helena Grant shrugged. 'Not exactly. I always feel more comfortable with a personal identification.'

'I'm not sure those involved would necessarily share your comfort,' McKay said. He knew he was being unfair, but he'd found the session with Bridget Young even more challenging than he usually found dealing with grieving relatives. It wasn't his strong point. He felt uneasy dealing even with his own emotions let alone those of others. His first instinct was to walk away and leave them to it, because that's how he'd want them to treat him if the situation were reversed.

Bridget Young had been more difficult than most. She'd spent the journey to Raigmore Hospital alternately denying that the body could be that of her husband and collapsing in tears at the certainty that it must be him. Neither response seemed entirely convincing to McKay. He had the increasing impression that the most important thing in Bridget Young's life was Bridget Young, and that her behaviour was more about drawing attention to herself than concern for her husband.

At the hospital, she'd initially declined to enter the mortuary, declaring the whole visit a waste of time. McKay had been on the point of acknowledging she might well be right, when Horton had succeeded in working her persuasive magic. She'd accompanied Bridget Young to view the body and returned just a few minutes later. Young's face gave nothing away but she looked at McKay and nodded. 'It's him all right. What the hell was he doing up here?' Her tone was that of a cartoon wife greeting her returning husband after a long session in the pub.

'That's what we need to find out, Mrs Young. We won't trouble you further for the moment, but we will need to talk to you again.'

She looked at McKay blankly, as if not taking in his words. 'I need to get home,' she said, her voice suddenly anxious as if he'd threatened to abandon her in the lobby of Raigmore Hospital.

'DS Horton will take you back,' McKay said. 'Is there someone who can be with you? I appreciate this must be an awful shock.'

'I'll call my sister,' Young said. 'She'll come over. I don't know how to explain–'

'I can do that for you, if you prefer,' Horton said.

Young nodded. She seemed emotionless, McKay had thought at the time, but then relatives often did when faced with the death of a loved one. It took them time to absorb what had happened, as if some part of their brain still believed everything would continue as before. The emotion often came later, triggered by some trivial reminder of the deceased.

'Are these private thoughts you're having,' Grant asked, 'or can anyone join in?'

McKay looked up, unaware how long he'd been silent. 'I was just thinking about Bridget Young and how she behaved after confirming the death of her husband.'

'Something suspicious?'

'Not in itself, no. It's just…' McKay stopped. 'I suppose she just struck me as a bit flaky.'

'We're all flaky when faced with that kind of trauma.'

McKay knew that Grant was speaking directly from experience, though he couldn't recall her seeming remotely unstable even at the time of her husband's death. Bridget Young had been something else again. 'I'm probably wrong. But it's maybe worth keeping an eye on her.'

'You think she's a suspect?'

'She has to be, doesn't she? Until we can prove otherwise. She tells us he's in Edinburgh. He turns out to have returned up here apparently without telling her. But it's not so much that. I just wonder about the state of their marriage.'

'That way madness probably lies,' Grant said.

'Aye, tell me about it. But it's more what it might tell us about Young's own lifestyle. And I'm wondering where he was killed. The docs reckon that the body hadn't been moved too far after death.'

'So it's most likely that he came back up here but didn't bother to tell his wife,' Grant said. 'We can presumably check with the studio and the band if his work down there was finished. From what you've said, he'd turned up unannounced before.'

'Apparently, though Christ knows why you'd do that.'

'In the hope of catching her out? Maybe he thought she was having an affair.'

'And maybe she was,' McKay said. 'Or maybe *he* was. Seems to have suited him to be incommunicado.'

'Lots of potentially fruitful avenues for you to explore then.'

'Let's hope so.'

'Have we found out who this band was he was working with?'

'Not yet. His wife couldn't remember. Get the impression that all that stuff isn't really her scene. But she's going to dig out the studio info and give it to Ginny.'

'So we should be able to find out when he left Edinburgh. Or at least when he was last seen there.'

'We should,' McKay agreed. 'But now you've done your level best to change the subject, let's go back to where we started. You were telling me that by the time I got up here with the news, you'd already confirmed his identity as Ronnie Young.'

'Aye, well. Like I say, nothing beats the personal touch. But, yes, it looks like he was already on the system. Fingerprints were a match.'

'Why was he on the system?'

'Because Mr Young had been in trouble with us before.'

'This go back to the stuff with the band? That was years ago. Surprised he was on the system from then.'

'No, this is slightly more recent. Up here. About twenty years ago.'

'Go on.'

'Allegation of sexual assault and rape. Woman he was managing at the time. It seems that as well as the pop star period and the production stuff, he also had a spell managing local talent. Not all that successfully, from the stuff I've seen on the file. They were local club acts or similar that he thought had potential. He took them onto his roster, did some demo recordings for them, managed them on the circuit, but also tried to get them their big break.'

'Just a wild shot in the dark,' McKay said, 'but were these mainly young women?'

'Jesus, you're an old cynic, Alec McKay. I don't know, to be honest. This is just stuff I gleaned from a skim of the file and a quick online search of the media coverage at the time. But it wouldn't surprise me. The woman who made the allegations claimed it wasn't an isolated incident and she could draw on supporting testimony from others who'd had similar experiences.'

'So what happened? As if I couldn't guess.'

'Never came to court. Procurator initially didn't think there was a realistic prospect of a conviction. Then the supposed supporting testimony seems not have materialised for whatever reason, and there were some uncertainties about the allegations that had been made.'

'Uncertainties?'

'Usual stuff, as far as I can see. Young raised questions about her motives. She was supposedly resentful about her lack of success under his management. He reckoned she was difficult to work with and she knew he was thinking of dropping her from his roster. So the allegations were just her way of getting her revenge in first.'

'The usual bollocks, in other words.'

'Quite possibly. Usual story anyway. It came down to her word against his. He'd already cast enough doubt on her motives to give the Procurator the jitters.'

'What about the supporting allegations?'

'Like I say, nothing ever materialised. Maybe that was just a bluff, or maybe the others couldn't be persuaded to take them forward. It takes a fair bit of bottle to bring a formal allegation. In any case, in the end the woman in question dropped the allegations herself. Some nonsense about how she must have misinterpreted the situation.'

'Aye,' McKay said. 'Not easy to bring allegations against a manager who might hold the key to your future success. Or at least has persuaded you that he does. I wonder what he promised her to make her drop the allegations.' McKay shook his head wearily.

Grant shrugged. 'Things are improving. Slowly. And we've never been blameless.'

'Christ, no. And we still aren't. But when you see people walk away scot-free...'

'You got one of those "This is what a feminist looks like" T-shirts hidden away at home, Alec?'

'No, but I've got one of those "This is what a serious copper looks like" ones. I just like to see justice done.' He paused. 'How long ago was this?'

'Like I say, over twenty years.'

'Do you think we should be looking at the woman who brought these allegations?'

'It's a bit of a stretch. If she'd wanted to take the law into her own hands, why wait so long?'

'If she was right about Young, it could well be that she's not the only victim. There could be more recent ones.'

'Anything's possible. Though how would that link to Jimmy McGuire? It's hard to imagine the two cases aren't connected.'

'I'm just asking questions,' McKay said. 'Don't expect me to have answers as well.'

'Aye, well, they're sound enough questions. And I suppose the first answer is that, yes, we probably should go and talk to the woman in question. Even if she's not a serious suspect, she may be able to give us some insights into Young.'

'From what you've said, she'll certainly be able to do that. What's her name?'

Grant flicked through the file in front of her. 'She was a bit different from a lot of the artists on Young's roster at the time apparently. A bit older, better established. Which is maybe why she felt more able to speak out than some of the others.'

'For all the good it did her.'

'She'd been a fairly big name on the local country music circuit. Was apparently hoping that Young could help her make the jump to mainstream success.' She paused in skimming through the pages. 'Here we go. Her name's Dowling. Henrietta Dowling.'

CHAPTER 28

Jack Dimmock always woke too late these days. He hated that, or at least he told himself he did. With the days growing longer, he wanted to rise early while the morning was still fresh. He wanted the sense of the whole day stretching before him, giving him real time to make progress with his work.

He felt that regret, that anger with himself, every day as he finally lurched out of bed around noon. He hadn't meant to do that. He'd set an early alarm, as he always did, every well-intentioned evening. When the alarm sounded, he'd just rolled over and turned it off, scarcely even conscious he was doing so. The next he knew, the morning had already gone.

His whole life was like this. An endless process of self-recrimination for actions he seemed unable to help. A series of seemingly involuntary actions that he almost immediately regretted. The reality was his life had long been out of control, and there seemed to be nothing he could do to get it back on track.

When he'd moved out here, he'd said it was because he was finally going to write the novel. He'd always promised he'd do that one day, even back in the days when he was successful. On the verge of being successful anyway. I won't do this forever, he'd told himself. I'll give it up and do what I really want to do. I'll lock myself away and just write. He was brimming with ideas for novels and stories, though he'd told himself then that they'd want him to do the autobiography first. Okay. He'd do that, just to prove he could. That he could do it himself, not through some bought-in ghostwriter. When that took off, he could turn to writing the stuff he really wanted to.

He'd been half right. He hadn't carried on doing that forever. In fact, he hadn't carried it on for much longer. That life had come to an abrupt juddering end when he'd been sent down. If that hadn't happened, they'd maybe have carried on and hit the heights he'd always thought they were destined for. As it was, there was nothing. Not for him. Not for Jimmy.

At least Jimmy had come away relatively unscathed, the bastard. Sure, his career had been wrecked too, but in the circumstances he could hardly be too resentful about that. He should just have been grateful he hadn't been shopped. It could easily have been both of them inside.

Jack knew that Jimmy was only too aware of that. Jimmy knew how close he'd been. Not that he'd ever said a word of thanks. But that was never Jimmy's way. He knew Jack Dimmock wouldn't spill the beans. Jack was loyal to his friends. He wasn't a grass. Or, as his ex-wife put it, he was weak as piss. But that wasn't the real reason. The real reason was that Jimmy could produce far more and worse dirt on him if he chose. *That* was Jimmy's way.

All Jack Dimmock could do was take the punishment, keep going, and try to find some way to rebuild his life. He hadn't exactly succeeded in the last of those, but he'd done the first and was trying to do the second. His wife had left him as soon as he was convicted, but that was hardly a surprise. Most of his friends had magically melted away when the accusations were made public, but that wasn't really much of a shock either.

It just meant that leaving prison had been a pretty bleak experience. He'd come out on licence and as a registered sex offender, so he hadn't even had much freedom of movement. He'd always been careful with his money and, unlike Jimmy, had a few quid stashed away from the glory days, and had even managed to keep some of that back from his lawyers and his ex-wife. What was left wouldn't keep him in luxury, but it was enough to tide him over until he could work out how else to make ends meet.

What he'd done in the end was go back to the writing. Jimmy wouldn't agree, but Jack had really always been the brains behind

Dingwall and McGuire. Jimmy had been the funny one, sure, but most of the time he'd been working with lines Jack had written for him. Jack had written almost all of their material, even if they'd honed it and improved it together. Jack had been a writer before he became a stand-up, producing material for others on the circuit. One of Jimmy's many resentments about their act was that, even at the height of their success, Jack continued to have a lucrative sideline writing for others. 'Why the fuck are you writing for the competition?' Jimmy had asked. 'Why are you wasting your best jokes on those bastards, rather than saving them for us?'

It didn't work like that, Jack had tried to explain. The jokes I write for them are different from the jokes I write for us. That was the trick of writing for stand-ups. You had to get yourself into the performer's head, imagine the kinds of things he or she might want to say. They were all different. Something you could imagine being hilarious delivered by one act would die a death if performed by another. So you wrote to suit their personality, the style of their humour, their delivery. Of course they'd tweak and refine the material further to suit themselves, but they were much more likely to buy it in the first place if they could see themselves saying it.

He'd got himself a reputation, even before the double act took off, as the comedian's comedian. He was the one that they came to if they were going through a rough patch, if they were looking to boost their career, if they'd managed to secure that first appearance on a TV panel show.

When the act took off, he cut back on the writing, not least to keep Jimmy happy. But he'd never stopped entirely. The work vanished as soon as he was sent down, of course. Even if he'd been in a position to continue, no one wanted to be associated with him. That had continued after he'd come out. But gradually he'd got in touch with former customers, former mates. They'd been wary of even talking to him at first, but he'd gradually persuaded them to listen.

He'd always been discreet when writing for others. Stand-ups want to leave the audience with the impression that the act is all their own work, that this humour just spills out of them. That was true of many of them. But others recognised that, funny as they might be, they didn't have the creativity or discipline to churn out the material needed to keep their acts fresh. This was where Jack came in. He could produce the material, and the deal he offered was that no one would ever know. 'I keep my head down and my mouth shut,' he said to clients. 'As far the audience is concerned, this stuff is yours. I'm just a facilitator.'

That had helped him gain work in the early days. More important, it helped him rebuild his business after he came out. 'I can understand why you don't want to be seen to be working with me,' he said. 'That's fine. But no one needs to know about me. I just send you the material, and you do what you want with it.'

They all knew he was good, and after a while the commissions increased. Other comics began to trust him, recognising that he had no interest in claiming any glory for himself. All he wanted was to make a living. And he was succeeding in doing that, more or less.

He'd moved back up here mainly to get away. There was nothing to keep him down south any more. He wasn't going to get back up on stage again – and, in truth, he'd never really enjoyed that even in the days when they were having a bit of success – and he could write anywhere. He still had one or two friends who'd stuck by him through everything, but no one close enough to keep him there. He wanted to put all that behind him, get on with the life he was living. Think about the future.

He'd always been a solitary type even in the old days. Most stand-ups, even if they were more introverted offstage, at least wanted to be the centre of attention when performing. But he'd always hated it. That had been why he'd worked so well with Jimmy. It was the usual odd couple set up – his own awkward stage presence providing the perfect foil for Jimmy's confident wisecracking. They'd fallen into it almost by accident. The original plan had been for him simply to write the material Jimmy would deliver. But Jimmy had quickly realised that it worked better if he could use Jack as a foil. Jack's discomfort on stage became part of the joke.

He wondered later if that had been one of the things that Jimmy resented. There was no question that Jimmy was the star of the show, the one with funny bones. The one who knew how to deliver a joke. But Jack's clumsy unease had been what made them distinctive. There were countless comics like Jimmy. There were few double acts like Dingwall and McGuire.

Dingwall. That had been Jimmy's idea too. Admittedly, Dimmock and McGuire would have sounded like a firm of estate agents. Dingwall had been Jack's hometown. But he'd still hated it as a stage name. It just felt wrong, ill-fitting. Not him at all. But that had been part of the joke as well.

At least, the stage name meant he really could put it all behind him. Now he was just Jack Dimmock, writer to the would-be stars, stuck in the back of beyond. That suited him fine.

He couldn't exactly say he was happy here. He probably wouldn't be happy anywhere. But he was surviving. When he'd heard from some friend of a friend that the house was available for rent, he'd jumped at the chance. It was cheap, it was comfortable enough. It was close enough to where he grew up that he could feel at ease, but not so close he was likely to run into anyone who remembered him. Above all, it gave him the solitude he wanted.

It was a beautiful spot too. Jack wasn't normally one for the scenery, but he had to admit that the sweep of the fields away to the firth was genuinely breathtaking. To the west, there were the mountains, still dotted with snow even this late in spring. From there, you could see the weather moving in – the grey haze of rain moving steadily across the hillside, the scudding low clouds, the morning haar that sometimes sat on the surface of the waters.

He'd set up his desk at the far end of the sitting room, where the large window offered the best view out to the firth. He sat there in the afternoons, trying to get himself inside the head of whichever comedian he was writing for. Sometimes it just flowed. Sometimes it was harder, and he found himself striding up and down the small living room, searching for the jokes that he knew were there somewhere, deep in the recesses of his head, waiting to be uncovered.

When it became really difficult, he'd take a walk outside and stand looking down at the firth, smoking one of his occasional cigarettes. It was extraordinarily silent up there. The only sound was the faint brush of the wind in the trees, the backdrop of birdsong.

The house itself was part of an old steading, converted and updated a few years before. The main part of the building had been transformed into two self-contained houses, used as holiday lets in the summer. The third part, where he lived, was a separate annex, converted for the same purpose. But, because it was relatively small and cramped, it had proved difficult to let to holidaymakers. The owner, a neighbouring farmer, had been looking for a long-term tenant and had responded to Jack's approach with enthusiasm.

For Jack, the place was ideal. He didn't want space, just somewhere he could lock himself away, get his head down and work. If he ever felt cooped up inside, he could just walk out and find himself in more space than he'd ever imagined.

He hadn't yet been there through the summer, but he assumed the place would have a different feel when the two adjacent houses were occupied. That didn't really matter. He had a small, separate garden overlooking the firth, and his own house was self-contained. If he wanted to avoid the holidaymakers, he could easily do so.

It could have been an idyllic existence. The only problem, as it always had been, was the booze. He wasn't as bad as he used to be. There'd been a time, when their careers were just taking off, when he'd been a full-scale raging alcoholic. He'd never been out of control, or at least that was what he told himself. He'd kept it under control, more or less, on days when they were performing. They'd only rarely had to cancel a gig because he'd been incapable of going on stage, and he thought there'd been only a handful of occasions when it had affected his performance. The irony was that what drove him to drink initially was stage-fright. He'd felt so anxious at the prospect of stepping out under the lights that he had a drink to calm his nerves. One drink had become two. Two had become several, and there you were. He performed much more comfortably and easily with a few drinks inside him. But that, in turn, simply made the act less funny.

Even so, he'd never thought it was a big deal. Jimmy thought it was holding them back, that word had got around that Jack was unreliable. If things weren't going well, Jimmy had the skills to hold it all together. But he didn't want to have to keep doing that just because Jack was fucking up. He'd told Jack that, repeatedly, in words of one syllable and four letters.

Jack had thought the criticism unfair. He did most of his drinking at times that weren't going to affect the act; on the days when they weren't working, or late at night after the show. At those times, he really had been unreliable. He was a bad drunk, truth be told, capable of almost anything when under the influence. But that was rare. Just the times when he needed to go on a bender. Most of the time he controlled it, kept it separate from his work commitments.

That was what he'd told himself. Looking back, he knew it was bollocks. If he'd ever had any control, it had been rapidly slipping away from him. There was too much from those days he simply wanted to forget. Too many embarrassments, too much damage.

He supposed that was what had put him inside, though he could barely remember the circumstances. It had happened, and he'd done it, he assumed. Just like he'd done lots of other things Jimmy had covered up for him. At the time, he'd thought that Jimmy was a pal, looking after him like that. It was only later he realised that Jimmy had simply been storing up ammunition. A shedful of material that Jimmy was able to pull out when he'd finally needed a favour for himself.

In that sense, being sent down was the best thing that could have happened, Jack supposed. It had forced him away from the drink, and he'd more or less sobered up.

More or less.

He'd never been through any kind of rehab process, probably because he was still reluctant to acknowledge the reality of his addiction. He told himself he despised all the AA twelve-step nonsense. He didn't need that. All he needed was willpower. That and a few years of prison discipline. There'd been alcohol available in prison, of course, if you wanted it – sometimes mysteriously smuggled in, mostly just home-made hooch brewed from fruit in a bucket by the radiator. But he'd never been that desperate. He'd kept his head down, followed the rules, and got himself out at the earliest opportunity.

And he still drank. That was the reality. He no longer drank all day, and he didn't drink spirits. Those urges were long gone. But when it came to the evening, he still wanted to sit down and pull open a can of beer or pour himself a glass of wine. Nothing wrong with that, except that once again he found that one glass quickly became two, two became several, and he was back in the old routine. He never got completely stoshied like he used to, but he still drank too much, dragged himself into bed in the wee hours, and slept until it was much later than he'd intended. Then he despised himself for wasting the day, and fell back into the old cycle of anxiety and self-loathing.

The result was that the promised novel was still firmly sitting on the back-burner. He managed to work effectively enough, but only on the material he was preparing for his clients, never on his own work. He had notebooks full of ideas for the novel, and he'd started the opening chapter more than once. He'd even wondered about returning to the idea of an autobiography. After all, his story now was considerably more interesting than when he'd just been the unfunny half of Dingwall and McGuire.

But he'd missed that boat. If he'd ever had any real notoriety, it had only been in that period around the trial. By the time he'd come out, he'd already been largely forgotten. No publisher would have wanted to touch the story then anyway, even if there'd been a public interested in buying it.

So here he was, spending his days writing crap for second-rate comics who allowed the world to believe they were producing this stuff themselves. And if they ever became successful, some idiot publisher would knock at their door to ask them to write a bloody novel of their own. Because that's what every stand-up does these days. And here was the poor sap who'd actually produced the bloody material for them, stuck up in a fucking hovel in the Highlands, making rapid progress towards nowhere.

He was supposed to be producing some material for a young Scottish comedian at the moment. Some wet behind the ears type who'd adopted a camp persona which Jack presumed represented some kind of ironic commentary on the Larry Graysons or John Inmans Jack recalled from his own youth. Jack had never worked out why the same material, presented in a supposed spirit of irony, was seen as less offensive than what it claimed to be satirising. But that wasn't really his business. His business was to churn out the jokes that the youngster, buoyed by his initial success, was unable to come up with by himself.

For some reason, Jack was finding this one hard going. He'd done what he usually did and sat through as much online footage as he could find of the comedian in performance. He hadn't found this one particularly amusing, but that was often the case. Jack knew the tricks. He could see the strings – the little techniques the act used to get the audience on his side, the way the stronger lines were used to skate over the weaker material, the obvious call-backs that flattered the audience into thinking they were party to some in-joke. This guy had got the stuff off pat. It was just that, like so many of them, he wasn't actually very funny.

Jack didn't care much about that. His job was to get inside the guy's head, or at least into his stage persona. Work out the things he might say, the lines that would sound funny with this personality, this delivery, this tone.

He'd get there eventually. It might not be his best work, but it would be okay. Better than most others could do. He just had to keep at it.

When he'd finally dragged himself back into the land of the living, fortified by a bowl of cereal and some over-strong coffee, he sat down at his laptop and reread the work he'd completed the previous afternoon. As was always the way, it was better than he remembered. It wouldn't all survive till the final draft, but there were some decent lines in there. Some that could even make him laugh.

As he always did, he started by revising the previous day's work. He'd found that was the best way of getting back into the right mood. He cut the obvious duds, refined and tightened the wording on some of the lines, added a few comments where he felt the material needed expanding or reworking more substantially. He'd leave that till the end, when he had a better sense of the whole routine and could decide what to keep or lose.

He came to the end of the revisions, but for once found that didn't provide him with the impetus he needed to continue. Somehow, it wasn't gelling. There were ideas and thoughts buzzing about in the back of his brain, but he couldn't immediately find the means to make them cohere into something that might actually make people laugh.

He tapped away in a desultory fashion for another ten minutes before finally acknowledging it wasn't working. Time for a break, he thought. A quick stroll around the garden, maybe a cigarette. Contemplate the views. Let his mind wander and wait for inspiration to strike.

It was another decent day outside. They'd had a sustained stretch of good weather, with clear skies and warm temperatures for the last couple of weeks. It wouldn't last, obviously. It wouldn't be long before the rain clouds swept in across the firth. But for the moment the whole scene looked glorious – the sunlight glittering on the waters, the green hills dotted with patches of yellow gorse, the last winter snows lingering on the summits of the mountains.

He lit a cigarette and sat drinking it all in, trying not to think too much about unfunny camp comedians. That was always the best way when it seemed not to be working. Think about something else. Anything else. The ideas would come.

The only risk, he thought, was that he might end up thinking about the past. The things he'd done. The reasons he was here. The life he was trying to leave well behind. He'd fallen into that trap before, and had been dragged back to the edge of the depressions he'd experienced when he'd first come out. He'd found ways to handle that, more or less. But he knew it was never gone. The abyss was there, waiting to pull him under, and there might eventually be nothing he could do to prevent it.

He was startled out of his reverie by the sound of the front doorbell from within the house. Who the hell could that be? This place was sufficiently remote that you didn't get passing callers. The only person he could think of who might visit without warning would be the landlord, and that was never likely to be good news.

Wearily, he pulled himself to his feet and made his way back through the house to the front door. He unbolted the door and pulled it back, unsure what to expect.

'This is the right place then? It's been a long time.'

Jack stared at the figure standing before him, conscious that the blood was draining from his cheeks.

'Hello, Uncle Jack. Aren't you going to invite me in?'

CHAPTER 29

T his is my life now, McKay thought. Accompanying grieving widows to identify their husband's corpses. Exactly the job satisfaction he'd hoped for when he'd joined the police. 'You're sure?' he said.

'Aye, quite sure,' Fiona McGuire said. 'That's Jimmy, that is.'

McKay nodded to the mortuary attendant and led Fiona back out into the corridor. 'Do you want to get a coffee somewhere?' he asked. 'Away from this place.'

She nodded, giving him a weak smile. 'That would be good.'

They'd brought her up there earlier that afternoon after local officers had visited her at the flat she'd shared with her husband on the outskirts of Edinburgh. She'd already been concerned. 'He was supposed to be back here by now. He always phones if he's going to be delayed.' She'd been on the point of calling the police herself, but had delayed for fear of appearing foolish, 'I kept telling myself there must be a simple explanation. Something wrong with his phone. He'd travelled up on the train, so he couldn't have been in a car accident or anything…'

She'd insisted on coming immediately to conduct the identification. McKay could tell, as they'd entered the mortuary, that she was silently praying the body would not be that of her husband. But she'd known immediately.

There were no tears. But her face was ashen, her eyes dead. McKay felt as if Fiona aged ten years in the last few minutes.

Unsure where else to go, McKay drove them to a nearby supermarket that he knew housed a café. The place was fairly busy but large enough for McKay to find them a table in a corner by the window away from the other customers. When he returned with two coffees, she was staring blankly out at the car park.

'You don't need to say anything,' McKay said, pushing one of the coffees towards her. 'We'll have to interview you formally in due course, but that can wait for the moment.' Inwardly, McKay wondered how long they could afford to delay. In any murder case, a partner has to be considered a considered a suspect in the first instance. Given the coverage the case was likely to receive, they couldn't let things slide, simply through consideration of Fiona's feelings.

'I need to talk,' she said. 'I mean, I'll probably just ramble but it's good to talk to someone about it all.'

'If we take you back this afternoon, is there anyone who can stay with you?'

She blinked, as if surprised by the question.

Most likely, McKay thought, *she won't have considered anything beyond this immediate moment*. Whatever future she might have been expecting had been cancelled.

'I can find someone,' she said. 'A friend, maybe.'

'We'll get someone to help you sort that out.' He paused, wondering how to start the conversation. 'You were surprised your husband hadn't been in touch. Was that unusual?'

'Very. Jimmy wasn't like that.'

'When did he last call you?'

'Just before the show. To let me know he'd got there safely and that it seemed to be a decent place, good crowd.' Her voice was toneless. 'I thought he'd call after he'd finished on stage. He often does that.' McKay could sense she was wondering whether to change the tense in what she'd just said, but instead she continued. 'I was surprised he hadn't. Particularly as it was his hometown. Then I thought he was probably just having a drink or two with someone and hadn't had a chance to call…'

'You never accompanied him when he was performing?'

'Not usually. Once or twice, if we decided to make a trip of it. We did that more when we first got married. But I didn't like taking advantage of what Jimmy was doing. It's work for him and I don't like to intrude on that. I think he preferred me to stay at home.'

'How long had you been married?' McKay asked,

'Five years this autumn.' She stopped, clearly thinking about the implications of what she'd just said.

'How long had he been away?'

'It was just a one-night stand. He's done a couple of tours over the last year or so, but this was just a single booking. So he was going to be away literally just for the night. That's why I got so worried.'

'Did he do many one-off gigs? I don't really know how these things work.'

She was silent for a moment. 'To be honest, Jimmy's not had the easiest time over the last few years. You know he had all that trouble? Or at least his partner did. It wasn't Jimmy's fault but he suffered as much as Jack did.'

Not quite, McKay thought, given he hadn't ended up in prison. 'That must have been difficult.'

'It was long before we met. But, yes. They'd been on the verge of some real success. You never know how far they might have gone, but they were beginning to appear on the TV, playing bigger venues. It all vanished overnight.'

'No one could blame your husband for what his partner did.'

'You'd think not, wouldn't you? But it never seems to work like that. Because they were partners, everyone assumed they were in each other's pockets. So Jimmy must either have been doing the same things, or at least known what Jack was up to. Anyway, they were a double act. Without Jack, they weren't anything, even if Jimmy was really the talented one.'

'Aye, I can see that.'

'So Jimmy was left having to start from scratch. From what he'd told me, they weren't easy years. Jimmy had his own demons. Drank too much, just when he was trying to make a comeback. Funny, that had apparently been one of Jack's problems. He liked the sauce too much and couldn't really handle it. Jimmy could handle it okay – up to a point. But he knocked it back too much. Got himself a reputation as unreliable, difficult to work with. It's really only been in the last year or two he's started to claw it back–' She stopped suddenly. 'Christ, he's dead, isn't he? I mean, that's a stupid thing to say. I've just seen his body. But somehow I hadn't believed it. That he really is dead.'

There was nothing McKay could say. He imagined it still hadn't really sunk in for her. It would, eventually, but there was no telling when or how. In his own case, it had been the sight of some childhood toy in Lizzie's bedroom. It hadn't even been a toy she'd cared for. Just a long-forgotten doll. Chrissie had found McKay sitting on the bed sobbing. The one time he'd really shown emotion about Lizzie's death.

'Can you think of anyone who might have wished your husband harm, Mrs McGuire?' It was the fatuous question they were always obliged to ask. McKay couldn't recall an instance when he'd received a useful answer.

'Jimmy? No. He wasn't always everyone's best friend, if you see what I mean. He'd got up a few people's noses over the years. But not to the point where anyone would actually want to harm him.'

'What about Jack? His partner. Had your husband heard anything from him?'

'Not for years, as far as I know. Don't think Jimmy ever really forgave Jack. When Jack went to prison – that was it. Jimmy just cut him off.'

'He didn't go to see him in prison?'

'That's what he told me. They'd never really been friends. It wasn't like some double acts where they've always known each other. This was a purely business thing. They'd realised the dynamic worked so they'd become partners. Jimmy always reckoned that Jack had been the perfect foil for him. He was funny enough on his own, but he worked best with someone to bounce off.'

'You've no idea where Jack is now? We'll need to talk to him.'

'I can't imagine he'll have anything useful to tell you.'

'We have to investigate every possibility,' McKay said vaguely. 'We'll need to get a formal statement from you in due course, I'm afraid.'

'There's nothing I can tell you, either.'

'There may be, Mrs McGuire. There may be details about your husband that might be pertinent.' He was conscious of keeping his words abstract, skating around the risk of distressing or offending her. There was no point in creating barriers he didn't need to.

'Nobody's even really told me how he died,' she said, after a moment. 'The officers who came to see me gave me the impression it was a mugging, but they couldn't give me any details.'

It wouldn't be possible to keep the full story from Fiona for long, but for the moment he preferred not to say more than he had to. 'We don't yet know the exact circumstances, Mrs McGuire. He was attacked in the street by person or persons unknown. It may have been an attempted robbery, but it doesn't appear that anything was stolen. That's something else we'll need to check with you in due course, but his wallet, credit cards, phone and so on appear not to have been taken.'

'So why would anyone attack him?'

'That's what we need to find out. It may just have been random, sadly. Someone who'd been drinking or was on drugs. As I say, it might have been a failed robbery.' He paused, wondering whether to continue then said, 'Or it might have been because your husband was targeted for some reason.'

Her mouth was open, and he wondered if he'd gone too far.

'I can't see why anyone would have wanted to hurt Jimmy.'

'That's most likely the case, Mrs McGuire. But we have to explore every avenue.'

'Someone must have seen it happen,' she said, as if changing the subject.

'We're checking all CCTV cameras in the vicinity, and we will be appealing for any witnesses to come forward. It was in the city centre, not too late, so we're hopeful we'll find something.'

'Why would anyone attack Jimmy?' she asked again, as if she hadn't heard his response.

'We'll find out, Mrs McGuire.' He could sense that the reality was beginning to strike her. 'Let me take you back to the station. We'll help you find someone to come and stay with you, then we'll take you back home.'

'I just don't understand why anyone would want to hurt Jimmy,' she said. It was as if, in the end, that was what she had to cling on to, McKay thought. That there was no reason for Jimmy's death.

The more she said it, the more he wondered whether it was true.

CHAPTER 30

Jane and Alicia spent the rest of the morning weeding the flowerbeds at the rear of the house. The beds were larger and more extensive than Jane had realised, and there was plenty of work to keep them busy. She supposed the task was worthwhile, though her unskilled eye could see only a minor improvement from the effort they'd put into it.

Halfway through the morning, Netty Munro had appeared bearing glasses of the home-made lemonade, which the two young women had gratefully accepted. The day wasn't overly warm but it was dry and bright, thin white clouds drifting slowly across the otherwise clear sky. The firth was a deep blue, dotted with occasional whitecaps from the breeze, and the mountains were startlingly clear. This was heaven, Jane thought. Better than anywhere she had ever been.

'I'll do some lunch for us about twelve thirty,' Munro said. 'Just something light.'

The lunch might have been light, but yet again it was different from anything Jane had previously eaten. There was bread which Munro said was home-baked sourdough, a platter of cheeses she mostly didn't recognise, and some sliced cold meat, fragrant with herbs. 'The cheeses are mostly local,' Munro said, as she set out the various platters. 'Apart from that one.' She pointed to a white cheese flecked with green. 'That's from the cheese shop in Cromarty. Dutch goat's cheese with sweet clover.'

As far as Jane was concerned, Munro could have been speaking a foreign language. But she sat herself at the table, spread salty butter on a slice of the bread, and felt more content than she could remember.

It seemed to be just the three of them for lunch – herself, Alicia and Netty Munro. There was no sign of Henry Dowling and still no sign of Elizabeth.

'How are you both feeling now?' Munro asked when they were all seated. 'Have you had a chance to settle in?'

It was clear Alicia wasn't going to volunteer any immediate answer. Jane said, 'I think so. It's all so different.'

'In what way different, dear?' Munro helped herself to a slice of one of the cheeses.

'I've never lived anywhere like this. I mean, I've only ever lived in the city.'

'In Inverness?'

'Yes.'

'But you must have been up here… out into the country.'

Jane felt confused for a moment. She felt that she ought to have done, perhaps as a child, maybe on school trips. If she thought about it, she perhaps had vague half-memories of passing through fields or visiting a beach. It seemed absurd she could have lived in a city as small as Inverness, surrounded by such extraordinary open countryside, and yet she'd never been out there. But that was how it was.

Her dad had never taken them anywhere. He wanted to stay at home and spend what little spare cash he had on booze. Her ma couldn't afford to take them anywhere, and couldn't even afford to pay the small amount needed for school trips. She made some excuse and kept her at home on those days.

She'd thought things might change when she married Iain. But almost nothing had. She just drifted into that, and had succeeded only in marrying a younger version of her dad with even less interest in taking her anywhere. She thought they must have had a few joint excursions when they were first going out together, but she couldn't recall anywhere more adventurous than some local pubs and nightclubs. Iain hadn't liked to drive, because if he drove he couldn't drink. There wasn't much more important to Iain than being able to drink.

So, ridiculous as it seemed, she'd never got closer to the open country than the glimpses of the mountains between the city's buildings, an occasional sighting of the Beauly Firth from the Longman's Estate. The saddest thing was that she hadn't even known she was missing it. Of course, she'd known there was something else out there. But it had never occurred to her that it was something she ought to be desiring. She was a city girl and that was the countryside. As far as she was concerned, the two never needed to meet.

Had she been brainwashed to think like that? In a way, she supposed. Her dad and her ma had always lowered her aspirations. She was a bright girl. She'd known that even then. She was hard-working, good at her schoolwork, not really interested in most of the silly stuff that obsessed her friends. She'd been seen as a bit of a swot. Oddly, the other girls hadn't despised or resented her for that. She'd felt herself almost protected by her schoolmates, like some rare and exotic creature who needed to be guarded from the tougher world out there. If anyone tried to bully her, someone would step in and prevent it.

The teachers had wanted her to go and do Highers, even think about university but her dad had made it clear that wasn't for the likes of her. He wanted her out earning a living at the earliest opportunity. In any case, that just wasn't what you did if you were from her background. It was as if, by displaying any interest in things outside his ken, she was somehow showing contempt for everything he stood for.

Maybe she was.

She hadn't really even thought to challenge him. They'd had rows about many things, her and her dad, but that hadn't been one of them. It was as if she'd accepted he was right.

So she'd done what was expected. She'd left school, got herself a job in one of the city stores, met and married Iain. Slipped into the routine that her mam had lived for years. She was beginning to realise what she'd missed.

She realised she'd been silent too long, contemplating how to answer Munro's question. 'No,' she said finally. 'I've never been up here. I mean, I might have done but I've no memory of it.'

Munro was staring at her, as if unable to believe what she was hearing. 'That's shocking,' she said. 'It would have been bad enough if you'd been brought up in London. But in Inverness, it beggars belief.' She turned to Alicia, who looked as if she'd been desperately hoping to avoid getting caught up in the conversation. 'What about you, Alicia?'

'I don't know. I've been out to the country a few times. Not up here, really. But when I was small we used to go to Nairn sometimes. And out around Loch Ness. Not often, but sometimes.' She glanced at Jane, her expression almost shamefaced, as if her words implied a reproach. 'But they were just visits, you know. I've never really stayed somewhere like this.'

'It's as if you were both trapped,' Munro said. 'It seems incredible, in this day and age.'

Not that incredible, Jane thought. Her own experience might have been more extreme, but she hadn't had the impression it was that different from a lot of her contemporaries. It occurred to her that it was possible for people to be living in relatively close proximity – geographically at least – but to have a very different understanding of how the world worked. Munro couldn't really begin to understand what hers or Alicia's background had been like. It wasn't exactly that Munro was privileged – though she no doubt was – but more than she was from a different world. A world where you had choices, could control your own fate. A world where you could make things happen rather than have to wait for it to happen to you.

That was her overriding impression of Netty Munro, Jane supposed. This was a woman who made things happen, who controlled her own life. She'd implied she'd been a victim herself, that she had some understanding of what Jane and Alicia had experienced. Jane had no reason to question that, but she suspected that Munro's victimhood might have been different from theirs.

'Still,' Munro went on, 'you're not trapped now. You're free. Free to do whatever you want.'

Jane glanced across at Alicia hoping to catch her eye, but Alicia was staring down at the table, as if hoping not to be pulled back into the discussion. Jane had no words to respond to Munro. She hoped it was true. She hoped this was freedom.

It didn't yet feel like it. Perhaps Jane didn't know what real freedom looked or felt like. Or perhaps she wouldn't know how to take advantage of freedom if she were offered it. But, for the moment, she still felt trapped. Trapped in a grander prison than she could ever have imagined, but still trapped.

It wasn't Netty Munro's fault, she thought. It was her own fault. She was her own jailor, scared to step out even when the cell door was unlocked.

The door was open, the sun streaming through, and Jane had been told she could step out at any time she wanted. Elizabeth seemed already to have done so, and Jane didn't know whether she was likely to return.

But Jane was already beginning to recognise she wouldn't be able to do the same. She was going to stay here. She didn't know for how long, or what that might mean. But she didn't have much doubt it was true.

Good material, she thought. Was that what she was, all she would ever be? Someone else's good material.

CHAPTER 31

'This is amazing,' McKay said.

Chrissie shrugged. 'Thought I should put in a bit of effort, you know. But don't go expecting it all the time.'

That statement carried all kinds of implications, McKay thought, but now didn't really seem the moment to explore them. 'You can really cook, Chrissie,' he said instead.

'When I can be arsed, yes. Maybe I should be arsed more often. I actually enjoyed doing it.'

'Not easy when you don't know what time your husband's going to get in from work though. You pointed that out to me a few times.'

'Aye, that's what I married, wasn't it? I knew fine well.'

This was certainly a new mellower Chrissie, McKay thought. He couldn't recall how many arguments they'd had because he'd been late from work and she'd had some dish ruined in the oven. But you could unpick that in countless different ways. The way, for example, they'd allowed themselves to drift into the same marital dynamic as their parents, with McKay as primary breadwinner and Chrissie as the wee woman who stayed at home looking after the house. Neither of them had wanted that and there was no real reason why it should have happened. Chrissie was a graduate. She'd had her own career as a hospital pharmacist.

She'd chosen to give that up when Lizzie had been born, at first supposedly just on a temporary basis. But the months and years had drifted by and Chrissie had ended up not going back. Even when she did eventually go back to work part-time she hadn't returned to her original profession but had taken routine administrative and reception jobs. It had been her choice, but

McKay recognised he'd just gone along with it. He'd never thought to question whether he should be contributing more to the marriage, to Lizzie's upbringing. Looking back, he suspected they'd both acted in bad faith, storing up resentment for the future.

They both seemed to have accepted that they were starting again. McKay hadn't exactly been invited back but they'd both assumed, without articulating it, that he'd be staying over tonight. McKay assumed that, for the moment, this would be just another one-night-only arrangement, but it felt like the start of something more permanent.

The truth was, of course, that this wasn't a new Chrissie. This was the old Chrissie, the one he'd married. The one he'd lost sight of since Lizzie's death, just as Chrissie had no doubt lost sight of the Alec McKay she'd once known. The question was whether they could sustain it, or whether they'd find themselves drifting back into those old recriminations.

So far there was no sign of it. They had an enjoyable evening, working their way through the smoked cheese soufflés, sea bass and cranachan that Chrissie had prepared, fortified by a few glasses of red wine and, after dinner, by a couple of single malts.

'So what happens now then?' Chrissie asked, when they'd repaired back to the living room, whiskies in hand.

'If it's like the old days,' McKay said, 'I get a call from the office telling me to come in to deal with some unexpected development.'

'You dare, Alec McKay.'

'Ach, I've told everyone, up to and including the Chief Constable, that it's more than their fucking life's worth to call me back in tonight. They'll bear that in mind.' In reality, short of another killing, there was unlikely to be any reason for him to be called back in tonight.

'I reckon they will,' Chrissie agreed. 'But I meant beyond tonight.'

'Ah.' He was silent for a moment. 'The ball's in your court on that, Chrissie. You know what I want well enough.'

'I know what you want. The question is do you want it enough to make it work.'

'I hope so. I reckon we've both got to help each other with that, don't you? It seems to be working okay at the moment. I don't feel as if I'm treading on eggshells, the way I did sometimes before. But I don't really know if I'm doing anything different.'

'You're being open, Alec. You're telling me what you feel. You'd stopped doing that.'

'Did I ever mention I'm a middle-aged Dundonian male?'

'Aye, many times. It was the smokescreen you hid behind. It fooled no one, Alec. You know that?'

'It fooled me.'

'You were the only one. But you have changed, Alec. I noticed it in the counselling sessions. You were taking them seriously. You dropped the jokes.'

He shuffled awkwardly on the sofa. 'I was missing you, Chrissie.'

'I was missing you too, Alec. More than I'd imagined.' She laughed. 'God, I hope no one ever overhears us talking like this.'

McKay said nothing for a moment, then reached out and took her in his arms. She offered no resistance. 'So am I being invited back then?'

'Looks like it, doesn't it? Only on probation, mind. If you start sliding back into your old ways…'

'You'll tell me, won't you?' He sounded genuinely worried.

'Oh, aye, Alec,' she said, pushing herself towards him. 'Trust me. I'll fucking tell you.'

***

It took him a moment to orientate himself. Not so much in location as in time. He'd thought he was dreaming and his dreams had some how led him back home, back to the marital bed. Back to Chrissie.

It took him a few seconds longer to realise that was exactly where he was. He was back in the only place he thought of as home. Back with Chrissie. And this time it seemed as if it might be permanent.

He realised his phone was buzzing away on the bedside table. Beside him, Chrissie said, 'You've set this up on purpose, haven't you? You're taking the fucking piss.'

'No, I–' he began defensively. Then he realised Chrissie was laughing rather than angry. He pushed himself up in bed. 'I'm not,' he said. 'But I reckon someone in the fucking office is.' He thumbed the phone. 'McKay. What the fuck time do you call this?'

'I call it 6.30am, Alec,' Helena Grant said. 'Almost mid-morning. You're missing the best part of the day.'

'I'm enjoying it much more where I am.'

'That right, Alec? I'm not sure I should enquire further.' There was a pause, which made McKay suspect this conversation was entirely pre-planned on Grant's part. 'Oh, right. Last night was the grand reconciliation dinner, wasn't it? I'm assuming it went well.'

'Aye, okay.' McKay glanced across at Chrissie. She was pretending to be asleep but McKay guessed she was straining to overhear the other end of the conversation. 'That the only reason you're calling me at this fucking time in the morning?'

'Funnily enough, no,' Grant said. 'Entertaining as that idea is. I'm calling to tell you we've found Jimmy McGuire's former partner. Jack Dingwall.'

'Oh, aye. Thanks for calling to share that with me. Do you want me to get my kecks on and come in to interview him?' His tone was facetious but he'd already concluded that Grant wouldn't have called at this time just to confirm they'd tracked down Dingwall's address. Who'd be working on that at this time anyway?

'When I say found, Alec, I mean just that. Stumbled across. Almost literally.'

'Oh, shit.'

'As you so rightly say, Alec.'

'From the fact that you've called me, I'm guessing this isn't just natural causes.'

'Unless you think having a garrotte pulled round your neck constitutes natural causes, I'd say not.'

'Fucking hell.'

'You're offering some lucid insights today, Alec. Yup, same MO as the other two.'

McKay had dragged himself round until he was sitting on the edge of the bed. 'Where was he found?'

'In a ditch, up near Dingwall. The town, I mean.'

'Don't tell me. Dog walker. What the fuck would we do without them?'

'Not this time. Dingwall's landlord, a farmer. He'd come out early to check on some livestock in the field next to Dingwall's cottage. Went to the edge of the field to look at some fencing that needed repairing. His eye was caught by something in the bottom of the drainage ditch next to the field. And Bob's your uncle.'

'And Jack's your corpse. We're sure it's him?'

'Guy who found him wasn't too squeamish about getting up close, being a livestock farmer and all that. So pretty certain it's him. That's also how we're pretty sure it's the same MO as the others.'

'Lovely. You want me to get up there then?' He was conscious Chrissie had rolled over in the bed behind him so that she was facing away.

'That's the thing,' Grant said. 'I just wondered if you might want a break for once. I could handle this one with Ginny, if you like. You could join us later.'

McKay bit back his instinctive response. 'This some sort of charitable impulse on your part, Grant?'

'I just thought this might be a good moment to remind you of the virtues of delegation.'

'So why disturb my sleep if you were just going to tell me not to bother coming in?'

'Because I know that if I hadn't told you, you'd have been even more pissed.'

'You're right about that.'

'Look, Alec, I'm dealing with what looks like a triple fucking homicide. I'm trying to do you a fucking favour. If you don't want to be helped, then, with the best will in the world, you know what you can do. The choice is yours.'

There would have been a time, possibly only the previous day, when McKay would have wanted nothing more than to leap out of bed, drag on his clothes and head up north to view a semi-decapitated corpse. It was what made him feel alive. There was a large part of his brain that wanted to do it. But there was another more rational part of his brain telling him not to be such a fucking numpty. There'd be times when he wouldn't have a choice, when the only option was to throw himself into the job. But this wasn't one of them. Helena Grant had given him an out. She was trying to help save his fucking marriage, for Christ's sake.

'If you're sure,' he said. 'If you think you and Ginny can handle it.'

He could tell she was stifling a laugh and wondered whether Ginny Horton was already there with her. 'I reckon we can just about handle it between us. Even though we're only women.'

'Aye, well, I know Ginny's up to it...'

'Bugger off, Alec. I'll text you the address. Come up and join us when you're ready. No rush.'

'If Jock Henderson and his pals are involved, we've got all morning,' he agreed. 'Okay. And, thanks.'

'No worries.'

He ended the call and lay back down next to Chrissie.

'You're not going in yet then,' she said from beneath the duvet.

'Looks like I'm not needed.'

'Jeez. It's the end of days,'

'Aye. Feels like it.'

'So how long before you need to get up?'

'Dunno. An hour of so, maybe?'

'So what are we going to do with all that time?'

'Not sure,' McKay said. 'Game of Scrabble?'

She rolled over to face him. 'If you insist. Though I've never heard it called that before.'

CHAPTER 32

'Turned a wee bit colder.'

Helena Grant watched Jock Henderson and Pete Carrick stride across the field towards her, laden with their cases of equipment. 'Morning, Jock. Pete. Aye, you get the breeze up here.'

She'd been standing looking out over the Cromarty Firth. The tide was full and it was looking glorious in the early morning sunshine, a deep blue under the clear sky. The wide basin of water around the old waterfront in Dingwall shimmered with flecks of light and she could see across to the Black Isle topped by the radio mast on Mount Eagle. The clean cold air was sharp in her lungs.

Grant had been here for ten minutes or so, accompanied by a couple of uniforms and the farmer who'd found the body. Ginny Horton was on her way, a few minutes behind Grant, and she'd watched as the examiners' van made its way cautiously up the narrow track to where she was standing.

The body was at the bottom of the field. She'd been down to take a brief look but hadn't wanted to risk compromising the scene. Not that it was likely to tell them very much. It was where the body had ended up, but she suspected that the killing had taken place elsewhere. When Horton arrived, they could check out Dingwall's cottage.

Not that his name really was Dingwall, of course. His real name was Jack Dimmock, and that seemed to have been how he was known up here. When she'd spoken to the farmer on arrival, he clearly had no idea of Dingwall's background. She hadn't bothered to enlighten him.

'How long's he been your tenant?' she'd asked.

'Not long. Just a few weeks. And then this.' He shook his head. 'I should have known he was hiding something. Living on his own in a place like that. Why would you do that if you didn't have something to hide?'

'We don't know that, Mr...'

'Campbell. Tom Campbell.'

'We don't yet know the circumstances of the death, Mr Campbell. It's better if we don't jump to any conclusions.'

'Aye. He seemed a decent enough chap, I'll say that. Looked after the cottage well enough.'

'This all your land, Mr Campbell?'

'All of it. From the boundary over there.' He gestured towards some invisible point to the east. 'All the way to that line of trees over there.'

'What about the cottages?'

'Up there.' He pointed further up the hill. 'Couple of outbuildings I converted a few years back. Made three cottages. Use two of them as holiday lets in the summer. Third one was a bit wee for the tourists, so I've tended to look for longer-term lets. Seems to be a shortage of decent lets even as far out as this, so I've generally been able to find tenants.'

'How long's Mr Dimmock been here?'

'Couple of months,' Campbell said.

'You hadn't known him before?'

'Not at all. Some friend of a friend had told him I was looking for a tenant. He phoned me up one day out of the blue. Place had been empty over the winter and I was keen to find someone to take it on. I got a reference from a previous landlord but that was about it.'

'Did he have many visitors?'

Campbell shrugged. 'I wouldn't know. I didn't go to the cottage all that often. In the summer I go in a bit more frequently to check on the gardens and the general state of repair. In the winter, I take the opportunity to do any odd jobs that need tackling. Otherwise, I just come up if there's a reason, or if I'm passing by on the way to the upper fields. But I've never noticed any cars parked outside Dimmock's house except his own.'

'When was the last time you saw him? Alive, I mean.'

'Just a few days ago, as it happens. Passed by in the Land Rover and saw him standing in the front garden, so stopped for a quick chat.'

'He seem okay? Not worried about anything?'

'Some hidden secret, you mean.' Campbell grinned. 'Not obviously. He was never the most forthcoming individual. But he seemed content enough. Writer of some kind, I believe.' Campbell spoke as if referring to some previously unknown species.

'When did you find the body?'

'This morning. I'm always out and about first thing, especially this time of year when the sun's up so early. It was only fluke I found him. Had some damage to the fence down there in the strong winds a few weeks back. Been meaning to go and check what needed doing. Otherwise wouldn't have seen him from up here.'

Grant nodded, taking in the implications. 'Why do you think he was down there?'

'Buggered if I know, pardon my French. Far as I know, he wasn't a great walker. And even if he was I'd have expected him to head uphill. There are some decent trails in the woods up there. Not much down here.'

Grant didn't yet know for sure how long the body had been there, but, as far as she'd been able to judge, probably not more than a few hours. There was no sign of decomposition or even the haze of flies that tended to indicate an older corpse. Her guess was that Dimmock's body had been there only since last night or early this morning, during the low temperatures of the night. It seemed unlikely he'd been walking down there, so most likely the body had been dumped after being killed elsewhere. Maybe even just rolled down the hill from up here, she thought.

If Campbell was right, it might have remained undetected for some time. She couldn't imagine there were many other visitors up here. It seemed that, like Young's body at McDermott's Yard, it was intended to be concealed. That in itself was potentially interesting. Three bodies, all with the same or a very similar MO. But two of them –presumably the first and third – with the bodies left concealed, while the second had been left, barely hidden, at the side of a city thoroughfare.

It might mean nothing. Perhaps just an accident of location. But if they were dealing with a multiple killer, she'd expect the same pattern to be followed or for the killer to become more careless over time. So there might be a reason McGuire's killing had been handled differently from the others.

She'd allowed Campbell to return home while she awaited the arrival of Horton and the examiners. She supposed he had to be treated as a suspect, but his connection with Dimmock, let alone with McGuire or Young, seemed nothing more than tangential. Not that their list of other suspects was exactly extensive.

Jock Henderson was peering down the length of the field. 'I don't suppose the bugger could have found himself a less convenient place to get killed?'

'Don't imagine it was his choice, Jock,' Grant pointed out. 'I suspect he wasn't killed down there anyway. I reckon we'll have to get you lot to take a look at his cottage too. I'll go and give it a once over when Ginny Horton gets here.'

Henderson raised an eyebrow. 'Alec having a duvet day then?'

The tone of his voice made Grant wonder whether he could have picked up something on the grapevine about McKay and Chrissie. That would have been impressive going even for Henderson. 'He's a busy man, Jock.'

'Too busy for the third garrotting in as many days? Christ, you lot must have some business on at the moment.'

'There's a body down there getting warm.'

'Aye, aye, ma'am,' he said, in a tone that steered just the right side of insolence.

Grant had a better relationship with Henderson than McKay managed, but she could see why he rubbed colleagues up the wrong way. But he was good at his job, which was all she really cared about. She left them to it, and made her way back to the farmyard, where Ginny Horton was climbing out of her car.

'Sorry to disturb your morning, Ginny.'

'No worries. I'm an early riser anyway. Just meant I had to cut the run short this morning.'

'Good to hear you're getting back into that.'

'Pretty much,' Horton said. 'Taking advantage of the light mornings.' She looked down towards the bottom of the field where the examiners were beginning to set up. 'I see Alec's not here. It'll be the first and last time, but good for him.' Grant had said nothing to Horton, but McKay's assignation the previous night had been common knowledge in the team.

'It won't last,' Grant said. 'Given what we're dealing with, I don't want it to. It looks like this is another.'

'Down there?'

'That's where the body is. I'm guessing that isn't where he was killed. Looks like the killer was attempting to conceal the body. It wouldn't have been undiscovered forever down there, but long enough to make our lives harder.'

'Where do you reckon he was killed?'

'His cottage is the first place to check out. I'm guessing either in there or somewhere outside it.' She led the way to the narrow road that wound up the hillside past the entrance to the farmyard. It was a public road, but it was single track without even any obvious passing places on this stretch. The sign at the bottom of the hill had indicated the road was a dead end, so presumably it led only to other residential properties. Something for them to check out in due course.

Dingwall's cottage stood near the summit of the hill, with the two holiday lets clustered close beside it. They were pleasant-looking, converted from what had previously been stone outbuildings. The two lets were both empty this early in the season. Dingwall's cottage looked more lived in, with a couple of tubs filled with spring flowers by the front door and another vase of flowers visible through one of the front windows.

The front door was closed but not locked. Grant pulled out the disposable plastic gloves she always carried and carefully pulled them on. She glanced quizzically at Horton, then, gesturing her to follow, she opened the door and stepped into the cottage.

The interior of the cottage matched the exterior – neatly if anonymously renovated. The furniture was mostly pine, real or artificial, and the stone floor was scattered with rugs. The room had a male feel, Grant thought. It was neat, elegant and functional, but it felt like temporary accommodation. There were no obvious personal touches, few pictures on the walls other than a couple that looked as if they'd been selected from the 'good taste' section in a local DIY store. Nothing to tell them that Jack Dingwall had actually lived here. At the far end of the room, there was a desk holding nothing except a vase of flowers and an open laptop. 'Something else for us to go through,' Horton pointed out.

'No sign of any struggle. And no obvious sign of any spilled blood.' Grant took another step into the room, conscious of the risk of contaminating a potential crime scene.

'Looks like he had a visitor though.' Horton gestured towards the coffee table in front of the sofa. There were two empty wine glasses and an empty wine bottle.

'Interesting. So if he had a visitor it must have been someone he knew well enough to be comfortable inviting them into the house for a drink.'

'Are we assuming the visitor's also the killer?'

'Who knows? But it's a coincidence. From what the landlord told me, Dingwall wasn't the gregarious kind. And I don't suppose many people would have popped in on spec to somewhere as remote as this.' Grant peered carefully round the room, not wanting to disturb it more than she needed to. Gesturing for Horton to stay put, she crossed the room to the small kitchen. Like the living room, it was neat and functional, with a cooker, fridge and washing machine and little space for much more. It had the air of being little used.

At the opposite end of the living room, an open wooden staircase led to the upper floor. Grant made her way up the stairs, trying not to touch the bannister. At the top, there was a single bedroom, which filled the eaves of the building. It had the same anonymous air as the rest of the house. There was a double bed covered by a floral duvet, a chest of drawers, a small wardrobe and little else.

She descended the stairs and rejoined Horton in the living room. 'Nothing upstairs. Landlord reckoned he was some kind of writer now. Presumably that's where he worked.' She gestured towards the desk with the laptop. The desk was positioned to give a view through the main window out over the firth. 'Decent office.'

Horton nodded. 'So what was he writing?'

'I suppose we'll find out when we check the laptop. We don't know much at all about Mr Dingwall at the moment.' She looked around the room again. 'Not even where he died. Let's have a look outside.'

That question was answered almost as soon as they stepped back outside. At the far end of the garden, a stone bench was positioned to take advantage of the views. There was a pool of blood beneath the bench, and splatterings of the blood on the surrounding stone. They could see that there were smearings of blood on the grass leading from the bench to the garden gate, presumably showing where Dingwall's body had been dragged.

'Would have required some effort to pull the body up there,' Horton observed. 'Then to drag it down to that next field. Wonder why they bothered.'

'Hoping to conceal the body, I suppose. At least for a while. I suppose if Dingwall didn't get many visitors the blood might not be noticed, and any rain would wash it away. But, aye, they must have gone to some trouble. Makes you wonder why they didn't go to more trouble to conceal Jimmy McGuire's body.'

'Assuming it's the same killer.'

'Assuming it's the same killer.' Grant was still staring round the garden, as if it might reveal some answers to their countless questions. 'Can't be a copycat though, given how little we've said publicly. There must be a link between the three deaths.' She turned back to Horton. 'Okay, let's go and break the news to Jock that he's got another site to examine once he's finished down there. The cottage and the garden.'

'He'll be pleased.'

'Oh, aye. I can't wait to see his little face light up.'

CHAPTER 33

Jane had set the alarm on her mobile phone and placed it carefully on the cabinet by her bed. Netty Munro had told her, once again, to sleep as long as she wished, but Jane was already feeling guilty about how little she was contributing to the household. She and Alicia had spent the previous afternoon still working on the garden, following Munro's sporadic instructions, but it had never felt like a substantive task. Jane and Alicia had struggled to fill the time. They'd spent much of the afternoon chatting, sharing their experiences. There was plenty to share – they were from similar working-class backgrounds, both with frequently unemployed fathers who drank too much, both subject to physical abuse from an early age with mothers who had been unable to protect themselves or their daughters. Both had been bright girls forced out of school too early. And both had saddled themselves with partners who perpetuated the abuse the two women had suffered their whole lives.

'So how did you end up in the centre?' Jane had asked. It was the question she'd wanted to ask everyone who'd stayed there but had never dared. She needed the validation of knowing her own circumstances were not unique.

'I couldn't take it any more,' Alicia said. 'I realised that if I married him, it would all carry on. And if I told him I wasn't going to marry him, he'd beat me up anyway. In the end I scraped together any money I could – I saved up bits and pieces whenever I could for months – and walked one day when he was at the pub. I didn't know where to go. And I knew he'd try to follow me, drag me back. One of my mates told me about the centre. Reckoned I'd be safe there.'

The Reynold Centre was a women's refuge, set up to provide shelter for women suffering from domestic abuse. It had been recommended to Jane by a friend too. It was amazing, once you started talking about it, how many women had been through similar experiences. Too often it went beneath the radar, not least because the women involved were too scared to make their problems public. But once Jane had begun to tell the truth to one or two of her closest friends, she found almost all of them had either experienced abuse themselves or had friends and family members who'd been through it.

She'd enjoyed staying at the centre. She'd been struck by the diversity of the women there, and she'd enjoyed listening to people chatting about films or TV programmes she'd never had the chance to see. She'd enjoyed being able to relax for the first time she could remember. And she'd enjoyed the sense of security, although she'd always thought it unlikely that Iain would pursue her up there. That wasn't his style. He'd grumble, bad-mouth her to his mates and then, quite soon, move on to some other potential victim.

Alicia had enjoyed the same sense of safety and relaxation there, even though her fears about her boyfriend had been well founded. But it had always been made clear to all residents that staying in the centre could only ever be a temporary solution. Eventually, they'd have to find some other way to take forward their lives. Jane had had no idea how she might do that with very little money and no friends who were in a position to help.

Then, unexpectedly, they'd received the offer from Netty Munro to come there. Munro had a long-standing relationship with the centre, apparently, though the available spaces were always limited. Quite why Munro had picked the two of them to benefit from her generosity was a mystery. 'She just thought you sounded like the sort of women who'd fit into her way of living, and who'd benefit from what she has to offer.'

Jane was still unclear as to what that offering actually was, but no doubt they'd find out over the next couple of days. All she knew was that it had given her the possibility of being able to reboot her life. Now she was here she wanted to do her fair share, to ensure she was justified in accepting whatever Munro might have to offer her.

Dinner the previous evening had been a simpler and lighter affair than the previous night. Elizabeth hadn't returned and Jane had felt unable to ask whether Munro still expected her to come back. There had been no sign of Henry Dowling so it had just been the three of them sitting round the table on the decking. The weather had stayed relatively warm, and they had been able to enjoy another *al fresco* meal as the evening had grown dark around them. Munro had roasted a chicken – which she said had come from one of the neighbouring farms – and served it with a green salad and new potatoes. It had been simple food but the chicken itself was delicious, more flavourful than any Jane could recall eating. Conversation had initially been stilted, with Jane and Netty Munro doing their best to keep it going while Alicia largely sat in silence. But there'd been more wine too, and after a few glasses, the exchanges had become more relaxed, and even Alicia had begun to chip in.

The consequence of the wine, though, was that Jane was now waking with a mild headache. Part of her wanted to roll over and go back to sleep. She could do that, she told herself. Netty Munro wouldn't mind. But that wasn't what she really wanted. It was important she should drag herself out of bed, get showered and then go and do whatever she could to repay Munro for allowing her to stay there.

Jane dragged herself to a sitting position and pulled the mobile towards her. It was earlier than she'd feared, only just after seven thirty. She was delighted that the wine and her own tiredness hadn't made her sleep longer.

She pulled herself out of bed and walked over to the window. Outside, it looked set to be another fine day. It was almost as if, since she'd arrived there, the climate itself had changed, as if she were no longer living in the dreich grey Scotland of her childhood. As if this house existed in its own unique space, a world conjured up by Munro just as she conjured music from the strings of her guitar. The sun was still behind the house, casting shadows down towards the firth, but the sky was a clear pale blue.

She pulled on the dressing gown and made her way across to the bathroom. The house was silent, Alicia's and Elizabeth's bedroom doors both shut. Jane had assumed that Munro would rise early, but perhaps that wasn't always the case. It didn't really matter. Presumably she wouldn't mind if Jane went down to make herself some coffee and toast.

She showered quickly and returned to her room to dress. She felt fully awake, and the headache had diminished. Today she'd try to persuade Munro to give her some real task. Jane wanted to prove she was serious.

Dressed and with her hair brushed but still damp, Jane made her way downstairs and crossed the hall to the kitchen. As she approached the closed door, she paused. She could hear voices from within. One was Netty Munro's but the other, as far as she could judge, was male.

She hesitated. The presence of a male in the house felt somehow unsettling. That was ridiculous. Of course there would be men visiting the farm. Munro had mentioned workmen, and they'd travelled up here with a male taxi driver just a couple of days earlier.

Even so, something about the proximity of the male voice made her uneasy. Or perhaps, she thought, it was the tone. She couldn't make out the words through the door, but she had the impression the exchange had been a serious one. Not angry, exactly, but emotional.

She coughed loudly then fumbled with the door handle for long enough to announce her presence. She heard the voices fall silent as she pushed open the door.

Jane had expected to find Munro and her unknown visitor sitting at the kitchen table. However, she opened the door to see Munro standing by the open back door and no sign of the man.

'Good morning,' Jane said, unsure whether to mention the voice she'd heard. 'I hope I'm not too early coming down.'

'Not at all, dear. I want you to feel entirely at home here. Come and go as you please. I hope we didn't disturb you.'

'Disturb me?' Jane was standing in the doorway, unsure how to proceed.

'We were talking a little loudly.'

Jane shook her head. 'No, not at all. I just heard voices from outside the door. I didn't hear anything from upstairs.'

Munro was filling the kettle at the sink. 'That's good. I sometimes forget how sound travels in this place. It's surprising what you can hear from the bedrooms.'

The last sentence felt freighted with meaning following Jane's accidental eavesdropping on Munro and Dowling. Jane crossed the room, feeling self-conscious. 'Shall I make some tea?'

'That would be nice.'

Jane busied herself at the Aga, putting the kettle on the ring, spooning tea into the pot, thankful to avoid looking Munro in the face. It wasn't that Jane felt guilty. She hadn't intended to overhear anything the two older women had said. It was more she felt she was betraying Munro's hospitality by not being completely open. On the other hand, what exactly was she supposed to say?

She'd hoped that Munro might reveal the identity of her visitor, but it was clear she had no intention of saying anything more. And why would she? He was probably of no relevance to Jane – maybe one of the men who'd supposedly done a shoddy job on the fencing. Perhaps that was why the conversation had sounded heated.

Jane finished making the tea and brought the pot over to the table, taking a seat beside Munro while she waited for it to brew. 'Any word from Elizabeth?'

'I believe she's back with us.'

Jane looked up in surprise. 'When did she arrive?'

'I'm not entirely sure what time it was. Sometime in the small hours. I'm a very light sleeper, and I heard someone trying the front door. I went down to let her in, but I didn't bother to check what time it was. I had the impression she hadn't expected me to open the door for her, so I don't know what she was intending to do otherwise.' Munro shrugged. 'But I'm not sure Elizabeth ever worries too much about the consequences of her actions.'

'Did she say where she'd been?'

'Of course not. She gave me a half-hearted apology for disappearing and told me she had some outstanding business to deal with. Nothing more than that.'

'You think she'll stay now?'

'For a while, I imagine.' Munro paused and smiled. 'This is the safest place for her at the moment, I think. I believe she understands that, whatever other instincts she might have.'

Jane had resigned herself to accepting that Munro had insights and ways of thinking she could never begin to share. She was happy simply to accept her role and do whatever she could to justify her presence. She picked up the pot and poured the tea. 'What would you like me to do today?'

Munro seemed surprised by the direct question. 'Oh, I don't know, dear. You could perhaps do a little cleaning in the house, if you don't mind. Some polishing and dusting in the main rooms. Perhaps some vacuuming. It's always hard to keep on top of things.'

To Jane's eyes, the rooms looked cleaner and tidier than any she'd ever seen, but there seemed little point in arguing. 'That's fine.'

'Excellent,' Munro said, as if she had just resolved some challenging conundrum. 'Now, would you like some breakfast? I've a yen for a bacon sandwich, and I think the smell will persuade the others to join us.'

CHAPTER 34

Helena Grant was unsurprised to find McKay sitting behind her desk, unashamedly flicking through the papers she'd left out. She was far too savvy to leave out anything that might conceivably be of interest to him, but she knew he lived in hope.

'I don't know what time you call this,' McKay said, glancing pointedly at the clock on the wall as Grant and Ginny Horton entered the office. He rose and gestured for Grant to take her seat.

'Very gracious of you, Alec. Managed to drag yourself out of bed then?'

'I've been here for hours. Doing real work. Not gallivanting round crime scenes like you two.'

'That right, Alec? Well, we can discuss the fruits of your labours shortly. Meanwhile, we've definitely got a third garrotting on our hands.'

'Oh, joy,' McKay said, in a tone that sounded less ironic than he'd presumably intended. 'A multiple killer.'

'Looks that way,' Grant agreed. 'Pretty distinctive approach certainly. But I'm intrigued as to why the McGuire death seems different.' She'd taken her seat back behind the desk and was double-checking to ensure she really had left out nothing compromising. Compromising, in this context, meaning anything, however trivial, that he could use to his advantage.

McKay nodded. 'Aye, the thought had occurred. Young's and Dingwall's killings appear to have been carried out somewhere isolated or private, as far as we can judge, and the killer seems to have gone to some lengths to conceal the corpses, at least temporarily. McGuire's happened in a public place, at a time when there was a risk that the killer might be interrupted by a passer-by, and no real attempt was made to conceal the body.'

Grant was always impressed by McKay's ability to be one step ahead of her own thinking. In this case, she was even more impressed, though not surprised, that he'd managed to get the gen on the Dingwall killing even before she and Ginny had arrived back. But McKay always had his sources. 'It's all guesswork though,' she said. 'Dingwall seems to have been killed in his back garden. Young could have been killed anywhere.'

'Aye,' McKay said. 'And multiple killers don't always follow neat patterns like they do on TV. Sometimes the killings are just opportunistic. Maybe McGuire was just unlucky enough to be in the wrong place.' He stopped. 'Which might make sense if these were random killings. But that doesn't seem to be the case, at least as far as McGuire and Dingwall are concerned.'

'What about Dingwall's visitor?' Horton asked.

McKay looked surprised. 'Visitor?'

'So there are some things you don't know,' Grant said. Presumably, she thought, because he'd talked to one of his uniformed mates before Henderson and Carrick had finished with Dingwall's cottage. 'It looks as if Dingwall had a visitor yesterday evening.'

'Friendly or hostile?' McKay asked. 'Or can't we tell?'

'Looks like a friendly visitor. Or at least someone he knew well enough to invite in for a glass of wine. There were two used wine glasses on the table.'

'Which may just mean that Dingwall was profligate with his use of glasses.'

'Nope. Multiple fingerprints too, according to Henderson.'

'Okay, sounds like a friendly visitor. So the question then is whether the visitor and the killer are the same.'

'Dingwall didn't get many visitors apparently. So two on the same night would be quite something.'

'But not impossible, especially if they are connected in some way,' Horton added. 'And it would be a pretty careless killer who left their prints behind, particularly on something like a glass where they're going to be easy to pick up.'

'We'll put them through the system,' Grant said. 'See if they match anyone we know. DNA too.' It was all sounding too easy, she thought. But sometimes it was. 'Anyway, what have you been slaving away at while we've been having fun with garrotted corpses?'

'A few things.' McKay briefly sat himself down opposite Grant, with Ginny Horton sitting beside him. Then, as he invariably did in Grant's office, he stood up and prowled round the edge of the room with the air of a caged animal. 'I've been trying to find out a bit more about Dingwall. What he's been up to since he got out. He served half his sentence. Model prisoner, by all accounts. Kept his nose clean, got himself out at the earliest opportunity. Looks as if he still had a bit of money stashed away so was in a better position than most ex-offenders. His wife had left him when the original scandal broke and they were divorced after he got out. I've an address for her and we'll need to speak to her, though it doesn't look as if she's had any contact with him since the split.'

'What's he been doing since?'

'It looks as if he went back to writing. Comedy writing, I mean. Material for other stand-ups.'

'Surprised anyone wanted to go near him,' Grant said.

'Aye, I was a bit too. This is just what I picked up from a bit of discreet ringing round this morning.'

'You didn't tell anyone about Dingwall's death?'

'How long have I been doing this job?' McKay asked.

'Long enough to have reduced my life expectancy by ten years,' Grant said. 'But go on.'

'I just spoke to that guy Drew Douglas at the comedy club. Told him we were still in the process of confirming McGuire's identity so not to say anything till it's officially announced.'

'You reckon he'll do that?'

'Not for a minute. He'll already have told everyone he can. But I'm one for observing the protocols.' He ignored Ginny Horton's derisive snort and continued. 'I just asked him if he could tell us any more about McGuire and Dingwall's background, or if he might know anyone who could. He seemed pretty knowledgeable himself so I've fixed up for him to come in to give us some more detailed background this afternoon. He said that Dingwall had always primarily been a writer who'd fallen into performing more or less by accident. Even in the double act days he'd written for other comedians, so he turned his hand back to that after he got out. I asked him whether Dingwall's reputation would have been a barrier to that, and he reckoned generally not. A lot of the stand-ups just want material.'

'I always assumed they wrote it themselves,' Horton said.

'Most do apparently. But as you start to become successful, some find it a big machine to keep feeding, so they don't mind a clandestine helping hand. Whatever else people might have thought of him, Dingwall was seen as one of the best. Not just new material, but helping to polish up the material others gave him. Looks as if he was also writing stuff for TV and radio, though most of that under an assumed name.'

'You can make a living doing that?' Grant said.

'Of sorts.'

'We've taken his laptop. So we can check all that out. Be interesting to see what else we find on there, given his track record. Okay, so you're seeing this Drew Douglas this afternoon? You reckon he's got anything useful to tell us?'

'Not sure,' McKay replied. 'I spoke to him briefly after we found McGuire's body, but that was really just to confirm details of McGuire's movements during and after the gig. But I got the impression today that he was quite steeped in the whole comedy and music scene, particularly the stuff with local connections. I thought he might be able to give us some insights into McGuire and Dimmock – and maybe even Young. It's not like we're exactly awash with leads at the moment.'

'That's true enough,' Grant agreed. 'Anything else?'

'One other thing,' McKay said. 'I've managed to track down an address for Henrietta Dowling.'

'Henrietta Dowling?' For a moment, Grant looked puzzled, then she said, 'The woman who accused Young of rape.'

'The very one. Took me a bit of time, as she's obviously moved about a fair bit. As you said, she seemed to have a biggish reputation on the country music circuit a few years ago. Even made some appearances on the telly. BBC Alba stuff. But in recent years she seems to have disappeared. Couldn't find any recent mentions of her performances, and she didn't show up on the electoral roll or any of that stuff. Thought at first she must have moved out of the area, but it looks like she's just retired and decided to keep her head down. Did a bit of phoning round and eventually found someone who remembered the name and did a bit more digging for me.'

This, Grant thought, would presumably have been one of McKay's mates on the local press. Fair enough, she thought. For all his posturing, McKay was old enough and wise enough not to get caught out. She imagined he got far more out of the journalists than they got out of him, even if he managed to leave them with the opposite impression. 'And?'

'She's living over in the Black Isle. Makes guitars these days. Once I knew that, I managed to track down her business details fairly easily. Just outside Culbokie.' He glanced across at Horton. 'Fancy a trip up there, Ginny? Or does Culbokie hold too many painful memories?'

'I came away without a scratch,' she said, referring to one of their recent cases. 'A lifelong deep-seated trauma, probably, but not a scratch. No, fine by me. Always helpful to bury a few more ghosts.'

McKay glanced at his watch. 'Drew Douglas isn't coming in till three thirty. So we've got time for a trip up there.'

'Lead on,' she said. 'I think it's your turn to drive.'

CHAPTER 35

'How's Chrissie?' Horton asked when they were in the car and heading out of town. Somehow, she'd still found herself driving. Not that she really minded. She'd long ago accepted that she made a better driver than a passenger. It was just that she didn't want McKay to think he could always get away with it, even if he generally did.

'Ach, she's okay.' McKay was staring out of the window so Horton couldn't read his expression.

'How are things looking? Between the two of you, I mean.' Horton knew she was walking on a minefield. It was always impossible to know how McKay would react to such questions. But she genuinely wished him and Chrissie well. She'd met Chrissie only a few times, usually at office events, but Horton liked her and thought her well matched to McKay.

'Not so bad, you know,' McKay said vaguely. Then he allowed her a smile. 'Think I might have wasted money on that fucking bungalow in Rosemarkie.'

'You're moving back in?'

'With immediate effect,' McKay said with satisfaction. 'I suppose we can use the bungalow as a weekend retreat till the end of the lease. I've always wanted a weekend retreat.'

'Chrissie deserves a few clandestine weekends away with you. She probably deserves a few clandestine weekends away with someone better than you, but she can't have everything.'

'Bugger off, Horton. Anyway, how are you and Isla? Everything settled down again now after all the traumas?'

'Never been better. If that doesn't sound too smug.'

'Trust me, it sounds too smug.'

'But, seriously, all that stuff brought us closer together. Meant we had to talk about everything, things from the past we'd skated around. It brought home how much we really cared about each other.'

'Jesus Christ, Ginny. Stop it. You're making me feel nauseous.'

She pulled out into the right-hand lane to overtake a lorry. 'Let's just say everything's okay now.'

'Aye, let's just say that.'

'Makes me nervous when everything's going well. Makes me think there's more trouble around the corner.'

'That's life though, isn't it? Every silver lining has a cloud.'

'Usually the way. Straight on here?' They were approaching the Tore roundabout.

'Aye, stay on the A9. Another mile or so.'

'Second time up here today.'

'They should award you some sort of medal.' Ahead of them, they could see Cromarty Firth and the solid mass of Ben Wyvis. 'This is the turning.'

They took a right onto the road into Culbokie, passing between stretches of farmland. The north side of the Black Isle had a different feel from the south. The south was fishing villages, most no longer working but with cottages clustered round once-busy harbours. The landscape was largely farmland, the villages strung out over fields and woodland.

Culbokie itself was little more than a gathering of relatively recent bungalows, interspersed with the occasional older cottage, mostly positioned to take advantage of the striking views out over the firth to the mountains beyond. They passed a village shop and a pub, a new primary school on their right and a church on their left.

'This one,' McKay said.

Horton turned left into a small estate of bungalows, probably dating from the 1970s or 1980s, fairly anonymous grey-fronted buildings with neatly maintained gardens.

'From the map, I think it's right at the far end,' McKay said.

Henrietta Dowling's bungalow was obviously a later addition than the remainder of the bungalows. It was a small but attractive building, designed in what McKay understood to be "steading" style. Chrissie had explained all that stuff to him when they'd been considering a house-move a few years before, but most of the detail had passed well above his head. There was a well-maintained garden dotted with spring blooms, and a small four-by-four car parked outside the front door.

'Nice place,' Horton commented. 'Must be an impressive view from the back too.'

She pulled up behind the four-by-four and they climbed out to survey the scene. A slight breeze blew in from the firth, but otherwise the place was silent. McKay walked forward and pressed the front doorbell.

He heard the bell sound somewhere in the depths of the house but there was no immediate response. He glanced at Horton and pressed the bell again, holding it for longer. This time, he saw movements through the frosted glass panelling. A second later, the door was opened a crack and a face peered out. 'Yes?'

'Henrietta Dowling?' McKay said.

'Who's asking?'

McKay held out his warrant card. 'DI McKay and DS Horton. I wonder if we could have a word.'

The door opened an inch or two further, and the face peered more closely at McKay's ID. 'What's this about?'

'We're just following up an enquiry. We'd like to speak to Henrietta Dowling.'

The door opened more fully this time. The face proved to belong to a middle-aged woman with long dark hair. She was wearing a faded tracksuit and looked as if she might have just crawled out of bed. 'I'm Henrietta Dowling. What's this all about?'

'May we come in, Ms Dowling? We just need a few minutes of your time.'

Dowling looked hesitant for a moment, then pulled the door open fully and gestured for them to come inside. 'I guess so. Come through.'

She was English, McKay thought, or at least she had an English accent, albeit with a burr that suggested she might have been living up here for many years. They followed her through into a living room. It was an attractive room, with a large picture window looking out over the firth. It was a while since the place had been tidied or dusted, McKay observed. The small coffee table was dotted with used glasses, a plate which looked as if it might have recently held an Indian takeout, and an array of books and CDs. There was an empty bottle of Scotch under the table. McKay wondered whether this was the result of a night with friends or a solo binge. From Dowling's appearance, the latter looked quite probable.

'Can I get you both a coffee?'

'Aye, why not?' McKay said. 'If it's no trouble. White, no sugar for me. Thanks.'

'No trouble. I need one myself.' Her words echoed McKay's own judgement. She looked like a woman who might be more responsive to their questions once she'd had a shot of caffeine inside her.

Dowling disappeared into the kitchen and McKay took a seat on the sofa, Horton perching awkwardly beside him. 'We woke her up,' Horton whispered, glancing pointedly at her watch.

'Not everyone goes running at sparrow fart like you, Ginny,' McKay pointed out. 'Some people have lives.'

'Well-lived ones.' Horton tapped the empty whisky bottle with her toe.

'It's called fun, Ginny. You wouldn't understand.'

A few minutes later, Dowling returned, bearing a tray holding a cafetière, three mugs and a jug of milk. There was even a plate of shortbread, McKay noted.

Dowling sat on the sofa opposite them and poured the coffee. 'Sorry. I'm becoming more civilised now.' She gestured round the room. 'Bit of a late one last night. Had a friend round.'

'No problem,' McKay said. 'I'm sorry if we disturbed you.'

'I was about to drag myself out of bed anyway. You just stopped me from procrastinating any longer.'

'Always glad to be of service.' McKay paused. 'I should warn you that we want to talk about an issue that might be distressing for you.'

Dowling pushed the coffee mugs towards McKay and Horton, gesturing for them to help themselves to the shortbread. 'Really? There's not much I find distressing these days.'

'It concerns a man called Ronnie Young. Ring any bells?'

'Young. That bastard?' She stopped and then smiled. 'Don't tell me someone else has finally come forward with more accusations against him?'

'I'm afraid it's not that. Mr Young has been found dead.'

She looked up at them. She looked surprised, but there was something else in her eyes that McKay couldn't interpret. 'What happened to him?'

'I'm not in a position to say too much at this stage. You'll appreciate that the enquiry is continuing. But we have reason to believe we're looking at an unlawful killing.'

Dowling took a sip of her coffee, taking this in. 'Is that why you're here? Am I a suspect now? For what it's worth, I haven't had any contact with Young for years. He was a bastard. But I've long moved on.'

McKay nodded. 'We appreciate that, Ms Dowling. You'll understand that we have to follow up any possible line of enquiry. At the moment, we're primarily interested just in finding out as much about Mr Young as possible. Any background that might throw up potential leads.'

'To be honest,' Dowling said, 'if you're looking for potential suspects you'll find dozens of them. A lot of them women like me. I was the only one who ever had the bottle to bring a formal complaint against him, but I wasn't the only victim.'

'You're saying that other women were assaulted by him?' Horton said.

'I don't know how many, but yes.'

'He was your manager?'

'For a time, yes. He was seen as a big thing in this neck of the woods in those days. He'd scout round the local talent – in every sense – and then snap up anyone with an ounce of talent. And one or two who didn't even have that but who appealed to him, if you get my drift. Then he'd feed you bullshit about how you were just a step or two away from the big time, and how he had the contacts and know-how to help you make it.'

'And did he?' McKay asked.

'Did he buggery. He was just a bullshit merchant. He had decent contacts locally so he could get you a few gigs. If you were any good, he could even find you the odd gig down south. But that was about it. He'd make demos – which in fairness he was good at –but usually at the artist's expense, and he reckoned he was sending them to his mates in the industry. But as far as I'm aware nothing ever came of it. It was mainly a ruse to get in your pants. And if you didn't succumb willingly, he had other methods of getting his way.'

McKay nodded. 'Was his roster exclusively female?'

'Not exclusively, but largely. Think the blokes were just there to provide cover for his real motives.'

'And in your own case?'

'I was making a decent living for myself on the country circuit. Slowly building a reputation, you know? I'd done a fair few gigs down south and was beginning to get noticed. It's a limited circuit but not that small. I was playing festivals here and even one in the US, had the odd appearance on BBC Alba. Anyway, after one of my gigs up here Young approached me and asked me if I'd thought about trying to cross over into more mainstream pop stuff. Sort of a Barbara Dickson deal. I told him I wasn't interested. I reckon the music world's moved on and the future probably lies more in the niche stuff anyway. I'm not even sure mainstream pop even exists in the way it did in the seventies or eighties.'

'So what happened?'

'He kept pestering me, reckoned I was missing out on a real opportunity. At the time I didn't have a manager, just looked after myself. In the end I said I'd give him a trial, see what he could come up with for me.' She smiled. 'I'm not sure that was what he was expecting. Usually he was the one who gave the artist a trial. I think at that point he realised he was up against someone a bit different from his usual innocents.'

'I'm taking it the trial wasn't successful.'

'Not so's you'd notice, no. I said I'd give him six months. We made some demos. Those were okay, and actually served me quite usefully later, which is just as well as I'd stumped up most of the cash for them. He still had the nerve to try to claim them as his property when we split. I told him to fuck off and walked out with them. Other than that, he got me a few gigs around the north which frankly weren't right for me. Lots of promises of record company interest which always came to nothing. And lots of attempts to try it on whenever we found ourselves alone together.'

'You accused him of attempted rape?' McKay said, deciding there was no point in skating round the issue.

She nodded. 'That came towards the end of our delightful time together. By then it was evident it was going nowhere. He knew I was going to bring things to an end and kept trying to persuade me to give it a bit longer. Lots of crap about how the big deal was just around the corner. I'd had enough by then. I thought if anything he was holding back my career because he was trying to present me as something I wasn't. I wasn't getting the right exposure. I wasn't playing the right venues. So I'd made it clear I was ending it.'

'He didn't like that presumably,' Horton said.

'It wasn't what he was used to. Normally, he was the one making the running. Offering little girlies the moon and kicking them out when he got tired of them. He definitely wasn't happy with me taking the lead. Anyway, he turned up at my flat one night – I had a small place in Inverness in those days. Didn't even try to ingratiate himself in the creepy way he usually did. Just barged his way in, grabbed me, threw me on the bed and tried to rape me. I'd been doing some self-defence training so he got a bit more than he bargained for. I ended up beating him round the head with a bloody bedside lamp. Christ, he was full of shit. Anyway, in the end he just walked out. I wasn't even upset at the time. I was just shell-shocked. I wished I'd done more – believe me, if he'd stayed a moment longer I'd have found some way of surgically removing his bollocks. It was only after he'd gone and I was sitting here that it really hit me, that I really understood what had just happened. What he'd tried to do. Does that sound crazy?'

'Not at all,' Horton said. 'I think it's a fairly common response. It's as if the brain shuts down, refuses to acknowledge what's happening. I guess it's a sort of psychological safety device. It's one of the factors that sometimes makes it even harder to prosecute rape. Because the victim can't even recall the detail of what happened.'

Dowling nodded. 'That was one of the difficulties I faced. I sat here for what must have been hours afterwards. It was only the next day that I decided to contact the police.'

'And how were we?' McKay asked.

'You were okay, actually. Better than I'd feared. Very sympathetic. Helpful. Took my story seriously. I had the sense that I might not have been the first to complain about Young, although no one ever said it in so many words. On the whole I think the police did everything they could.'

'That's something,' McKay said, thinking how often he'd heard the opposite. 'But it never came to court.'

'Young denied it, of course. Didn't deny he'd come round that night. Said it was just a business meeting, and that he'd come to break the news that he was going to sack me from his roster.' She laughed. 'He reckoned I'd taken it badly. He claimed I'd attacked him – and of course he was able to show the bruises to prove it – and that I'd promised to get revenge on him.'

'So it became your word against his?' Horton said.

'There was no physical evidence he'd assaulted me. I had no real proof. And there were some inconsistencies in my story. Just minor things on timing, which I think were the result of that shutting down that we talked about. I thought it must have happened later than it did, for example, so the account I gave to the police didn't tie in with CCTV evidence about when Young's car was in the area. It was all explicable, given the circumstances, but you could imagine a smart lawyer ripping it apart.'

'So the Procurator decided not to proceed?'

'Didn't even get that far. It was looking more promising to start with. The police did a great job of tracking down a couple of other victims who'd had similar experiences with Young. As I say, I think there'd already been other complaints that hadn't gone anywhere because of lack of evidence. The police were hoping that, if they could find enough parallel cases with victims who could independently corroborate Young's behaviour, they might have a chance of pulling it off.'

'But that didn't happen?'

'I'm not sure exactly what happened. Maybe the other victims got cold feet. Maybe they were warned off. Young still had quite a lot of influence in the business locally, and I imagine he wouldn't be averse to calling in a few favours to help protect his arse. Remember that these other victims would have been young wannabes who still believed they could make a career in the industry. They wouldn't have wanted to get on the wrong side of local promoters. Whatever the reason, the other accusations melted away and I was left as the only woman standing. At that point, I was persuaded to drop it.'

'By the police?' McKay asked.

She shrugged. 'By this point, it was looking likely that the prosecution wouldn't proceed. But it was really family and friends who talked me out of taking it further. They thought I was unlikely to succeed and that the trial would harm my career more than Young's. They were probably right. Young was slippery as a greased weasel. Christ knows what kind of crap he'd have come up with if it had come to court. In the end, everyone seemed content to let it drop.'

'Have you had any contact with Young since then?'

'What do you think?'

There was something in Dowling's tone that caught McKay's attention. He had the sense there was something she wasn't saying. 'So what happened after all this? In terms of your business relationship with Young.'

'There wasn't one. Simple as that. I'd taken care of all that at the start. That it was up to me to renew the arrangement at the end of the six months. If I didn't do that then by default everything reverted to me. I didn't want to get into any protracted legal wrangles. I walked away. There were a couple of outstanding gigs, which I honoured. But I didn't have any more contact with Young.'

'He didn't try to contact you?'

'Not at all. Once I made the complaint to the police he was presumably advised not to try. But after it was all dropped, I wondered whether there'd be something, if only to taunt me. But nothing.'

McKay nodded, still feeling there was something missing. 'You said there'd be dozens of potential suspects for Young's death. Did you mean that?'

'I was joking. But not much. Young made more enemies than friends. He was a ruthless bastard. He enjoyed screwing people over, I think. Not just the young women he took advantage of, but people he ripped off in business deals. Artists who never got paid. You name it. Probably even his dealers.'

'Drugs?'

'Oh, Christ, yes. Cocaine, mainly. The drug that deludes you into thinking you've got talent. From what I picked up on the grapevine, that had got worse in recent years.'

'Since he moved into producing?'

'Exactly. In fairness to him, that was where his real talents lay. He was a decent producer. He knew how to take whatever you were doing and make the best of it in a studio. Nothing very sophisticated and he talked a load of pretentious bollocks while he was doing it, but there was a gift there all right. He liked working with all these young bands. Reckoned he had to throw himself fully into it. Take on their lifestyle, really get on board with them. Which as far as I can see just meant he locked himself in a studio with piles of drink and drugs and got everybody shit-faced while they recorded.'

'And that worked?' McKay asked.

'Young saw it as an excuse to relive his youth. I remember chatting to the lead singer of a band he'd worked with. The kid just thought Young was an embarrassment. Like having your granddad getting down with the kids. But Young never twigged that they were mostly laughing at him rather than with him. Christ, if I carry on like this, I'll end up feeling sorry for the old bastard.' She shook her head. 'But, yeah, the whole producing thing looked to me like a high-profile midlife crisis, but he was successful enough at it. Not A-list, maybe, but not far down the B-list.'

McKay glanced at Horton. 'That's been very helpful, Ms Dowling.' He gestured towards an acoustic guitar propped up in one corner of the room. 'Do you still perform? I'm sorry, that's probably an insulting question. I ought to know the answer, but country music isn't really my scene.'

'Not sure I blame you. I've mixed feelings about it myself, and I've spent most of my working life in it. No, I've pretty much given up the performing. In public anyway. I focus on building guitars these days. Only play them when I have to demonstrate how brilliant they are to prospective customers.'

McKay pushed himself to his feet. 'We still don't have a confirmed time of death for Mr Young. But we'll probably need to double-check your movements at the relevant times. Just routine.'

'Yeah, just routine for suspects. Shouldn't be difficult. Here, mostly, for the last couple of weeks, mainly sitting in my workshop next door. Downside of which is that I don't have much of an alibi for most of it. But not much I can do about that.'

Dowling led McKay and Horton back to the front door. 'Seriously, I've no time for Young and there's no point in pretending I have after what he did. I might even be prepared to offer a gentle round of applause to whoever did top the bugger. But it wasn't me. I'm happy to co-operate with you in any way I can to prove that.'

'That's much appreciated, Ms Dowling. I suspect we may well need to talk to you again.'

They walked back to the car, McKay looking back in silence to where Dowling was still standing watching them. As Horton reversed out of the drive, McKay said, 'What did you make of that?'

'Not sure. In some respects, she seemed very straightforward. Maybe too much so for her own good. On the other hand...' Horton slowed as they approached the junction with the main road.

'Aye?'

'I'm not sure. She seemed to know an awful lot about Young for someone who claimed to have no interest in him.'

'I noticed that. Though maybe not so surprising given the history. But, aye, interesting. Maybe the blunt speaking was just a double-bluff. And I had the sense that there were things she wasn't telling us.'

'You reckon she's a suspect?'

'Who knows? Sounds as if half of Scotland might be on that list. But worth keeping an eye on. There's something there. I'm just not sure what it is.'

'The other question,' Horton added thoughtfully, 'is who her visitor is.'

'Visitor?' McKay had managed to extract a strip of gum from somewhere deep in his jacket pocket and was painstakingly unwrapping it.

'As far as we know she's single, right?'

'Found nothing to suggest the contrary.' McKay slipped the strip of gum into his mouth and carefully folded the foil wrapping for reuse.

'So she has a male visitor.'

'I'm not aware there's any law against it,' McKay observed.

'Not at all, and it's none of our business.'

'Unless it turns out it is, of course.' McKay was chewing steadily. 'Anyway, how do you know she had a male visitor?'

'Has,' Horton corrected.

'Go on, Sherlock. You're about to tell me he's a six foot tall sailor with a pronounced limp and a deep suntan from his years spent working in the South Seas.'

'Size eleven shoes anyway. Or something like that.'

McKay was silent for a moment. 'The boots in the hallway.'

'You noticed them then?'

'Can't say I did, but I'm assuming it was something like that.'

'Smart arse. But, yes, a pair of male shoes in the hall.'

'Could have been there for ages.'

'Might well have been. But they'd been worn this morning.'

'You reckon?'

'Definitely. They were damp and had traces of grass on them. Someone had obviously worn them to walk on a wet lawn or a field. So either the visitor was still there, or they'd left that pair of shoes there earlier this morning.'

McKay was gazing out of the window, watching the sun flickering through the trees as they pulled onto the A9. 'Like I say, no law against having visitors. Might even explain why she was still in bed at this time of the day. But there's definitely something interesting about Henrietta Dowling. I've a feeling she may be worth a little more attention.'

CHAPTER 36

Netty Munro's prediction proved accurate. Shortly after she'd begun to fry bacon on the top of the Aga, the kitchen door opened and Alicia walked in, rubbing her eyes. 'Sorry if I'm late,' she said, glancing nervously around the room. 'I must have overslept.'

'No worries, dear,' Munro said. 'It's still early. We're making bacon sandwiches. Help yourself to tea or coffee. There's tea in the pot and the kettle's just boiled.'

'Sounds good.' Alicia crossed the kitchen and spooned coffee into a mug. 'Did I hear Elizabeth come back in the night? I thought I heard her bedroom door opening.'

'Yes, she's back,' Munro said. 'I don't know if she'll join us for breakfast. I imagine she's rather tired.'

It occurred to Jane that there was something remarkable about Munro's patience with Elizabeth. After just one day here, and despite Munro's hospitality, Elizabeth had disappeared without warning. She'd returned in the middle of the night without any explanation. She'd shown no gratitude for the generosity she'd received but seemed happy to continue accepting it. Jane had always seen herself as a tolerant individual – far too tolerant through those years with Iain – but she felt she'd have lost patience with Elizabeth by now. Somehow Munro seemed as serene as ever.

There was something odd about that, Jane thought. Admirable, certainly, but also strange. It was as if either Elizabeth had some hold over the older woman or, perhaps more likely, Munro had some ulterior motive for wanting Elizabeth to stay there.

Jane was increasingly feeling that there was a great deal about the set up there she did not understand. Her initial inclination was simply to take it at face value. She'd been offered a gift horse, and there was little to be gained from peering between its jaws. But the sheer strangeness of the set-up was beginning to nag at her. Why was Munro so keen to offer such hospitality to a group of women she'd never previously met?

As if to illustrate the thoughts running through Jane's head, the door opened and Elizabeth entered the kitchen. 'Something smells good. Any bacon going?'

Munro looked up momentarily from the pan. 'Bacon sandwich for everyone. Jane, can you slice some bread please?'

Jane rose, relieved to avoid Elizabeth's eye. She finished slicing the sourdough bread that Munro hand-baked freshly every day. Jane couldn't imagine why or how you'd do that, but Munro seemed to derive pleasure from the process. Jane had watched her kneading the dough the previous day, noticing how the rhythm seemed to take the older woman almost into a kind of trance. There was the same expression on her face when she was playing the guitar.

Elizabeth had made herself an instant coffee and sat back at the table, watching the other two young women with something close to amusement. 'Made yourselves useful yesterday, I hope?'

'We were here,' Alicia said pointedly. 'Where did you get to?'

Elizabeth shrugged. 'I had some business. Things to attend to.'

Netty Munro carried the cast iron frying pan over to the table and set it down on a trivet in the centre. 'Help yourselves to bacon,' she said. 'Couple of rashers each. There's butter and ketchup in the fridge for those who want them.'

Jane took the opportunity to fetch the items from the fridge, content for Alicia and Elizabeth to continue without her contribution. Behind her, she heard Munro say: 'You're free to go wherever you want to, dear. It's none of our business. Next time, it might be courteous to let me know though, eh? Just for catering purposes and suchlike, you understand.'

Jane turned to see Elizabeth's expression. She clearly was not happy at being challenged and looked, at least for a moment, as if about to respond aggressively. Finally she said, 'Yes, I'm sorry. It was all a bit short notice. Something I wasn't expecting.'

'Apart from anything else,' Munro went on, 'if you want to go somewhere, just let me know. I'm happy to give you a lift to the station in Dingwall or even into Inverness if I've nothing else on. I'm glad you managed to make it back okay.'

'It was fine,' Elizabeth said.

Jane returned to the table and helped herself to the last two slices of bread and rashers of bacon. The bacon was locally reared, Munro told them. Not here on the farm, but elsewhere in the village. Jane assumed this was a good thing even if she was unclear why. It tasted good though.

'What are you planning to do today, Elizabeth?' Munro asked.

'I don't know. Do you need me to help out somewhere? Happy to do what I can.' The response wasn't what Jane had expected, and she wasn't sure how seriously to take it.

Munro had clearly decided to take the answer at face value. 'I can always find something. Henry was going to come in today and give me a hand with that fencing I was complaining about. Those buggers who came round to mend it reckon they've done everything they can. I haven't the time or energy to argue with them, so I thought we could do a "before" and "after" photo and fix it properly ourselves. Then I'll refuse to pay their bill and send them copies of the pictures to show why. The bastards can take me to court if they want.' She paused, clearly satisfied with her rant, and added, 'You can come and give us a hand with that, if you like.'

Jane found herself feeling almost irritated. As on the previous day, she and Alicia would be stuck with some makeweight task while Elizabeth was given real work to do. Jane realised immediately that was idiotic. She had no idea what kind of task Munro might allocate to Elizabeth, or what her motives might be. It could well be she was going easy on Jane and Alicia because she recognised their relative vulnerability. It could also be that it was her way of punishing Elizabeth or simply a means of keeping an eye on what she might be up to.

It was futile to speculate, and it was equally futile to feel resentment for a non-existent slight. Jane simply wanted to feel a part of the household, someone who was critical to its day-to-day operation, rather than a guest passing through. Despite her dismissive behaviour, Elizabeth seemed somehow to be more fully accepted there than she or Alicia were.

Elizabeth herself seemed uninterested in what Munro had said. 'Yeah, sure. Whatever you say.' She opened up her sandwich and squirted another shot of ketchup onto the bacon.

Jane had finished her sandwich and swallowed the last of her tea. 'Where do you want me to start?'

Munro looked up, her expression suggesting she had momentarily forgotten what Jane was talking about. 'With the cleaning? In the sitting room, I suppose. You can do some dusting in there, if you like.'

If you like, Jane thought. She turned to Alicia. 'That all right with you, Alicia? Netty was suggesting we do some cleaning indoors today.'

Alicia shrugged. 'Sure. Happy to help.'

Munro looked more content, as if an outstanding problem had been resolved. 'That's good, dears. I'll get you both sorted with polish and whatever else you might need.' She trailed off vaguely then turned to Elizabeth. 'We can head off down to the lower fields. Not sure when to expect Henry, but she'll join us when she gets here.'

For a moment, Elizabeth looked as if she might be about to protest after all. Then she smiled and said, 'Fine. Whenever you're ready.'

CHAPTER 37

'Quieter than I expected.'

McKay looked around the almost empty lobby. 'Aye, we no longer encourage Joe and Jenny Public to trouble us with their many problems. Far too disruptive to smooth policing if we have to start listening to people out there.' The offices, which previously had included a public enquiry desk, had been closed to the public some months earlier. McKay had felt ambivalent about the move. He'd welcomed not having to wade through a mass of humanity whenever he entered the building. On the other hand, the move had once again widened the gap between the force and the public it supposedly served. In any case, he rarely resisted the temptation to give management a public kicking. That, he reasoned, was what management was for.

Drew Douglas laughed, though he looked unsure whether or not McKay had been joking. McKay led the way through a set of double doors into the rear of the building. 'Good of you to take the time to come in, Mr Douglas.'

'No worries. We don't have a gig on tonight, so it's relatively quiet. I've left the bar in Morag's capable hands. Happy to do whatever I can to help. I'm not that keen on our acts being bumped off. Doesn't reflect well on the club.'

This time it was McKay's turn to wonder whether Douglas was joking. Probably not, he thought, or at least not entirely. It was the kind of light-hearted comment you made when you felt rattled. No doubt Douglas had felt some responsibility for McGuire, even if not for his death.

McKay had booked one of the formal interview rooms. He liked having meetings in there. The presence of the recording equipment reminded people of what normally went on in that or similar rooms. That usually helped to concentrate the mind of even the most innocent interviewee.

Douglas looked nervously around the room. 'This isn't anything formal, is it?'

'Not at all. Just a chat. About our investigation into McGuire's death. Though we also have another enquiry now. Into the apparent killing of Mr McGuire's former show business partner, Jack Dingwall.'

'Dingwall? What's happened to Dingwall?'

'I'd be pleased if you treated this as confidential,' McKay said, 'until we've advised any next of kin. But it looks like he was killed in the same way as Mr McGuire.'

'Jesus. Where?'

'I'm not in a position to release any more information at this stage, Mr Douglas, but the two deaths were very similar. Similar enough for us to treat them as part of a single enquiry at least.'

'I see.' Douglas was silent for a moment, as if absorbing what he'd heard. 'How can I help?'

'I want to pick your brains. When we spoke earlier, I had the impression you had a good understanding and knowledge of the comedy scene.'

'It partly goes with the job.' Douglas looked mildly embarrassed. 'What's coming up, what's going down. But it's an interest as well. Always has been. I grew up with stand-up. My dad was in the business. He was a musician. Guitarist. Various bands but mainly session and backup work. He worked with a lot of the up-and-coming comics at the time, and he loved that world. Ended up managing some of them. Anyway, I caught the bug. Used to go see acts in the theatres and in the clubs when I was far too young to do so, and of course you can find loads of stuff online these days. Then it became a bit of a hobby. Tracing back the history. I started with the British stuff, especially with the alternative comedians in the 1980s–' He stopped suddenly, clearly aware that he'd let his enthusiasm run away with him.

'That's really interesting, son,' McKay said, in a tone that implied the interest wasn't one he shared. 'What about the Scottish scene?'

'It's always been a bit hit and miss. There's always been lots of good Scots comedians, but only the odd Billy Connolly's managed to break through to the real mainstream. Some tend to be a bit too Scottish. Others get further but sometimes by burying their Scottishness. But there's a few getting through to the big time now. Kevin Bridges. Frankie Boyle. Very different styles.'

McKay nodded, though the names rang no more than the faintest bell of recognition. 'You got ambitions in that line yourself?'

Douglas looked embarrassed. 'I don't fool myself I'm in that class but I enjoy getting up there on stage. It's always a buzz when it goes down well. I do the compering at the club and I've done the odd set when we've a gap to fill.' He laughed. 'Maybe one day, eh?'

'And what about Dingwall and McGuire? Where do they fit into the great Scottish comedy tradition?'

Douglas shrugged. 'At one point they looked as if they might make it apparently. Like I said the other day, Jimmy McGuire was a genuinely funny man in his way. Dingwall was a bit weird. In some ways, he was the brains behind the act. He did most of the writing. But as far as I know, he'd never had any desire to go on stage himself. But McGuire saw something in him, and thought it was worth a shot. And McGuire was right. Dingwall was awkward, clearly didn't want to be there, prone to forgetting his lines – but with McGuire keeping the show on the road it worked. They got bigger and bigger bookings. Some TV work here in Scotland, and the promise of stuff down south.'

'But it never happened.'

'That's the business. Obviously, the stuff with Dingwall put the lid on it, but their moment had passed anyway. Just never really took off. And Dingwall was having drink problems – probably because he didn't want to be on stage in the first place. And even before Dingwall's arrest there'd been rumours…'

McKay looked up, as if he'd been only half-listening up to that point. 'Rumours?'

'This is only what I've gleaned second-hand,' Douglas said. 'This is before I was born. But I've heard some people say the stuff with Dingwall was only the tip of the iceberg.'

'Some iceberg, given that Dingwall was prosecuted for rape.'

'Exactly. But there were stories of young girls – I mean, underage girls – being traded backstage. Deals being done with groupies. Not just the comedy acts. People like Dingwall and McGuire weren't exactly groupie magnets, except that anyone appearing on the telly has a bit of cachet. But some of the bands too. Word was there was a bit of a network, grooming youngsters. Male and female.'

McKay was silent for a moment, wondering whether any of this had reached the ears of the police. It would be before his own time in the force. It might be worth checking the files. 'You've no evidence for this, presumably?'

'No. It's just gossip. Stuff I've picked up from blethering with people over the years.' He paused. 'I've been thinking of writing a book about it. The history of the comedy scene in Scotland. So I've just been amassing stuff where I can, chatting to some of the older guys on the scene. Would have liked to have spent some time with Jimmy McGuire–' He stopped. 'That's not going to happen now, is it?'

'Not without the services of a medium,' McKay agreed. 'You think there might be something in this? The idea of a network.'

'Who knows? It's come up a few times with people I've spoken to. But always second-hand. Stuff they've heard on the grapevine.'

'On the other hand,' McKay said, 'nobody's going to admit to being part of it, are they? You fancy naming any names, son? This is a murder investigation, after all.'

Douglas shifted in his seat. 'I don't know. It's nothing more than hearsay. I can't remember who said what, exactly.'

McKay sat back in his chair, watching the young man. 'Name Ronnie Young mean anything to you?'

'Young? The record producer, you mean?' Douglas had dropped his head down, staring at the desktop, but McKay thought he'd caught something, some flicker of expression in the young man's eyes, in the moment before he'd looked away.

'Aye, so I understand. Producer. Former manager. Former rock star of sorts. You come across him?'

'Not really. I mean, I know of him. But I don't think we've ever met. Why?'

'Another killing, son. Another death that we think might be connected. Again, just between ourselves for the moment. I was wondering if there might have been any connection between him and Dingwall and McGuire.'

Douglas had still not looked up. 'Not that I'm aware of. I mean, there's always been some overlap between the different circuits. But as far as I know Young had focused on the production stuff in recent years.'

'What about Henrietta Dowling? Have you come across her?'

This time Douglas did look up. McKay couldn't fully read his expression, but there was something beyond bafflement. 'Henry? What about her?'

'You know her?'

Douglas hesitated. 'The singer? A little. I've been trying to get her at the club but she doesn't perform much these days.'

'I didn't know you put on acts like that.'

'We put on all kinds of things. Mainly comedy, but some music. Acoustic stuff. A few bands. Acts that fit the ethos...' He trailed off, as if unsure what he was saying.

'Ethos?'

'It's hard to explain. I mean, we're not a rock venue. There are other places in town that do that better. We're not really an acoustic music venue, for the same reason. We put on people who'll give the audience a decent night out. Fairly relaxed, a few laughs.'

'And Dowling would fit into that?'

'Yes, she would.' Douglas sounded almost defiant, as if McKay had challenged his professional competence. 'She started out as a country singer, and she does that really well. But she's also funny on stage, you know? Deadpan delivery, but nice jokes between the songs. Where does she fit into this anyway?'

'She came up in passing in the enquiry,' McKay said vaguely. 'You'll appreciate, Mr Douglas, that this isn't exactly my world. I'm just trying to get an idea of how it all fits together.'

He was about to say something more when the door opened and Ginny Horton peered into the room. 'Alec. Sorry to disturb. Can you spare a moment?'

McKay hesitated momentarily then turned to Douglas. 'I think we've just about finished here, haven't we, Mr Douglas? That's been very illuminating. I'm grateful for your time.' He rose and ushered Douglas to the door. 'Back in a sec, Ginny. I'll just show Mr Douglas out.'

He led Douglas back through the double doors to the lobby. He wasn't entirely sure what instinct had made him want to take Douglas off-site before responding to Ginny Horton. But something about Ginny's expression had told him she had something significant to share. And something about his discussion with Drew Douglas had made him uneasy about the young man's continued presence. McKay wanted time to think about what Douglas had said to him.

McKay returned to Horton, who was watching him quizzically. 'Useful interview?'

'I'm not sure.'

'You seemed keen to get rid of him.'

'I just had the sense you had something more important to share with me.'

'I reckon so. Pete Carrick's got them to pull out all the stops on the Jack Dingwall killing.'

'Good for Pete. I'll remember to mention it to Jock Henderson. And?'

'We have a match for the fingerprints on the glass used by Dingwall's visitor on the night of his killing. Looks like a DNA match too.'

'Someone on the system?'

'Someone on the system,' Horton said. 'Someone by the name of Elizabeth Hamilton.'

CHAPTER 38

By the time Carrie Baillie reached the front door, she'd stopped swearing under her breath. Now, she was swearing out loud, the expletives clearly audible to anyone who might have been passing by. Fortunately, in the middle of a sunny weekday afternoon, the road outside was deserted and there was no one to hear her in the leafy garden other than the occasional sparrow. The taxi driver would have heard, but he'd already been subject to an extended diatribe all the way from the airport. She'd felt obliged to give him a larger than usual tip just for putting up with it without complaint. Presumably he'd become well accustomed to tuning out his more objectionable passengers.

'You fucking fucker,' she said, for perhaps the twentieth time as she approached the front door. 'You fucking fucker of an absolute fucking fuck.'

As she reached the front door, she set her wheeled suitcase back upright. The door was wide open. 'Christ, you fucker,' she added. Either he was out somewhere and hadn't bothered to lock the front door, or he was inside and had simply forgotten about her. Either was quite possible, particularly if one of his numerous young bits on the side was involved. She didn't really care about the reason – all the possible causes were already well factored into her valuation of the marriage. All she cared about was that, whatever the reason, he'd not given her priority. That, as he well knew, was unforgivable.

The bastard had left her standing at the airport. Literally standing in the pick-up area with her wheeled suitcase, looking eagerly at each new car entering the slip road with the air of someone who didn't want to admit they'd been fucking stood up. It wasn't the inconvenience so much as the humiliation. That was the deal. He could do pretty much whatever the hell he liked as long as he put her first and did nothing that would make her look stupid.

She pushed open the front door. After the warmth of the afternoon, the house felt cool inside. That was the other thing. She'd been hot and uncomfortable at the airport. She'd initially been expecting him to be at the arrival gate. Failing that, if he was running late, she'd expected a text and for him to sweep into the pick-up zone in his big air-conditioned executive car. There'd been no text, and no sign of a fucking executive car. In the end, she'd had to traipse over to the taxi rank and sort out her own sodding transport.

Her first thought, once she was inside, was to call his name. Her second, almost instantaneous thought was: bugger that. She was thirsty. She wanted a drink and a sit down. In the taxi, she'd been contemplating the prospect of nothing stronger than some iced water or maybe an orange juice. Now she was back, she felt as if she needed something like a tonic water, maybe fortified with a very large slug of gin.

Abandoning her suitcase in the hall, she entered the kitchen. It had been left fairly tidy, but that was Tom's way. He had countless faults, but untidiness wasn't in the top ten. There was a cereal bowl and a plate in the sink, which she assumed were the remnants of that morning's breakfast. She wouldn't have been particularly surprised to have seen two sets of crockery in there, but maybe that would have been careless even for Tom.

She found herself a glass, a slightly tired looking lemon, and some chilled cans of tonic. The gin took a few moments longer, as Tom had taken it out of the kitchen. She eventually found the bottle on the large coffee table in the sitting room. Luckily – for both Tom and her, she thought – it was still nearly half-full. Picking up the gin bottle, she walked over to the patio doors and peered out into the garden.

The garden looked glorious in the late spring sunshine. This open space was her personal pride and joy. Admittedly, these days she did little of the maintenance herself –and why would she, given that they could afford to pay for professionals? – but the concept, the design, those were very much hers. It looked good at almost any time of the year, as the different blooms came and went. Sometimes, in the summer, she would just sit out there, her eyes closed, drinking in the sunshine, the scents, the fragrance of the flowers.

She made her way back into the kitchen, clinked some ice in her glass from the American-style fridge, poured a generous slug of gin and tipped in the can of tonic. As an afterthought, she cut a slice of lemon and dropped it carefully on top.

Perfect, she thought, as she took the first sip of the bitter-sweet liquid, enjoying the scent of the gin, the sharp fizz of the tonic, the tap of ice against her teeth.

So where the hell was he?

She already had a sense that, despite the open front door, the house was deserted. It just somehow felt empty. If he'd been upstairs, even if he'd been in bed with some little tart, she'd have expected to have heard something. She'd made plenty of noise entering the house. He'd have been down by now, even with his trousers halfway round his ankles, at least metaphorically.

She took another sip of the gin and slumped down on the sofa. Half of her wanted to sit there and never move again. But after a moment, she found herself making her way back out into the hallway. Where the hell was he? He was feckless enough and had been known to miss appointments with people more important than her. But he wasn't usually this useless. Usually, he'd remember just in time to send her an apologetic text, grovelling about his own stupidity and promising to turn over a new leaf. Which would last as long as it took for him to forget the next appointment.

Maybe something had happened to him. That was a new thought. He wasn't getting any younger, and he could hardly be said to take good care of his health. Maybe it had finally caught up with him. She hurried up the stairs, half expecting that he'd be up in bed at death's door, or maybe even through death's door. Either that, or she'd find him in bed with one of those floozies.

Their main bedroom was deserted. The bed had been slept in, and a half-hearted attempt made to tidy it up, which suggested to her that Tom might well have shared it with someone else. If so, or even if it was just a possibility, she'd make him drag the bedclothes down to the washing machine. There was no way she was spending a night inhaling someone else's knock-off perfume, let alone any other scents that might have been deposited there.

The other three rooms, used mainly for guests, were undisturbed. The bathroom, similarly, showed no more than the expected signs of recent use.

So where the bloody hell was he?

She made her way down the stairs. The truth was he could be almost anywhere. It was possible he'd headed into the office to deal with some business issue. Tom always liked to think his presence was indispensable even though most of the team were probably more capable than he was. Bugger him.

She picked up the gin and walked through the kitchen to open the back door. What she could really do with in the unaccustomed warmth was a breath of fresh air. She stepped out onto the decking, enjoying the breeze on her cheeks.

She recognised almost immediately that there was something strange about the garden, but it took her a moment to work out what it was. It was an oddly designed garden to start with, which was one of the qualities that had attracted her to the house. The lawn rose in a gentle slope from the back of the house then fell in a steep slope at the far side of the garden as the land dropped towards the nearby River Ness. She'd had the slope reconfigured as a series of gentle terraces, dotted with appropriate shrubs and flower plants, and with garden seats at intervals among the terraces. There was no view to speak of, other than the tops of trees and other neighbouring houses, but it provided a shady and welcoming place to sit on a day like today.

There was a line of shrubs across the top edge of the lawn which marked the boundary of the terraced slope. The two nearest shrubs had both been crushed, as if a heavy weight had been thrust against them.

She deposited her drink on the picnic table and stared up at the damage. What the bloody hell had he been doing while she was away? Had he had some bloody stupid party out here?

She strode up the lawn to the summit, peering down into the area beyond. The damage continued down the terraces, shrubs and flowers crushed in parallel lines down the hillside. At the bottom of the garden, wedged against the far fencing, she could see what had caused it. A human body, dressed in black, had been rolled down the terraces to end up smashed against the wooden panels.

She looked further along the fencing. As the daughter and granddaughter of old-time variety performers, her instinct when uncertain was to cling to showbiz stories. For some stupid reason, as she stared down into the well of the garden, the thought that sprang into her mind was the old tale about the double act playing the Glasgow Empire – Mike and Bernie Winters, was it? Like the heckler from the back of that audience, her immediate reaction was to mutter: 'Oh, Christ. There's two of them.'

CHAPTER 39

'We're sure about this?' Helena Grant asked.

'Sure as we can be,' McKay confirmed. 'Several prints on the wine glass. All clearly defined. Full prints, not partials. Perfect match with Elizabeth Hamilton.'

'A DNA match from the glass too,' Ginny Horton added. 'There doesn't seem much doubt.'

'Sounds too good to be true,' Grant commented. 'Life's not that helpful. Ours isn't anyway.'

'That was my first thought,' McKay said. 'And Hamilton may be many things but she's never struck me as stupid.'

'Some sort of set up then?'

'Anything's possible. But it would mean someone got hold of a glass with her prints and DNA on it, and then planted it there without leaving any trace of their own contact. The only other traces on there match with Dingwall.'

'Not impossible.'

'Not impossible. But convoluted. Seems better to start with the evidence that's in front of us. Occam's razor and all that.'

'Aye, Alec. You're always the one for the philosophical approach. I hope this isn't just about unfinished business with Hamilton?'

'We've all got unfinished business with Hamilton. But what else do you suggest? We've clear evidence here. We can't ignore it. We have to start by taking it at face value and seeing what Hamilton has to say.'

'I hope you're not trying to teach me to suck eggs, Alec McKay?'

McKay grinned. 'I wouldn't dare. And I'm resisting any of the obvious jokes at this point. But I'm right, aren't I?'

'Aye, of course you're right. You're always sodding right. Except of course when you're steamingly, outrageously, unbelievably sodding wrong and I have to dig you out of the shite.'

'Aye, but that's only now and again. So... Hamilton?'

'I've been trying to track her down. She seems to have gone to ground after the trial, maybe not surprisingly. She gave that one newspaper interview, just to stir up the crap for us. Then she vanished. I've been onto her solicitors.'

'And?'

'They started by giving me lots of bollocks about harassment and how they hoped their client wasn't going to become a target for police victimisation.'

'Oh, for Christ's sake.'

'Aye. I told them that we had a legitimate need to interview Hamilton in connection with an ongoing murder enquiry and that if they weren't able to help me they'd have to consider their own positions very carefully. It looks as if, after the trial, she went to stay in The Reynold Centre in Inverness.'

'The Reynold Centre?' Horton said. 'The women's refuge?'

'That's the place,' Grant said. 'Most of the residents are women who've experienced domestic violence and who need active protection.'

'So why would Hamilton need to stay there?' McKay looked puzzled. 'I mean, she's a survivor of abuse and violence, and she might well need support, but she's not actively under threat. Not any more.'

'As far as we know,' Horton said. 'We know she was abused by her father and by Denny Gorman–'

'Who're both dead. Thanks to her.'

'Not proven,' Horton said. 'But, yes, both dead. It's possible they weren't her only abusers.'

McKay made no immediate response but jumped to his feet and made his familiar prowl of Grant's office. 'I suppose that's possible,' he said finally. 'I'm just thinking about what she said about her father.'

'Go on,' Grant said.

'Remember she told us her father used to attract these young women as his counselling clients. Then he'd... groom them is the only word, I suppose. Manipulate them and get them infatuated with him to the point where they'd do anything for him. Then eventually he'd get sick of them.'

Horton nodded, clearly following McKay's thinking. 'Hamilton reckoned he had a network of business contacts, as she put it, who he used to get them out of his hair. Some of them ended up in new lives working in Manchester and other places.'

'And we know that some of those ended up dead,' Grant said grimly. 'But we still don't know if there were other victims we've never discovered.'

'Exactly,' McKay said. 'But maybe some of those "business contacts" of his weren't just there to facilitate a move down south. That's another thought that's been nagging away at the back of my mind but I hadn't recognised till now. Why would these contacts be willing to help Robbins out like that? What was in it for them? Maybe it was just Robbins calling in favours. But maybe...'

'Maybe we're talking about a network of abusers? And these women got handed to the next in the pecking order. Jesus.' Grant looked genuinely horrified.

'In which case,' McKay went on, 'there might well be people out there who Elizabeth Hamilton has reason to be scared of. Maybe people who abused her. Maybe people who don't want the full story to come out.'

Grant nodded. 'I suppose it's quite possible that one of those people might have been Jack Dingwall. He had the history, after all.'

McKay was still thinking. 'You all know my views on cheap psychology...'

'We know your views on all types of psychology, whatever the price,' Grant said.

'Aye. It just strikes me that if Hamilton did kill another of her abusers, she might not be too fussed about concealing her identity.'

'After all the effort she put into avoiding being convicted for Robbins' and Gorman's deaths?' Grant said.

'Maybe that's the point. Maybe this was unfinished business. And now it's done maybe she doesn't much care any more.'

'It is a point of view,' Grant conceded.

'So is she still in the centre?' Horton asked impatiently.

'That's the thing,' Grant said. 'I phoned them. They're reluctant to give out any information on the phone. To get any real information we're going to have to go in person, I reckon.'

'You did tell them this is a murder enquiry?'

Grant sighed. 'Aye, Alec. Oddly enough, I did think to mention it. But I'm guessing they've heard every kind of claim from abusive men trying to get information on their victims, don't you? I got a firm "I don't doubt you're who you say you are, but even so…" They suggested I go through the formal channels – there's a designated liaison officer, apparently – but it'll be quicker just to turn up on their doorstep with ID.'

'I suppose that's their job,' McKay conceded. 'You want me to go down there then?'

'Tell you what, Alec. Why don't you let Ginny ask the questions? I've got a hunch that in this particular case she might handle the sensitivities a wee bit better than you.'

'You do realise that's sexism.'

'That so, Alec? I'll take my chances.' She looked as if she was about to offer a few further choice thoughts on the subject when the phone buzzed on her desk. She held up her hand to silence McKay. 'DCI Grant.' There was a long silence as she listened to what was being said at the other end of the line. 'You're kidding me.'

She held the phone to her chest and looked up at McKay and Horton. 'Now we're really neck deep in the shite. We've two more bodies. Two more fucking garrottings.'

'*Two* more?' McKay said.

'Aye. Two more. Brothers. Tom and Colin Baillie.'

CHAPTER 40

J ane looked around the room. 'Do you think that's good enough?'

Alicia was still crouched down, polishing the front of a cabinet that seemed to contain more bottles of spirits than Jane had ever seen even in most of the local bars. She'd lost count of the number of different single malts. Most of the bottles looked unopened. 'I've no idea,' she said. 'Even before we started, this place looked tidier than any room I've ever been in.' She pushed herself to her feet and looked around. 'It smells more of beeswax now, but it looks more or less the same.'

Jane nodded. 'Aye, that's pretty much how I felt. I couldn't find any actual dust to, well, dust. And I couldn't see anything on the floor even before we'd started vacuuming.'

'You know Netty has a cleaner comes in twice a week,' Alicia said. 'I'd have said this room's been cleaned already in the last few days.'

'I don't suppose it gets used very much.'

'Even so, you'd expect a bit of dust to build up if it was left for any length of time.'

Jane knew Alicia was right. She couldn't understand why Munro wouldn't give them real tasks to do, rather than these superfluous duties. Jane would have preferred to do something much more arduous, as long as she could have felt it was worthwhile.

'What do we do now?' Alicia said.

Jane glanced at the clock on her mobile. It was still only around 11.15am. She didn't expect that Munro and Elizabeth would be back up for lunch till around 1.00pm. That seemed to be the usual pattern for the day. 'We could do another room or two?' she offered.

'But Netty said not to do any more than the ones we've done,' Alicia pointed out. Munro had implied that the other rooms were either private – including the rooms that were used as bedrooms by Netty herself or by guests such as Henry Dowling – or contained work or other documents that might get misarranged if the rooms were tidied.

'Aye, you're right. So what do we do?'

'Should we go and get a drink in the kitchen? Netty told us to just help ourselves.'

'Why not?'

Jane followed Alicia through to the kitchen. The back door was open, and there was sunlight glittering on the path outside. The kitchen felt airy, a faint breeze blowing through to counteract the warmth of the Aga. 'Do you smell something?' Jane asked.

'What sort of something?'

'Not sure. A burning smell. Something charred.'

Alicia stopped and sniffed the air, with the appearance of a dog seeking its quarry. 'Maybe. Do you think it's the Aga?'

Munro had told them that one of the downsides of the Aga – one of the *few* downsides, she'd emphasised – was that it was difficult to smell what was cooking inside. 'That might be a good thing,' Jane had pointed out, 'depending on what you were cooking.'

Munro had laughed, but said that she missed the old scent of baking bread from her previous cooker. 'It's things like that. The kind of scents you want filling a house like this.' The odd thing was, she'd added, that because of the way the Aga flue worked, you could sometimes smell those scents more strongly upstairs or even out in the garden than in the kitchen.

Jane stepped out of the back door and stood breathing in the morning air. There were a few fluffy white clouds drifting across the sky, but otherwise the day was as bright as ever.

She *could* smell something, she thought. As Munro had said, it was more detectable out there. A definite smell of burning. Perhaps, she thought, burning bread.

She re-entered the kitchen. 'There's definitely a scorched smell,' she said to Alicia. 'It's more obvious out there, so it must be something in the Aga.'

'Do you think we should check?'

Jane hesitated. The answer was clearly yes. If there was something burning in the oven, then Munro would want to know about it. On the other hand, Jane still felt this was a world she didn't fully understand. Perhaps some things were meant to be left to char. Perhaps if she interfered, she'd be getting it wrong and Munro would be unhappy with what they'd done. 'I suppose so,' she said finally. 'I mean, things aren't supposed to do that, are they?'

'I wouldn't have thought so,' Alicia said, in a tone that suggested that she was no more confident of the rights and wrongs of the place than Jane.

Jane crossed over to the Aga and gently opened the hot oven door. As she did so, a cloud of acrid smoke filled the kitchen. 'I'm sure it shouldn't be doing that.' She reached over and grabbed a pair of oven gloves.

For a moment, she had a disconcerting sense that whatever she was about to pull from the oven would be something truly horrible. Afterwards, she couldn't explain where the idea had come from or why. But, just for the merest instant, she had felt it must be true. It was like a moment in a dream when you know that what you're about to find is something you're truly dreading, something you've long imagined but now, just at that terrible instant, can no longer recall.

'It's a loaf, isn't it?' Alicia said.

It was, or at least it had been intended to be. It was difficult to be sure now, but it seemed to be the remnants of one of Netty Munro's sourdough cobs. Now, it was little more than a charred shrunken boulder. A meteorite that had burnt up on its long journey through the atmosphere, Jane thought, fancifully. She stared at it for a moment. 'That's a pity.'

'Netty must have put it on before she went out with Elizabeth,' Alicia said. 'It's not like her. She's normally very well organised about that sort of thing. I've noticed it when she's cooked supper for us. It's always amazing how she can juggle all this stuff and know exactly when to get things out of the oven.'

'Maybe she got distracted by something. It's easily done.' Jane could feel a growing sense of unease. It was connected, she thought, with the odd sensation she'd had a few moments earlier. The sense that she was about to witness something awful, something she'd never seen before. 'Do you think we should throw it away?'

'I'm not sure. Netty might want to see it.'

Jane couldn't really think why Netty might want to do that, but she shared Alicia's uncertainty. 'I'll leave it on top of the Aga. I don't think any of it's salvageable but you never know. Do you think we should go and tell Netty?'

'Can we have a drink first? I'm parched.'

Jane pulled open the fridge and peered inside. There was none of Munro's home-made lemonade. Even that, in Jane's current frame of mind, seemed oddly significant, as if the few norms she had become accustomed to in the house had already shifted. She pulled out a carton of orange juice. 'This okay?'

'Fine for me,' Alicia said.

They found glasses, added some ice from the freezer, and poured themselves each a glass. Alicia's judgement had been sound. As soon as Jane tasted the cool sweet juice, she instantly felt calmer. Perhaps she'd allowed herself to become a little dehydrated, overheated, while they'd been working. Whatever the reason, she hadn't been thinking clearly. Why would anyone care about a burnt loaf? It was a mild irritation, nothing more. Netty would probably just make another one.

'Do you think Netty would mind if we had another glass?' Alicia asked. 'I hadn't realised how thirsty I was.'

'She said to help ourselves,' Jane said. She poured two more glasses, and they both sat drinking them in silence, sipping more slowly.

'Pity about the bread,' Alicia said. 'Do you think Netty will mind?'

'It's only bread. She can make more. I imagine she'll be mainly cross with herself for forgetting about it.'

'I hope she doesn't blame us.'

'Why should she blame us? We didn't even know she'd put a loaf in the oven.'

'Perhaps she meant to ask us to keep an eye on it.'

'We're not mind readers,' Jane said. Then a thought struck her. 'She didn't ask you to, did she?'

'No, of course not. I just meant…' Alicia shook her head. 'I just meant that it's not like her, that's all.'

'Everyone makes mistakes,' Jane said. 'She's only human.' She finished the last of her juice. 'Do you think we should go and find her?'

'To tell her about the bread, you mean?'

'Partly. But I was thinking we could also ask her what else she'd like us to do. I don't like just sitting around and doing nothing. I feel as if I ought to be earning my keep.'

'Me too. Though I didn't really feel we were doing that this morning, even though we were working hard.'

'Let's go and track her down. We can see if we can persuade her to give us something more useful to get on with.'

They placed their two glasses in the dishwasher as Munro had shown them, and made their way out into the garden. 'Where do you reckon they'll be?' Alicia asked.

'Not sure.' Jane stopped and looked around. 'She said it was the fencing on the lower fields. So presumably that's towards the firth.' There was a field filled with the first burgeoning shoots of barley between them and the stretch of fencing below. 'Down there, I suppose.'

There was no immediate sign of Munro or Elizabeth, but the fencing stretched the length of the land ahead of them, disappearing into a cluster of trees at the far end of the barley field. From what Munro had told them, her land extended some distance beyond that, so Jane assumed that the work must be taking place somewhere beyond the trees. 'I'm not sure how we get there,' she said.

They walked along the edge of the barley field. There were farm buildings to their right and somewhere Jane could hear the sounds of mooing cows, but there were no visible signs of life. At the end of the field, there was a time-worn path leading down towards the lower ground. Jane gestured to Alicia, and they made their way down the hillside.

The sun was high in the sky and the day was beginning to grow hot. The tide was low in the firth and much of the bed was exposed. The stretch of water that remained was utterly still, reflecting the landscape above and around it. Jane could hear no sound but the tread of their own footsteps, the occasional caw of a gull, and the counterpoint of more melodious birdsong in the hedgerows around them.

They reached the lower fence and Jane looked along it, hoping to see Munro and Elizabeth, perhaps with Henry Dowling. But there was no one. She glanced back at Alicia, and then set off to follow the line of the fence. There was no real footpath, and the ground was rough and overgrown under their feet. They passed the trees, pushing back some undergrowth to force their access, and found themselves in an open space.

It looked as if it was little more than woodland. Perhaps it was one of the wildlife areas that Munro had talked about. There were various parts of the farm, she had said, that she'd deliberately left uncultivated to encourage birds and other wildlife. 'At least,' she'd added, 'that's what I tell the neighbours. They don't really approve of me not extracting every square metre of value from the place. They just think I'm mad.'

Jane peered around. Then she saw, at a point just ahead where the fence wiring seemed to sag inwards, a toolbox left on the ground, with a hammer and some other implements scattered beside it. Perhaps they'd somehow managed to miss Munro and Elizabeth, Jane thought. Perhaps they'd already headed back up towards the house. If they'd gone directly back up towards the farmhouse, their paths wouldn't necessarily have crossed, though Jane was surprised she hadn't heard any sound from them.

She took another step forward and she stopped.

Her grandmother had had a phrase. She'd always reckoned that she had a touch of second-sight, and that her dreams were filled with meaning, if only she was able to decipher them. Occasionally, she'd pick up on something Jane had said or done which she claimed had been prefigured overnight. 'Oh. You've broken my dream,' she'd say.

That was how Jane felt now. You've broken my dream. Not a real dream though, but the uneasy disturbing sensation she'd felt in the kitchen only a short while earlier. The sense that at any moment she was about to witness something dreadful.

And now she was. Something more dreadful than she had ever witnessed before.

She took a step back and gestured to Alicia. 'Keep back, Alicia. There's something here. Something—' She stopped, trying to force her mind to work. 'We'd better call the police.'

CHAPTER 41

'So you're from the police?' the woman behind the desk said, with a note of scepticism in her voice.

Christ, this was proving hard work, Ginny Horton thought. Helena Grant had made the right call in asking Alec not to handle this one. 'DS Horton,' she said patiently.

'And you have ID?'

Which I've already shown to at least three of your staff, Horton said to herself. 'Of course.' She slid her warrant card across the cluttered desktop.

'That looks in order,' the woman said, though she hadn't obviously even glanced at the card. 'You'll understand we have to be very careful, DS Horton.'

'Of course.'

'Even with the police. Not all of your colleagues are above reproach. Not all of them come here with entirely professional motives.'

Horton had little doubt this was true. She could easily imagine some officers she'd encountered in the force as potential abusers. She could equally imagine they might not be too punctilious in exploiting their status. 'I can ensure you my motives are entirely professional,' she said. It was difficult not to find yourself echoing the officialese you encountered in places like this. She imagined they adopted that manner of speech to avoid getting too emotionally entangled in the cases they were dealing with, day in, day out.

'I'm sure.' The woman suddenly seemed to decide she was content to accept Horton at her word. Her face broke into an unexpected smile. 'Ann Callaghan,' she said, as if offering her name as a talisman of goodwill. 'How can I help you?'

'I'm trying to trace the whereabouts of a woman called Elizabeth Hamilton.'

Callaghan was silent for a moment. 'May I ask why?'

'We need to speak to her as part of an enquiry,' Horton said. 'A murder enquiry. We need to speak to her urgently.'

'Is Ms Hamilton a suspect in your enquiry?'

An interesting conclusion to jump to so quickly, Horton thought. 'She's one of a number of key witnesses we need to talk to in connection with the enquiry,' she said, knowing Callaghan would be fully aware her question had remained unanswered.

'You know that Ms Hamilton has an… interesting history?'

'We've been fully informed about her background, yes.'

'Is that history one of the reasons you want to speak to her?'

Horton was sorely tempted to respond, as she had no doubt McKay would have done by now, that she was the one asking the questions. 'Not directly, no. We have substantive grounds for believing she can assist us with the enquiry. Is Ms Hamilton still staying here?'

Callaghan was silent again, her expression suggesting she was considering the options available to her. 'I'm afraid Ms Hamilton's no longer with us. She's moved on.'

'Are you able to inform me where?'

'We have an… associate,' she said, after a pause. 'She sometimes offers places to women here who have nowhere else to go.'

'And that was the case with Hamilton?' Horton was still unclear about Elizabeth Hamilton's circumstances. It was possible she'd inherited her father's estate, given her acquittal for his murder, but it was perhaps more likely Robbins had excluded her from his will. Another line for them to check out in due course.

'As we understood it, yes. She had no friends and other family. Her father… well, you know about him.'

'So she's moved on to stay with this associate you mentioned?'

'A woman called Netty Munro. Look, I have to ask you to treat this with as much discretion as you're able.'

'Of course.' In practice, Horton thought, that might not be much discretion at all, depending on how it all panned out.

'Netty helps to provide women with a route back into normal life. That's one of the problems we have here. The women who come here have often developed a dependency relationship with their abusers. That's how the abusers work – manipulation, gaslighting, grooming, until the target of their abuse comes to believe they have no option but to stay with the abuser. The abusers withhold money, confiscate possessions, ensure the victim is entirely reliant on them. So, however bad the abuse becomes, the victim has little option but to stay. And of course there are usually threats that the abuse will increase if the victim tries to escape.'

None of this was exactly news to Horton, but it was a shock to hear it spelled out so baldly. 'So if they do get away, they come with nothing?'

'More often than not. Sometimes they've managed to squirrel away a few pounds over the years. But almost never enough to start any kind of new life.'

'So what can they do?'

'We can help them in small ways. Sometimes with limited financial help – perhaps the money for a deposit on a flat, or the travel costs needed so they can go to stay with relatives elsewhere. Sometimes we can help them find employment. Mostly it's finding ways of getting them out of the orbit of their abuser, if you see what I mean. But it's rarely easy.'

'And this Netty Munro?'

'Netty's lovely. I don't know how or why she does it. I believe she has her own history. But she was one of the luckier ones, in the sense that at least she had her career and money stashed away, and the means to make the escape. I assume she just wants to help those who don't have that.'

'It sounds admirable.'

'It is. I mean, she can afford to do it. But not many would choose to use their money that way. She has a farm over in the Black Isle. She takes the women in there, provides them with accommodation and food. Lets them stay as long as they wish, and tries to help them find practical ways to restart their lives. She has good contacts in the music and entertainment world–'

'Music and entertainment?' It was strange how they kept coming back to that, Horton thought. Music. Comedy. Show business.

'She used to be a singer. Guitarist. Quite a big name, I believe, in her day, though not really my sort of thing. Natasha Munro.'

The name rang a bell with Horton. She vaguely recalled seeing Natasha Munro on Top of the Pops sometime back in the 0s. Throaty-voiced country singer-songwriter with a rocky edge. Some Christian angle in there too, Horton thought, which might explain what she was doing now. 'Must have a bob or two then presumably?'

'Exactly. She's pretty much retired from all that, as I understand it. But it's a working farm, not a vanity project. She seems to do well from it. But she's chosen to use her wealth for this.'

'Do the women work on the farm? The women who move there from here, I mean.'

'You mean is this just a way of recruiting cheap labour?'

'Well…'

It was the police officer's lot to be the voice of cynicism, Horton thought. Sometimes she wasn't proud of that.

'That's not the way I understand it,' Callaghan went on. 'I think she asks them to do a few tasks around the house in return for their bed and board, but fairly light stuff. If they want to work on the farm, she pays them the same as her other employees. But only does that if they volunteer for it. She's always said to me her objective is simply to provide a safe space for recovery.'

Horton felt appropriately chastised. 'Sorry. I didn't mean to sound critical. I was just trying to understand the set up. Do you have contact details?'

'This is where I need you to be discreet. Netty doesn't have the same kind of security as we have here, though she has some. We keep her location and identity as confidential as we can.'

'I understand.'

Callaghan turned to her computer and tapped on the keyboard for a few moments. A printer on the far side of the room disgorged a sheet of paper, which Callaghan rose to retrieve. 'Here you are.'

'And as far as you know Hamilton's still there?'

'Netty would have informed me if she wasn't.'

'Thank you for your help in this. It really is important that we speak to Hamilton.' Horton paused. 'This may or may not be relevant, I'm not sure. But can I ask you why Hamilton was here in the first place? We're aware of the history, of course, but we weren't aware she was facing any kind of threat now.'

Callaghan frowned. 'She was referred to us by social services after her… after the trial. They said she was in a fragile emotional state and she believed there were still threats to her physical well-being. She refused to be explicit about the nature of those threats, but our understanding was that they related to acquaintances of her late father. In that kind of situation, we carry out whatever due diligence we can to ensure there isn't some ulterior motive for wanting access to the centre, but to an extent we have to take such claims at face value.'

'She hadn't reported any of these concerns to the police,' Horton pointed out.

'We encouraged her to do so, but we could do little more than that. She perhaps had reasons for not entirely trusting the police, if you'll forgive me saying so.'

Horton recognised there was little point in arguing. She rose and held out her hand for Callaghan to shake. 'Thanks again for your time and for the information.'

'I hope I've done the right thing.'

'You have. We're conducting a murder enquiry. All we're trying to do is get to the truth.'

'The truth can often be painful,' Callaghan said.

Horton nodded. *Perhaps more than you know*, she thought. *Perhaps even more than you can imagine.*

CHAPTER 42

'Christ. Of course,' McKay exclaimed as they pulled into the roadside in one of the leafier quarters of Inverness.

'You just got religion, Alec?' Helena Grant asked. 'About time.'

'I'm been trying to think why the Baillie brothers rang a bell,' he said. 'I knew I'd heard it somewhere recently.'

'Go on.'

'They're the owners of the bloody comedy club. The bar where Jimmy McGuire performed before he was killed. I checked out the ownership at the time.'

'Interesting coincidence.'

'Isn't it? Wonder whether Mr McGuire was acquainted with the Baillie brothers.'

'The other question,' Grant said, 'is whether Elizabeth Hamilton was acquainted with the Baillie brothers.'

'Aye, that'll be an interesting one. Any word from Ginny yet?'

'Not so far. I'm guessing it'll take time even for Ginny to prise any information out of that bunch.'

They climbed out of the car and stood for a moment gazing at the house, a detached villa in one of Inverness's more desirable suburbs. The river was close by and the neighbourhood seemed eerily quiet for somewhere so close to the city centre. The house was set in a decent sized garden, thick with mature trees. The ground was a tapestry of green shade and golden sunlight.

'Nice looking place,' Grant commented.

'People with a few quid to spare.' McKay looked around him. 'Hamilton's father's place was around here somewhere too, wasn't it?'

'Just along from here, aye.'

'Another coincidence.'

'This is where the well heeled tend to end up in this town,' Grant said.

'Fair point.' The drive was blocked by marked patrol cars, blue lights still pulsing. 'See the uniforms have done their best to keep it discreet,' McKay commented.

They'd been told the bodies had been discovered at the rear of the house. Horton and McKay followed a path that led round the side of the building, and found themselves in a large rear garden. A woman with bright blonde hair was sitting at a picnic table, sobbing, apparently uncontrollably, comforted by a female uniformed officer. Three more uniformed officers were milling about on the lawn, clearly unsure of their role. There was no real need to protect the crime scene, except perhaps from nosy neighbours, and little more that could be done pending the arrival of the examiners.

The nearest of the uniforms had glanced up as McKay and Horton turned the corner, poised to challenge their presence. But Grant was already brandishing her warrant card. 'Afternoon, Charlie.'

The PC in question, Charlie Keen was familiar to Grant from previous enquiries. She'd always found him helpful and co-operative, which was not something she could say for all his colleagues. He walked forward to meet them, gesturing discreetly towards the blonde woman. 'That's the wife. She's in a bit of a state. She was the one who stumbled across the bodies.'

McKay looked around. 'Where are they? You've not touched them?'

Muir emitted a derisive snort. 'We're not all utter numpties, you know. They're over the wee hill there. Nobody's been near them since they were found.'

'Did the wife disturb the scene at all?'

'She's not really been in a state to ask, but I doubt it. She got close enough to confirm the identities but that was about it, as far as I can tell.'

'She's sure it's her husband and his brother?'

'Seems to be. As I say, difficult to be entirely certain as she's been like that since we arrived.'

Muir led the way up the gentle slope of the lawn. When they reached the point where the garden dropped down towards the far boundary, he stopped and gestured. 'There.'

Grant nodded and turned to McKay. 'Shall we try to have a word with the grieving widow?'

'She seems to be doing a fair bit of grieving. Almost too much, you might say.'

'You might. But you've said it yourself many times, Alec. You can't judge anything from the way people respond to these kind of events.'

'I know. It sends the copper's instincts buzzing, that's all.'

They walked back down the lawn and approached the woman sitting at the table. 'Mrs Baillie?'

She looked up and stared at them with tear-reddened eyes. 'Aye?'

'DCI Grant and DI McKay,' Grant said. 'Do you feel up to talking to us for a few minutes?'

'I suppose.'

'We just need a few words for the moment, Mrs Baillie. Just to understand what's going on—'

'I've no idea what the fuck's going on,' Baillie snapped. 'Who'd want to do that to poor Tommy. And Colin. Someone's going to have to tell his wife too. Poor Rona…' The tears had returned and she collapsed back into silence.

'We'll deal with all that, Mrs Baillie. We'll get the contact details from you and arrange for someone to break the news.' Grant paused, wondering how far it would be possible to take this. 'Can you tell us when you found your husband, Mrs Baillie?'

'I don't know. I mean, I called you pretty much straightaway. Half an hour ago?'

'You'd been out of the house?'

'I'd been away. Tenerife. With a girlfriend. For the last week. We flew back separately though, to Gatwick together but she was going to visit some friends in London, so I flew back up here by myself–' She stopped, as if unsure why she was telling Grant so much. 'I was expecting Tom to meet me at the airport. But he didn't, so I got a taxi. I thought he'd…'

'What did you think, Mrs Baillie?'

There was silence for a moment. 'I thought he'd forgotten. I tried to phone him, but it just went to voicemail. So I thought maybe he'd had to go into the office for some reason or, I don't know…'

Grant exchanged a glance with McKay. 'What does your husband do, Mrs Baillie?'

'He's a company director. They both are. Tom and Col. They own various bars around the city. But they've stepped back from the business a bit in the last year or so, so he's often around the house.'

'Would you have expected your brother-in-law to be here?' Grant asked. 'I mean, did he visit often?'

Baillie seemed taken aback by the question. 'Not really. I mean, we occasionally have them over for supper, but not often. Tom reckoned he and Col spent enough time in each other's pockets at work as it was, so we tended to do our own things outside that. He hardly ever came over apart from that. If they had a business matter to discuss, they'd do it in the office. Tom liked to keep work and home separate as much as he could.'

Grant nodded. 'I don't like to push you on this, Mrs Baillie, so don't feel that you need to answer. But you're sure it is your brother-in-law?'

Baillie blinked but answered immediately. 'It's definitely him. He was the one I checked first. He was rolled against the fence but I could see his face quite clearly. For a moment, I'd thought it was Tommy, then I realised it wasn't. It was Col. There was dried blood all round his neck. Then I knew the other one must be Tommy…'

The tears were returning but Grant felt she had to continue with the question. 'And you're sure it's your husband there, too?'

'Aye, it's Tommy right enough…' She was sobbing again deeply.

Grant gestured to the female PC who had been standing a discreet few metres away. 'Thank you, Mrs Baillie. I'm sorry we had to trouble you with these questions. We needed to be certain of the situation. We'll leave you be for the moment. Is there someone we can contact to be with you? A family member or a friend?'

There was no immediate answer. As Grant and McKay rose, the PC took Grant's place. 'I'll find someone,' she said. 'Leave it with me.'

Grant nodded her thanks and led McKay to the far end of the decking. 'What do you think?'

'Question is why were both brothers here,' McKay said. 'And I know you can never fathom other people's marriages – Christ, I can't even fathom my own – but I got the impression that maybe the Baillies might have been a little semi-detached.'

'The solo holiday, you mean? Not that unusual, especially with business types who can't get time off together.'

'Baillie wasn't exactly a pub landlord. He could presumably take time off when he wanted. But it wasn't just that. It was the way she talked about him not meeting her at the airport. That she thought he might have forgotten. You don't forget that your wife is coming back from holiday.'

'You don't have a memory like mine,' Grant said. 'But point taken.'

'Maybe I'm adding two and two and making who knows what, but I had a sense Baillie might have been engaged in extracurricular activity. Maybe his wife wasn't necessarily the first thing on his mind.'

'An affair?'

'Something worth looking into. Something to push his wife on, maybe, when she's in a state to be pushed.'

'She said there was blood around the brother's neck.'

'Looks like we have another garrotting special then. Which suggests a link with McGuire, Young and Dingwall.'

'Which in turn puts Elizabeth Hamilton firmly in the frame. At least until we have reason to think otherwise. Speaking of which…'

Grant pulled her mobile from her pocket and glanced at the screen. 'I felt it buzzing while we were talking to Baillie. Ginny.' She thumbed the call back button. 'Any luck?' There was silence as she listened to what Horton had to say. 'That sounds straightforward. Are you heading up there? If so, stop when you get to Culbokie. There's a car park by the village shop. Pull in there and wait for us. We don't know if Hamilton's potentially dangerous.' She felt the phone buzz in her hand. 'Hang on, Ginny. I've another call coming in. Stay there while I take it in case it's relevant.' There was almost always a moment like this, Grant thought. The point where the enquiry takes off and everything happens at once. She switched calls and spoke. 'Grant. Yes. Oh, for Christ's sake. When was it called in? Don't let anyone go up there, uniform or plain clothes, until you've heard from me. No, I'll sort that with the powers that be. I'm heading back to HQ. We'll regroup there and decide next steps.' She flicked back to Ginny Horton. 'Ginny. Change of plan. Don't go to Culbokie. Head back to HQ. New developments. We're not going into this without backup. See you in my office.'

She ended the call. McKay was regarding her quizzically. 'New developments?'

'Aye. Just the sort we don't need.'

'Another body?'

'You fucking psychic or something? Aye, another body. And Ginny's found out where Elizabeth Hamilton's staying. So, Mr Mentalist, have a wild stab at guessing where this new body's been found.'

CHAPTER 43

The two young women had backed as far as they could from the body, while still keeping it in sight.

'What did they say?' Alicia said.

'They asked if I was sure it was a dead body. I said I was as sure as I could be. That it was definitely human. That there was blood on the ground all around it, and it was showing no sign of moving. They asked me to check for a pulse and I tried–' She stopped, shivering as if she'd been struck cold despite the warm morning sunshine.

'Could you find one?'

'No. I was probably doing it wrong. But I'm sure she's dead.' Jane looked as if the real meaning of that word had only just struck her. 'She didn't move. She didn't respond at all. They asked me if I knew who she was, and I said I thought I did.'

'Netty?'

'I told them it was Netty Munro, and I gave them her address here. They asked me if I knew how death had occurred. I said we'd found her like that. Maybe there was some kind of accident... Anyway, they told me to leave the scene untouched and step away as far from it as I reasonably could. So they can do the forensic stuff, I suppose.'

'Does that mean they think it's murder?'

Jane could hear the tremble in Alicia's voice. 'I imagine they have to be careful, just in case.'

'Do *you* think it was murder?' Alicia spoke the words as if Jane was the fount of criminal knowledge.

'Why would anyone want to murder Netty?'

'I can't think why anyone would. She's such a lovely warm generous person.'

Jane knew there was little point in arguing with that. But she knew what she'd seen, and she knew that, however Munro had died, it wasn't the result of any accident. She couldn't think much beyond that, couldn't begin to process who might have done this or why.

The two young women had backed away as far as the fencing. The firth was behind them, glittering blue under a clear sky. It was hard to imagine that anything bad could happen on a day like this.

'Do you think we should go back to the house?' Alicia said.

Jane didn't know what they should do. She had a vague sense they ought to stay near to the scene, though the police operator hadn't really said that. She'd just said the police and an ambulance were on their way and would be with them very shortly. The operator had asked if Jane wanted to keep the line open until the police arrived, but Jane had felt too exposed, unsure what she ought to be saying. She wondered whether that had been the right decision.

She felt bewildered, but the reality of what had happened was slowly percolating into her mind. Someone had killed Munro, and that someone could still be there, perhaps somewhere among these trees. Watching her and Alicia.

It was only then that the second thought struck her, although it had been the obvious question from the start. Where was Elizabeth? Was she lying somewhere in the grass nearby, another victim of whoever had done this? Or...

Jane couldn't begin to deal with the implications of that thought. It would be sensible to head back up to the house, wait there for the police. There must be other people working on the farm. They should seek help there.

Instead though, she felt paralysed, unable to move from this spot, with no option but to wait until help arrived. Alicia seemed to be in the same state, although she was perhaps waiting for Jane to provide some lead.

'What's going to happen now?' Alicia whispered.

'How do you mean?'

'To us. What's going to happen to us? If Netty's dead.'

That was something else Jane hadn't considered. They were staying here as Netty's guests. If Netty Munro was dead, they couldn't remain. Who knew what would happen to the house and the farm? Presumably it would be bequeathed to some relative of Munro's, who might want to live there or to sell it, but who wouldn't want the likes of herself or Alicia anywhere in the house. They weren't tenants. They had no legal rights, presumably. In short, they would be back where they started. At the centre, with nowhere to go beyond that.

Jane felt guilty even thinking about those issues with Munro lying dead just a few metres away. But it was another part of the reality they were going to have to live with. In the few minutes since they'd left the house, everything had changed.

'Jane!'

She looked up, startled, at the sound of the voice through the trees. She glanced at Alicia, and placed a finger to her lips as a sign she should keep silent.

'Jane!' the voice called again.

Involuntarily, Jane took a step back against the fence, half-pulling Alicia along with her.

'Jane. It's me, Elizabeth. Are you there?'

Jane's instinct had been to keep quiet and try to hide, moving back from the sound of the voice. But she knew it was already too late. The woodland was too sparse to conceal them. Elizabeth stepped out of the shadows. 'Jane?'

'What's happened, Elizabeth?' Jane called. Her voice sounded steadier than she'd expected. 'What happened to Netty?'

Elizabeth was watching them in silence. There was something in her hand, Jane thought. Something that moved and glittered in the sunlight.

'What happened to Netty?' Jane called again.

Elizabeth said nothing. After a moment, she took a step forward, and Jane thought she was intending to approach them.

She looked around at Alicia, wondering what to do, whether they should try to make their escape to the farmhouse. But when she looked back, Elizabeth had already turned and was moving away from them, into the trees.

A moment later, Jane heard what Elizabeth had presumably already picked out from the birdsong and the whisper of the breeze in the leaves. The sound of a police siren, growing louder.

CHAPTER 44

'I didn't even know this place was here,' McKay observed as Horton pulled the car in alongside the two marked cars that had arrived just ahead of them. An ambulance was following behind, but the paramedics would be going nowhere until the police had worked out exactly what had happened.

'This Netty Munro's obviously got a bob or two,' Grant said from the back seat. They'd reconvened at HQ as arranged, and Grant had organised backup before they'd set off up here. One of the marked cars contained two armed officers. She had no idea what they were dealing with but with six deaths already reported, she was taking no chances. The journey had been punctuated by a series of calls to senior officers and the communications team to clear the lines of authority before they went further. A Chief Super was travelling up somewhere behind them, but had accepted that they shouldn't delay taking action.

They stood for a moment in the sunshine, the team of uniformed officers mustering around them. Somewhere in the distance they could hear the sound of farm machinery, but otherwise the place was silent, as if even the birds had ceased to sing.

'The caller said they'd found the body at the rear of the house,' Grant said. 'She didn't know the cause of death but said there was a significant amount of blood. We can't take any chances. If our various killings are the work of a single individual, we're dealing with someone who's highly dangerous.'

'The killings so far have all been garrottings?' one of the armed officers said. His tone suggested he could hardly believe it.

'So far. I'm assuming that requires an element of surprise, so keep alert.' Grant made her way towards the house. She directed a couple of the uniforms and one of the armed officers to remain at the front. 'In case our killer tries to make a break for it,' she said. 'But for Christ's sake don't shoot unless really necessary. We've already got the media breathing down our necks on this.'

She pressed the front doorbell and held it down, hearing the shrill ringing from inside the house. Better to go through all the protocols, she thought. She gave it a few more seconds, then banged heavily on the door.

'Police!'

She could hear no movement from within. She tried the door handle but the door was locked. 'Okay. Let's head round the back.'

With McKay alongside her, Horton a step behind, and a following trail of the armed officer and two uniforms, Grant made her way around the side of the building. At the rear, there was a working farmyard with open storage buildings to the right. Beyond the farmyard, a track led down past the edge of a barley field towards more grassland and a thicket of trees.

Grant peered along the track. To her left, at the bottom of the barley field, she could see two figures standing by the fence. 'Police! Make your way up here slowly, with your hands above your heads!'

The two figures jerked into motion and slowly shuffled up the edge of the field. As they drew closer, Grant saw they were two young women. Both looked terrified. Grant waited until they'd reached the track, then gestured for them to stand apart. 'Who are you?'

The woman at the front said, 'I'm Jane McDowd. I'm the person who called. We found the body–'

The other woman jumped in. 'I'm Alicia Swinton. It's true. We found the body.'

Grant nodded. 'Okay, you can put your hands down now.' The two women were both dressed in jeans and flimsy T-shirts. It was clear neither was carrying any kind of weapon. 'Where's the body?'

'In those trees to the left of the track.' Jane paused and gulped down a breath. 'Elizabeth's down there too.'

'Elizabeth?' Grant nodded to McKay and Horton.

'She's staying here too. Like we are. She was working with Netty…' Jane trailed off.

'Netty Munro's the owner of this place?'

'Netty's dead,' Alicia said, and for the first time her voice quivered on the edge of tears. 'It's Netty's body.'

'You're sure this Elizabeth is still down there?' Grant said.

'We saw her,' Jane said. 'Just a few minutes ago.'

'Okay.' Grant turned to one of the uniformed officers. 'Can you look after these two? The rest of us will head down and see what's going on.'

The sun was high in the empty sky, and there was not even a breath of wind. The only sound was the rasp of their own footsteps on the rough ground. Not much chance of approaching surreptitiously, Grant thought.

For all their caution, Elizabeth's appearance was still unexpected. She stepped slowly out of the shadow of the trees, a slim figure dressed in black. Her face was pale and her eyes looked dead, expressionless.

Ginny Horton would say later that Elizabeth Hamilton's expression was the same as when Horton found her on Rosemarkie Beach on the rain-soaked night when she'd drowned her father and Denny Gorman. Her face was blank, the look of someone who had lost contact with the world, who no longer felt any responsibility for anything she might have done.

There was something in her left hand, Grant saw. Something that glittered and writhed in the afternoon sun. As Grant took a step forward, the object dropped onto the track. A long wire.

'Elizabeth?'

Elizabeth Hamilton blinked.

'Where's Netty Munro, Elizabeth?'

There was a prolonged silence, then Hamilton turned to point into the trees. 'She's there. She's dead.'

'Did you kill her, Elizabeth?'

'She needed to die.'

'Why did she need to die?'

'She was one of them.' Hamilton's voice was as dead as her eyes. 'Or she might as well have been. He wouldn't accept that. Didn't want to believe it. Wouldn't believe it.'

'Who wouldn't believe it, Elizabeth?'

'He wouldn't. I couldn't persuade him. Just like he wouldn't believe me about Jack.'

'Jack?'

'He was wrong about Jack.'

Grant was as sure now as she could be that Hamilton was unarmed. She took a step forward, took Hamilton gently by the arm, and led her over to the two uniformed officers. 'Take her back up to the car. Make sure she's secure and we'll deal with the formalities in a bit. First priority is to check out Netty Munro's condition. Send the ambulance down here. They should be able to get it down this track okay. Tell them to bring it as far as the trees and we'll meet them there.'

McKay had produced an evidence bag and a pair of disposable gloves – Grant was always bemused by what he managed to carry in his pockets – and was bending down to retrieve the object that Hamilton had dropped to the ground. He was obviously experiencing some difficulty in getting it into the bag without risking any contamination. He finally succeeded, winding the wire carefully into a loop. He looked up. 'Looks like a guitar string.'

Grant nodded. It made as much sense as everything else in this enquiry, she thought. 'Okay, Let's go and track down Netty Munro.'

CHAPTER 45

'It doesn't make sense,' McKay said. 'I mean, it would make our lives a hell of a lot easier, but I just can't see it.'

Grant leaned back in her chair and peered at him through narrowed eyes. 'You like to make things difficult, don't you, Alec? Always keen to add your little extra layer of complication.'

'I just like to make sure we've got things *right*. Just because I'm the only one around here with standards.'

'Aye, that'll be it, Alec. Not because you're the only one who's a major pain in the arse.'

'I'm sure this constitutes some form of bullying. What do you reckon, Ginny?'

Horton was watching the exchange with her familiar bemusement. 'You're not seriously expecting me to express a view about that?'

'So what have we got?' Grant said. 'We've charged Hamilton with Netty Munro's murder. We're on pretty safe ground with that one, given she was found holding the murder weapon. One of Munro's own guitar strings.'

'She was found presiding over the dead bodies of her father and a man who'd abused her,' McKay pointed out. 'She still managed to get herself acquitted. She didn't actually confess to Munro's murder. She just said that she had to die, whatever that meant.'

Grant nodded, wearily. It had been a long day already, and they weren't at the end of it yet. She wondered, tangentially, whether McKay had taken the trouble to call Chrissie to let her know he'd be late home yet again, and she wondered how Chrissie might have taken this start to their rebooted married life. 'Okay, but accepting she might still pull off a "one leap and she was free" deal, we should be on safe ground. Even the Depute Procurator agrees.'

'Bound to be fine then,' McKay said sardonically.

'So what about Jack Dingwall? We have clear evidence she was in Dingwall's house on the night he was killed. Killed using the same or a similar method as that used to kill Munro.'

They'd found Munro's body in the patch of woodland, just as Jane had told them. The cause of death was the same as that of the previous victims. The steel guitar string had been pulled round her throat and tightened until it had cut deeply into her throat. The removal of the string had released the blood spread copiously around the body. In the end, they'd had to leave the paramedics cooling their heels, awaiting the arrival of the examiners.

'What was it she said about Dingwall?' McKay said.

'Assuming that it was Dingwall she was referring to, she said something about a "he" being wrong about him, just as this "he" had been wrong about Munro. So who's the "he"?'

'McGuire, maybe?' Horton offered.

'Maybe, but did McGuire know Munro? He might have done, I suppose. But that just brings us back to the question of how all this fits together.'

'Time for us to go and interview Hamilton some more?'

'Aye, once the doc's finished with her and given us the all clear. We need to make sure we do this by the book.' Hamilton's solicitor had argued she was in no state to be interviewed and had insisted that her condition should be reviewed by a doctor.

'Ach, she's fine,' McKay said. 'This is just her up to her usual tricks. It's like the guy who kills his parents and claims mitigation because he's an orphan.'

'Nevertheless,' Grant said. 'We do it by the book. Don't want anyone to accuse us of being – what was it? – "acerbic and unsympathetic".'

'Bugger off,' McKay said. 'What about the other killings then? McGuire and Young, and then the two Baillie brothers. Do we really think she's capable of that?'

'You thought she might have been capable of committing the Candles and Roses killings,' Grant pointed out.

McKay nodded. 'Aye. All that still keeps nagging at me. On the one hand, I don't have much doubt she'd have been capable of those killings and these ones. Psychologically, I mean. She's a genuine psychopath. There's something about her eyes, about the way she looks at you. There's no warmth, no feeling. No sense she's anything but utterly calculating and manipulative.' He paused. 'Her father's daughter, I suppose.'

'But?'

'But it's whether she'd have been capable of it physically. I mean, she's a wee slip of a thing.'

'But isn't that the thing with the garrotting?' Horton said. 'It depends more on the element of surprise than physical strength. If you get the wire round the victim's neck, they don't have much of a chance to fight back.'

'I'll bow to your expertise,' McKay said. 'I'm sure you're right. I was thinking more about the physical effort involved in dragging Young's body into McDermott's Yard or dragging Dimmock's body down the hill to the field where it was found. Or even dragging the two Baillie brothers' bodies up to the top of that bloody garden to push them down the other side. The same's true of the Candles and Roses killings. Whoever was responsible managed to get the bodies out past the Clootie Well, out to the caves in Rosemarkie, up to the top floor of that old retirement home. None of that would have been easy.'

'She managed to drag her father's and Denny Gorman's body into the car and then down to Rosemarkie Beach,' Grant said. 'People are often capable of more than you expect.'

'Maybe,' McKay said. 'Let's just say it's left me with a few doubts.'

'You think she didn't do these murders?' Grant paused. 'Or the Candles and Roses ones?'

'I don't know. The Candles and Roses killings we had pinned on her father anyway, so maybe we can forget about those. Maybe.

These killings – I don't know. The evidence points to her, but I just can't quite see it.'

'So if you're right,' Grant said. 'Then either she didn't commit the other murders or…'

'Or she had an accomplice,' Horton said.

McKay nodded. 'Which might explain the "he".'

'But–' Grant stopped as the phone buzzed on her desk. 'Grant. Yep. You're sure about that? Happy to put your name and your professional reputation behind it? Aye, well, I appreciate that the latter probably isn't much of a sacrifice. But thanks anyway, Rob. That should make life a little easier.' She ended the call and turned back to the other two. 'That was the doc. Clean bill of health with regard to Hamilton. He reckons she might have been suffering from a touch of shock.'

'Aye, shocked that she'd just put a fucking guitar string round some bugger's neck,' McKay muttered.

'And she might be in a fragile emotional state, but he says she's perfectly fit to be interviewed as long as we don't push her too hard. Reading slightly between the lines, I had the impression that he thought she was putting it on a bit, but he could never prove that.'

'Let's go then,' McKay was already on his feet.

'Sit down, Alec. I reckon, in the circumstances, that I should lead the interview with Ginny. You can watch from the viewing room.'

'Oh, for–'

'"Acerbic and unsympathetic", Alec. Which by coincidence is also the name of every firm of solicitors I've had to deal with. Look, we're doing this by the book. I don't want her to have any chance of slipping out of this one on a technicality, even if your ego gets bruised along the way.'

'It's not about my ego,' McKay said. 'It's just about making sure the job's done properly.'

'You're saying that Ginny and I aren't capable of doing that?'

'No, no. Of course not. It's just–'

'Stop digging, Alec,' Horton said. 'You'll only make it worse.'

'Okay then, you two go and do your best. I can always step in and sort it out if I need to.'

'Don't be holding your breath, Alec,' Grant said. 'Tell you what, why don't you go and make a nice cup of coffee for those of us who are doing the real heavy lifting.'

CHAPTER 46

Grant went through the formalities of starting the tape and introducing the interview, then turned to Elizabeth Hamilton. Before she could speak, Hamilton's lawyer, a skinny balding middle-aged man with reading glasses he left permanently balanced on the end of his nose, leaned forward. 'My client isn't prepared to answer any questions relating to the death of Natasha Munro.'

'Is that so?' Grant said slowly. 'Why would that be, Mr…?' She consulted the card which the lawyer had handed her earlier. 'Why would that be, Mr Bannatyne?'

'For the moment, she doesn't wish to add anything to what's already been said.'

'Which is very little indeed. But for the moment that's fine. Ms Hamilton, can I ask you about Mr Jack Dimmock. Also known by his stage name of Jack Dingwall. I believe from what you said earlier that you may be acquainted with Mr Dimmock. Is that correct?'

Bannatyne leaned forward to whisper something into Hamilton's ear. Her expression suggested she'd decided to ignore his advice, whatever it might have been. 'Yes, I know Mr Dimmock. I've known him for years.'

'How do you come to know him?'

There was a brief silence before Hamilton responded. 'He was a friend of my father's.'

Grant hadn't been expecting that. 'How did he come to know your father?'

Hamilton shrugged. 'I'm not sure, initially. Probably because my dad gave him some therapy. He's the sort who always needs therapy. But he became a sort of – friend of the family.'

'Have you seen him recently?'

The lawyer leaned forward again, but Hamilton waved him back dismissively. 'Aye, couple of nights ago.'

'Where did you meet him?'

'At his house. Up in the hills.'

Grant caught Horton's eye. 'Why did you go to see him?' Horton asked.

There was a hesitation this time. 'I went to have a brief chat with him. About some business.'

'What sort of business would that have been, Ms Hamilton?' Grant asked.

Bannatyne leaned forward again, clearly intending to be heard this time. 'Look, I'm sorry, but does this have any relevance to the charges you've brought against my client?'

'That's what we're trying to ascertain,' Grant said.

'You don't need to respond to any of these questions if you choose not to,' Bannatyne said to Hamilton.

Hamilton was staring at the table, her expression unreadable.

'When we found you at Natasha Munro's house,' Grant said, 'you said that "he" was wrong about Jack. By Jack, you meant Jack Dimmock?'

'Aye.' Hamilton's voice was almost inaudible. Bannatyne looked as if he was about to intervene again, but Grant shot him a look and he settled back into his seat.

'Who was wrong? Who's "he"?'

'Jack wasn't one of them. He wasn't like that. He tried to protect me.'

'What do you mean by "one of them"?'

More silence. Grant sat back, content to let the silence build. Bannatyne looked as if he was desperate to chip in with some worthless two penn'orth, but Grant's glare seemed to persuade him otherwise. Hamilton was still staring at the table, as though she could see something there that was invisible to the others in the room. At last, in a voice that was little more than a whisper, she said, 'I went there to warn him.'

'Warn him of what?'

'That he was in danger. That his life was in danger.'

'Why was his life in danger?'

'Because–' Hamilton stopped suddenly, as if up to that point she'd forgotten where she was, who she was talking to.

In the resulting silence, Bannatyne tried again. 'I really don't see what relevance–'

Grant looked up at him. 'Mr Dimmock was found dead. We believe he was unlawfully killed, and the manner of his death is very similar to that of Natasha Munro. We have clear evidence of your client's presence at Mr Dimmock's house on the evening of the killing.'

Bannatyne looked deflated. 'What kind of evidence?'

'Fingerprint evidence. DNA evidence. Unequivocal.'

Bannatyne looked as if he might be about to challenge that assertion, but Hamilton spoke again. 'I've already told you I was there. I went to warn him. He gave me a glass of wine. He was kind like he always is. But I could tell he wasn't taking me seriously. He never did until it was too late. That was one of the problems.' She paused, her expression suggesting she'd only now registered what Grant had said. 'He's dead?'

Grant nodded. 'He was killed the night you were there.'

Hamilton was staring at her open-mouthed. 'But… he was alive when I left. I told him to take care. I told him to take what I'd said seriously.' Her expression shifted suddenly to one of anger. '*Shit!* That stupid stupid fucking bastard…'

It wasn't clear to Grant whether this comment was directed at Dimmock or someone else. 'Just to be clear for the record,' Grant said, 'you're saying that Dimmock was alive when you left his house?'

'Of course he was fucking alive. I didn't think anything would happen that night. For Christ's sake.'

'What time did you leave?'

'I don't know. About ten, I suppose.'

Grant consulted the notes from the interviews they'd already conducted with Jane McDowd and Alicia Swinton, the two other young women who had both been staying in Netty Munro's house. Both had been provided with temporary accommodation until their futures could be resolved. 'According to Jane McDowd, you left Natasha Munro's house early that morning. What had you been doing for the rest of that day?'

There was another long silence before Hamilton said, 'I took the bus back into Inverness. I needed to think. I spent most of the day just walking by the river.'

'Thinking about what?'

'About what was happening. He'd called me. Told me it had started. What we'd always talked about.'

Another mention of the mysterious "he", Grant thought. She had the sense that Hamilton didn't want to say more, didn't want to expose this other individual. Her instinct was to approach the issue obliquely. She didn't want Hamilton to clam up entirely. 'What had you always talked about?'

'Revenge,' she said. 'Proper revenge. Full revenge. Like we'd already done with my father.'

Grant decided to leave that particular avenue unexplored for the moment. 'Revenge for what?'

'For what they did. For what they all did.'

'What did they do, Elizabeth?'

It was the first time Grant had used Hamilton's forename in the interview, and Hamilton looked at her as if she'd used some term of affection. 'They traded us. They used us. They exploited us.'

'Who are they?'

'All of them. My dad. McGuire. Young. The Baillies. All the bastards.'

Grant exchanged a look with Horton. 'But not Dimmock?'

'Not Dimmock, no. He tried to stop them, when he realised the extent of what was happening. He was going to blow the whistle. That's why they stopped him.'

'Stopped him?'

'Framed him. It was a set up. The woman who accused him was one of theirs. One of us.'

Grant frowned, unsure she was entirely following this. 'So why didn't he expose them anyway? He wouldn't have had much to lose by that point.'

Hamilton laughed unexpectedly. 'You think? They'd concocted a whole lot more on him. Worse stuff. Stuff that would have got him sent down for much longer. He'd already lost credibility, and he had a reputation for drinking anyway. Even if he'd tried to expose them at that point, no one would have believed him. So the deal was that he did his time, kept his head down and his mouth shut. He did, and they left him alone.'

'Until now.'

'But that wasn't them. That was the point. That was Andy.'

Grant tried to keep her face expressionless. 'Andy?'

'I told him Jack wasn't one of them. That Jack was different. He went along with that, or he pretended to, but I knew he didn't really believe me. He wanted to take Jack down along with the rest of them. He thought he deserved it…' She looked back up at Grant. 'So you're saying he went there that night after I'd been there? The stupid, stupid bastard…'

'You said you spent the day wandering round Inverness, just thinking,' Grant said. 'So what made you decide to go up to Jack Dimmock's house in the evening?'

'It was Andy. Like I say, he'd phoned me earlier to tell me it had started. He told me he'd dealt with Young. That he'd left the body where it wouldn't be found for a while.'

Grant nodded. The detail of Ronnie Young's death hadn't yet been made public. 'Did he say where, Elizabeth?'

'He said he'd left it in McDermott's Yard, that place near the airport.'

Grant drew in a breath. They were making progress. 'Okay,' she said. 'So you knew that Andy had… dealt with Ronnie Young. Why didn't you head up to Dimmock's straightaway, if you wanted to warn him?'

Hamilton gazed back at her as if the question was nonsensical. 'Andy told me he was going to do it slowly, take his time. Minimise the risks. I thought there'd be time.' Her eyes were brimming with tears. 'He hadn't told me about McGuire…'

'McGuire?'

'I only saw it because I was in town, though I suppose I'd have seen it on the news soon enough. I'd been walking down by Ness Islands and then I walked back up the river into the centre later in the afternoon. I saw all the police activity going on. Something big, obviously. I stopped and asked one of the police officers what was going on. He told me it was a murder.'

Grant cursed inwardly, wondering what numpty had said that to a passing member of the public. 'You thought it was McGuire?'

'I knew he'd been performing at the club in town. Andy had told me about that, and we'd wondered whether it would give us the opportunity. But Andy's plan had been to do it more discreetly, later. He'd done that with Young. Kept an eye on his movements. Caught him outside his home when he was returning from Edinburgh. Had him dealt with and in the back of Andy's car before he even knew what was happening. He told me he was planning for the longer term with McGuire. If he was up here performing for longer, there'd be more time.'

'So what happened?'

'I don't know. I phoned him and asked him what had happened to McGuire. He wouldn't tell me at first. Then he got angry. He said that McGuire hadn't changed at all, and that he'd decided he had to be dealt with straightaway. Something to do with the way McGuire had behaved at the club. I panicked and thought he'd go after Jack Dimmock next. I told him not to, kept telling him that Dimmock wasn't what he thought. But I knew he wasn't listening. He just thought I was infatuated with Dimmock, that I didn't recognise that he'd groomed me.'

Grant had been half-expecting that Bannatyne would try to intervene while Hamilton was talking. But he looked as if all the fight had gone from him, as if he could scarcely believe what he was hearing. Grant couldn't really blame him. 'So you decided to warn Jack Dimmock? How did you get up there?' Grant wasn't sure why she asked this question, except that she wanted to understand the sequence of events as fully as possible. The other women staying with Netty Munro had said that Elizabeth had no transport, and she herself had mentioned getting the bus into Inverness.

Hamilton laughed. 'I took my dad's old van. It was still there at the house. The house itself was all locked up, but I could get into the shed where the van was kept and the keys were still sitting in there. Took me a few goes to get it going.'

Bannatyne leaned forward. 'My client's father died intestate. Following her recent acquittal, my client was expecting to inherit his estate though clearly it will have to go through probate.'

If Bannatyne was trying to mitigate his client's apparent car theft, Grant thought, then he really hadn't understood what was going on. 'So you drove up to Dimmock's,' she said to Hamilton. 'What happened there?'

'He was friendly. He's always friendly.' Grant noted the present tense. 'He invited me in, gave me a glass of wine and a sandwich. I hadn't eaten all day, though I hadn't really noticed. I told him about Andy. I told him about what was happening. I don't think he believed me. He said he'd seen nothing on TV about any murders.'

At that point, Grant thought, *we hadn't yet discovered Young's body and the McGuire killing was still under wraps*. There'd just been some anodyne report on the local news about a body being found in the city centre, with no reference to foul play. 'I begged him to take care, go away for a bit. He said he'd be careful but he'd only just moved into this place so no one even knew he was there.'

'You must have known he was there,' Horton pointed out.

'We'd kept in touch. He'd sent me a text with his new details on.'

'Did you share those details with Andy?'

'No. Not knowingly. But Andy's good at winkling out that sort of information. He probably got hold of my phone at some point and found the text.'

'Okay,' Grant said, trying to get her mind around the whole story. 'So you warned him and he didn't listen. Then later that same night, unknown to you, this Andy pays him an unannounced visit so he can deal with him.'

'That must be what happened.'

'You expect us to believe that? That you went there on your own to warn Dimmock. That you didn't go with this Andy. That you didn't participate in his killing.'

The tears finally came and Hamilton dropped her head to the table, sobbing. Maybe this was real, Grant thought, or maybe it was just another act. Finally, Hamilton raised her head and stared at Grant through reddened eyes. 'It's true. What I'm saying. It's all true.'

Grant nodded, her expression giving nothing away. 'So you left Dimmock's house at… what, about ten? What happened after that?'

'I just drove around for a bit. Went to the beach at Rosemarkie.' She glanced across at Horton. 'Just sat there for a while looking at the waves. For old times' sake, you know? Then eventually I thought I might as well head back to Netty Munro's house. I'd nowhere else to go. I dumped the car in one of the back lanes round there, then went the rest of the way on foot.'

'Were you already intending to kill Natasha Munro then?'

Bannatyne was about to interrupt but Hamilton said, 'I didn't know what I was going to do. I was waiting for Andy to get back to me. I wasn't sure it wasn't all talk. I wasn't sure that he really had killed Ronnie Young. I mean, this was all different again from what happened with my father.'

'What happened with your father, Elizabeth?' Grant flicked a look at Bannatyne, daring him to speak.

Hamilton looked surprised at the question, as if Grant had changed the subject. 'The idea was to frame him. He didn't kill those women. We did. Me and Andy.'

CHAPTER 47

Grant glanced towards the door. McKay was in the next room, listening in to all this. It sounded as if his second thoughts might have been correct all along. 'You mean the killings last year?'

Hamilton looked at her as if she barely understood the question. 'Yes,' she said finally. 'Those three women. We killed them. We left the candles and roses there. As a sort of tribute, I suppose. Me and Andy. It was us.'

'Why did you kill them?'

'Like I say, partly to put my dad in the frame for the killings. I was sick of him getting away with what he'd done. Leaving all those victims in his trail. And him living in that big house of his, making more and more money, having more and more success. I wanted to bring that to an end.'

'You told us your father was the killer.'

'That was the idea. I still think he had killed people. Other young women. Maybe the ones he couldn't pass on to his mates. And even if he didn't kill them literally, he destroyed them inside. That was what he did to me. He wrecked me, he wrecked my life. I went through life thinking it was my fault, that I'd somehow allowed it to happen. I'd nothing but those awful memories of what he'd done.' She stopped. 'That was the other reason we killed them. I wanted to release them from all that. I wanted to take them to the only places they'd been happy. I wanted them to be remembered for who they were, not what had happened to them.'

Exactly what McKay had suggested, Grant thought. God, maybe the old bugger was more sensitive than she'd given him credit for. 'But you didn't just frame your father, Elizabeth. You killed him. And Denny Gorman.'

Hamilton shook her head, as if to deny this. 'That was Andy too. He decided to have one more go at my dad. Try to get a bit more cash out of him before it was too late.'

A bit more cash, Grant thought. She wondered whether Robbins had been blackmailed by his daughter for longer than she'd initially suggested to them. 'So what happened?'

'We went round to his house, that last day.'

Grant could see that Bannatyne was on the point of interrupting, so she pre-empted him. 'That isn't what you said under oath in court, Elizabeth. You said he'd snatched you.'

Hamilton shrugged, as if this no longer mattered. 'I was lying.' To her left, Bannatyne dropped his head into his hands, his whole body a picture of submission. 'We went round there. My dad hadn't seen Andy face to face since… for years. Didn't know who he was at first. Then when we told him what we wanted, he got angry. Andy dealt with him. The same way we'd dealt with the women.'

Grant drew in a breath, startled by the calm way that Hamilton was speaking. Grant had noted the one momentary hesitation in Hamilton's story. Robbins hadn't seen Andy since… since what? Out loud, Grant said, 'And Denny Gorman?'

'He was nothing,' Hamilton said. 'But we were both angry with him. Andy was going to deal with my dad, so we decided we'd deal with both of them.'

Horton had been following everything with obvious fascination. She raised an eyebrow to Grant, seeking her permission to ask a question. They both knew how delicate the interview had become, the importance of keeping Hamilton talking. 'Where was Andy,' Horton said, 'that night on the beach? You were on your own.'

Grant herself had begun to wonder whether Andy might be some figment of Hamilton's imagination, perhaps some manifestation of whatever mental disturbance had enabled her to do all this.

'He was there, watching. He'd wanted me to leave with him, abandon the bodies in the water. But I wanted to stay there. Make sure it happened. Make sure they really were dead. He said he was going, but I don't think he did. He didn't take the car, and I don't think he could have got very far when you arrived. He stayed to watch.'

Grant could see that, even now, Horton was disturbed by the thought that there might have been a third presence, watching while she had grappled with Hamilton in the water. 'So why didn't he come back?' Horton asked. 'Why didn't he come back to save you?'

Hamilton gave an unexpected smile. 'That's not Andy. That's not what he does. He doesn't really care about anything. Not even me. Not me at all, in fact. He's gone beyond that. I think he cared about Netty, in his own weird way, which is why he didn't want to believe the truth about her. Didn't want to believe she was as bad as the rest of them. He thought things were different with her. He couldn't even accept the way she'd manipulated her own sister. Henry was the only really innocent one in all of this, but Andy wouldn't believe that. He thought I'd got it the wrong way round. That I'd dealt with the wrong one.'

'You told him you'd dealt with Munro?' Grant said, her mind recoiling at the way they were all accepting this euphemism.

'I called him. After I'd done it. Told him what I'd done. He was angry. But I hung up. I didn't care any more. I just want us all dealt with. We all deserve it. I don't care what he does.'

Grant felt a chill in her stomach, prompted less by what Hamilton was saying than by her dead, expressionless tone of voice. She wondered whether Hamilton knew yet about the Baillie brothers, who were somehow presumably also part of this. She wondered what else Hamilton might know.

The silence in the room grew. Bannatyne was staring at the ground, clearly wanting to be anywhere but where he was. Hamilton was gazing blankly into the air.

Grant looked across at Horton, and said to Hamilton, 'You need to tell us, Elizabeth. Who is Andy?'

Hamilton's blank look remained unchanged. After a moment, she said, 'He's my cousin.'

CHAPTER 48

McKay had been listening to a relay of the interview in the next room. He'd been joined, much to his irritation, by Chief Superintendent Gerry Tarrant, who'd recently been transferred to the region on a promotion and was now at least notionally their collective boss. So far, his approach had been largely characterised as 'hands off', which suited McKay perfectly. Today though, he'd insisted on joining them, presumably wanting both to ensure his backside was well and truly covered if anything went wrong and that he could claim his share of the credit if everything went well. Fair enough, McKay thought. That was what the management classes were for.

To his credit, he'd mostly sat in silence. In the latter stages, he turned to McKay. 'What do you reckon?'

McKay shrugged. 'I reckon I've largely been proven right about Hamilton, though too late. Helena was right. I should have said something at the time.'

Tarrant looked baffled at this response, which was what McKay had been aiming for. 'So what do you think we're talking about here? Some sort of paedophile ring?'

'It's looking that way. I don't know how much of it was underage, but I'm guessing some of it was. Maybe prostitution too. A network operating in the entertainment industry. Young women, and presumably young men, assuming this Andy actually exists, being passed around for the pleasure of the artistes.' McKay spat out the last word in disgust.

'Jesus,' Tarrant said. McKay had heard on the grapevine that, for a senior officer, Tarrant appeared to have lived an oddly sheltered life. Public school and one of the more upmarket 'ancients', McKay guessed, but he hadn't bothered to check. 'And one of them was Hamilton's own father?'

'Robbins? Looks like it. He wasn't really a showbiz type, but on the fringes of that world. Supposedly a therapist of some kind, originally, but did the whole motivational speaker bit. My guess is he was the main fixer behind all this.'

'And these two have been picking them off one by one?'

'Seems so.' McKay had been musing on what Hamilton had been saying, his brain barely engaging in the conversation with Tarrant. 'The question is, whether they've all been picked off yet.'

'How'd you mean?'

'I've just got an uneasy feeling this isn't done.' McKay had pushed himself to his feet and was beginning his usual prowl around the room. 'Look, I'm going to go and check something out. Just a stupid hunch. But if I'm right, I might save a life. If I'm wrong, I might waste an hour or so and look a bit daft. Wouldn't be the first time for either.'

'I don't understand—'

'Don't worry,' McKay said, biting back the suggestion that he didn't really expect Tarrant to understand.

'The interview's not finished yet,' Tarrant pointed out.

'I know,' McKay said. 'But I may have a spoiler. Just tell Helena to give me a call on my mobile as soon as she's finished. Tell her it's urgent.'

'Yes, but—'

'As soon as she's finished,' McKay repeated as the door slammed behind him.

He scurried down the stairs, deciding to take his own car rather than wasting time picking up a pool vehicle. If he was right, there was a chance he might already be too late.

It was late afternoon and the traffic up to the Longman roundabout was tailing back. It occurred to McKay that he hadn't updated Chrissie on what had happened and its likely impact on his getting home. He hesitated a moment and dialled the number.

'Let me guess,' Chrissie said immediately. 'You're going to be late home?'

'Aye, well, just a bit. Look, I'm really sorry, pet. You know how much we've got on–'

She laughed but it didn't sound like the cynical laugh she might once have offered in response. 'Don't worry, Alec. I've told you. I know it goes with the job. That's never been the problem.'

'You're sure?'

'Of course I'm sure. Just keep me updated when you can. I'll keep something warm for you.'

'You don't need to do that.'

'But I will anyway. If you're very lucky I might save you some food as well.'

It was McKay's turn to laugh. 'I don't deserve you.'

'Obviously not, but you're stuck with me again. And Alec…?'

'Aye?'

'Take care, won't you? Whatever it is you're up to.'

She ended the call before he could ask how she knew he was up to anything. That was another thing about Chrissie, he thought. They almost never discussed the detail of any investigation that he was involved in, but somehow she could always tell if he was about to do something outside the norm. Something that might involve a level of risk. Even then, she rarely said anything explicit. Just asked him to take care.

For the first time in a long while, it occurred to McKay to wonder quite what it must be like for Chrissie. Sitting there at home, waiting for his return, not even knowing what he was doing but knowing that – not often, but often enough for her – this might be the time he didn't come home.

The lights changed and he pulled away from the roundabout, picking up speed as he crossed the Kessock Bridge, the Beauly Firth glittering in the afternoon sunshine. He was being sentimental, of course. Most of the time, there was little risk in his job. He'd face more danger if he was back in uniform, patrolling the city centre on a wild Saturday night.

The traffic cleared as he crossed the bridge, and he pulled into the outside lane, putting his foot down on the accelerator, keeping just within the speed limit. There were sometimes police cameras or even cars waiting for those who accelerated too much away from the bridge. The last thing McKay wanted was to be pulled over by one of his esteemed colleagues.

He reached the Tore roundabout and continued on up the A9 until he reached the right turn off to Culbokie. As he was waiting to turn, the phone rang.

'Afternoon. Helena. All done?'

'Where the hell are you, Alec? Why do I have a bad feeling about this?'

'Just heading into Culbokie.'

She was silent for a moment. 'You didn't wait for the end of the interview?'

'Ach, I could see how it was going to end.'

'Hamilton finally told us who this Andy is.'

'Aye. Drew Douglas.'

'Fuck sake, Alec. You doing the psychic thing again?'

'Not really.' There was finally a gap in the traffic and he pulled onto the Culbokie road. 'It had been nagging at me. When I spoke to him, he seemed to have too much knowledge of that whole scene, all the stuff that had happened before he was born. Spun me some bollocks about writing a book, but it didn't feel right.'

'Some people are just anoraks, Alec. You must have met them.'

'Aye, people like Jock Henderson. This didn't feel like that. But the clincher was in the interview, when Hamilton said they were intending to delay dealing with Jimmy McGuire until he came up for a longer stint at the comedy club. The only person who could guarantee that that would happen is the guy who does the booking there. Andrew fucking Douglas. Andy. I'm guessing he thought Drew Douglas was a better stage name for a would-be master of fucking mirth.'

'Smart arse,' Grant said. 'So if this mere mortal can keep up with your lightning brain, I'm guessing you're heading up to Henrietta Dowling's place?'

'There's hope for you yet. Aye, that's me. I caught the bit about Hamilton and Douglas being cousins. I'd been bothered about the whole set up with this Netty Munro and Henrietta Dowling, and why Hamilton had gone there. Or, more to the point, why Munro was willing to have her staying there. She didn't seem to fit the profile of the people Munro normally took in. Jane McDowd and Alicia Swinton seem to have felt the same. They thought there was something odd about Hamilton's behaviour to Munro. So I wondered if there was another reason she was there–'

'If you'd listened to another ten minutes of the interview with Hamilton, you'd have found out, Alec,' Grant pointed out.

'That Netty Munro was her mother, aye. I'm right, aren't I?'

'Anyone told you no one likes a smart-arse?'

'You've told me, more than once. So the sad thing is that Munro thought she was taking Hamilton in to protect her.'

'Looks like it. Hamilton had contacted her to say she didn't feel safe. She told Munro that, after what had happened with her father, some of the other members of the network would have her in their sights. That was why Munro didn't let on to the others that Hamilton was her daughter.'

'That's another tiny thing that should have troubled me from the start. Though I never got round to thinking about it properly. What had happened to Hamilton's mother. By the time she was arrested, it didn't matter. I'd assumed Robbins was a widower or that she'd walked out on him and he'd got custody. Mr Respectable.'

'Simpler than that,' Grant said. 'Munro and Robbins were never an item. Just a one-night stand and Elizabeth Hamilton was the result. Good Catholic Netty Munro didn't want an abortion, but also didn't want anything to impede her career which was just beginning to take off in the US. Robbins was the white knight charging to the rescue. Munro took a few months out of the limelight before the pregnancy showed. She still wasn't a big enough name for the media to pay any attention. Robbins took on the fatherly role, no doubt supported by a decent stipend from Munro, and there you were.'

'And Elizabeth Hamilton never forgave her.'

'Seems not. As far as Hamilton was concerned, Munro was always part of this. She was always on the list.'

McKay had reached the centre of the small village of Culbokie. He passed the village shop of his right, the pub on his left. There wasn't much more to the village than stretches of farmland and scatterings of houses. 'And she didn't trust Douglas to do the deed.'

'That's what she said. But he'd always been closer to Netty Munro than she had. Which raises some interesting psychological questions in itself. But she reckoned Douglas had never really seen Munro as part of the network, though it looks as if, at the very least, she'd been happy to turn a blind eye to it.'

'Not to mention persuading her own sister not to expose it.'

'Henrietta Dowling? I assumed you must have worked that out. That why you're up there then?'

'That's it. You think I'm wasting my time?'

He could sense Grant hesitating at the other end of the line. 'Maybe not. She's the only one left on the list now, from what Hamilton told us. Whether she really deserves to be is another question.'

'As is the question of whether Douglas would be prepared to kill his own mother, if he was reluctant to kill Netty Munro.' McKay had reached the turn off into the small estate of houses.

'Hamilton said that was why she'd done it. To show him they had to go all the way. Eradicate them all. That was the word she used. Eradicate.'

McKay had reached the end of the estate. In the driveway ahead of him, there was the four-by-four he'd seen parked here before, with a battered old Volvo estate behind it. That guy down at McDermott's Yard, Gordon Stewart, had mentioned seeing a Volvo estate. 'I'm here,' McKay said. 'Wish me luck.'

'I've done more than that, you numpty. I called out backup as soon as I heard where you'd gone. There's a team coming down from Dingwall, so they won't be far behind you.'

'Okay. Thanks,' he said, conscious he sounded more grudging than he'd intended. 'No, you're right. I shouldn't be doing this on my own.'

'Of course you bloody well shouldn't. But you're Alec fucking McKay, aren't you, so what else are you going to do?'

'That's the way I see it.'

'And you might be right. We can't afford to delay if there's a chance you're right. But, Alec...'

'Aye?'

'Take care, won't you?'

CHAPTER 49

He ought to do this by the book, he thought. Ring the bell, wait for a response. Take it step by step. Don't go blundering in until you've an idea of what you're blundering into.

But that was the trouble. He had no idea what was going on in there. He had no idea what he might provoke even by ringing the doorbell. Depending on Douglas's state of mind, something as trivial as that might be the only catalyst needed.

McKay retrieved his baton from the rear of the car and made his way slowly round the side of the bungalow. Ahead of him, the land opened up and fell away, the wide blue waters of the Cromarty Firth mirror-like in the afternoon sun. As he rounded the corner, he saw the rear patio doors were open. He moved closer, straining his ears for any sound.

At first, he could hear nothing. Then, as he stepped forward, he could make out a strange, indecipherable noise. It was two parallel voices, not exactly in harmony but in an eerie counterpoint, both murmuring or whimpering. He could make out no words, just an unsettling keening.

He moved further round, trying to find a line of sight into the room without exposing his own presence. But a thicket of bushes to the left of the patio prevented him from seeing into the room without moving on to the lawn beyond. He hesitated for a moment, then moved quickly around the bushes, jumping up onto the decking. Then he stopped.

Henrietta Dowling was sitting on the floor with her back to the sofa. Douglas was behind her on the sofa. It took McKay a moment to work out what was happening. Then he caught the glitter of the wire around Dowling's neck. Douglas was holding it pressed hard against her throat, but hadn't yet pulled it tight.

The weird keening appeared to be coming from both of them. Dowling had her eyes closed and was whimpering, a long continuous inarticulate sound that dripped with terror. Douglas looked and sounded little different. His eyes were shut and he was murmuring something to himself. A wordless incantation, as if he were trying to summon up the state of mind needed to complete the act. It wasn't clear that either of them had registered McKay's presence. Behind him, somewhere in the distance, he could hear the faint sound of a police siren.

McKay took another few steps forward and entered the room, blinking at the relative gloom. He'd moved as silently as he could, but Douglas's eyes snapped open. Involuntarily, his hand jerked and the wire tightened on Dowling's neck. The whimpering increased in volume, although Douglas had fallen silent, staring blankly at McKay.

'Let go of the wire, eh, Andy?' McKay said. 'She's done nothing.'

'She gave me to them,' Douglas said. 'She let me go. She never cared.'

'She's your mother, Andy.' McKay took another cautious step forward, trying to work out how he could make Douglas drop the wire without harming Dowling.

'She never cared,' Douglas repeated. 'Netty was the only one who cared. The only one who ever looked after me.'

'This won't help anyone, Andy. Just let go of the wire and I'll take care of you.' Somewhere outside, McKay could hear the sound of sirens growing closer. If the uniforms burst in here, he had no idea what Douglas's response might be. He took another step towards the sofa.

Douglas looked up sharply and his hand twitched again bringing another gasp of pain from Henrietta Dowling. 'You don't understand. I have to do this now. I have to finish it. I have to make it complete.'

McKay was never sure whether, at that moment, Douglas really did intend to pull the wire tight. He saw the young man's hand grip the wire, its end wrapped around some kind of wooden stick, and he saw the muscles in Douglas's arm tense. He slammed the baton hard down on the back of Douglas's hand, desperately hoping that Douglas would release his grip rather than pulling tighter. Then he stuck a second blow to the right of Douglas's head, sending him falling in Dowling's direction. As Douglas fell, he heard a scream from Dowling and he turned to see the wire cutting deeply into the flesh of her neck.

CHAPTER 50

'We'll have to go through the process, that's all,' Grant said.

'You mean *I'll* have to go through the process.'

'We all will, Alec. They have to make sure everything was handled appropriately.'

'Aye, but I'm the one who went off-piste, aren't I? Went up there to deal with it by myself.'

'Which was the correct thing to do. You made the right call. We couldn't have delayed another minute.'

'I should have got some backup to come with me.'

Grant was silent for a moment. 'Aye, that may be your one weak spot but that wouldn't have helped.'

'It might. Anyway, I should have handled it differently. Not go charging in there like a bull in a porcelain factory.'

'You had to go in, Alec. You had no other choice.'

'I still should have handled it differently.'

'There was nothing else you could have done. You did the only thing possible.'

'Aye, but—'

'Oh, for Christ's sake, Alec. She's alive. She survived.'

'No thanks to me. What if he'd tightened that wire a bit more?'

'He didn't because you'd knocked him unconscious.'

'But if he'd not been properly knocked out, or if he'd fallen the wrong way, or—'

'None of that actually happened. You've nothing to reproach yourself for.'

'That's not how they'll see it.' McKay had finally jumped to his feet and begun his familiar circuit of Grant's office.

'Alec, it's a routine enquiry. They're only doing it because they want to pre-empt any attempt by Douglas or Hamilton to do what Hamilton did in her last trial. They're just covering their arses.'

'Aye, and I'm the one who had to hand over his trousers.'

'It'll be fine. Main thing for us is to put the story together as clearly as we can for the trial. I'm struggling to get my head round some of it. So you reckon that Ronnie Young was Douglas's father?'

'That's what he said. He knew nothing about the circumstances, but the timing fits with Dowling's initial claim that Young raped her.'

Grant sat up. 'So you're saying—'

'I'm saying nothing. We need to see what Dowling says once she's in a condition to tell us.' The wire had cut badly into Henrietta Dowling's throat. It was likely that her life had been saved only because McKay had managed to hold the wound shut until the paramedics arrived. She was in hospital, but expected to make a full recovery. 'But the timing works.'

'So why would she drop the complaint against Young?'

'Because Netty Munro persuaded her to. I suspect Munro was very persuasive. Dowling's career was struggling at that point. She was in the same position as Munro in that an abortion, whatever the circumstances, would have damaged the following she'd begun to build up on the country scene in the US. She and Munro were both seen as clean-cut Christian country rockers, and that wasn't going to play well with any of this. So Munro persuaded her to keep the baby who grew up to be Andy Douglas. Dowling was no more maternal than Munro, and she was quite content for Douglas to be used in the same way as the network's other victims.'

'Christ. But Douglas had had the idea that Munro had protected him.'

'Maybe she did,' McKay said. 'Though not for his benefit, I imagine. My impression is that Munro was the smartest and most ruthless of all of them. I wouldn't be surprised to discover she was the one behind the whole thing. If she took greater care of Andy

Douglas, I think it's because she recognised he was the flakiest of all of them. The one who needed to be protected to protect the rest of them.'

'She was right then.' Grant watched him prowl around the room. 'So what about all Munro's supposed good works. Taking in all these poor young women from the refuge centre. Was that just a way of grooming more victims, or had she turned over a new leaf?'

'I suppose we'll have to do some digging into that,' McKay said. 'Some of the previous woman who've stayed there seem to have done okay. Got out and rebuilt their lives. But there's a number we haven't been able to track down yet. Munro had more or less retired from her singing career. Maybe she'd decided to settle down and apply some of these Christian principles, after all.'

'What about that stuff that Jane McDowd overheard? The idea that they'd be "good material"?'

McKay shrugged. 'Could go either way, couldn't it? Good material for the network, or good material for Christ's eternal salvation. Alleluia and all that.'

Grant nodded. 'Christ, I don't envy the Procurator on this one. Especially if Hamilton starts playing the same games as last time.'

'I would say that was a trick she could only pull once,' McKay said. He finally sat back down in the seat opposite Grant and fumbled for a stick of gum. 'Except we're talking about Elizabeth Hamilton, and I'd put nothing past her.'

'That's what scares me.' Grant paused. 'By the way, speaking of Christ's eternal salvation and all that, I've heard you've suddenly turned to performing charitable acts in your old age.'

'It's a foul slander,' McKay said. 'Whatever they're saying.'

'Jane McDowd and Alicia Swinton. I hear they've found temporary accommodation.'

'That's what you've heard, is it?'

'Little bungalow up in Rosemarkie. No longer needed by its primary occupant.'

McKay had reddened slightly. 'It was just going to waste…'

'Thought you were going to take Chrissie up there for dirty weekends by the coast?'

'My weekends are none of your fucking business, Grant,' McKay said. 'But, yes, I discussed it with Chrissie. Those poor wee lasses had nowhere else to go. Christ knows what's going to happen to Munro's farm – the lawyers are still arguing over that one, given that she'd apparently bequeathed it to Elizabeth Hamilton in her will and it's not clear who's next in line assuming Hamilton's found guilty.'

'Assuming.'

'Aye. The bungalow was going to be standing empty. I had to clear it with the letting agent and the landlord, but they were okay as long as I continued to pay the rent. And it's amazing how persuasive the mention of a police rank can be sometimes. They're there until the end of the year's contract, so there's a good few months still to run. It'll tide them over till they can get themselves sorted.'

'I thought you'd taken the bungalow on a renewable six month contract?' Grant said.

McKay had reddened a little more. 'Aye, well. That was part of the deal I did with the agent.'

'So you and Chrissie are paying for them to stay there for the next six months? How does Chrissie feel about that?'

Grant half-expected that McKay would once again tell her to mind her own fucking business, but instead he just offered her a sheepish smile. 'She's grand with it, to be honest. They're fine wee lasses. They invited us over, offered us a nice little lunch as a thank you. And we've invited them back. It'll bring a bit of life to the house, you know?'

Grant knew. It was what she missed herself, living in her neat little house in North Kessock. It was fine, mostly. She'd never been a gregarious individual. But sometimes the silence, the emptiness in the house, felt too much for her. She thought about McKay and Chrissie and the daughter they'd lost, the silence that had grown between them after that, and she felt pleased for them.

Pleased that they'd come through. Pleased that they'd found a way of filling the silence.

After her husband Rory had died, Grant had even harboured her own vague fantasies about a future with McKay, but that had always been a ridiculous idea. Instead, she'd mainly just thrown herself back into the job, and that had been okay. But now, suddenly, she felt as if she'd been treading water for too long. 'That's great,' she said. 'Really pleased it's all going so well for you and Chrissie. You both deserve it.'

McKay looked at her. 'You okay, hen?'

She looked down at her watch, conscious that there were tears brimming somewhere behind her eyes. 'Aye, Alec, I'm grand. It's late. We've had a hard week. So why don't you just fuck off home to Chrissie, eh? She'll be waiting for you.'

END

NOTE AND ACKNOWLEDGEMENTS

The first DI Alec McKay book, *Candles and Roses*, ended on a deliberately ambiguous note. The crime was solved, justice was served, but McKay was left with some lingering doubts.

At the time, I hadn't intended to take the story any further. I hoped that the book's resolution was satisfying to the reader, but provided one further twist to reflect the kind of uncertainty that can bedevil any real police enquiry or criminal trial. I didn't know whether or not McKay's concerns were justified, and I assumed I never would.

Then my mum read the book.

She told me she'd enjoyed it (but then she's my mum so she has to say that), but she wanted to know who the killer really was. I replied that I knew no more than she did – I was just the author – but she refused to believe me. 'You *must* know,' she said. 'You *wrote* it.' But that's not how it works. The truth was I really didn't know.

You can't ignore your mum, though. So when I sat down to think about the third book in the series, I found I'd also become curious to know what really happened after the end of *Candles and Roses*. So I decided to revisit the story and find out what happened next. And it turned out that there was a lot more to the story, and to the enigmatic Elizabeth Hamilton, than I'd ever imagined…

I've tried hard to ensure that *Their Final Act* works as a standalone book, whether or not you've read *Candles and Roses* (though, like most crime series, you'll probably get a little more out of the books if you read them in order). But if you have read the first book, I hope you enjoy where the story goes next.

So thanks to my mum for making the book possible (and to her and my dad for making everything possible). Thanks as ever to Helen for being my first and best critic, and for the support in writing and everything else. Thanks to all those who advised on the book, and apologies for any liberties I've taken with what you told me. Thanks, as ever, to Betsy, Fred, Sumaira, Sarah and everyone else at Bloodhound Books for their unfailing support. And thanks to all the good people of the Highlands and the Black Isle for allowing me, yet again, to clutter this glorious landscape with fictional corpses.

11012723R00182

Printed in Great Britain
by Amazon